the RIDGE

David B. Clark

GSPH

Published by

GSPH GENERAL STORE PUBLISHING HOUSE

1 Main Street Burnstown, Ontario, Canada K0J 1G0
Telephone (613) 432-7697 or 1-800-465-6072

Layout Design by Gerry Langill
Cover Design by Leanne Enright
Cover Photo: "Photos for Canadian War Museum by William Kent"

Copyright © 1994
General Store Publishing House
Burnstown, Ontario, Canada

No part of this book may be reproduced, stored in a retrieval system or transmitted in any form or by any means electronic, mechanical, photocopying, recording or otherwise, except for purposes of review, without the prior permission of the publisher.

Canadian Cataloguing in Publication Data

Clark, David B.
    The ridge

Includes index.
ISBN 0-919431-70-4

    1. World War, 1939-1945—Personal narratives, Canadian. 2. World War, 1939-1945—Campaigns—France—Normandy. 3. Canada. Canadian Army—History—World War, 1939-1945. I. Title
D811.C515A3 1993 940.54'2144'2 C94-900066-3

First Printing February 1994

ACKNOWLEDGEMENTS

I wish to acknowledge with deep gratitude the following persons, without whose encouragement, assistance in preparing the manuscripts and critical advice, this novel would not have seen the light of day:

My wife Flora; my professional associates, Mary Ellen and Rose-Marie; Brigadier General S.V. Radley-Walters; Mrs. M. Patricia Radley-Walters; Brigadier General W. Denis Whitaker; Colonel Strome Galloway; and John A. Stevens, my editor, and Tim Gordon, publisher at General Store Publishing House.

I wish to thank the Directorate of History, National Defence Headquarters, for permission to quote the passages from Colonel C. P. Stacey's Official Histories of the Canadian Army in World War 11; also the Canadian War Museum, for permission to use a copy of Bruno Bobak's painting "Carrier Convoy After Dark" for the front cover.

Although The Ridge *is based on historical fact, the main characters are fictitious, and are not intended to bear resemblance to any person, living or dead.*

This novel is dedicated to the soldiers of the Canadian Army who fought in Normandy in 1944, and to the memory of those of its ranks who gave their lives on the battlefields, so that Canadians today could live in freedom.

"*Their Name Liveth For Evermore.*"

"Three miles or so south of Caen, the present-day tourist, driving down the arrow-straight road that leads to Falaise, sees immediately to his right a rounded hill crowned by farm buildings. If the traveller be Canadian, he would do well to stay the wheels at this point and cast his mind to the events of 1944; for this apparently insignificant eminence is the Verrières Ridge. Well may the wheat and sugar-beet grow green and lush upon its gentle slopes, for in that now half-forgotten summer the best blood of Canada was freely poured out upon them."

Colonel C.P. Stacey, <u>The Victory Campaign.</u>

TABLE OF CONTENTS

PART ONE - Normandy, July 1944

Chapter One	11
Chapter Two	27
Chapter Three	42
Chapter Four	57
Chapter Five	76

PART TWO - London, Ontario May 1959

Chapter Six	95
Chapter Seven	107
Chapter Eight	119
Chapter Nine	126
Chapter Ten	146
Chapter Eleven	157
Chapter Twelve	165
Chapter Thirteen	174

PART THREE - London, Fall 1959

Chapter Fourteen	187
Chapter Fifteen	196
Chapter Sixteen	203
Chapter Seventeen	210
Chapter Eighteen	222
Chapter Nineteen	231

PART FOUR - Normandy, April 1986

Chapter Twenty	245
Chapter Twenty-one	254

PART ONE

NORMANDY JULY 1944

CHAPTER ONE

At high tide on a July morning in 1944 a landing craft edged slowly towards the pebbled beach. Her light grey hull, with "LCIL 284" painted in large black lettering on either side, reflected the summer sun. This small ship, like her many sisters which had already touched down onto the beach, was classified as a "Landing Craft (Infantry)", whose mission was to convey troops across the channel from England to the battlefields of Normandy, where the Allied forces had landed barely a month ago.

The LC(I) belonged to the Royal Navy, but on this crossing she carried Canadian troops. Her captain had steered her skillfully past the twisted hulks of sunken ships and the grotesquely shaped steel obstacles which still protruded above the gentle swell, a grim legacy of the violence of the assault landing. Ahead lay the narrow beach with its low outcroppings of rock left by the high tide. Beyond were sand dunes, littered with coils of barbed wire. Blown, burned-out concrete casemates, some with their guns still protruding, stood like macabre landmarks towards which the ship headed. Along the beach, on the dunes and in the green countryside beyond were thousands of khaki-clad troops in battle gear, with tanks and military vehicles of all descriptions. To the left, a few hundred yards away, was the Seulles River, with the fishing village of Corseulles at its mouth. From the distance could be heard the continuous drum-roll of artillery. This was "Mike Green", one of the landing beaches in the Canadian JUNO sector. The battle front was a mere seven miles inland. The captain was firmly convinced that this was an unpleasant and unhealthy place for any naval officer to be, and he anxiously hoped for a quick off-loading of his human cargo, so that he could return to his home port at Tilbury, in the estuary of the Thames, from which he had weighed anchor the previous evening.

"LCIL 284" carried an entire rifle company, consisting of five officers and a hundred and twenty other ranks. This was Able Company of an infantry battalion, which was part of the Second Canadian Infantry Division, now assembling in Normandy. Designated a "build-up division", it was to join the Canadian formations which had landed on D-Day, to form the new Second Canadian Corps.

As the landing craft approached the beach, the soldiers stood in battle order, crammed together on the open deck. Each wore a steel helmet covered with camouflage netting, and webbing over the khaki battle-dress blouse, on the back of which was strapped a large pack, gas cape, entrenching tool and water bottle, with ammunition pouches on the front. Most carried the .303 Lee Enfield rifle slung over a shoulder, with its sheathed bayonet attached to the web belt on the left side. Others carried the Bren light machine gun, the two inch mortar, the Thompson submachine gun or Sten gun. All wore the blue rectangular divisional patch on each sleeve of the battle-dress blouse, just below the regimental shoulder flash. The other ranks wore their battle-dress blouses open at the neck. The khaki shirt underneath had no collar. The officers wore collared shirts, with a khaki tie.

The landing craft touched down on the beach. The captain momentarily reversed his engines, bringing the craft to a dead stop. He reached for the microphone close to the wheel. "Are you hearing this? Are you hearing this?" blared from the loud-speaker. "All troops prepare to debark! All troops prepare to debark!" The sailors swiftly rolled down the gangways, located on either side of the deck, deftly landing each close to the water's edge.

Major Dick Mitchell, the officer commanding Able Company, stood by the port railing and observed with relief that his company would land without wading through the water, heavily encumbered as each soldier was with personal kit and fighting gear.

"O.K., men, get ready to move off! Platoon commanders and N.C.O.'s, make sure every man has his gear properly strapped down." Turning to Lieutenant Jim Niles, the subaltern in command of Able Company's Three Platoon, he said: "Lead off with your platoon, Jim. Follow the guide from the beach party waiting down there. I'll join you as soon as we are all off this tub!"

"Right, sir, we're on our way. Sergeant Banfield!"

"Sir!" The platoon sergeant had already positioned himself at the end of the platoon file, having carefully checked each of the men, for whom he felt personally responsible. Although he could hear the distant roar of guns, this landing was disturbingly different from the Dieppe landing two years ago, when his battalion had been badly mauled by the enemy before they could even get off the beach.

Most of his present platoon were raw recruits, arrived from Canada as replacements after the Dieppe disaster, and who had never been in battle. He knew that no amount of training in England had really prepared them for what lay ahead. He also felt a pervasive uneasiness about his platoon officer, who had been posted to the battalion two months previously. The lieutenant, at twenty-two a year younger than himself, had arrived on a draft from Canada, recently graduated from the Royal Military College in Kingston. He had remained aloof from his men, and apparently uncaring. Bob Banfield wondered what sort of leader this officer would prove to be, once they were committed to battle. "Ready to move off, sir."

"Then let's go!"

Three Platoon clattered down the gangway in single file. For these young men, this was their personal "invasion landing". They were leaving the relative security of the ship, to embark upon an unknown and hostile shore, to fight an enemy whom most had yet never seen, but whom their leaders warned were tough, professional soldiers, and so they were expected to be tougher and more professional. Each had conjured up in his mind his own particular spectre of the monstrous Hun. But these fears had rapidly dissipated with the rambunctious chatter and aggressive bravado of the barrack-room in England. Now, as these young Canadians stepped off the gangway onto the soil of France, their natural spirit of adventure and curiosity were tempered with more sober reflections regarding what they were getting into. How would they react to going into battle for the first time? Would they let their chums down? Would they be killed?

The British sailors of the crew of "LCIL 284" were there on the foredeck to bid farewell to their erstwhile passengers. "Cor, you blokes don' 'alf look like a scruffy lot! Bloomin' 'ell, gonna scare ol' Jerry 'alf to death, is yer?"

"You're doggone right! We're gonna beat the stuffin' out of them and be back home in Toronto for Christmas!"....... "So long, you limeys! Great boat ride — beats the ferry to the Island!"....... "Hey, youse should get another cook! Man, that swill you served us — yeach!"....... "Hey, sailor, my buddy and me's gonna send you one of them dirty postcards from Paris — after we've tried a little of that French nookie!"...... "Hey, remember me to that broad who works in the pub off Picadilly — you know, Susie? The pub with them golden balls?"

"That's enough! Watch your step! Two Section, close it up! Bren gunners, keep your weapons held high until we get past the sand dunes!"

Good old sarge ... we can depend on him. He was at Dieppe, and knows all about this killing and fighting stuff. We better stick close to him. But Mr. Niles .... well, that was different. None of the men of Three Platoon felt they could trust their young officer. He was cold and distant. They sensed that he resented them, and in turn, they disliked him.

On the beach to meet them was their commanding officer, Lieutenant Colonel Phillip Bryson, with battalion headquarters staff. Lieutenant Niles, at the head of his platoon file, approached the colonel and saluted.

"Welcome to France, Jim!"

"Thank you, sir. Major Mitchell will be down when the rest of the company has disembarked."

"Good enough. Don't wait, Jim. Move off ahead with your platoon. Mr. Reid will guide you to the forming-up place."

"Right! Follow me, Mr. Niles, sir!" Regimental Sergeant Major Stuart Reid walked off with the lieutenant, the platoon still in single file, trailing behind. RSM Reid was a large man, with a bushy, red moustache. On this momentous occasion for the battalion, he looked exactly as he did on parade in England; his uniform was immaculate, and his boots gleamed. The men glanced furtively in his direction. All too frequently they had been victims of his bellowed invective; they feared and revered him. Real nice of the "Old Man" to choose that son-of-a-bitch to lead us off this beach personally! Things can't be that snafu'd after all.....

The platoon marched through a gap in the dunes which had been bulldozed through by the army engineers to facilitate rapid exit from the beach for disembarking troops. As they emerged on the other side, the noise of distant artillery fire sounded louder and closer. They followed a dirt road inland for about two hundred yards, and there before them, where the road crossed the coastal highway, the arriving rifle companies of the battalion were gathering. Each had been herded into columns of platoons, three ranks deep, facing the left side of the road. There was no sign of their support company with its vehicles and heavy weapons, and the rest of the unit's motor transport, which had been routed in their landing ship to the "Mulberry" artificial harbor at Arromanches, eight miles further west.

The fields around were pitted with shell-holes. Here and there were wooden crosses to mark the temporary graves of the soldiers of the Canadian Scottish battalion who had been killed in this area during the D-Day battle. Elsewhere were signs of larger graves, where dozens of German dead had been buried together. There had been no time to identify the bodies of the fallen enemy, only enough time to bury the corpses before they decomposed in the summer sun.

Three Platoon was brought to its allotted position and immediately formed into ranks, one for each of its sections. The remaining two platoons of Able Company — the last of the battalion's twelve platoons — were right behind them. The officers were called away to their first "Orders Group" in Normandy; Sergeant Banfield was left in charge of the platoon. Again he checked out each man, to make sure he was ready for the march inland. The men were required to "stand easy" on the road, still maintaining their ranks. This was not a "rest stop", but a "gathering of the clan", all five hundred of them, before moving off.

Within a half hour, the officers returned to their respective companies and platoons. Lieutenant Jim Niles spoke with Sergeant Banfield alone, then the sergeant turned to face his men. "O.K., you lot, get ready to move. We're going to march in column of platoons through the next village, then on to another village called Creully, where the battalion's assembly area is located, where we will likely remain for the next few days. About a five-mile march."

There were mutters of relief. This was after all not going to be another twenty-mile "piss cutter", to which they had become all too accustomed in the endless "schemes" in England. But they were moving up to the "sharp end". This was how it was to begin. The riflemen slung their Lee Enfields over their shoulders, and adjusted the straps. The Bren gunners hoisted their awkward weapons onto their shoulders. The commands rang out, first from the colonel, and then down the line from the company commanders: "Move to the right in threes! Right turn! By the right, quick march!"

The battalion marched in step along the dirt country lane in a southwesterly direction, paralleling the front lines. The marching troops raised a great cloud of powdery white dust, which coated their sweating faces and their uniforms. Frequently, despatch riders on motorcycles roared past them, which made matters worse. The men chuckled as they passed the first of the many signs which had been erected by the provost - the military police in the Canadian Army - which read: "Dust Means Death!" Fortunately, on this clear day, British and Canadian fighter aircraft patrolled the skies overhead, and no German spotter plane ventured to locate this marching column for their artillery.

As they approached the first ancient stone-built village, St. Croix-sur-Mer, they were met by the provost, in their khaki berets and white web-belts and holsters, who guided them through the narrow, tortuous streets. "This way, sir!" a provost sergeant called out to Colonel Bryson, who led the battalion column. "If you turned the wrong way down there, you would have had to learn German quick, like!" The village was deserted, its houses and courtyard walls were pockmarked with bullet holes. Littering the little village square were a number of burned-out German command and signals vehicles. A month ago, there had been a firefight here, as Canadian troops moved inland after clearing the beaches.

The march continued along the road, lined on either side with trees, many of which had been badly damaged by shellfire. Whole boughs had been shot off, and often only a shattered trunk remained. The troops were learning about Normandy, with its myriad stone villages, some no more than a mile apart. The fields in between teemed with troops, tanks and other vehicles, and vast supply dumps, camouflaged by nets and tree branches, the very sinews of modern war, which had drawn so many men together, to be consumed together in the holocaust of the Normandy battlegrounds.

In places, beyond the verges of the road, were abandoned slit trenches, recently occupied by soldiers of either side desperately attempting to find some cover and concealment from the murderous fire around them. Those who had succumbed to grenade, mortar bomb and bayonet were buried in shallow graves in the fields close by. To the horror of these green troops, the hands and boots of some of the dead protruded from their graves. For the first time, the sickly, sweet smell of decaying bodies, so characteristic of the Normandy battlefields that summer, invaded their nostrils. There were more little wooden crosses:...."H 23140 Pte. Johnson, DR, Royal

Winnipeg Rifles, 6 Jun 44...." The odd steel helmet hung on some of the crosses. On some graves were empty ration tins, holding long-wilted wild flowers, which comrades had gathered and left as a final farewell before they moved on.

Within a few hundred yards of Creully, the terrain dropped slightly to a shallow valley, through which ran a small stream. The road crossed the stream over a stone bridge. The men of Three Platoon could see the companies ahead of them turn left and right off the road once they had passed the bridge. When Able Company drew up, they saw their colonel standing by the bridge. He waved to Major Mitchell. "Dick, this is where we bivouac. Take your company over the bridge, and then move off over there to the left close by those buildings. We're about five miles from the 'sharp end' to the south-east. Get your men to dig in before nightfall. We're within range of Jerry's medium guns, and the Luftwaffe has a habit of raiding before sun-down. There is a battery from our 3 Light Ack Ack just beyond your locality; there may be a lot of shrapnel flying around. Get your sigs people to net in your Company H.Q. with my Tac H.Q. Brigade will be bringing in "compo" rations shortly. Also, I want you at an "Orders Group" at Tac H.Q. in that clump of trees close to the bridge, at 2200 hours."

"Yes, sir. That will give me time to set up a company defensive perimeter before it gets dark. What about Support Company?"

"They have been held up in a royal traffic jam just outside Arromanches. The scout platoon took it upon itself to put its training into practice by hot-footing it across country, and got here before we did. Great map-reading, and great 'Indian tactics' to get past traffic control without being spotted! These lads have pegged out a harbor for the guns and vehicles over in those woods by the road. Should all be here soon."

Dick Mitchell was not impressed. This colonel seemed to take all of this as quite a lark. A banker from Windsor, Ontario, he had served in the militia before the war. He was politically well connected, and after the Dieppe raid, when the battalion had lost its colonel and a great many others, he was given command. He revelled in his privileges of senior rank, excelled at "playing soldiers" during the many training exercises in England, and was ever an impressive social success at ceremonial functions. But like so many of the senior Canadian Army officers at that time, he lacked any awareness of the seriousness of winning this war, and the appalling sacrifices it was taking.

"Well, sir, I had better get going." Dick saluted the colonel, and then, turning to his men, said: "Able Company, follow me. We're home!" He led his company over the little bridge, off the dirt road, and across the field to the company's area. Having surveyed the terrain around him, he located his three platoons in a rough circle with his headquarters in the center and ordered them to dig in.

....

Three Platoon was allotted the south-end portion of the perimeter, close to the edge of the village of Creully. Lieutenant Niles found an old slit-trench which had been dug there previously, commandeered it for himself, ordered his batman to clean it out, and then ordered Sergeant Banfield to get on with supervising the rest of the platoon at the job at hand. This annoyed Bob Banfield, and served to confirm his uncomfortable impressions of his officer, who showed no more concern for his men now than before they had arrived at this battle zone, with the imminent likelihood of being committed to the front lines. In battle, without strong leadership from his platoon commander, the responsibility for controlling the platoon would fall heavily on him.

Concealing his nagging doubts, Bob Banfield ordered the men to stack their weapons and gear, and then showed each of the sections where he wanted them to dig in. For these young soldiers, the digging of slit-trenches had been one of the more detestably onerous tasks they were required to perform in their infantry training, but they were now learning that in a battle area, this was how to stay alive. With a soldier's eye, he ensured that each trench was sufficiently deep, that there was no obstruction to the firing of weapons, and that there were interlocking fields of fire between each of the platoon's trenches and those of neighboring platoons. He instructed his men to "recce" the farm buildings close by, to find straw to throw down into the trenches for the comfort of the occupants, and also boards or planks which could be used for overhead cover from rain — or enemy bomb fragments. The shadows were lengthening; they would have to work fast.

At twenty-three, Bob Banfield was a well-built young man of medium height, and, like the rest of his platoon, at the peak of physical fitness. His clean-cut features revealed a maturity beyond his years. His five years of service in the infantry had hardened him physically and strengthened his character. Bob was an only child, whose mother had died when he was nine. Since his father, who was employed as a locomotive engineer with the C.N.R., was often away, he was raised by his maternal grandparents. His crusty old grandfather had served in the Boer War with the Royal Canadian Regiment, and had fought at Paaderberg. It was from the old man that Bob had acquired an interest in the military. He enrolled in the cadet corps in his high school in Barrie, Ontario; after completing his grade twelve he enlisted in the Canadian Army.

His leadership qualities soon became apparent during his basic training in the armories of Toronto, and at the brigade concentration at Camp Borden. He adapted rapidly to army life, thrived on the discipline and sense of purpose it provided, and easily tolerated its perverse idiosyncracies and inane regulations and customs. He was determined to excel at his trade as an infantryman. He went overseas with his battalion, as part of the Second Canadian Infantry Division, whose first mission was the defence of Britain against a German invasion which never came. As a lance-corporal, his sole experience of actual combat had been in the Dieppe raid. There, in a very short time, he saw most of the officers and N.C.O.'s fall in battle, and he assumed command of the remnants of his company. During this terrifying day in August of 1942, the men about him drew strength from his imperturbable calm. He had convinced himself that fighting was his stock in trade, what he had trained for all those years, and he was going to make the best of this total military disaster which had befallen Canadian arms. Back with his battalion in England, as the replacement drafts arrived, he was sent on leadership courses, and was promoted, first to the rank of corporal and then to sergeant; hence to his Three Platoon.

The corporal in charge of the platoon's second section of ten men was René Charlebois. The same age as Bob Banfield, he was also a lance-corporal at Dieppe. René came from the Lafontaine area of Central Ontario, part of the French-Canadian enclave around Penetanguishene. He was raised on a small farm, the third of nine children. He never attended secondary school, because his father needed him to work on the farm, and to help to raise his large family. When war came, his older brother joined the RCAF. Within a year, René left home and hitchhiked to Toronto to enlist in the Army. His father had been with the Canadian Corps at Vimy Ridge in the First War, and grudgingly accepted that it was now the turn of his sons to serve. However, his mother had no illusions about the utter futility and waste of war. René had always been her favorite, with his dark, curly hair and deep-brown eyes, and she mourned at his departure, harboring a premonition that she would never see him again. In time, the Charlebois' lost their son in the RCAF, killed in a bombing mission over Hamburg. That did not daunt René's two younger brothers, who join the Army after him, when they came of age. For René, to serve in the Army meant adventure, and the chance to get away from the humdrum of life on a farm. Most French-Canadian volunteers preferred to enlist in French-speaking units, but René decided that he wanted to sample the delights of Toronto, and what better way than to join up there?

Short and stocky, René possessed a farm boy's simple outlook on life; there were no stirring sentiments about serving king and country, but he willingly took orders, learned what the Army taught him, and as far as infantry tactics went, this was "nuthin' more than huntin' in the bush". At Dieppe, he showed the courage which comes with the lack of a vivid imagination, did what he was told, survived the disaster, and the Army rewarded him by sending him on the same Junior N.C.O. course that Bob Banfield attended. To be a corporal with two stripes on his sleeves was the height of his military aspirations. He was delighted to serve under Bob, "that guy from Barrie". In the years since he left Lafontaine, he had seldom written letters home, but whenever he permitted himself a moment of nostalgia, he thought of his little sister, Laura. Laura was the youngest; she was six when he left. She was a delightful kid, full of fun; he loved to pull her pigtails, and they shared a deep affection. Laura, above all else, was what he missed from home. When the war was over, he would find a doll for her, to bring back with him. In his heart, she remained forever six.

The long Norman twilight arrived, but it did not quell the booming of the guns in the distance. The proximity of Three Platoon to the front lines lent an unsettling urgency to the task of digging slit trenches to the satisfaction of Sergeant Banfield. Most of these trenches were about three feet wide and six feet long, usually occupied by one soldier. Some, however, were in the shape of a "V", with the arms extended outwards from the perimeter, shared by two or three men. On his round of inspection, Banfield noticed one such trench, which became the temporary home of three of the men in Two Section, whom Major Mitchell had dubbed the "Soldiers Three". These lads, all nineteen, were inseparable. As he passed, he was greeted by a voice from the bowels of this trench, which he could have recognized anywhere.

"Sarge, an' when will we be expectin' grub? All this fuckin' marchin' an' diggin' make me stomach feel like me throat was cut!"

"Jesus, Brennan! Can't you think of anything but your stomach?"

"Sure, Sarge, them broads we left in England!"

"You just concentrate on what you're supposed to be doing, so you can protect your damned Irish ass, if the stuff starts flying! The Company C.Q. will be up soon with the "compo" rations."

B156728 Private Brennan, Thomas. The bastard son of some Irish whore in Toronto! Practiced scrounger, in fact a downright thief. Smooth-talking little son-of-a-bitch. Self-designated barrack-room lawyer and company trouble-maker. Perennial joker. Repeatedly on orders parade before Major Mitchell, who Bob felt was far too lenient with the wiry scoundrel. The major seemed to have a soft spot for this codger, and he got away with a great deal of plain mischief by sweet-talking the major with his Irish wit. The platoon tended to shun him, but somehow he was "adopted" by the Two Section's Bren-gunner, Jack Sipulski, and his "number two on the Bren", Ronnie Matthews. These three were blatantly dissimilar, yet they were fast friends.

As Bob Banfield peered into the trench, his gaze was met by a grin from Jack Sipulski, sitting cross-legged on a pile of straw, busily engaged in his favorite pastime, oiling and polishing his Bren gun. A tall, powerfully-built lad with tow-colored hair, wide cheek bones and enormous hands, he appeared blissfully content and totally oblivious to the incessant booming of the Canadian artillery in the distance. The Army had been good to Jack. He was the sixth child, born to a destitute Polish immigrant family in Hamilton. He did poorly in school. At fourteen, to the relief of his father, who then had one less mouth to feed, Jack left home at the height of the depression, and "hit the rails" to find work to keep body and soul together. He crossed the country several times. When he turned sixteen, he presented himself to the recruiting sergeant in Toronto to enlist. He handed over a crumpled letter from his mother, on which was scrawled: "Please take my boy in army. Is good worker, need job." The sergeant noted that he was cold and hungry. His large size was impressive; this was what the infantry needed, he was processed and attested into the Canadian Army. But after his basic training, he was kept behind, employed in orderly-room duties, until he turned eighteen, when he was sent on a draft of reinforcements to England, and posted to this battalion. For Jack, to have three square meals a day and a comfortable, warm cot to sleep in was all he wanted. In England, on the ranges, he demonstrated that he was a deadly shot, and was particularly adept at firing the Bren .303 light machine gun. "Sipulski," Major Mitchell informed him, "if you continue to shoot this well, with no 'Maggie's drawers' (missing the target in his groupings), we'll make you into a Bren gunner yet!" Thus he was eventually issued his own Bren, and this was his greatest achievement. He truly loved his weapon, his most cherished possession; it became the abiding purpose of his life.

Jack never spoke much. In England, when he was given a pass from the barracks, he would inevitable head for the nearest pub and get very drunk. He would then become belligerent, and as inevitably get into vicious brawls with whomever would oblige. The military police would be called in, and were it not for his friend, Ronnie Matthews, he could have frequently ended up in serious trouble. Over all others, he would listen to Ronnie, who to him possessed a remarkable ability, with his long English words, to get him out of tough spots. There were many nights when Ronnie conveyed him back to barracks, his face bloodied and bruised. Ronnie would clean him up, so that he would be reasonably presentable at parade the following morning. Ronnie, the "English" from Toronto who had "good education", was his "number two on the Bren". He would gladly give his life for his friend.

The ration truck arrived. Ronnie Matthews helped Corporal Charlebois distribute the "compo" rations, never a favorite with the Canadian troops, who regarded this "limey shit" as one of the necessary drawbacks in belonging to the British Empire, and being a part of the Second British Army. The men had not had a hot meal since they had disembarked from the landing craft. They were soon to realize that "compo" rations were to be their main diet in the battle zone, when often as not the battalion's cooks were unable to get hot meals to them. While the others of the section grumbled and cursed, Jack Sipulski wolfed down his share, and that of any of the others who would contribute.

Bob Banfield was glad to have Ronnie in his platoon. Tall and slim, with sad, grey-blue eyes, he had been posted to the battalion at the same time as

Tom and Jack. He was a serious youth, kindly and thoughtful, who provided a stabilizing influence over the young hot-heads. When the "Dear John" letters arrived, it was Ronnie the lads came to for advice and solace. As time passed, many felt that they had lost contact with home and Canada. The men bitterly resented the news from Canada, about what was happening in the political scene, and what the politicians were not doing regarding any adequate form of conscription. As the casualties mounted in the subsequent months, and the units often had to fight gravely understrength, their sense of isolation grew. Many of the men had married English girls. The English had suffered badly in the five years they had been at war. Millions of their servicemen and women had been overseas for years, fighting Germans and Japanese in far-flung theaters of war, and many were never to return. The English welcomed the young Canadians, who had left their own homes, many thousands of miles away, to defend England. The friendship extended by these people had helped to assuage the painful homesickness experienced by many of the soldiers; England quickly became a second home. But, above all, the Canadians identified strongly with their respective units. Each was a close-knit clan to itself, and the young men in each were much concerned that they should never let their unit and their comrades down, when the time came for battle. The unit was their family, their home away from home.

Private Ronnie Matthews had been raised in a middle-class family in Toronto. Because he had just completed his grade thirteen when he enlisted, he was urged to apply for the officer candidate course, leading to a commission in the Army. He had declined. He had joined the Army because he was deeply convinced that his country needed him to fight against Nazi tyranny, which had to be defeated by force of arms. There was no other way. Being of a sensitive nature, he abhorred violence in any form, and constantly struggled against nagging doubts that he could survive the obscene ravages of the battlefield. He believed that he lacked the courage to be an officer.

On the passage over to Normandy, he could not sleep. When the landing craft touched down, and the order came for him to descend the gangway onto this alien land, his stomach knotted, and his legs shook. He fought against an overpowering urge to run back into the ship, and plead to be taken back to England. It was the determined voice of Sergeant Banfield telling his section to close up which propelled him forward.

On the march to the Creully assembly area, it sickened him to see the evidence of violence about him. The sight of the smashed buildings, the gutted tanks and other vehicles which littered the countryside, and above all the countless graves with their pathetic crosses, horrified him. How could civilized people do this to each other? His paramount fear was how he would act when called upon to kill other human beings. He prayed that somehow, as Jack Sipulski's "number two", his job would be to hand over the heavy Bren gun magazines which he carried in pouches attached to his webbing, so that he could avoid that hideous duty. But what if Jack were killed or badly wounded......?

....

Dawn broke early on their second day in Normandy. For many, it had been a sleepless night. Thoughts of the events of the previous day intruded on their minds; the artillery had maintained a continuous, desultory fire all night. If this persistent banging kept them awake, perhaps it had the same effect on Jerry, they concluded.

Support company had arrived during the night, and with them the vehicles of the headquarters troops, including the field kitchen trucks. The cooks swiftly set about to prepare a hot breakfast for the battalion on their "dixie" stoves. The company quartermaster sergeants delivered eggs, toast and hot tea, to the delight of all ranks. The men wrote letters, some to wives in Canada and mistresses in England. Ronnie Matthews, the "brains" of his platoon, was asked to help a number of the lads compose heartrending love letters to the many girls in England they had left behind. They cleaned their weapons yet another time, although up to now none had been fired in anger at the foe.

As the day drew on, the traffic around them thickened by the hour. Whole regiments of Sherman tanks rumbled down the road through Creully, kicking up clouds of dust. A battery of 7.2-inch medium guns hauled by Quad tractors, rumbled past, followed by numerous ammunition trucks. The gunners proceeded to align the twelve guns in the field beyond them, erecting their camouflage netting over their huge weapons, stocking up vast piles of shell cases next to the guns, and busily netting in their wireless sets with their regimental headquarters and the forward observation officers in the front lines. Periodically, groups of infantry in company strength marched through their lines, headed for the front, wearing the grey patches of the Third Division. These men had been in action since the D-Day landing, and to the fresh troops of Three Platoon, they looked dirty and bedraggled. Something big was obviously going on. It was none less than the final assault to capture Caen, and once this was completed, it would be time for the new Second Division to take over its part of the front lines.

"Hey, you guys, the hell are you headed for?" called out Tom Brennan.

"To kick fuckin' Jerry in the ass again, you stupid crud!" was the answer. "Where the hell have you jokers been? What took you? About fuckin' time you got over here! Second div, second to none, eh? You're fuckin' second to us!"

In the late afternoon, swarms of rocket-firing Typhoon fighter-bombers roared overhead, and they could hear the explosions ahead of them, as the rockets hit their mark. Then, as dusk was falling, hundreds of heavy bombers, Halifaxes and Lancasters, with their bomb-bays open, flew over them, and discharged flaming death on the city of Caen. The noise of the bursting bombs was both frightening and exhilarating to the green troops. From the city some ten miles ahead, sheets of flame shot to the skies, black smoke rapidly spreading over the whole area.

The men of the battalion stood above their slit-trenches and cheered and waved at the airborne armada which swept over them. Never had they seen anything like the pyrotechnics they were witnessing now. How could Jerry survive this type of pasting? they thought. Perhaps when they got to the sharp end, it would be "duck soup" for them!

Throughout their second night, it seemed that hell itself had opened up before their eyes. Thousands of guns fired round after round of shells towards the German lines. The noise became deafening, as the medium guns close by added to the barrage. They could hear a bombardier with a high-pitched voice yelling into his radio microphone all night. "Mike target! Mike target! Figures one zero niner three two niner. Fire! Fire! Fire!" The ground shook beneath their feet.

At dawn the following day, the Third Division went into the attack. From their position in the rear of the battle lines, the men of Three Platoon could not see what was happening, but they discovered that the noise of battle was taking on a different tone. As the artillery barrage eased off, they could hear the sound of small arms fire, the dull crump of exploding mortar shells, and the deep thudding of hundreds of Bren guns, as they opened up on the enemy. The Germans, however, despite the bombing of the previous evening and the devastating artillery fire which came down upon them during the night, were defending the approaches to Caen with vicious resolve. The rapid, high-pitched fire from their automatic weapons was added to the chorus of battle. Nervously, the young men of the platoon waited during the day for some news about what was happening.

By midafternoon, long convoys of trucks and jeeps with red crosses painted on white circles on their canvas covers, bearing the wounded from the raging battle, drove through Creully, past their lines towards the casualty clearing stations and field hospitals located closer to the beaches. They were horrified to hear the cries and moans of the wounded, loaded to capacity in the vehicles. Trucks carrying replacements drove in the opposite direction, towards the battlefield. The idle chatter died among the men of Three Platoon. They were witnessing war in its hideous insanity. This was the meat-grinder of Normandy, and soon enough they too would be led into the cauldron of hell.

CHAPTER TWO

It took two days for the Canadian Army to capture Caen, in the final assault. The prize, which had eluded the Allied forces since the D-Day landings a month ago, was gained at a fearful cost. Thousands of French civilians also perished in the battle. The ancient Norman university city was now a shattered, smouldering ruin. The Third Division, supported by armor and British brigades to the east, drove the remaining German defenders through the rubble-strewn streets, and over the Orne, which separated Caen from its suburbs of Vaucelles and Colombelles. But it was not a rout; the enemy was frantically engaged in throwing up new lines of defence, to prevent a further advance by the Canadians beyond the river. The main objectives of the Third Division had been attained. It was now the time for the recently-arrived Second Division to take its place in the extended Canadian front.

To the men of the battalion in its assembly area, the noise of battle from the direction of Caen appeared to subside and an uneasy quiet descended over the battleground to the south-east. During the day, there were sporadic exchanges of gunfire. At night, they could occasionally hear the popping and rattling of small arms, as probing patrols from both sides engaged each other in the murky darkness. However, there was no end to the procession of ambulance convoys, which drove through Creully and passed by the battalion on the dirt road leading to the rear areas. For the green troops, the repetitive spectacle of these vehicles, conveying the maimed and mangled bodies of their own countrymen down the road, was unnerving. Was this how they would eventually depart this fearsome place?

On the morning of their fifth day in Normandy, down the same road came a long column of dusty, dirt-covered, dishevelled soldiers clad in field-grey uniforms. They carried no packs or weapons, no belts or steel helmets. They were escorted by a single Sherman tank, which brought up the rear of the column. The commander sat upright, out of his cupola, training his 50 caliber machine gun on the column. The soldiers appeared dazed and exhausted. Utter dejection, yet also defiance, showed on their gaunt faces.

The men of Three Platoon stared at them with curious fascination. Except for the Dieppe veterans, most had never seen the face of their enemy before.

"You bastards," said Corporal René Charlebois quietly to himself as he gazed in their direction. "So we meet again. You could have fuckin' killed me at Dieppe if your aim was better. And you're going to get the chance pretty soon again. If it happens, I'm going to make damn' sure to take as many of you with me as I can."

The word rapidly spread that the prisoners were on their way to England, and some to Canada. "Geez, sarge," they asked Bob Banfield. "Is it true that they're goin' to Canada? How come *they're* goin' and not us? Was it them guys who done those bad things to the wounded of the Third Division?"

Sergeant Banfield felt no enmity for these Germans. They were soldiers, like he was. They had undoubtedly fought well, and were captured. This was far better than to have been killed or badly wounded. Some day, after it was all over, they would return home. But over the River Orne he and his platoon would surely have to go. There these lads would learn the true horror of battle. And when they saw their own chums killed, they would learn to hate; to kill or be killed. And this would go on until they defeated the German Army, once and for all. Such, for this young sergeant, was the profession of arms. He would do his job the best way he knew how.

....

That evening, the battalion received orders to strike camp; they were moving up to the front. Across the fields where they had bivouaced for the past five days, the men scrambled to pack their gear. As each company marched off towards the road, there were many last wistful glances at the network of slit-trenches which had been their first safe but mosquito-infested home in this foreign land. They wondered what their circumstances might be, when the next day dawned.

A column of fifty universal carriers clattered up the road, churning clouds of dust, which turned a fiery red in the light of the setting sun. Each of these squat, tracked, lightly-armored vehicles, with no overhead protection, bore the blue and yellow tactical sign painted on one mud-guard, and the crusader's cross on the other, which identified it as being part of a troop transport company from the British Second Army. The British, having brought these Canadians over to France, were now to transport them into battle. Coming to a halt, the column divided itself into packets of twelve carriers, one for each of the four rifle companies.

Major Dick Mitchell assigned four of his vehicles to each of his platoons. Lieutenant Jim Niles ordered Sergeant Banfield to load the men of Three Platoon, and then climbed into the seat next to the driver of the lead carrier. The soldiers were heavily encumbered with combat gear. They were jammed aboard, with little room to move; this promised to be an uncomfortable ride. After a final check of his men, Bob Banfield discovered that there was no place left for him. He jumped onto the rear bumper of the fourth carrier, and held tightly to the ropes which bound the rolled tarpaulin above the ammunition box. Privileges of rank. The officer gets the seat to himself, and the sergeant hangs onto whatever he can......

Colonel Bryson and the battalion headquarters staff drove past in their jeeps, and positioned themselves at the head of the column. In front were two provost on motorcycles, who were to guide the battalion to its destination. The provost started their motors with a roar. The whole column of carriers shuddered, and lurched ahead. The battalion was on its way. Since they were in a battle zone, and approaching ever closer to the front lines, the convoy was in black-out drill, and as it got darker, the muted red tail lights on each carrier were barely visible.

The column wound its way through the narrow streets of Creully, and then headed out into the country, following twisting country roads. At every turn, there were provost stationed to provide accurate direction. With each successive mile came more vivid evidence of death and destruction. In the pale moonlight, the men of Three Platoon, in their crowded, jolting carriers, could see close by the burned-out wrecks of Sherman tanks and German Mark IV's, some with their turrets blown completely off and lying at a distance. Many of the wrecked Shermans had clean holes driven through their armor, the calling card of the dreaded German 88mm guns. And everywhere, the graves.....

They drove through the village of Secqueville-en-Bessin. Many of the stone houses had been badly ripped apart by shellfire. Rear area troops, quartered in whatever buildings were still standing, looked impassively at the long line of universal carriers, loaded with combat infantry. Outside Secqueville, on the flat plain, was a group of large marquee tents, each with huge red crosses painted on white squares. This was a casualty clearing station, being set up. Ambulance vehicles were parked in neat rows in its transport compound, waiting for the next offensive operation.

They reached Bretteville-l'Orgueilleuse, on the Caen-Bayeux paved highway. This village had been totally destroyed. There was no house standing. Slowly and painfully, the carriers negotiated the rubble-filled streets.

"Jesus Christ, what a fuckin' mess!" exclaimed Tom Brennan.

"Yeah," retorted Corporal Charlebois, sitting uncomfortably behind him. "Don't it remind you of your home in Cabbage Town! And for Chrissakes, Brennan, sit still. Your fuckin' pack is gougin' my eye-balls!"

Jack Sipulski stared out with emotionless eyes, cradling his Bren gun, munching on a chocolate bar he had saved from his rations. But this evening drive had torn into the very bowels of Ronnie Matthews. Over and over again, the word *why* echoed in his mind. The peaceful, ordered world which he had known seemed to be collapsing around him. For him, the ride on the carrier was a descent into a personal hell, from which there seemed to be no possible reprieve or redemption. Raw fear gripped his whole being. He was shaking violently, holding his steel helmet tightly over his eyes, as if to blot out the scene of destruction around him.

The others in the carrier were too preoccupied with their own thoughts and fears to notice Ronnie. But Jack did. "Hey, Ronnie! take it easy, buddy! Don' worry. I'm gonna look after ya. It ain't that bad, O.K.?" He put his hand on Ronnie's shoulder, still gripping his Bren with the other.

"Yeah, thanks Jack". Privately, again, he prayed that he would never be called upon to contribute to this fearful destruction, above all to kill another human being. Please God, keep Jack alive.....

The carrier column turned left on the highway — in the direction of Caen. The pavement had been torn up badly in the recent fighting, but with courage and dogged persistence, the Canadian army engineers had patched it up whenever possible. The road was crowded with troops and vehicles, who loudly protested to being ordered off to the side by the provost, as the battalion drove through. In the distance, the men could see the city of Caen, lit by the many fires which were then still raging. Caen, the city of death and ruin, brought by the Canadians — and the British bombers — who came as liberators.

Lebourg. Franqueville. Totally pulverized. Then, within three miles of the outskirts of Caen, the column turned off the highway to the right, trundled into the village of Carpiquet, and came to a stop. Orders were passed down the line to de-bus. The respective companies were gathered together by their company commanders, and told that from this point onwards, they would be going on foot, in single file. They were now very close to the front, and there was to be no talking. Able Company to lead off.

....

Carpiquet. Until now, another insignificant Norman village, in an unremarkable corner of the Département of Calvados. Its name was to be etched forevermore in the annals of Canadian arms, synonymous with desperate hand-to-hand fighting, with no quarter given on either side, the scene of unsurpassed heroism tarnished with the worst of obscene barbarity.

Two days before the battalion landed near Courseulles, the Canadian Eighth Brigade of the Third Division, reinforced to a total of eight thousand all ranks, was committed in Operation WINDSOR to capture Carpiquet, and its airfield, hangars and control buildings to the south and east of the village. This would place the Canadian forces at the back door of Caen. The Germans, as expected, would have none of this. Caen was the hinge of the entire Normandy campaign. To stop the Canadians, they committed a hundred and fifty teen-agers of the 12 SS Hitler Youth Panzer Division, who occupied the village and the thick concrete casemates across the airfield. Tanks from the panzer regiment were hastily despatched to assist the panzer grenadiers. The Canadians were repulsed in their efforts to take the airfield, but they drove the enemy out of the village. This in effect placed them in a highly vulnerable salient, which stuck into the German defence lines and threatened Caen. The Eighth Brigade converted the village ruins into a fortress, from which it repelled attack after fanatic attack by the Hitler Youth to regain this ground. Two days previously, when the other Canadian units were fighting their way into Caen, this brigade broke out of Carpiquet, and advanced a distance of one mile to the banks of the little Odon River, a tributary of the Orne, where the Germans had again succeeded in stabilizing the front. In so doing, they had captured the airfield, the hangers and the casemates.

The men of Able Company, leading the battalion, passed by the makeshift fortified strongpoints, which had been constructed from the ruins of stone buildings, reinforced with mounds of dirt, wood doors and furniture, and whatever else was available. Late into the night, burial parties labored at their gruesome task, collecting the bodies of the dead Germans, who had fallen heaped against the emplacements. The smell of death was everywhere. The young men were sickened at the sight of the mangled bodies, their mottled camouflage smocks caked with blood, heads and limbs missing, and intestines spilling out. They had seen German prisoners. Now they saw German dead. As they crossed the shell-pocked airfield, they were rapidly approaching the front lines, where they would be facing live Germans, whose sole function was to kill Canadians with all the skill and determination they could muster.

Bretteville-sur-Odon, yet another dismal collection of ruins, loomed before them in the dark. The North Shore Regiment, which had fought its way into the village the previous day, was starting to pull out. The battalion was assigned to relieve them in the line. As Three Platoon reached the village, stumbling over the shell-holes and battlefield debris, a platoon from the North Shore, also in single file, passed them, on its way to the rear areas for a well-deserved respite from battle. This platoon consisted of about fifteen men, led by a corporal; half strength, with no sergeant or lieutenant. The significance of this struck home; it was now their turn to enter the killing ground.

"Well, ain't it about time!"..."Here comes the 'baby blue boys'!"..."Hey, does your mother know you're out late?"..."Lot's of luck you poor bastards, it ain't no hotel out there, with fuckin' Jerry breathing down on you all the time!"..."Hey, do you know what a Kraut smells like real close? Better learn in a hurry!" Grim, fearsome, bitter remarks, uttered in barely perceptible murmurs, were their welcome to the battle front.

As Three Platoon entered the village, Major Mitchell was standing by a truncated lamp-post, holding his flashlight closely by his map-case. He addressed the platoon commander. "Jim, get your platoon into these four houses. There are still a few North Shores remaining there to acquaint us with our new surroundings. Take over quickly. Get your Brens out on the flanks. Keep your 2 inch mortar with your platoon H.Q., in case you need defensive fire in a hurry. Company H.Q. will be in that house over there. Report back to me when you're settled into your position."

"Yes, sir. Sergeant Banfield, get your men in there fast". Major Mitchell heard this order, and frowned. He was becoming increasingly uncertain about his junior officer; he was not showing adequate leadership at all. It was just as well that Sergeant Banfield was with him. Dick Mitchell had also been at Dieppe. They understood each other. The sergeant might prove to be the redeeming factor when this platoon was committed to battle.

The houses had no roofs. In fact, there was very little left of their walls. But their shattered remains provided cover and concealment, which was as much as the infantryman in Normandy could ask for. This was how he lived, and where he often died. There was very little by way of creature comforts. Sleep was snatched whenever he could, always with an ear to the next enemy attack. Frequently, he went for days, even weeks, without taking his boots off, and when he did, his socks were fairly rotting. His world shrank to the confines of his section or platoon position. He neither knew nor cared about the grand strategy which was in progress in the campaign. Whenever he was provided any information by the brass, he listened without comment, harboring no illusions as to what these officers wanted. It always meant one thing, that he was expected to go out to kill the enemy, and somehow survive himself. The enemy was whoever stood out there against him. He did not concern himself with what the rest of the Canadian Army or the other Allied forces were facing, other than to wish on them circumstances as uncomfortable and dangerous as his own.

Two Section was assigned to the left flank of the company locality, which in turn was on the battalion's left. A North Shore sergeant was there to greet Bob Banfield. Lean and gaunt, his battle-dress torn and caked with mud, Bob noted that he was clean shaven. Well, now, these New Brunswickers are a real disciplined lot! Shave every morning, and a cup of tea —- no matter how tough things are!

"Get your Brens forward in those dug-out positions, in front of the platoon F.D.L.'s. Better field of fire for them, covering the ground beyond the stream. Keep an eye on those woods to your right front. Jerry has some kind of machine-gun nest in them. Uses the woods as a base for his recce patrols at night. Our lads have had a few tight scrapes with him in that vicinity. And, by the way, you will find out soon enough in the morning that your battalion is holding a salient, and Jerry hates salients. He'll try to infiltrate his tanks at night around your flanks, to shoot up anything that moves in your rear. Hope your antitank platoon and your PIAT men are up to scratch! Well, so long, Ontario! And, as the Brits say — keep your pecker up!"

With that, the North Shore sergeant and the few of his men still remaining left. Bob Banfield turned to René Charlebois.

"You heard the man, *mon cher caporal*. I think Sipulski and his Bren should set up, like now, in that cubby-hole over there. Get your riflemen in position along this wall. Good firing positions over these window sills. I'm off to check the rest of the platoon. No firing unless attacked. Stand down some of your men if it stays quiet. But stand-to at first light."

"O.K., *mon sergéant*, your word is my command!" But before he could get another word out, Jack Sipulski had moved ahead, with Ronnie Matthews behind him, and sited his light machine gun on the rubble, so that he could fire it from a standing position.

"Brennan, get in there with them. Looks pretty lonely out that far. Your rifle may come in handy, if we get into a fight."

....

It was a restless night for the lads of Three Platoon. Fortunately, the German enemy was not aware that the Second Division was now in the line. Their intelligence had misled them to believe that Patton's Army Group was poised across the English Channel at its narrowest part, facing Calais, that this was where the main Allied assault on the shores of the continent would be made, that the Normandy effort was still merely a diversion, and that the Second Canadian Infantry Division would be part of this other force. They sent no patrols out that night, to Bob Banfield's relief, because this meant that there would be a little more time to "shake down", before his platoon would be involved in combat. However, he could hear the guns roaring, and the machine-guns chattering, some miles to the west, where the British were again attempting to capture a height of land, Hill 112, which dominated not only the British troops advancing from the Odon valley, but also provided total observation over any Canadian operation beyond the Orne River.

Dawn came early. The hot sun soon dissipated the morning mist. Ronnie Matthews peered over the Bren parapet, and made out a low-lying ridge about five miles to the south-east. On Lieutenant Niles' map, this feature was designated the "Verrières Ridge", although no French farmer who lived on it ever called it that. Ronnie could not then have possibly known that in nine days he would be out there on that ridge facing the severest trial of courage and endurance of his young life. Now, he was with his two chums, in their own private hole in the dirt, his nerves taut, anxiously waiting for what the new day would bring.

Tom Brennan was the first to notice an ominous form, lying about twenty yards in front of them, on their side of the stream.

"What the Christ is that?"

"I dunno," replied Jack Sipulski, "But it ain't movin'."

"Shit, I think it's a Kraut!" All three strained their eyes in its direction. As daylight broadened, the form indeed proved to be a German soldier, lying motionless, his rifle held in front of him.

"Jesus, let's shoot the fucker!"

"Naw, we ain't supposed to shoot without no orders! Ronnie, go get Corporal Charlebois, quick!"

When Charlebois scurried over to the Bren position, he knew exactly what they were seeing. It was a German soldier, very dead. His face and hands were badly bloated, and flies crawled out of his empty eye sockets; he must have been dead for some days. Patches of orange showed through his field grey jacket, where once bright red blood had spilled, when the soldier fell and departed this life.

As the sun rose in the sky, the light breezes in the direction of the platoon position brought an overpowering stench of decaying flesh. The men attempted to cover their noses with their khaki handkerchiefs tied behind their heads. All of this was unhinging Ronnie Matthews. Finally, there was a loud popping sound, as the gases erupted from the corpse, and he could stand it no longer. He ran from his position, but was grabbed in time by Charlebois, who prevented further flight.

"The hell do you think you're going, Matthews?"

"Corporal, I can't take this any longer. It's all so horrible! Why didn't the North Shores bury the German soldier?"

"Look, lad, you're going to see worse before you're finished with this man's army, one way or t'other!"

"Then let me get out there and bury him myself!"

"Don't you fuckin' get any crazy ideas, Matthews. You poke your fuckin' head out there, and you'll get it blown off! We don't want your stinking corpse added to his! I need every man in this God-damn section alive for as long as possible. Now get to hell back to the Bren position. That's an order, Matthews!"

Ronnie dutifully returned. Shaking with horror he grabbed at his stomach in the effort to stop it from aching. Soon after that, a hot breakfast was brought up to Three Platoon. Ronnie refused his rations.

....

The battalion remained in its location in the front lines for a week. Their mission was essentially defensive, to hold fast while the Allies attacked further to the west, until their turn eventually came, to participate in offensive operations. With each subsequent day, these green troops were provided a little more time to learn their trade in the battlefield, although their front was relatively quiet. There were episodic artillery and mortar duels, and active patrolling in front of their positions, particularly at night, became standard procedure.

The battalion incurred its first casualties. Mortar bombs blew apart some of the slit-trenches and fortified weapon sites, killing and maiming young Canadians, who until then had been in top condition, robust and alive. This had a sobering effect on their comrades; they mourned the loss of their friends. The German out there was determined to kill them, and they had to get him first. Patrols returned at dawn, struggling back with their wounded, dog-tags in their pockets, removed from those who had been killed in fire fights, and left out in the woods and fields until their bodies could be located and buried, when the areas had been captured. These young men were learning to hate; having been taught for so long how to kill, they now convinced themselves that they wanted to kill.

At first light and last light, the entire battalion was required to stand to, when every soldier had to be at his post, alert to any enemy intentions, because it was at these times that attacks frequently came. On one occasion, at dawn, Three Platoon was standing to, closely watching its front, when before them, out of the mist which shrouded the shallow valley below loomed the unmistakable figures of four German soldiers, wearing their steel helmets. Corporal Charlebois was with Jack Sipulski and Ronnie Matthews at the Bren position. At any moment, he expected them to rush the position, firing their Schmeisser machine weapons, and hurling grenades.

"Sipulski!" he yelled. "Target in front, thirty yards, fire!" Jack pulled the trigger of the Bren, which came to life with its dull, thudding sound. The rounds went through the Germans, and they were thrown to the ground. The young Canadians stared in fascination and revulsion at the sprawled, bleeding grey-clad bodies before them. Tom Brennan turned to Jack, with a look of confused disbelief. He had never seen his friend kill anyone before. "Shit," he thought, "so this is war....." Then one of the Germans began writhing, and yelling in pain. *"Mutti, Mutti, hilf mir!"*

"The hell is he saying?" muttered Jack.

"He's calling for his mother! Them Krauts do this, when they're hurt bad! Master race for you!" spat Charlebois contemptuously.

Then, behind the Germans, emerged a lone khaki figure, holding a Thompson sub-machine gun. "Don't shoot! I'm from Dog Company! God damn you bastards! Our patrol captured these Jerries for questioning, and you've just killed them! And look what the fuck you did to me!" He held out his left arm, which was bleeding badly, yet another victim of Jack and his Bren. "In future, I'd be most obliged if you kept your fucking hands off my fucking prisoners!"

This stunned the Canadians. The men jumped out, and at the risk of exposing themselves to enemy fire, dragged the young, blond German into their weapon pit. He was in severe shock from chest wounds, and was retching and coughing blood. The other three were dead. Ronnie Matthews ran off for help. Within minutes, a jeep ambulance from the Regimantal Aid Post drove up, and the prisoner was removed on a stretcher. The soldier from Dog Company crawled painfully into the seat next to the driver, and they were off.

Ronnie Matthews held his head. "God, will he make it? I don't want him to die!"

Jack Sipulski turned to his comrades. "Funny, ain't it?" he said. "They tell us we have to kill them Krauts, but if we don't kill them right then we have to take care of them. It don't make no sense....."

....

On the evening of the battalion's twelfth day in Normandy, its ration trucks left "B Echelon" — the unit's rear administrative area — with compo rations for the troops in the front lines. They were repeatedly held up by the provost on traffic control, and arrived very late, to the consternation of the young soldiers. Tom Brennan was sent back to the center of the village, where the rations were being distributed, to pick up what his section was entitled to — and whatever else he could scrounge. He collared the driver of one of the trucks, to glean what information he could regarding what was happening "on the outside". He was startled to hear from the Army Service Corps lance corporal that there were great things afoot, that convoy after convoy had driven across his route, all in the direction of Caen. The entire Second Division was on the move. One of the division's field artillery regiments had been diverted to the Carpiquet airfield, a half a mile behind them. The twenty-four twenty-five pounders were being dug in, with their muzzles pointed in the direction of the battalion's position.

Rumors flew that these guns were there to support them in an imminent attack. Here was finally their chance to get out there after the Hun, and drive him to hell. However, these aggressive aspirations were quickly dashed, when, after their meal, each platoon was briefed by its commander that they were still to hold fast, to provide a "firm base" from which another unit, the Royal Regiment of Canada, was to attack the next day. The Royals were to capture Louvigny, about a mile to the south-east, on the Orne River. The men were told that the purpose of this operation was to clear the triangle between the Orne and Odon Rivers, to protect the right flank of their Fifth Brigade, which was to cross the Orne at Vaucelles the following day, part of a major Canadian offensive, called Operation ATLANTIC. They were told that they were to be part of the division's reserve; their turn to get at the Germans would soon come.

Outwardly, the young Canadians expressed a great deal of anger and frustration, and made comments about being "always the bridesmaid, never the bride". Inwardly, however, they felt relief that once again it would be someone else who was going to go out there across the open fields to assault the enemy.

"Oh, fuck it!" muttered Charlebois. Then, with a more audible voice: "Fuck 'em all!" He gazed at the men of his section. A broad grin showed on his face, as he started singing in an exaggerated baritone the old, ribald song of barrack room and pub back in England, which had come to be the unofficial anthem of the battalion:

> "Fuck 'em all, fuck 'em all,
>
> The long and the short and the tall!
>
> Fuck all the sergeants and W.O. Ones,
>
> Fuck all the corporals and their bastard sons!
>
> For we're saying good-bye to them all,
>
> As back to our barracks we crawl.
>
> There'll be no promotion this side of the ocean,
>
> So cheer up my lads, fuck 'em all!"

Before he reached the fourth line of the chorus, the entire section had joined him. This impromptu a capella choir, in the midst of a battlefield, rapidly expanded in numbers and volume, as platoon after platoon, from company to company, all the way down the line were belting out the verses, each more vulgar than the last, as the young men released their tensions and fears with this raucous rendition of their familiar ballad.

....

Three hundred yards away, on the other side of the Odon, in the clump of thick woods, two Germans manning a Spandau machine gun, well hidden in the foliage, listened to the refrain in three-quarter time, which drifted towards them.

"Herman, was gibt es mit dem Lied?"

"Weiss nicht, Helmut. Sie singen, aber ich kenne das Lied nicht. Ach! Zum Teufel mit diesen ferrueckten Kanadiern!" So what were these crazy Canadians singing, anyway? No matter, to the devil with them!

There was very little firing on that front, that night. But for the Germans in the woods, and the Canadians in their forward defence lines, the morning would herald the beginning of the final Calvary of Normandy, which many would not survive.

....

Shortly after first light on that clear, bright morning, the men heard the droning of aircraft engines to the north of them, becoming louder and more deafening by the minute. Overhead, the sky was darkened by hundreds and hundreds of bombers. Their target areas were south and east of Caen. As the bombs rained down on the hapless defenders below, whole villages were obliterated, and smoke, dust and fire shot into the sky. The black clouds drifted across the battlefield, and reduced visibility for miles. The earth shook. Many bombers were hit by anti-aircraft fire, and spiralled to their fiery doom. Then the bombers flew home, and the artillery took over; battery after battery added to the continuous thundering roar. Once again, it seemed as if the very bowels of hell had opened.

Through the battalion's lines came a group of officers from the Royal Regiment of Canada. Their task was to "recce" the ground in front of them, in order to plan their attack to capture Louvigny. But the choking dust and smoke which spread across the scene before them obscured everything. Thus it was not until early evening that the Royals were committed to their attack. Then, company after company marched through the lines, deployed as they crossed the Odon, and advanced on the village and chateau to the north of the stream in arrow formation of sections. The men of the battalion had a ring-side view of the attack, and watched with mounting consternation as the khaki figures fell in heaps. The enemy was striking back. The artillery regiment positioned behind them fired their shells ahead of the advancing infantrymen. They could hear the roar of the guns, the shells screaming over their heads, and the explosions in the distance. For the Royals, in their first battle since Dieppe, it was a costly affair. Their casualties streamed back to the battalion's lines. The battle lasted through the night and most of the following day, before all of the objectives had been taken. The men of the battalion watched helplessly at the slaughter in progress in front of them, and were again reminded by their officers that this was not their show. Typical of the foot soldier in Normandy, they were too preoccupied with what was happening to the Royals to care about the rest of the Allied offensive. They did not know that, although the Third Canadian Infantry Division was slowly fighting its way to its objectives, the British armored divisions on their left, whose task it was to break out into the plains south of Caen, had in fact been badly mauled by the German defenders, and could advance no further.

In the meantime, their Second Division's own Fifth Brigade had crossed the Orne, linked up with the Third Division, had taken the villages of Fleury and Ifs, and the Calgary Highlanders were now ensconced on Point 67, a small hill half way to and in full view of the next objective, the Verrières Ridge.

With the Royals now in front of them, the battalion was no longer in the front lines. The men bedded down for the night; but they were not to sleep for long.

CHAPTER THREE

Shortly before midnight, on the battalion's fourteenth day in Normandy, a jeep pulled in to the lines, and the driver was immediately challenged by two soldiers on picket duty, who converged on the vehicle with fixed bayonets. He was a young lieutenant, with a khaki tam-o-shanter, and the shoulder flashes of the Cameron Highlanders of Canada above his blue divisional patches. He identified himself as a staff officer from Brigade Headquarters, and it was of utmost urgency that he speak with Colonel Bryson. He parked the jeep, climbed out, and followed his guide over the rubble and debris of Bretteville-sur-Odon to Battalion Headquarters. This was located in a small house on the northern edge of the village. It had no roof. On the bullet-riddled door, which hung precariously on one hinge, was a wooden sign, on which was painted "BN HQ". Outside the house were two jeeps and a carrier, each of which bore the blue and white tac signs of the battalion. On the doorstep sat a bleary-eyed lance-corporal, cradling a Thompson sub-machine gun in his arms. When he saw the officer, he got up quickly and saluted.

"Good evening. I am Lieutenant Summerby from Brigade, to see Colonel Bryson."

"Yes, sir, go on in. Turn right past the orderly room. You'll find his room, but I think he has already hit the sack."

"Thank you, corporal." The young officer found it humorous, that this particular unit, right in the middle of a battle area, would have an orderly room at its headquarters. Undoubtedly some idiosyncracy of Bryson's, he concluded, who was wishfully pretending that he was back in England, with all the amenities of garrison life! He opened the door, and walked in. A tarpaulin had been stretched between the crumbling walls, to provide protection from the elements. A naphtha lamp swung from a pole, which provided a fitful illumination of the dismal surroundings. Two signal corps corporals sat by their field telephones and "eighteen" radio sets. Battle maps had been pinned on the walls, with colored chinagraph markings on them. Sitting on the makeshift tables, made from empty ammunition cases, were clipboards stuffed with half-completed forms and typed orders — the eternal paperwork of the Army, even on the field of battle. A private soldier sat crosslegged on the floor, cleaning a pair of brown boots. Lieutenant Summerby recognized this lad to be the "Old Man's" batman — for no private owned brown boots. The men in the headquarters stood to attention.

"Carry on, please. I'm from Brigade. Your C.O. — he's in that room over there?"

"He just turned in, sir. I'll get him for you," said the batman. He pushed aside a grey army blanket draped across the entrance to what might have been a kitchen in better times. Lieutenant Summerby smiled, when he heard the batman's efforts to awaken the colonel. "Sir... sir... wake up. An officer from brigade to see you.."

"What... Who... yes... yes... send him in..."

Lieutenant Summerby walked in. Colonel Bryson was sitting on the edge of his cot, in his shirt and battledress pants. The lieutenant saluted.

"Good evening, sir. I'm Summerby, G.S.O. 3 from Brigade. Brigadier McNeil's compliments, sir. He sent me to summon you to Brigade H.Q. soonest. It is a matter of top urgency."

"Yes, is that so... eh.. Somerset, is it?..."

"Summerby, sir!"

"Very well, I'll get my driver..."

"No, sir. I am to take you there in my jeep. Rather difficult to locate in the black-out. I know the roads."

"Right.." The colonel grabbed the half-polished boots from his batman. He pulled on his battledress blouse. On his way out, he lifted his steel helmet from under his cot, strapped it on his head, and departed with the staff officer.

Lieutenant Colonel Phillip Bryson, erstwhile banker and week-end soldier, political hack ever held in high esteem by his party's riding association back home, was on his way to his personal rendezvous with destiny. Already his peacetime enthusiasm about soldiering was beginning to pale, now that he was confronted with the realities of the battlefield. All of this was hardly what he was prepared to endure. There were no dress parades, no teas with diplomatic functionaries and senior generals and admirals in which he was so proficient, no playing at war when he could manoeuver his companies at will, and from which he could return at the end of an exciting "scheme" to the luxuries and comforts of the Officers' Mess. In England, no one had been killed — except for those silly little men who had been in vehicle accidents, inevitably causing a mountain of paperwork.

This was different; living here in Normandy was downright dangerous. It was dirty and uncomfortable — and ever so boring, so far. No grand charges with bayonets fixed. In fact, no glory whatsoever. And the noise and the stench was most disconcerting. Why couldn't his powerful friends in Ottawa have posted him to a higher headquarters job? Canadian Military Headquarters in London would have suited him admirably. His talents were totally wasted in this type of nonsense, something which really should be left to those degenerate Permanent Force men, who knew how to do nothing else anyway.

And what did the brigadier consider so important, to haul him out of his well-deserved sleep, at this inane hour? In the jolting jeep, the thought crossed his mind that perhaps this was to be a sudden transfer, even a promotion, to a more fitting position. Then the spine-chilling possibility occurred to him, that he and his battalion were to be committed to the offensive now in progress. Surely not — his battalion was supposed to be in divisional reserve. Good God...what in Hades was happening out there? He began to shake.

....

Brigade Headquarters was located in the village of St. Germaine-la-Blanche-Herbé, on the western fringe of the city of Caen, and on the Caen-Bayeux highway. During the month of stalemate on the Normandy front, it had served as a center of command and communication for the fanatic Hitler Youth Division, and as such merited persistent attention from the Canadian artillery. Now its pathetic ruins became the temporary home of this brigade headquarters of the Second Canadian Infantry Division, still relative newcomers to Normandy, in the process of committment to major offensive operations.

Wherever any house in the village was at least partially standing, and deemed habitable for headquarters personnel, it was put to use. Elsewhere, a variety of tents, large and small, had been pitched. A number of wooden signs, painted white with black lettering, had been nailed to posts, identifying the functions and offices of this formation headquarters: "BDE MAJOR", "DAA and QMG", "BDE COMDR".

The brigade commander, in command of some four thousand Canadian soldiers, was Brigadier Walter McNeil. Brigadier McNeil had turned thirty-six two days before he and his brigade had sailed out of Tilbury, bound for the shores of Normandy. He was a quiet, pensive man of medium build, with a wide face, a moustache which never seemed sufficiently trimmed, and large ears which stuck out incongruously from under his khaki beret. On the shoulder tabs of his battledress blouse, he wore the crown and three pips which designated his rank, with the red gorgets of a field commander attached to his collars, campaign ribbons above his left pocket, and the badge, "CANADA", above the blue patch on each sleeve. He rarely wore his web belt, or the regulation boots. His informal style of command exuded quiet confidence and consummate skill in conducting the dirty business of war.

The first two days of Operation ATLANTIC had been disconcerting for the brigadier. He had been called to attend several conferences, both with the division commander and the corps commander. Up-to-date briefings had been provided, and operational orders issued. He was relieved to know that the Canadian Third Division had captured all of its objectives after desperate fighting, and that the Fifth Brigade of his own Second Division had successfully crossed the Orne, and was firmly consolidated beyond the suburb of Vaucelles, and, in fact, had one unit on Hill 67, two miles south of the river. The Royals had cleared the triangle between the Orne and the Odon, which included the village of Louvigny. But then came the dismaying news that the British corps of three armored divisions, to the left of the Canadians, had been stopped dead in its tracks, having lost some four hundred Sherman and Cromwell tanks. The British armor, having failed in its mission to break through the German defences, was now withdrawing from the battlefield, leaving the smoking wrecks of its tanks behind. Now, the British Second Army commander had issued orders for the Canadian Third Division to relieve the battered armored units in the front line, and to take over what ground the British had captured. This meant a shift in the

Second Division's front. He began to sense that the Canadians were to be sacrificed to keep the German panzer divisions pinned down, while the British tanks to the east were to be pulled out, and also so that the Americans to the west would have an easier task in breaking out southward to capture Brittany and make a run for the Seine River.

So far, the Second Division had been committed piecemeal in this great offensive. The brigadier was convinced that the principles of war were being violated with abandon. There was neither concentration of effort, nor surprise. The organization appeared confused in the extreme, and he was to learn the following day that the intelligence regarding enemy defensive dispositions was badly faulty. So also was administration wanting, in that the division's units were being committed to the assault without being properly fed.

Late that evening, he received word from Major General Foulkes, General Officer Commanding the Second Division, that the Sixth Brigade was to assault the Verrières Ridge, the next objective, with all three battalions up front at the same time. The Sixth Brigade therefore had no reserve battalion to provide a firm base behind its attacking units. He, Brigadier McNeil, was ordered to detach one of the battalions from his brigade for this purpose. It would mean a night march through the ruins of Caen, to get the troops to the battlefield in time for the attack, scheduled to go in at noon the next day. The closest battalion available was Colonel Bryson's. Thus, in the upcoming supreme test for this unit, still fresh to battlefield conditions, the brigadier would not be able to command it himself.

Walter McNeil was a graduate of the Royal Military College in Kingston. He had served as a career infantry officer in the tiny Permanent Force of the Canadian army before the war. He went overseas with the First Canadian Infantry Division, and was with this formation first in England, and then in Sicily and Italy. He rose rapidly in rank, eventually commanding a battalion in the Italian campaign, and then was sent back to England to attend a crammed staff college course, which led to his promotion to brigadier. He was posted to command this brigade of the Second Division, which was still receiving replacement drafts from Canada after its disastrous experience at Dieppe. Brigadier McNeil was determined to do his utmost to re-train the brigade, to bring it to the highest standard of fighting proficiency possible, before it was once again committed to battle. Following the Army's precept of commanding "two down", he made sure he knew personally not only his battalion commanders, but the individual company commanders as well. In England, he busied himself with frequent visits to each unit, to ensure that all the men of the brigade recognized him, and knew him for what he was — a no-nonsense commander who nevertheless cared personally for the men serving under him.

His experience with Colonel Bryson left him with grave doubts about his subordinate. The colonel possessed none of the necessary personal strengths and characteristics which the brigadier felt were essential for the successful leadership of an infantry battalion in battle. Bryson, he felt, lacked military professionalism, and was essentially a politician in a colonel's uniform. To win this war, the brigadier was convinced that there was no place for infantry commanders playing at soldiers. The German foe was always superlatively led in battle, and the Canadians had to be better than the Germans when it came to a show-down. Regardless of any superiority in artillery fire-power, air support, or even tank strength, ultimately it came down to the man at the other end of the rifle and bayonet, and he had to be led with courage and expertise. After the brigadier despatched Lieutenant Summerby to bring Bryson to his headquarters, he paced up and down in his marquee tent, and the mug of coffee which his batman had brought went cold on the table, untouched.

....

The jeep pulled up to the headquarters' parking area, and Lieutenant Summerby cut the motor. The two officers climbed out, and headed directly to the brigadier's command tent. Colonel Bryson walked in first, still with his steel helmet on his head. He saluted the brigadier.

"Good evening, sir!"

"Oh, good evening, Phil. Sit down, will you? And take that tin hat off!"

"Yes, sir." The colonel was still shivering with anxiety about the purpose of this nocturnal summons.

"There's been a rather important new development." He explained to the colonel the military situation now in progress south of Caen. His remarks were punctuated by the booming of the guns in the distance. A constant chatter was audible, from the signals tent across the way, as messages were coming through both on the wireless sets and by field telephone. The colonel listened with obvious dismay. This was to be no posting to a cushy job. McNeil was in fact ordering him into a damned battle with his battalion, and he was going to have to lead them all the way through Caen, on foot, in the dark, to go into the attack the next morning! Damn the luck of it all!

Brigadier McNeil completed his briefing. "Mr. Summerby will drive you back to your unit. Waste no time in getting your men out of your location, in battle order, and march them single file along this route which I have marked out for you on your map. Traffic control will assist you where possible. Your battalion's vehicles will have to take this more detoured route. With some luck, they should arrive a short time after you do, at your assembly area at the village of Ifs —here." He pointed to the map. "The Black Watch from Five Brigade are firmly dug in around the village. Keep your marching companies close together, or you will lose them in the ruins of Caen and Vaucelles. You have no time to lose. Report to the commander of Six Brigade when you arrive, for further orders. When your mission is completed, you will revert to my command. I expect you to do justice to our brigade. I will try to get over there in the next couple of days, to see how you have managed. These are good soldiers, Phil. Don't let them down! Do you have any questions?"

"No sir, I got the picture. Eh ... wilco! ... I'm on my way!" He saluted the brigadier, then discovered that he had no headdress on, and military protocol forbade saluting without headdress. He quickly jammed his helmet on his head again, saluted once more, and hurriedly left, with Lieutenant Summerby close on his heels.

Brigadier McNeil stared after the colonel, and slowly shook his head. Although he had never openly discussed his feelings about Colonel Bryson with his brigade staff officers, none had any illusions about the limitations of this field officer, and shared their commander's grave concerns at this critical time. The Brigade Major approached the brigadier.

"You've done all you can, sir. You had to comply with the G.O.C.'s orders. Bryson's battalion was the only unit available in the circumstances. Now it is up to him."

"I know, John. It's the men .... damn it, if they had decided to fight us as a brigade, I could have kept close tactical control over Bryson. The man scares the hell out of me, even more than the bloody Hun! If they could only have had a little more time .... and a competent C.O. I wish to God I could have been the one to lead this battalion in its first offensive operation. John, keep me informed, will you? Any news, no matter how trivial..."

"Of course, sir. Now I'd suggest that you turn in. Big day in the morning. We'll keep an eye on things for you."

....

It was two in the morning when Colonel Bryson got back to his lines. Runners were despatched to haul every officer and Senior N.C.O. out of his bedroll to attend an immediate Orders Group outside the Battalion Headquarters. In turn, these people saw to it that every soldier in the battalion hurriedly packed his belongings and fell in by platoons for the night march. The colonel sent on ahead the men of the scout platoon, his personal "Imperial Guard", great favorites of his, since their escapade after their landing at Arromanches. He provided them with explicit orders to stay close to the designated line of march, and to warn the main body of the battalion, fast behind them, of any unforseen eventualities. Able Company came first in the order of march with Three Platoon in the lead, its Two Section directly behind the colonel, Major Mitchell, the O.C. of Able Company, and Lieutenant Niles, the platoon commander.

The night was sultry and humid, and pitch dark. For over a mile, they marched along the badly-cratered road, north-east, in the direction of Caen. To their right, they could hear the intermittent booming of the guns, and they saw winking flashes on the far horizon, like lightning in the distance. None of these young Canadians knew then that the flashes were caused by shells, bursting on the Verrières Ridge, where, by this time the next day, many would be lying, dead or dying.

The leading company entered the city of Caen. The night march became an exhausting obstacle course, as they stumbled over the debris of the devastated city. Whole blocks had been totally demolished; five- and six-storey buildings lay in huge piles of rubble before them. Panting and cursing, the men climbed over large slabs of concrete, stones and half-charred wood beams, flooring, doors and windows, with shattered glass everywhere. Some of the street signs were still hanging on the crumbling walls. "Rue Guillaume le Conquerant" —- God, if poor William could have seen his city now, a thousand years later! On the right was a large church, St. Etienne, ancient beyond comprehension to these soldiers from the New World, its priceless stained-glass windows blown out, its lofty stone walls riddled with shell and bullet holes. St. Etienne was used as a place of refuge for the Cannais, rendered homeless in the cataclysmic battle for their city. A Canadian field dressing station had been erected on its grounds. Under the dim light of its lanterns, medical personnel were working into the night to provide aid to civilian casualties. Here and there, the French civilians were picking their way through the ruins, trying to save something of value from their bombed-out homes. All too often, the provost forcefully ordered them away, to let the marching column through. "Rue d'Ecuyère", typical of the narrow, winding streets of this medieval city, was by some strange fate spared from total devastation. The old buildings loomed ominously over them in the darkness, their battered walls threatening to engulf them at any moment. All this was the price of liberation.

René Charlebois led his section, leaping from pile to pile of fallen debris. It was all that Jack Sipulski could do to keep up, with his large frame, carrying the heavy Bren gun clutched tightly in his hands. For Ronnie Matthews, this march through Caen was a terrifying nightmare. Caen was a city of the dead, and the hideous wanton waste and utter purposeless madness of its destruction screamed at him from each of the city blocks he passed. And the relentless persistent question stabbed at his very soul: Why? Why? Why?

Repeatedly, the column was halted by army engineers, who were attempting to clear a road through for them, with Sherman tanks equipped with bulldozer blades. On these forced rest stops, the men sat down where they could, with their packs and ammunition pouches still strapped to their webbing, too exhausted to talk, waiting for the command to move on again. They were now veering southward. The sound of the guns in the night was becoming louder.

They eventually arrived at the Orne River. All the bridges had been blown as the Germans had retreated out of Caen. The river, separating Caen from its drab suburb of Vaucelles, had become the front line for a week, over which Canadians and Germans had shot it out, night and day. Assault crossings were launched at the start of Operation ATLANTIC, two days before, following which the Canadians fought their way southward to clear Vaucelles of the enemy. Under heavy fire, the Canadian army engineers had thrown several military bridges across the Orne. One of these, plainly signed on the Caen side as "CUBE ONE — COURTESY OF 2 DIV

ENGRS", was a Folding Boat Equipment Class 9 structure, and it was across this that Colonel Bryson led his battalion out of Caen and into Vaucelles. To the east, silhouetting the shattered buildings, the new day was dawning, heavy and overcast.

Closely following the route marked out for him by the brigadier, the colonel turned left at the second intersection, the battalion column trudging along behind him. On they went, along the badly damaged street, debris everywhere. The bodies of dead Canadian and German soldiers were strewn about; rivulets of half-congealed blood streaked across the sidewalks and along the gutters. They passed a German supply wagon train which had been caught in the crossfire. The horses were all lying dead, still harnessed to the upturned, smashed wagons; guts protruded from their torn bellies. Many had had their legs shot off. The stench of death pervaded all.

Then, ahead of them, the young men of Two Section heard the sharp reports of rifle fire. A corporal from to the battalion's scout platoon raced back towards Colonel Bryson, his hob-nailed boots clattering on the cobbled street.

"Sir, don't go any further! There's a sniper up there in that building ahead, on the third floor. The bastard got three of the Maisies over there, rear ech types — one of them's dead! We're providing covering fire, and Sergeant Silverstein is trying to flush him out! He's in the building now!"

The words were hardly out of the corporal's mouth when the popping sound of a Thompson sub-machine gun was heard, in three bursts. Out of the window a body fell, hitting the street with a sickening thump. Three scout platoon men emerged from cover, and cautiously approached the stricken enemy, their rifles pointed ahead.

The scout platoon sergeant emerged from the front entrance to the apartment building, holding his automatic weapon in his left hand. He walked slowly to the colonel, and saluted. In the pale light, his features were ashen, his jaws clenched.

"Jesus Christ, sergeant, what was that all about?"

"Sir, I have just killed a girl. She couldn't have been more than twenty. I didn't know it was a girl, for God's sake! I burst into the room, and fired. She was at the window, with a German rifle. She turned around and tried to shoot me. I fired two more bursts. The impact knocked her through the window. There was a picture of a young German officer on her dresser. I thought the French were our allies, sir! Why the hell did she do this?"

"God Almighty!" exclaimed the colonel. "Well, we won't have to get into any paper work with this type of thing.....damned good thing that this didn't happen in England....Eh....get back to your platoon, sergeant. We have to push on."

The sergeant ran ahead with his men and the column started moving again. As Ronnie Matthews was passing the girl, he noted with horror that she was still alive. He was there in time to hear the last sobbing gasps from her bloodied, crumpled body. He ran over to the corpse, which a moment ago had been a young and vibrant human being, with her whole life to look forward to. "Oh, God! Oh, God!" he cried. "Not this! Why did we have to kill her? She lived here! What are we? — Barbarian killers, we destroy everything, people, their homes, their cities and villages! What for?"

"Get back into line, Matthews!" yelled Corporal Charlebois. "She's dead! She would have killed you, for Chrissakes, if she wasn't fuckin' killed herself!"

Further down the street, the column passed the dead body of the private from the Régiment de Maisonneuve. This lad from the Quebec battalion could not have been more than seventeen. He lay on his back, blood oozing from his chest, shot through the heart by a girl from the land of his ancestors, which he had come to liberate. There was a look of surprise in his sightless eyes and open mouth. Close by, propped against a wall, were his two wounded compatriots. Two stretcher-bearers from a casualty collecting post just outside Vaucelles had driven up in a jeep ambulance, and were attending to the "Maisies". The bulky shell dressings, khaki on the outside and salmon-colored inside, were applied to their blood-soaked limbs.

"Eh, mes gars, vous êtes forts blessés, 'lo'?" called René Charlebois, as he walked by.

"Ah, oui, mais pas trop fort!" was the reply. "Assez pour retourner au Canada, je pense!"

"Bon chance, les maudits Maisonneuves. Mes souhaits au Quebec!" René wondered whether these "gars" were aware of the identity of their assailant. Perhaps it was best if they did not. What a crazy war! He thought about the French girl. Did she have a German lover? Had he been killed?

What possessed her to fight for the other side, knowing that she would surely die? Magnificent courage — or abject stupidity? He dismissed the incident from his mind. Soon he would have to fight Jerry in a big battle. *C'est la vie, comme la vie!*

....

The battalion column emerged from the desolate ruins of the built-up area, after an all-night march. In front of them lay a flat plain of low ground. The highway from Caen to Falaise lay to their left — the Canadian Army's own "Voie Sacrée", which so many soldiers would follow into eternity during the next few weeks. Beyond the highway was the village of Cormelles, held by units of the Third Division. Beyond the village lay the burned-out hulks of the British tanks, littering the open fields. The column passed the casualty clearing post, where the medical corps was frantically at work, as ambulances brought in the Black Watch wounded from the village of Ifs, half a mile ahead, the forming-up point for the marching troops. The heart-rending cries of the wounded portended a similar horrible fate for themselves.

The fields behind Ifs were crammed with vehicles from the Sixth Brigade, whose infantry had already arrived and dug in, in front of Ifs, close to their start-line. Several squadrons of Sherman tanks could be seen re-arming and re-fueling in their laagers. Battery after battery of the division's twenty-five-pounder guns were being dug in, shell cases from the ammunition trucks piling up beside each gun. Six and seventeen pounder antitank guns were being lined up limbered to their carriers, ready to move against any German counterattack.

The Germans for their part were far from idle. Since dawn, there had been constant harassing mortar fire on the forward positions. The men of the Sixth Brigade dug deeper into their slit-trenches.

As the battalion wound its way into Ifs, it passed burial parties from the Black Watch, in the process of burying their dead. The bodies were lined up, wrapped in grey army blankets. As each shallow grave was dug, the dead soldier was lowered into it, and the grave was immediately filled with dirt. The unit chaplain was there, his surplice over his battledress uniform, performing the brief last rites before each grave.

The Black Watch, which had captured Ifs late the previous evening, had fought all night to beat off repeated attempts by the Germans to re-take the village. They were still ensconced in their perimeter slit-trenches around the southern edge of the village, too exhausted to move out. The German dead lay sprawled in heaps outside the perimeter.

As company after company arrived, they filled every house, barn, street and lane. They were ordered to stand down, to wait their turn to advance. Three Platoon found itself in the courtyard of the little stone church in the center of the village. Around the courtyard was a ten-foot stone wall. The young Canadians dropped their weapons and gear, and collapsed on the grass between the time-worn tombstones. The walls of the church had been chipped by small arms fire, but the quaint bell-tower and steeple were still intact.

Jack Sipulski and Tom Brennan, both officially Roman Catholics, wandered into the church. They walked over to the font, where each dipped his fingers into the water and crossed himself. The interior of the little church had also been involved in the fire fight. Its walls had been shot up, and the pews were in disarray. Two dead German soldiers lay where they had fallen in the nave. This was enough for Tom Brennan, and he started backing out.

"For Chrissakes, Tom, you ain't superstitious or sumpin'? They ain't goin' to hurt ya!"

"You can stay, buddy. I got better things to do!"

Jack lingered in the church for a few minutes. Simple as he was in mind and spirit, an uneasy foreboding gripped him. Maybe he should have attended church more often. He tried to pray: "Hail, Mary, full of grace. The Lord is wit' yer...." If there had been a priest, he would have wanted to make his confession.

....

The brigadier of the Sixth Brigade had established his command post in a farmyard, enclosed by a stone wall, on the southern edge of Ifs. Behind the wall, the brigadier and his staff officers looked through their binoculars, observing intently what was transpiring in front of them. The brigade signallers stood by with their wireless sets. Colonel Bryson was invited to join them, with his company commanders. The colonel had managed to overcome his initial revulsion at the prospect of leading his battalion in an attack. Since the village was "in defilade" from the Verrières Ridge, he could not see his objective. But brigade intelligence had informed him that they faced demoralized defenders of inferior combat caliber, and that once the fighter bombers did their work and the artillery hit the ridge with its creeping barrage, it would be a cake walk for the infantry. Colonel Bryson was heartened by this news, and hoped that after a reasonably bloodless battle, he might very well become a hero, and even be promoted and transferred to a more civilized job. He was dead wrong in his expectations.

The sky continued overcast, and rain threatened. This precluded any air support. Furthermore, a British tank unit had strayed over its divisional bounds, and actually got onto the Verrières Ridge, before recognizing its error and pulling back. The Germans, awaiting bigger and better prey, held their fire and remained concealed in their ingeniously camouflaged positions. All of this resulted in a delay in the attack, which was postponed to three in the afternoon, and would have to go in without the fighter bombers.

The Canadian soldiers waited, and so did the Germans. The Canadians had had very little by way of breakfast or lunch, but there was a great deal more than food on their minds, as each man had to come to terms with his own unsettling fears, before closing with the enemy. The Germans, although the Canadians did not know it, had reinforced their infantry during the night with powerful elements from the First S.S. Panzer Division, the cream of their army. For the Germans, this was to be the chance to despatch this green Canadian division, once and for all.

At 1500 hours, dead on schedule, the assault barrage opened up. The seventy-two twenty-five pounders of the divisional artillery had been reinforced by many more guns detached from the Third Division and the corps artillery. Low over Ifs the shells screamed, and within seconds the loud drum-roll of continuous gunfire added to the cacophony of death. Beyond the rise, the shells found their target, the close, humid air reverberated with the explosions, and large plumes of smoke and dust rose into sight. This was a creeping barrage, which would precede the advancing infantry, and lead them onto their objectives. The men were required to "lean into the barrage". The rifle companies of the entire Sixth Brigade climbed out of their slit-trenches, and moved rapidly ahead in extended order, the thin, khaki line stretching almost two miles. Soon they crossed their start-line and disappeared over the rise.

"My God, isn't that superb!" exclaimed Colonel Bryson, as he stared through his binoculars, shifting his vision from flank to flank. "It's the Canadians at Vimy Ridge all over again! Yes! Yes! Like Pickett's charge at Gettysburg! My God, I can't wait to get my boys into the fray as well! We're going to knock the Boche clear to Berlin!"

The brigadier had decided to give the South Saskatchewan Regiment, in the center of the advance, time to get ahead and on to its objectives, before he committed his fourth battalion, which was ordered to follow the path of the SSR, from its start-line to a dirt road running across the axis of advance, a little more than a mile away, where it was to dig in, to provide a firm base for the rest of the brigade. It was to advance in box formation, with two companies forward in extended order, and two companies behind, and Battalion Headquarters in the middle.

The brigadier turned to Colonel Bryson. "Phil, prepare to move your battalion out now to the start-line. You have about an hour. Stay close to your radio on the brigade net. When I give you the order, move as quickly as you can onto your objective. Be sure to provide me with periodic SITREPS. Good luck, and good hunting!"

Colonel Bryson decided to hold his battalion Orders Group then and there in the farmyard, while he and his company commanders were still together. His orders were for Able Company to be the forward company on the left, and Charlie Company on the right, with Dog Company behind Able, and Baker Company behind Charlie, to complete the box formation which the brigadier required. The axis of advance, as it was for the South Saskatchewan Regiment, was the unfinished railway line running due south of Ifs. The colonel then provided orders regarding the supporting elements for each rifle company. During the advance, his headquarters and the Regimental Aid Post would move up in the center of the box. There would be a little time for the officers to brief their sub-units in turn, before the troops moved off to the start-line.

The battalion's officers scurried off, leaving the brigadier and his staff in his command post, from which the brigade battle was to be controlled. The abbatoir of the Verrières Ridge was beckoning.

CHAPTER FOUR

The men of Able Company stood huddled together, jammed into the narrow street outside the churchyard. The young Canadians waited anxiously for the return of their company commander from his Orders Group with the colonel. They were in battle order, with their steel helmets on their heads, their packs and other gear firmly strapped on, and their weapons slung over their shoulders. For the past hour, they had stood by, waiting for orders to move out, sweating in the oppressive heat. During this time, the artillery delivered its barrage over their heads with unabated fury. The thundering drum-fire was accompanied by the screaming of shells, rending the air above them. The reverberating explosions of the shells gradually became more distant, as the barrage crept ahead of the attacking infantry units, but with increasing frequency came the sound of small-arms fire. The intermittent rhythmic thudding of Bren guns, interspersed with the high-pitched, irregular sizzling of the German MG 42's — the Spandau machine guns - and bursting grenades, added to the tumult of the raging battle ahead of them.

With few exceptions, none of them had been involved in a major assault on the enemy before. Despite the heat, a cold fear gripped them. Their throats felt parched, and their stomachs churned, as they waited for the order to move out. They wondered what was happening to the battalions already in the thick of it. There was some comfort in knowing that their comrades were all there with them, yet each soldier felt very much alone with his thoughts and fears. Would his luck hold out and would he survive? What if he were badly wounded? Would it hurt? Each wanted to hide or run from the ordeal facing him, but it would be even worse to let his chums down. "God Almighty," each thought, "I'm too young to die in this fucking battle. I haven't even started to live....."

Major Dick Mitchell walked briskly over to them. He had anticipated the frightened, anxious look on their sweaty faces. This was how all soldiers reacted, before a major attack. If they survived, it would not matter how many start-lines these lads would cross, the gripping fear would always be the same. For a moment, he thought of his wife and the two little daughters he had left behind; he needed them badly now. He had taught history in a secondary school in Oshawa, before he was mobilized with his militia battalion into active service and sent overseas to fight. Now he was *making* history, not teaching it. And his present job was to lead this rifle company into battle, to destroy the enemy and its detested regime, and if he survived, return home. If he survived..... He could not allow his men to detect any of the fear and uncertainty which gnawed at his own innards. He had made up his mind that he would brief and provide orders to his entire company, officers, NCO's and privates included, all together.

"All right you people! Gather around me. We don't have much time. We're soon going to be moving out in single file by platoons to our start-line, just beyond this village. When the C.O. gives the word, we will advance up the gradual slope towards what they call the Verrières Ridge. We will be doing this in box formation. Now you guys know all about it; you practiced it God knows how many times back in England. You know the drill. Quite simple. Able Company will be on the left, and in front." A murmur of dismay came from the ranks. "O.K., steady up, you guys. No sweat! Why has the C.O. chosen us to be up front? Well, we're the best damn company in the battalion, agreed? So this means we will be on our objective before Dog Company, behind us. The objective is a dirt road running across our front, half way up the slope, a little more than a mile from here. When we get there, we're going to dig in. We're going to dig in fast and we're going to dig in deep. And we are going to hold that position, while the rest of Six Brigade clears its objectives ahead of us. We're going to play defensive back in this game, just in case Jerry pulls something unexpected.

"Supporting elements. Anti-tank Platoon will be pulling up into our lines, as soon as we get dug in. Carrier Platoon will be moving up on our left, so don't mistake them for Tiger tanks and shoot at them! Come on lads, what's the matter? No sense of humour?

"Platoon commanders and platoon sergeants; stay in the center of your platoons. Have your Bren men on your flanks, and keep your mortar man and your runner close to you. I want Three Platoon on the left, One Platoon in the center and Two Platoon on the right. Get into your positions as soon as we reach the start-line. On the colonel's command, we will cross the start-line in extended order. I don't want to see any of you bunching up — let's not give Jerry any more of a target than we have to."

"L.O.B.'s - those to be left out of battle: CSM Tenute and CQ Howes - to make sure the chow is brought up, when the battalion cooks have the chance to get around to it and get it to us. Our Company 2IC, Captain Werner, will be here in Ifs - just in case some enterprising Kraut knocks off your Major! Come on, guys, a smile!

"Any questions?"

"Yes, sir! Can we double our service insurance?"

"O.K., wise guy! I'll take it up with the adjutant! Any other questions? All right, let's go!"

With that, Able Company marched in platoon files to the start-line. The men deployed in extended order. Behind them were the slit-trenches which the SSR had occupied before they moved out. As the shells continued to roar overhead, the men fought the irresistible urge to jump into these empty trenches, where there was some protection. But they stood fast, painfully conscious of the fact that their khaki uniforms were all they had between flesh, blood and bones, and the bullets and shrapnel awaiting them.

Major Mitchell stood close behind the center of the Company line. His signaller with the Eighteen RT set held the earpiece of the receiver tightly to his head. Within minutes, he handed the receiver over to the major. "Sunray on the net, sir!"

"Nan Item to Nan Item One, Two, Three and Four. Do you read me? Over."

"Nan Item One to Nan Item", responded Dick Mitchell. "Loud and clear!" He heard the replies from the other three company commanders. "Nan Item Two to Nan Item. Loud and clear." "Nan Item Three to Nan Item. Loud and clear."....

"Nan Item to all call signs. My Big Sunray has informed me that our little friends have reached their objective. It is now our turn to catch up with them! All call signs, move now! I say again, all call signs move now! Out!"

Major Mitchell handed the receiver back to the signaller. He turned to his men, and called out loudly: "Able Company, fix bayonets! Prepare to advance!... Advance!" The young soldiers followed their company commander into the fields of waist-high grain, their axis of advance identical to the one followed by the South Saskatchewan Regiment two hours previously.

....

Three Platoon was on the extreme left of the battalion's two forward companies. The men moved rapidly across the wheat fields, which stretched in front of them as far as they could see. The terrain ahead gained elevation gradually, almost imperceptibly, for about two miles, and beyond the crest of the ridge it dropped into a small valley. This height of land stretched for some two miles across their front, west of the Caen-Falaise highway. On the military maps, this was called the Verrières Ridge, named after a small village on its north-east corner. The land undulated gently towards the ridge, so that at the start of the advance, the platoon was marching across "dead ground", or were "in defilade", meaning that there were low rises which prevented the enemy directly observing them from the crest of the ridge. Furthermore, at first the Canadians could not see the crest and the battle which was raging across it with increasing fury. But as they approached the last rise, the sounds of battle became louder with every yard, and the explosions of the bursting shells from the barrage came ever closer.

Sergeant Bob Banfield positioned himself in the center of Two Section of the platoon, with Corporal Charlebois on his left. The platoon commander, Lieutenant Niles, early in the advance, began falling back behind the platoon line. This grated on Bob Banfield. Their officer should be up front with his men, particularly in that this was the first time these green troops had been on offensive operations. They would soon close with the enemy, regardless of the fortunes of the Sasks in front of them. As they marched across the fields to the roaring of the guns, Bob Banfield recognized that he must assume leadership responsibility. Repeatedly, he checked the deployment of his men in their extended order, calling to the sections if they were lagging behind, or had moved ahead of the line. Periodically, he glanced to his right, to ensure that his platoon was in line with the rest of the company, and to maintain some visual contact with the Company HQ section.

With the practiced eye of the professional soldier, Bob Banfield searched the terrain before them for any possible cover. There was none. No trees, bushes or farm buildings could be seen. It was monstrous, he felt, for the Army brass to have committed infantry in an assault over bare fields, before an alert, well dug-in and camouflaged enemy, highly skilled in exploiting any tactical error on the field of battle. The sooner they arrived at their objective on the reverse slope of the ridge, the better — if they had time to dig in.

The platoon soon crossed the artillery's barrage line, where the creeping barrage, preceding the Sasks, had started. From that point on, the wheat fields were pocked with fresh shell holes. A few cows lay dead in the wheat, having strayed there and been killed by artillery fire. There were also dead Germans, caught by the barrage, sprawled beside their demolished mortars and machine guns.

"Jesus H. Christ!" Bob heard René Charlebois, the farm boy from Lafontaine, exclaim. "What a hell of a waste of wheat! Ain't goin' to be no harvest after we get done with these fields!" For the French, Bob thought, there would be another season for harvesting, and another, but war's harvest on the lives of young soldiers was final and permanent. For them, there would be no other season.....

To their right, about a half mile away, was a small hill. Bob recognized this to be "Point 67" — the furthest the Canadians had advanced the previous day. The Calgary Highlanders were still manning their slit-trenches, dug around and on top of the hill. Their role on this day was to provide the firm base for the Cameron Highlanders of Canada, whose mission was to capture the twin villages of St. Andre-sur-Orne and St. Martin-de-Fontenay, a mile ahead off on the steep western edge of the Verrières Ridge. Behind the hill, immobile, stood several Sherman tanks. Bob concluded that they were safely sheltered there from the dreaded German 88's which could destroy at a considerable distance any Canadian tank which ventured out onto these bare fields, into their field of fire. So this was to be an infantry battle. All very well — unless Jerry had tanks and chose to use them. He wondered where their anti-tank platoon was, and their carrier platoon, which was to protect their left flank.

As Three Platoon crossed the last gradual rise, the very heavens above them opened up. Added to the din of the battle, lightning flashed across the heavy skies, followed by thunder and a lashing rain drenched the troops. There was no time to pull on their gas capes. In the rain storm, they could not see the violent battle which was in progress on the crest of the ridge, a mile away. Neither, it transpired, could the artillery's Forward Observation Officers, who had accompanied the infantry to direct fire from the guns, dug in behind Ifs. Furthermore, their radio sets became inoperable in the rain storm. Fearing that they would hit their own advancing troops, the artillery men were forced to curtail the barrage. About this time, all radio contact with Brigade Headquarters in Ifs broke down. All four Canadian infantry battalions were no longer controlled by Brigade in this crucial battle; they were completely on their own.

As the forward companies of the battalion plodded across the last five hundred yards of rain-sodden grain, the whole hideous panoply of the battle lay before them. In the fields lay the dead bodies of the Saskatchewans, blood-soaked and torn apart. Stretcher-bearers with red cross armbands attended to the wounded, and struggled to remove them from the battlefield, on stretchers, and on their backs. Many of the SSR carriers were churning down from the crest, loaded with wounded. A number of Sasks walked down towards them, without weapons, dazed. There seemed to be no control by their officers. These were men who wore the same khaki uniform, with the same blue divisional patch on their sleeves, with whom the battalion had trained those long years in England, and with whom there had always been a friendly rivalry. They were bewildered and horrified.

René Charlebois turned to Bob Banfield. "Christ, it looks like a fuckin' balls-up, Bob. Too damn' much like Dieppe, eh?"

Bob Banfield could sense the panic and utter demoralization of the SSR troops. What had happened to them beyond the crest of the ridge? They were to have reached the forward slope, and held their position there. A terrible disaster must have befallen them. These were signs of more than a repulse — it was the beginning of a total rout. If so, it would mean that his own battalion would be into the fighting very shortly.

To his left about a half mile away, a clump of buildings came into view. This was the Beauvoir Farm, one of the initial objectives of the Fusiliers Mont-Royal. A vicious firefight was in process out there. The FMR obviously had been halted in its advance, and was locked in a death-grip with the German defenders. Then, in the gap between the FMR and the Sasks, Bob recognized the shapes of German tanks, blurred by the rain as it came down in sheets. The Sasks had in fact been flanked by German armor. High on the gradual slope of the ridge, directly ahead, he saw the Sask anti-tank guns being frantically pulled into position by their carriers. But before the six pounder guns could be unlimbered and brought into action, one by one the guns and carriers, and the crews with them, were methodically blown to pieces by accurate 88 fire from the eastern face of the crest. The bodies of the gunners were hurled like rag dolls into the air. The tanks then swung towards the Sask rifle platoons which were already starting to pull back, down the slope from the crest. The Mark IV tanks opened up with cannon and machine gun fire; this surely meant the end for the SSR.

The German defenders were now confident that the attack by the SSR had been bloodily defeated, and that they were retreating in disorder. All the while, they had observed closely the advance of the other Canadian battalion on the heels of the Sasks. Now was the time to engage it and to defeat it in turn. Their mortar and field artillery weapons were well dug in and concealed on the other side of the crest. For the gunners and mortar crews, this was truly a defensive fire task beyond their fondest hopes — to engage infantry deployed in extended order, advancing across bare fields with no protective cover. The target area had previously been accurately ranged in. It did not matter that it was raining hard.

Mortar bombs began to whistle down onto the advancing companies. The bombs detonated on impact with a loud crump. Able Company started taking casualties. Young soldiers were being blown to pieces, their uniforms and skin ripped off their bodies, revealing lacerated muscles and sinews — like peeled oranges. The terrified screaming of the wounded resounded over the bursting bombs. "Stretcher-bearer!" came the repeated, frantic calls from down the line. Instinctively, the young men went to ground, hugging the sodden dirt, paralysed with terror. Shortly thereafter, the German artillery started firing air burst, with high explosive shells, which peppered the prone, mud-soaked khaki figures with shrapnel from above.

Throughout all of this, Major Mitchell never appeared to flinch. He ran from one platoon to the other, deliberately exposing himself to the flying steel fragments, urging his men to get up on their feet and move on. "Keep moving, lads," he yelled. "If we stay here, we'll all be blown to hell! Come on, now, let's go! Follow me!"

Bob Banfield pulled himself into a crouching position. Looking around, he was alarmed to see how many casualties there had been in Three Platoon. The men who still survived lay prostrate in the mud, desperately trying to get as close to the ground as possible, holding their steel helmets tightly over their heads. Lieutenant Niles was nowhere to be seen. Bob concluded that the officer was either dead or badly wounded. Without hesitation, he knew that he must now assume command of the platoon. Also without hesitation, he must obey the company commander's order and follow his example. He stood up, clutching his rifle tightly, and yelled: "O.K., Three Platoon! You people heard the major! Now get the hell off your butts, and let's move it!" To his relief, the men clambered onto their feet, the mud and grain coating their faces and uniforms. With a wave, Bob Banfield ran after the major, and his men followed. No longer was there any semblance of a straight line of advance. The men raced ahead in groups over the remaining distance to the objective. Before them, the narrow dirt road came into view. This road started in the twin villages to the west, out of view below the incline, where the Camerons were fighting desperately to capture the villages. It ran eastwards past the Beauvoir Farm, where the Fusiliers Mont-Royal struggled to gain possession of the farm buildings; and then on, out of sight, past the Troteval Farm and on to the Caen-Falaise highway. They must hold this road at all cost, to form some sort of continuous front against the counter-attacking enemy, or the whole brigade front could collapse.

On they ran, taking more casualties. The lead platoons of Able Company crossed the road. Major Mitchell called out: "We're here, lads! Now dig in!" But as the first entrenching tools struck into the sticky mud, the men came under devastating fire from the German Spandau machine-guns, sited on the crest of the ridge. Their sizzling, high-pitched rattling, added to the bursting mortar shells, caught the young Canadians in their frantic attempts to dig for cover.

"Get down! Get down quickly!" was the next order from Dick Mitchell. The men needed no second warning. Once again, they went to ground, as the machine-gun bullets clipped the wheat stalks above them, like a monstrous harvesting machine, dropping the grain on top of them. They were, in effect, pinned down, and nakedly vulnerable to infantry assault. Then, the German barrage began to slacken. The machine-guns fell ominously silent. To Bob and René Charlebois, this meant only one thing;

they would shortly be assaulted by the German infantry. Through them and over them, the remaining survivors of the routed Saskatchewans ran, some carrying their wounded, down the slope of the ridge. Many carried no weapons. For these panic-stricken men, only one purpose remained; to escape from this hideous scene of destruction as fast as their legs could carry them. Their officers were running with them.

Major Mitchell crawled on his belly over to Bob Banfield. "Where is Mr. Niles, sergeant?"

"I don't know, sir. I've taken over command of the platoon."

"O.K., that's how I want it. How are you off with your Brens and PIAT's?"

"We have two Brens operational. I have sent Sipulski with his crew over to the left flank. All three PIAT's still operational. I'm holding them in the center."

Dick Mitchell was relieved. Here was an N.C.O. he could rely on, regardless of what was happening. And Charlebois was with him. Three Platoon, he knew, was prepared to fight. "Sergeant Banfield, keep your men down until they are close enough. Then stand up, and let 'em have it! We have had the shit kicked out of us all day. Now it will be our turn to dish it out. Try to keep in contact with me. Good luck, Bob!"

Half on his side, Bob Banfield managed to salute his major. In this fearsome situation, like his company commander, he was able to maintain his calm. The men must never see him otherwise. "Corporal Charlebois!"

"Yes, sarge! Us chickens are here ready and waiting!"

"Wait for my order to stand up. Make sure Matthews has his Bren mags in his hands, to re-load Sipulski's Bren quickly! Keep Brennan close by those two. They'll need some protective fire when Jerry shows up!"

"I read you, Bob." These were the last words the two veterans from Dieppe, close friends, both from Simcoe County in Ontario, were to exchange.

....

Jack Sipulski lay on his back, once again lovingly cradling his Bren gun. The safety catch was off. He made sure to keep the muzzle pointed away from the dirt. A strange calm had come over him. He was the section's Bren gunner, and proud of his status with them. He knew he was good at his job, which had provided him with the only important purpose he had had in his young life. He was here to kill Germans, and he would do his duty with blind determination. After all, that was what the Army wanted. He thought of nothing else.

Tom Brennan was on his left, holding his rifle tightly. Silently, he cursed his luck to be in such a dangerous predicament. Nothing to scrounge in this corner of flaming hell. Christ, what a bloody way to go!

For Ronnie Matthews, sheer, stark terror gripped him. His mouth was badly parched, and his stomach in tight, painful knots. Lying on his face in the mud and grain, he shook uncontrollably. What was to become of them? "Lord, I don't want to die! Why is all of this happening? Why? Why?" Yet, terrified that he would be killed, he feared even more that he would be required to kill Germans. Horrifying doubts assailed him, that he would let his section down when the time came.

They waited. When the hell were the Germans coming? Then, behind them, they heard the unmistakable churning and grinding of their carrier platoon, moving up towards them, on their left. Suddenly, over their heads, came the deafening, cracking sound of 88 shells. One by one, the carriers were hit by the flat trajectory, high velocity fire from the crest. None of the carriers, with their Bren guns, survived. Those of the carrier crews who were not hit raced across the field to join the troops of Able Company. They had lost their flank protection in a matter of minutes. Against the 88's, the Bren carriers did not stand a chance.

Down the slope came the victorious German infantry, charging straight at them, firing their Schmeisser sub-machine guns at the hip. On they ran, yelling like fiends from hell itself. As Bob Banfield peered over the wheat stalks, he observed that the enemy soldiers did not wear the standard field-grey uniforms of the German infantry, but instead they wore speckled camouflaged smocks, with camouflaged helmets. On the lapels of their smocks were the black patches, with silver "SS" markings. They were SS panzer grenadiers. These men were from an SS panzer division, whose battle group must have been transferred during the night to bolster their defenses against the Canadian offensive. This would account for the Mark IV's which had smashed into the SSR. And if so, their Panther tanks, huge killing machines impervious to six-pounder anti-tank fire, could not be far behind. A fresh Canadian infantry division had thus been committed against the elite of the German Army. How was their battalion going to hold against this lot?

As the German soldiers closed within thirty yards of the Canadians, Bob Banfield yelled: "Stand up. Target in front! Rapid fire! Rapid fire!"

"Two section! Let's give it to them bastards!" echoed Charlebois. He jumped up, firing his Thompson sub-machine gun at the charging enemy. Jack Sipulski immediately followed, and brought his Bren to the firing position, from his hip. He pulled his trigger, and the Bren thudded to life. With deliberation, he swung the Bren, spewing bullets, from one side to the other. German soldiers started falling in heaps before him, writhing in the wheat field.

"Yah!" Jack yelled. "I'm gonna get you fuckers good for what you done to some of my buddies!" He fired in bursts until the bolt mechanism slammed shut after the last round was expended. Deftly, he pressed his thumb against the empty magazine, ejecting it. He turned to Ronnie: "Gimme another mag, Ronnie, quick!" With trembling hands, Ronnie handed over one of the loaded Bren gun magazines he carried. Jack started firing into the Germans again. All along Able Company's line, the young Canadians fought back, with a frenzy born of fear, shock and revulsion at what they had been forced to experience. Here was the opportunity to assert their very identities, which they felt they had lost in the relentless confusion and carnage of the last two hours. Here was a tangible enemy, and they intended to annihilate him.

The German panzer grenadiers recoiled at the ferocity of the defence put up by the Canadians. Having previously systematically destroyed the fighting capability of the SSR, they had fully expected this new battalion to fold and run in turn. They began pulling back, firing as they retreated, until they disappeared over the rise. The men of Three Platoon cheered lustily. Sweating and panting with tense excitement, they looked at each other, elated that they were still alive. They had discovered that these German "super-men" were made of flesh and blood like them, and were far from immune to death from bullets.

Their exultation was short-lived. From their left front came an ominous clattering of metal and grinding of gears. Four Mark IV tanks appeared on the crest. At first, they stood still, like great beasts of prey, scenting the air. Then, slowly, they began to move down the slope. Along the company line, the word "Tanks!" spread alarm and consternation. Major Mitchell, half crawling up and down the line, called out to each platoon: "Tanks to your front! PIAT men, load your weapons. Stand by! No firing until they come within your range!"

Then, once again, they could hear carriers churning across the fields behind them, moving towards them. The anti-tank platoon had arrived just in time! As the six-pounders were unlimbered from the carriers, they could hear the commands ring out: "Action front! Three hundred yards! Load! Prepare to fire!" Sergeant Banfield watched as the gunners went through the prescribed drill. These guns would even out the odds for them. The rifle platoons could take on the panzer grenadiers — but tanks and infantry attacking together could result in a dangerous situation for them, as the Sasks before them had learned. However, once again, the German 88's found the range, and fired first. Again, gun after gun was knocked out, the men in the crews somersaulting in the air with each shuddering explosion. The gunners never got close to the forward companies, and in fact were behind the reserve company lines, when they were hit. They saw the tanks, they unlimbered out in the open, and they were destroyed.

The Mark IV's moved gradually towards the left flank of the Canadian position, their co-axial machine guns firing widely over their heads. Then, over the crest, swarmed the panzer grenadiers, this time with twice their previous numbers, and they charged headlong at the forward companies. Orders were given to the Canadians to stand firm. The leading enemy infantry was engaged with rifle and Bren fire, and began falling. But more followed, and they were closing fast.

Ronnie Matthews crouched behind Jack Sipulski, with a pile of loaded Bren magazines at his feet, salvaged from the destroyed Bren carriers. He could see Tom Brennan firing off round after round from his Lee Enfield rifle, working the bolt frantically to eject each casing after firing. Ronnie was convinced that Tom was not aiming accurately, but blindly shooting into the mass of advancing enemy. Jack, however, was deadly with his Bren, no matter how he held it. The sweat poured down his broad features. There seemed to be no fear in him. He grinned, as if he were back on the ranges in England, scoring well in his shooting.

Jack suddenly jerked, and fired off the rest of the magazine in an arc in the air. Slowly, he collapsed on his back, beside Ronnie. Blood was pouring out of a bullet wound through his forehead. His arm muscles twitched, and then he was still, his eyes wide open and rapidly glazing, as his life ebbed to its end. Ronnie removed his helmet, tore open the shell dressing which was tucked under the camouflage netting, and held it over the wound. "Jack, Jack, for God's sake, don't die!" He repeated this over and over.

"Quit doin' that, Ronnie! Jack's dead! The fuckin' Krauts killed him!" Tom's blunt remark stunned him. The Germans had killed his friend! A blinding rage seized him. He was no longer afraid.

"Matthews, pick up that Bren! Get up and keep firing!" René saw how Jack had died. He needed his number two on the Bren to man this vitally important weapon.

"Yes, corporal!" Ronnie loaded a new magazine, stood up and fired into the enemy. As he saw the German soldiers crumple before his bullets, an animal savagery took over. Ronnie, the quiet boy from Toronto, who had shunned violence and killing, had become an exultant killer.

The Germans closed with the Canadians. A violent melee ensued; bayonet and rifle butt, fist and entrenching tool. The slaughter raged unabated. Soldiers of both sides fell dead and dying across the Canadian position, spilling blood, brains, guts. None of them had a moment to reflect what their young lives might have come to. On this bitterly contested, blood-soaked field in Normandy, far from their homes, many young Canadians and young Germans were dying horribly.

To the left of the attacking panzer grenadiers, their Mark IV's lumbered forward, down the gradual slope, towards Three Platoon's left flank. Sergeant Banfield rushed two of the PIAT men to the threatened corner. The first man stood up and took aim. He fired at the lead tank, but the rocket missed and exploded harmlessly in the dirt beyond the tank. The turret of the tank turned, and the co-axial machine gun fired a long burst, cutting the PIAT man in two, at the waist. The second PIAT man stood up and fired. This time, the round hit home. It penetrated the tank on the left side, above the bogey wheels and in front of the engine compartment. The tank "brewed" instantly. Clouds of thick black smoke poured out. The crew attempted to bail out, their black uniforms on fire, and they screamed horribly. Those who made it away from their burning tank were killed by rifle fire. On the Verrières Ridge, there was no quarter, given or taken. The other tanks veered away from Three Platoon, and moved off towards Ifs, between Dog Company and the FMR behind Beauvoir Farm. There was nothing to stop them.

Major Mitchell surveyed the strength of his company. Two platoon officers had been killed, one was missing, and he had lost a number of NCO'S. All three platoons were now commanded by sergeants. Of the hundred soldiers he started the day with, he had less than thirty effectives left. He could not hold much longer. He contacted Colonel Bryson on his Eighteen radio set. Should he withdraw across the dirt road? He could not obtain clear orders from the colonel, who sounded confused, even incoherent. Dick Mitchell began to doubt whether his politician colonel could hold the battalion together, the way things were going.

The panzer grenadiers pressed attack after successive attack with relentless determination. The forward companies started to give way. Only a dozen men remained in Three Platoon, still able to fight. Some of these were wounded, but were as relentlessly determined to fight it out to the end, at the side of their comrades. Charlie Company on the right was virtually annihilated. Dick Mitchell then decided on his own initiative to give the order for Able Company to withdraw. The remnants of Charlie Company followed. Sergeant Banfield waved to his section commanders, pointing rearward.

Corporal Charlebois acknowledged Sergeant Banfield's order, by waving back and nodding. Quickly, he looked around. There were dead and wounded Canadians and Germans everywhere. The rain, now a drizzle, did little to wash away the pools of blood at his feet. "Jesus!" he muttered. "What a fuckin' mess this has turned out to be!" There were six men left in his section, including himself. One young soldier was sitting beside his dead comrades, trying to prop himself up with his elbows, staring at his shattered right leg, where the blood was oozing through the shell dressing, and soaking his trouser leg. "This one," thought René, "we're going to save out of all of this."

"Matthews.....Brennan.....Smith.....Ferraro — we're pulling out! Crouch as low as you can. Take it slow. When we get over the road, we will be joining up with Dog Company. Matthews, keep a sharp look-out with your Bren, in case the bastards try to rush us. Brennan, stick with him. Smith,

Ferraro, see if you can lift Helder up. Try to carry him out with you. Get going first. Get him to the R.A.P. as soon as you can. I'm going to hold them off as long as I can here. Now move! Move!"

As Ronnie Matthews was backed off, his Bren held tightly in both hands, he saw René Charlebois slam a fresh ammunition clip into his Thompson sub-machine gun. The corporal glanced back to make sure his section was on its way. With a final "Get going, Matthews!" he turned towards the enemy. They were attacking again. A stick grenade was hurled at René, exploding close to him. The shrapnel tore into his left shoulder. Blood spurted out, drenching his uniform. He grimaced with pain. He did not turn. Instead, he advanced towards the enemy, firing his Thompson with his right hand. René knew he was going to die. If he was to be sacrificed in this battle, he was determined that he would make the sacrifice worthwhile. If it helped his section to withdraw, then what could be better......

A burst from a Schmeisser ripped through his chest. As he crossed the dirt road, Ronnie Matthews saw his section corporal fall. The farm lad from Lafontaine, whose fervent hope was to be able to bring home a doll to his little sister, was dead.

....

The sky, heavily overcast with drizzling rain, was beginning to darken, as the remnants of the forward companies clambered into the slit-trenches of the reserve companies behind the road. The violent hand-to-hand fighting had bought time for the men of Dog and Baker Companies to dig in. They apprehensively watched the movements of the Mark IV tanks, which had broken through the Canadian lines, and were roaming at will across the wheat fields, shooting up any target in sight, particularly when any effort was made to bring up food, ammunition and replacements to the beleaguered front-line troops. However, as dusk descended, the tanks did not tarry long. Darkness was something every tanker feared, when infantry could creep up on them with anti-tank rockets. Having done all the damage they could, the panzers clattered over to the Caen-Falaise road, down which they drove with all haste, back to the protection of their own lines.

As soon as he could, Major Dick Mitchell found Colonel Bryson at Battalion Headquarters. The colonel sat in the corner of a slit-trench, his gas cape pulled over him, dripping with rain. The battalion signallers were in the trench with him, desperately attempting to re-establish communication with brigade. The colonel seemed to be totally withdrawn, disinterested in any messages, garbled as they were, which came through.

"Sir," Dick Mitchell said, "we have lost most of Able and Charlie Companies. What are your orders now? Do we hang in here for the night, or do we pull back further? There's an SS panzer battle group out there, which will likely attack us again by nightfall. If they hold back, then you can be sure they will be on top of us in the morning with tanks and infantry. Have you heard anything from brigade? Any word of reinforcements? What about our tanks? Any SITREP's regarding the FMR's and Camerons?"

The colonel did not answer. The destructive confusion and hideous butchery he had witnessed was quite beyond his personal resources even to begin to cope with. In this, his first test of battlefield leadership, he had been found utterly wanting. He was no longer capable of command control. He made the most crucial decision in his short-lived combat career. With slow deliberation, and in silence, he climbed out of the slit-trench. There was a carrier standing behind the Battalion Headquarters. Although its crew had all been killed, it was still functional. The colonel lifted himself into the driver's seat, started the motor, and drove off in the direction of Ifs, away from the scene of ghastly carnage, out of battle and to safety. He abandoned his battalion.

Dick Mitchell was stunned. He cursed silently as the colonel drove off. The battalion's 2 I/C was "left out of battle", and until he was brought up, the senior company commander would be required to assume command of the battalion. The awesome conclusion struck home. He was the senior major. It was his duty to take over command. Before any panic set in following the precipitate departure of Colonel Bryson, he would have to act quickly. He assembled the shaken battalion headquarters staff, and informed them that he had taken over command of the battalion, until further orders. He urged the signallers to spare no efforts to contact brigade. He was now on his way to check with each of the company HQ's, and would start with Dog Company. They were to reach him there, if they got brigade on the net. Dick Mitchell's strong leadership immediately changed the morale of these soldiers. They now worked for an officer whom they trusted, and whom they were convinced could pull them through.

Crawling and sliding over the shell-torn wheat field in the fading light, Dick Mitchell soon located Dog Company's HQ, where Major John Epstein was waiting for him. Fully expecting an enemy attack at last light, Epstein had just concluded an inspection of his company forward defence lines, where he had his platoons dig in a perimeter defence. When Dick Mitchell had led the survivors of Able Company into Dog Company lines, the men were formed into one composite company. Now that Mitchell had taken over command of the battalion, Epstein would command the composite company. John sensed an understandable reluctance in the Able Company commander to relinquish his men. He reassured Dick with some humour that they would be treated with respect and dignity, that he was not to fret, and far better was it that Dick now had the responsibility for the entire battalion, rather than John.

When Dick reached Baker Company on the other side of the unfinished railroad, he was dismayed to discover that their slit-trenches were badly scattered. On the advance up the slope, they had been cruelly mauled by the enemy counter-barrage, and the men dug in where they could. They had absorbed the few men from Charlie Company who had been able to get away. The young captain, temporarily in command of Baker Company, waited anxiously for orders. Dick Mitchell saw the danger on the battalion's right flank, and ordered Captain Lederman to shift his men eastwards, and to consolidate their positions close to the rest of the battalion. Fields of fire had to be integrated. They had to move quickly, and dig in again, fast. It was a calculated risk. Dick prayed that the Germans would not choose this time to attack.

The Germans, however, had had their fill of slaughter for the day. They had driven the Fusiliers Mont-Royal out of the Beauvoir and Troteval Farms. They still held onto the southern fringes of St. Andre-sur-Orne and most of St. Martin-de-Fontenay. In the center, they had destroyed the Saskatchewans as a fighting unit and had driven back the forward companies of Dick Mitchell's battalion. For the Germans, it had been an eminently successful day. The night seemed a good time to re-supply and reinforce their exhausted troops. And most likely, the morning would see the collapse of the entire Canadian front. A concerted attack would be all that was needed. What they did not know was how weak the Canadian defenses were that night, and had they had sufficient reserves to push through, they could easily have reached Vaucelles, and the Orne River beyond.

For the young Canadians in the battalion, having lost half their comrades, it was another sleepless night. They were cold, wet and hungry. Rain water pooled at the bottom of every slit-trench and shell-hole. Straining their eyes and ears for any sign of activity which might herald another enemy attack, they shivered in the cold drizzle, which persisted most of the night. Where it was necessary, they dug in deeper. In the dark, they succeeded in locating two six-pounder anti-tank guns which could still fire, which they manhandled into position.

During the night, a convoy of carriers finally made it up the gradual slope to the battalion's lines. Led by Regimental Sergeant Major Stuart Reid, the carriers had been loaded with ammunition, drinking water and compo rations. The men had not eaten all day. They cheered loudly, as the wooden cases were broken open, and the tinned rations were being distributed. The "M and V" (meat and vegetables) was consumed cold. B echelon had come through for them; they were not forgotten.

....

RSM Reid found Major Mitchell at Battalion Headquarters. "By God, sir! I'm glad to see you! But you'll never pass muster on parade, looking like that, sir!" he exclaimed, as he scanned the mud-coated apparition before him.

"'Fraid I wouldn't at this time, Mr. Reid...you'd have to give me a chance to freshen up first! We've been in one hell of a dirty, bloody fight with Jerry!"

Dick Mitchell listened intently as RSM Reid briefed him on the events which had occurred during that tumultuous evening. Brigade Headquarters had lost all communication with the advancing units because the radio sets could not operate in the rain storm. It was not until the straggling survivors from the SSR had reached the rear areas that the plight of the advancing troops finally became known. Frantic efforts were made by the officers from brigade to rally the men. They were now assembling north of Ifs, were being re-organized and were already taking on replacements. Fearing an imminent breakthrough by the enemy, the Black Watch had been alerted, and the regiments of the Canadian Second Armored Brigade, for a possible counter-attack.

When Colonel Bryson arrived in Ifs, he was interrogated, and summarily despatched to Division Headquarters under guard, for further disposition. Major Tolchard, the battalion's 2I/C, immediately set out in the jeep to locate the battalion to take over the command, but a 75mm shell from one of the marauding Mark IV tanks struck the jeep, killing his driver and wounding him badly. He was evacuated forthwith. Major Mitchell was to continue in command of the battalion.

Most important of all, Dick Mitchell was informed that brigade had ordered him and the battalion to hold their present position at all cost; there were to be no reinforcements.

....

RSM Reid went out to the platoon positions, to visit his young soldiers. He did wonders to cheer and encourage them, speaking freely with each of them. He was deeply saddened to discover how many of the battalion's men had been killed. He located Three Platoon, down to no more than a section in strength. He was relieved to find that Bob Banfield now commanded this platoon, and that he still had Ronnie Matthews with him, now their Bren gunner. He was even glad to see that Tom Brennan had survived so far. Brennan in his eyes was always "that dirty little man", and poor Tom had never looked dirtier!

The carriers left with the wounded; Stuart Reid stayed behind. This was his battalion, and more than ever, they needed him.

CHAPTER FIVE

As the men of the battalion peered into the dark void in front of their slit-trenches, they saw the first glint of light in the distance, outlining the flat, featureless crest of the Verrières Ridge. Dawn arrived on the wet, cold battlefield, gradually dispelling the inky darkness which had held unseen terrors during that seemingly interminable night. The intermittent rifle and machine gun fire, the Very lights periodically illuminating the murky sky, the moans and cries of the wounded who still lay out there with no possibility of rescue, and the cold drizzle which persisted all night, had made sleep impossible. As first light arrived, they clutched their weapons, hands stiff with cold and fatigue, and waited for the enemy to make his move. But the enemy did not appear at dawn. He bided his time, until better visibility facilitated the task he had set himself, to drive the Canadians back and destroy them.

A few of the young soldiers ate of the rations they had saved during the night, anxiously watching for any movement to their front. Then, from beyond the crest, came a hollow rushing sound from the enemy mortar emplacements, as the lethal bombs were propelled from the barrels in a high trajectory over the crest, to descend onto the Canadian positions.

"Take cover!" Within seconds, the first bombs exploded on impact with their dull "WHOMP", shaking the ground around. The men cringed in the bottom of their trenches. The mortar barrage continued without let-up. Where there were direct hits into trenches, the soldiers occupying them were blown to bloody fragments. The enemy was obviously intending to soften up the Canadian defenses, preparatory to a full-scale attack.

Before the barrage halted, they heard the ominous clattering and grinding of gears, as the German tanks appeared on the crest. Their large size, with their long, protruding guns, sloped frontal glacis and squared-off backs, identified them as Mark V Panthers, enormous engines of destruction, far superior to any tanks the Allies possessed in Normandy. Their thick armor was virtually impenetrable by anti-tank fire, unless they were hit in vulnerable places at close range. Their nemesis, the rocket-firing Typhoon fighter-bombers, still could not operate effectively in the heavy overcast and misty conditions. Some thirty of these behemoths roared down the slope. They were closely accompanied by hundreds of smock-clad panzer grenadiers. The enemy was attacking in force, and this time was employing tanks and infantry in a combined assault. Yelling and screaming, the German soldiers fast approached the Canadian lines. The terrified defenders prepared themselves for the next onslaught.

"Target in front! Two hundred yards. Fire!" Major Mitchell had carefully planned his battalion perimeter defence, with Bren positions sited to deliver interlocking fields of fire. The battalion's mortars had been ranged in, so that mortar fire was brought to bear on the attacking infantry. The mortar barrels were elevated almost to ninety degrees, to range the short distance. The panzer grenadiers were being cut down, and their advance slowed. This tactic would effectively separate out the infantry from the tanks, which could then in turn be engaged with tank and anti-tank gun fire. But none of these weapons were available, except the two six-pounders and the PIAT's; the battalion was desperately out-gunned. The Bren machine-gun fire splattered against the German tanks, with no apparent effect. Their hatches had been slammed shut prior to the assault. They came on, their infantry lagging behind. There was nothing to stop them.

The leading Panthers lurched their way through and over the Canadian forward defence lines, their coaxial and hull machine-guns spraying everything before them. They rolled over the slit-trenches, crushing whomever stood in their way. The crews of the six-pounder anti-tank guns engaged the enemy tanks, but their armor-piercing shells bounced off the thick, sloped armor, ricocheting off in all directions. One shell knocked the track off a Panther, which slewed crazily to one side, its engines roaring, like some wounded prehistoric beast. The Panthers which followed immediately spotted the anti-tank guns, and demolished them, with their crews, with converging rounds from their 75mm cannons. Another Panther was struck in its underbelly, as it loomed over a slit-trench, where a soldier had discharged his PIAT rocket at close quarters. It burst into flames, sending dense clouds of black smoke into the air. Other tanks were also hit by PIAT's, and some were badly disabled. The courageous young soldiers with PIAT's stood up to these monstrous machines, until every last one was killed.

The German tanks tore wide gaps through the Canadian position, and then roared on ahead, northward, across the shell-torn wheatfields, towards Ifs. The panzer grenadiers caught up, and closed with the Canadian defenders. Once again, the Germans and Canadians swung into each other, in an orgy of frenzied butchery. The Germans set about to blow the Canadians out of their slit-trenches with stick grenades, then to shoot them down with machine pistols, before they jumped in with the bayonet. Many Canadians and Germans transfixed themselves on each others' bayonets, and bled to death together at the bottom of the trenches.

Dick Mitchell left his command post, and ran from one end of the crumbling line to the other, urging his men to stand up to the enemy assault. He saw with alarm that many of the young men were jumping out of the trenches, attempting to get away. Without any cover, caught between the German infantry behind them and the Panthers in front, they were instantly cut down. The survivors of the battalion began to give way. The men abandoned their beleaguered positions, and withdrew down the slope. Many attempted to fight back from the cover of shell-holes, but the screaming German infantry, with the smell of victory in their nostrils, ran after them, determined to destroy the battalion to the last man.

A number of the wounded gave themselves up to the doubtful mercy of the German SS troops. This was the signal for others to follow, choosing to risk the lot of a prisoner, over certain death in this abbatoir on the slope of the Verrières Ridge.

The battalion as an effective fighting unit had ceased to exist. However, Major Mitchell and RSM Reid rallied some of the survivors, and fighting a desperate rear-guard action from shell-hole to shell-hole, eventually made their way back to Ifs.

There was now a dangerous salient in the center of the Canadian front. Frantic efforts were made by Sixth Brigade to shift what resources they had available to form a blocking position before the Village of Ifs. Squadrons of Sherman tanks from the armored brigade rapidly deployed in hull-down positions, and engaged the stampeding Panthers in a furious tank battle. To assist them were the seventeen-pounder guns of the divisional anti-tank regiment, which were quickly dug in to support the Shermans. Then, the weather started clearing, and the Typhoons returned to the battlefield. Like the cavalry of old, these fighter-bombers saved the day. The marauding Panther tanks became the prey themselves, as the rockets found their marks.

It was all too close; the German breakthrough attempt had been foiled, but the salient remained. Another Canadian battalion had been sacrificed in an ill-prepared, poorly-organized attempt on the Verrières Ridge. And already a third battalion, the Canadian Black Watch, was preparing an assault up the same slope, to recover the few acres of blood-soaked wheat fields which had been lost.

....

In the swirling fury of the German assault, their main tactical concern was to smash through the center of the battalion's front, expecting that there would be a precipitous rout, and the Germans could then destroy what remained of it in the open. The flanks of the position mattered little to them. On the extreme left flank, Sergeant Bob Banfield and what was left of Three Platoon had dug in. The men saw and heard the battle raging with ever increasing violence immediately to the west of them. The Panthers thundered through, followed by the yelling panzer grenadiers. Gradually, the shouting and firing, the exploding grenades and the clashing of rifle, bayonet and entrenching tool drifted past them. The cacophony of battle became more distant. By some bizarre combination of circumstances in the "fog of war", Bob's platoon had been left behind. Very cautiously, he crawled out of his slit-trench. The entire Canadian position before him lay in ruin. Several Panther tanks were burning furiously. The dead and dying littered the ground. Here and there, German and Canadian wounded, with all enmity discarded, tried pitifully to help each other. German stretcher-bearers were scouring the area, and had started to carry the wounded back up the slope. Fresh German infantry platoons were scurrying down the slope and across the captured position, to reinforce their attacking comrades. No one noticed him. Now was the time to move out, and if possible make it back to the Canadian lines.

"Come on, you men. Quietly. Hug the dirt. Let's try to get the hell out, before the Krauts discover us!"

Without hesitation, the handful of men followed him. On their bellies, they crawled through the wheat, dragging their weapons with them. Some fifty yards beyond the abandoned position, they came across a clearing in the wheat field. The Panthers, as they had churned about, had flattened the wheat stalks with their wide tracks. There was a gaping laneway of about twenty feet. Bob knew that they could not remain where they were. They had to get across, if they were to have any chance to make it back over this terrain, held as it was by the enemy.

"Matthews, Brennan. I want you to go with me first. Run like hell when I say. The rest of you, wait until we're across. When I wave, get over fast, and hit the dirt once you're into the wheat again. Clear, everyone? O.K., first group, let's go!" The three men fairly flew over, and disappeared into the wheat. There was no enemy reaction. Bob crawled to the edge of the wheat stalks, and waved for the others to follow. As the three jumped out, a burst of Spandau machine-gun fire caught them. They fell, twitching and bleeding in the clearing, and then were still.

"God damn you fucking bastards!" rasped Bob. He slithered over to Ronnie and Tom. They heard excited German voices, yelling out commands and directions, to the west of them, where the Spandau section must have been located when they opened fire. They had no time to lose. "Come on, lads! Let's high-tail it, before they catch us!"

There was a shell-hole some distance away. Panting with exhaustion and cold, gripping fear, their hearts pounding in their ears, the three Canadian soldiers, all that was left of Three Platoon, dropped into the shell-hole, landing in the soft mud at the bottom. Ronnie still had his Bren, the other two their rifles. They could hear the German troops rushing about. Above the din of machine-gun and rifle fire, there were now the sharp cracks of high-velocity tank cannon fire. Bob recognized that there was a desperate tank duel in process. "Bloody armor," he muttered. "Where the hell were they, when we needed them up there the most? Sounds like now they're being used to save the brigadier's ass!"

Bob Banfield looked at the two privates, who were shaking with fear. This, he felt, was as far as they should try to go. They could very well die in this muddy ditch, but to try to move any further in this raging battle was to die for certain. These boys were totally exhausted. "Well," he thought, "this is where Three Platoon makes its last stand"....."O.K., you guys, we're staying put right here!"

The three of them huddled in the mud at the bottom of the shell-hole, and waited. Their torn battle-dress uniforms were coated with the grime and mud of that battlefield in Normandy, where they had witnessed such horrors of unremitting butchery, the cruel insanity of man's uncontrolled barbarity, beyond anything they could have imagined in their young lives. This experience had caused them to doubt their own humanity. They were like sewer rats, clawing and wallowing in the mud, and though they had survived thus far, they had abandoned all hope of surviving further. As the storm of steel flew in all directions above them, they no longer felt fear, but rather a numb resignation, born of utter exhaustion. Paradoxically, as the day dragged on, they seemed to find a semblance of peace. They could not go any further. And if they were discovered, or blown to eternity by another shell landing in this same place, then so be it.

They could hear the voices of German soldiers, as they ran past them, towards the north, too preoccupied with staying alive themselves to notice the three lone Canadians. A German mortar team set up barely twenty yards from them. The *gefreiter,* on the radio set was calling out azimuth and range. *"Feuer!"* he yelled, the bombs were dropped down the tubes, followed by a loud rushing sound, as the bombs fired out of the tubes and took flight. To their relief, the mortar section moved off, seeking a tactically better location. They could hear the Panthers clanking and churning in the distance, seeking positions of vantage to engage the Canadian tanks defending Ifs. Solid armor-piercing shells tore into the ground close by, when the Canadian gunners missed their targets.

"Stay awake, lads!" called Bob Banfield. "Keep alert! I don't want either of you falling asleep on me — not until I get you home!" Bob was determined to maintain control, even though only two of his platoon remained. He must not show them any semblance of doubt that he would get them out alive.

As the weather began to clear, the unmistakable drone from the skies above heralded the arrival of the R.A.F. fighter bombers. The aircraft shrieked towards their prey, loosing their rockets at the German armored vehicles. Then, as Bob Banfield looked up, he saw a flight of three Spitfires, high in the sky above them. Down they came in steep dives, and began machine-gunning the German infantry. Bullets thudded into the ground, very close to the shell-hole, where the three cowered. They could hear the agonized cries of the wounded Germans, as the Spitfires took their toll.

Suddenly, a young German soldier lurched into view above them, and fell into the shell-hole, landing on top of Tom Brennan. Much of his right shoulder had been shot to shreds, and the gushing red blood drenched Tom. "Ah, Christ!" Tom yelled in horror. "Get the fucker off me! Shoot the bastard!"

Bob Banfield swung his rifle towards the fallen enemy. His trigger finger tightened. He stared at the young German. He was a lieutenant in the panzer grenadiers. These were the people who had killed almost all of his platoon. He wore no helmet. His young, blond face was rapidly becoming deathly pale, as beads of sweat broke out on his brow. His machine pistol had dropped into the mud.

"God damn it, no!" Bob shouted. "There has been enough killing for all of us! Enough of all of this God-damned carnage. If it's the last thing we do, we're going to help this man! Matthews, help me pull him off Brennan.....easy now.....easy."

The three Canadians worked frantically to save the life of their enemy. Bob removed shell dressings from under the netting over their helmets, and deftly and gently applied pressure dressings to the gaping wound. He placed his pack under the young officer's head. He took off his water-bottle, and held it to the German's mouth. The German gulped down the water.

"Danke...Danke sehr....."

These young Canadians, who during the last two days would have killed any German on sight, labored to save this young German's life. And in so doing some of their humanity, which had been so violently stripped from them, returned. To their surprise, with the battle raging about them, they had discovered a purpose which transcended that which they had been rigorously trained to discharge and was exclusively demanded of them. The badly wounded young German officer was no longer the hated and feared enemy, to be destroyed. They felt a strange kinship with him. For the moment, this was sufficient.

The German smiled weakly at them. Pointing at Tom and Ronnie with his left hand, he said: *"Wie alt sind Sie?"*

"The hell is he saying?" asked Tom.

"*Alt*.....I think he means 'old'," replied Ronnie. "I think he wants to know how old we are.....Nineteen! Do you understand? Nineteen!" He held out ten fingers, then nine.

"Ach, ja. Ich verstehe...Ich bin auch neunzehn...."

"Shit!" exclaimed Tom. "The fucker's nineteen like us!"

Ronnie looked at him with a deep compassion. Although a commissioned officer in the army of the enemy, this lad was very much like himself. He had been called upon to fight for his country, as Ronnie had been. He had shared the same horrors, and no more wanted to die before he had ever lived than Ronnie did.

"Comrade," said Ronnie quietly.

"Ja," was the immediate answer. *"Kamerad, wir sind alle Kamaraden...."*

Beyond the shell-hole, they heard a clattering rumble which grew louder until the earth around them began to shake. There appeared above them the huge steel form of a Panther tank, as it backed into full view. The tank stopped moving, its engines still roaring. It was painted a tan color, with irregular green patches sprayed on for camouflage. On the turret were the large letters "R O 1", in black on white. Next to the hull machine-gun, on the frontal glacis, was a painted symbol which looked like a key imposed upon a crest. Bob Banfield recognized the tank as belonging to the commander of the panzer regiment from the 1st SS Leibstandarte Adolf Hitler Panzer Division. He concluded that they had been up against a battle group from this elite division, which had crossed the Orne from the British front, to block the Canadian offensive on the Verrières Ridge. An officer of senior rank stood in the cupola of the turret. He was dressed entirely in black. He wore earphones over his peaked cap, and the wires dangled down the front of his dusty, oil-stained uniform as he scanned the battlefield with his binoculars. Eventually, he lowered these, glanced to his side and then down into the shell-hole. The Canadians froze. Quickly, the German officer climbed out of the cupola, jumped from the tank, and walked towards them, his Luger pistol drawn.

Gripped with terror, they stared at this apparition above them. He had gaunt features. Below his eyes, where his goggles had been, his face was covered with smoke and powder grime. He wore the rank markings on his shoulders of a lieutenant colonel, or in the nomenclature of the SS, an "Obersturmbannfuehrer". Various medals were attached to his jacket, including the Iron Cross. Around his waist was a plain brown leather belt, with a simple metal buckle. He wore the black ankle boots of a tank officer. To the Canadians, he was the personification of death itself.

In perfect English, the colonel addressed them. "You men down there, do not move, or I shall kill you. Remain sitting. Now throw your weapons out. Quickly." The Canadians obeyed.

The colonel noticed the wounded German lieutenant. His tense features appeared to relax. For a moment, it seemed that he could not believe what he saw. When the Canadians threw out their weapons, he holstered his Luger, and spoke to the young officer. *"Um Himmels Willen, Leutnant! Es efreut mich dasz Sie nicht todt sind! Aber schwer verwundert....und der Feind hat Ihnen Hilfe gegeben! Unglaublich!"* Turning to Bob Banfield, he exclaimed: "I am indeed grateful to you, sergeant, for what you and your men have done for our lieutenant. My good God, in this damned war, there is chivalry yet, not so?"

The German colonel was soon joined by the gunner from his tank crew, also attired in a dusty, tarnished black uniform, with the rank markings of an "SS Oberscharfuehrer". The colonel rapped out orders. The N.C.O. left, and shortly returned with stretcher-bearers. These men jumped into the shell-hole, and worked to remove the seriously wounded lieutenant. The Canadians provided assistance, and the Germans muttered *"Danke"*, without giving them a second glance. As the lieutenant was borne away, he waved to the Canadians with his left arm. *"Nochmals vielen Dank....Ich werde es Ihnen nicht vergessen...."* He thanked the Canadians and vowed he would never forget them. The Canadians hoped he would make it home.

"Well, as you know, we all have a battle to fight - more is the pity! - and I must be going. I have decided not to take you prisoner. Our forces will soon be withdrawing from the salient. If I may predict the minds of your generals, there will be another attack on this ridge. When it comes, we shall destroy it like the others. Such a waste of fine infantry. We know you are from a new division. You have fought magnificently. If we had men like you Canadians — under German generals — we would easily win this war. You may wear the English uniform — perhaps a shade darker, yes? — and you have their organization and equipment. But you make far better soldiers. You go into an attack — shall we say — like hockey players!

"Your next attack will of course be preceded by your artillery barrage. No precision aiming! We call these 'fire-rollers'. They smash everything in their path. Stay down in your shell-hole. If you survive your barrage, your infantry will soon find you when they get up here.

"One final request. Our panzer grenadiers have captured one of your junior officers. He was hiding in the wheat. He had no weapon. We believe he deserted his soldiers. If he was a German officer, we would have shot him. I want you to take custody of this officer. Your commander will know what to do with him.

"Well, good luck, chaps! The war will not last forever. Perhaps we shall meet again!"

The Canadians were stunned. Everything seemed to be happening too fast. Why had the Germans spared them? Chivalry, the colonel had mentioned, a moment of truce and good will in the living hell of a battlefield. Where was the sense of it all?

Bob looked at the colonel. "Thank you, sir" he replied, with a mixture of gratitude, relief and hesitant admiration. Bob concluded that, in the horror and chaos of war, this was a true military professional. Still sitting, he saluted the colonel. The black-uniformed enemy smiled, returned the salute and walked off. He and his gunner N.C.O. climbed into the Panther. Roaring as its gears engaged, the behemoth backed away and disappeared.

Within a few minutes, two panzer grenadiers appeared before them, dragging a man in khaki uniform between them. Not too gently, they pushed him into the shell-hole and departed. The Canadians stared in disbelief. The officer was their platoon commander, Lieutenant Jim Niles.

Jim Niles said nothing. He sat down with the others, and gazed ahead, with empty, despondent eyes. Bob Banfield fought to suppress his anger at his officer, who had abandoned the platoon at this critical time. He struggled to account for what had happened. Had Niles suffered from concussion from the German counter-barrage, and blacked out in the wheat fields? In the confusion of the final rush to their forward defence position, had he lost contact with them, and was with another company during the fighting? The officer shared no more with them now, than he had ever done. Bob Banfield concluded that Jim Niles was in no condition to resume command, even over three men.

"Mr. Niles," he said, quietly and deliberately. "We are all that is left of Three Platoon. In your absence, I have had to assume command. I do not think you are fit to take over again. We are in a bad situation. I am determined to get us out of here somehow. You will remain with us, and you will take my orders until we return. Do you understand?" There was no reply.

....

The brigadier of the Sixth Brigade, stalwartly ensconced in his command post on the outskirts of the village of Ifs, followed the battle with mounting apprehension. It had been an exhausting and trying two days for him and his over-worked staff. Not content with their repeated frantic calls on the field telephones, both the division commander and the corps commander periodically descended on the brigadier, usually unannounced, to confer with him as desperate efforts were undertaken to manoeuver units into line, to prevent the German counter-offensive from rolling through the center of the Canadian front. Out of perilous military exigency, finally and rather late, came some semblance of coordination and cooperation from all arms, so lacking when the original assault was planned and executed. Like the Battle of Waterloo, it was a "near run thing".

The brigadier eventually found himself in command of what amounted to the best part of a makeshift Canadian "panzer grenadier" division, in the field. Two of his original infantry battalions still tenaciously fought it out, on each of the flanks of the Canadian front. The two other battalions, badly mauled and depleted, were now held in reserve in the rear areas, re-organizing and taking on replacements as fast as fresh troops arrived from England. He also now had under command the entire Canadian armored brigade, as well as the divisional reconnaissance unit and the anti-tank regiment, now heavily committed to fighting off the German panzers, which threatened to break through the center at any time.

One final infantry battalion was made immediately available to him, and that was the Black Watch, the Royal Highlanders of Canada. To them was to fall the task of clearing out the enemy salient. Only the infantry, the "Queen of Battles", could conduct this type of operation. The Black Watch was now moving out of Ifs to the same start-line as their two preceding sister battalions. They were to deploy in extended line, in the same manner. Their advance would be heralded by a creeping artillery barrage, and the Black Watch was ordered to "lean into the barrage", also in the same manner.

The artillery was ready. Battery after battery north of Ifs stocked its ammunition behind the guns, and awaited the signal. Major Mitchell pleaded with the brigadier to hold back the creeping barrage, until he could retrieve as many survivors from his battalion as possible from the battlefield. The brigadier consented, but could not wait long. By this time, the German panzers had furtively begun to pull out from the salient, and they were already digging in on the crest of the Verrières Ridge, anticipating the next Canadian assault. A screen of their infantry remained to absorb and slow down the attack.

Finally, with the Black Watch straining to get going, the order came for the guns: "Fire!".

....

The "fire-roller", predicted by the German tank colonel, came crashing down on the devastated battlefield. Bob Banfield heard the explosions of twenty-five pounder shells coming closer and closer to where he and the three others crouched in the shell-hole. Very soon, the ground about them was torn up with cataclysmic violence. Clods of mud and dirt fell on them, half burying them where they lay. Dust filled their mouths and noses, and choking off breath. Terrified, they waited, expecting to be blown to pieces by their own guns, their bodies ripped apart by the razor-sharp, red-hot shell splinters. Every muscle and nerve was taut and vibrating. Above the frantic pounding of his own heart, Bob could hear animal-like whimpering from the two young privates. But, through all of this raging maelstrom, Jim Niles sat upright, indifferent.

A heavy body arced across the shell-hole, and fell on top of them. It was the hind half of a cow, maggots swarming out of its bloated intestines. Ronnie Matthews retched and vomited. Shaking violently, Tom Brennan pulled himself away from the stinking carcass.

"Ah, Christ, sarge, I can't stand this no more. I'm getting out!"

"Stay where you are, Brennan!" yelled Bob, grabbing him tightly by the shoulders. "I told you, you bastard, that I'm going to get you out of here, when the time comes. Don't make it any harder for me!"

The barrage rolled on past them, churning up the fields beyond the dirt road, and over to the crest of the ridge. Covered with debris, they lay there gasping. They were still alive. Perhaps there was a chance after all.........Soon they heard Canadian voices, commands being yelled out, above the sound of the exploding shells.

A young Canadian sergeant, holding a Sten gun, appeared above them. "Holy shit!" he muttered in disbelief. Then: "Major Fraser! Over here, sir! There are four Canadians in this here hole! I think they're still alive!"

The major, with a Browning GP35 pistol in his hand, rushed over. "My God! We were told that there were none left alive from your unit out here! Lieutenant, are any of your people wounded? There are medics coming up behind us. Lieutenant, can you hear me? Lieutenant!....."

"Sir," interjected Bob Banfield. "The officer with us can't answer you. I think he is in a state of shock...."

"O.K., sergeant. God Almighty! You people must have been through a terrible time! You have done your part. It is up to us now. So get the hell out of there, and start making tracks back to Ifs! Your unit is re-forming in Vaucelles right now. Take your officer with you, and get him the care that he needs. Good luck to you, lads!"

" Yes, sir — thanks a hell of a lot for getting us out of here....."

"Sergeant, get going! Now!"

Bob hauled Jim out of the shell-hole. He looked around for their weapons, which were nowhere to be seen. "Brennan! Matthews! I told you all along, I'd get you out of this! Pick up your packs! We're going home!"

Wearily, the four soldiers trudged back across the remaining mile. They passed through the Black Watch platoons, advancing in extending order with bayonets fixed, who stared at their filthy, bedraggled figures in amazement. "Jesus Christ, what happened to you guys? ... Got the shit kicked out of you, eh?" ....."Hey, Mac, anyone else come out of this fuckin' mess from your outfit? .... We been passin' your dead guys ever since we crossed the start line...." Even Tom Brennan, usually full of wise-cracks, was too exhausted to answer.

Everywhere on their way back across the battlefield lay the broken bodies of dead Canadian and German soldiers. Scattered about were the burning hulks of German armored vehicles, some blown apart and lying upside down in the wheat fields with black, oily smoke still pouring out of them.

They passed the Black Watch carriers, towing their anti-tank guns. There were dozens of Sherman tanks, squealing and clanking behind the advancing Black Watch infantry, testimony that this time Brigade Headquarters had made certain the infantry was closely supported. They passed a 40mm Bofors battery, their gun carriages limbered to their 60cwt. Quad tractors. The young captain commanding the battery surveyed the panorama of death and destruction, and silently wept.

Major Dick Mitchell and Brigadier McNeil were anxiously waiting outside Ifs. The major was convinced that there were still more of his men yet to return. When he saw the four men walking towards him, he ran over to them. Bob Banfield and the two privates came to a halt. Bob saluted. "Sir, Three Platoon reporting for further orders. All ranks present and accounted for. Sir!"

"Sergeant Banfield! God, I'm so damned glad to see you, Bob! I was afraid that I had lost you. I'm so damned glad you made it back!" Tears streamed down his face, as he embraced the sergeant. He turned to the others, and clasped their hands with both of his. "Matthews! Brennan! I'm so damned glad..." Since he had made it back to Ifs, he had agonized over the fate of the men of the battalion, and particularly his Able Company. Brigadier McNeil, as deeply concerned with the fate of the battalion, had left his headquarters at St. Germaine-la-Blanche-Herbé, and joined him. The two officers were there to contact the survivors as, singly and in little groups, they made their way back.

The major fought to compose himself. "Sergeant Banfield. What you boys need now is a damned good bath and a shave, clean uniforms, a hot meal and time to catch up on some sleep. Now I want you to get yourself and Matthews and Brennan over to that jeep parked over there. The driver will take you to Vaucelles, where the battalion is being assembled. RSM Reid and Captain Werner will show you to your quarters. Staff Howes has laid on a good hot meal with the cooks.

"I am now Acting C.O. of the battalion. We are taking on replacements, straight from England, with no combat experience. There is a shortage of officers, so I want you to remain in command of Three Platoon. Matthews and Brennan will stay with you. Now get going! I have business here to attend to. I'll be back with the battalion later this evening."

"Very good, sir!" replied Bob. They climbed aboard the jeep, and were off.

Dick Mitchell joined the brigadier, who was questioning Jim Niles. The young lieutenant was virtually incoherent. To the brigadier's disgust, Jim repeatedly whimpered: "I was afraid ..... I never wanted to serve in the infantry ..... I don't want to be responsible for troops in battle ..."; he had folded into himself. The experience he had lived through had totally unraveled him, and deeply wounded his very soul. Guilt engulfed him. He found himself sinking into black despair. He was a coward beyond salvation, and he wanted to die.

The brigadier concluded that Jim Niles was suffering from battle exhaustion. This was forgivable for other ranks, but it must not happen to an officer; this young man was unfit for command in battle. He chose the most expedient way to remove him from overseas active service.

"Major Mitchell, my orders are for you to arrange for this officer to be conveyed to Thaon, where he is to be admitted to Number Six Field Dressing Station, at present operational for battle exhaustion casualties. I intend to consult with the division commander, and request that he be returned to Canada for further duty."

Mitchell had no recourse but to comply. He had lost another officer to the Verrières Ridge.

....

The driver pulled up at the battalion's assembly area in Vaucelles, and the three men jumped off. A row of bombed-out houses across the street which ran along the south bank of the Orne, had been commandeered for billets. A mobile bath and laundry unit had been set up on the street, with hoses drawing water from the river. The battalion cooks were hard at work over their bubbling "dixies". The men of the battalion were lining up for baths, new uniforms, and food. And all the while trucks were arriving from the JUNO beaches, with fresh replacements. These young soldiers were met by their new platoon N.C.O.'s and marched off to their respective company billets as soon as they climbed off the trucks.

Bob smiled at his two bedraggled companions, starkly contrasting with the polished, parade-ground look of the replacements. "Well, you guys, we've got a job to do, to break in this lot, before we're back to it again."

Captain Werner met them and directed them to the Able Company lines. A dozen men, freshly fed and in clean uniforms, were sitting outside the houses. For them, the ruins of Vaucelles were a paradise, beyond anything they could have hoped for a few hours ago. Just to be alive was a celebration to them. For the moment, they were safe from the mortar bombs and shells, the 88's and the Spandaus. They had survived.

As the three soldiers walked towards them, they heard the familiar refrain, belted out in three-quarter time:

"Fuck 'em all, fuck 'em all,

The long and the short and the tall!

Fuck all the sergeants and W.O. Ones,

Fuck all the corporals and their bastard sons..."

Bob felt his tired body tingle with pride in his battalion. They had lost their colonel and all but two majors, and most of their junior officers and N.C.O.'s. They had lost many of their closest comrades. But they were undaunted. Bob was convinced, given any reasonable odds, that they could beat the German army, and bring the war to a close. They had learned from their bitter defeat, and he hoped the brass had learned too.

Bob found his thoughts drifting back to that hell on earth which was their battlefield, where the bodies of René Charlebois and Jack Sipulski and the many others still lay, unattended. He mourned the death of these young Canadians, who would never return to their homes again. But without any doubt, he saw himself as a soldier, and this was a job which had to be done.

"....For we're saying good-bye to them all,

As back to our barracks we crawl.

There'll be no promotion this side of the ocean,

So cheer up my lads, fuck 'em all!"

....

Within four days, the battalion, back to sufficient strength with its replacements, was once again committed to the front lines. This time, they were assigned the role of providing a firm base, as the other units of the Second Division in turn assaulted the Verriéres Ridge, and failed to capture it, with appalling losses. The Black Watch, which had rescued Bob

Banfield, Ronnie Matthews and Tom Brennan and Lieutenant Niles, was badly repulsed and shattered. Then there was Operation SPRING, regarded by the generals as "partially successful with limited gains".

Two weeks afterwards, came Operation TOTALIZE. This time, finally, innovative tactics were employed. The attack went in at night, without a barrage to warn the enemy. The battalion rode into battle in "Kangaroos", the first armored personnel carriers ever used by any army. These vehicles were modified from self-propelled artillery; the guns had been removed, and armor plating welded on in their place, to provide protection for the infantry. The attack was successful; the Verrières Ridge had finally fallen.

PART TWO

LONDON, ONTARIO MAY 1959

CHAPTER SIX

Spring came early to southwestern Ontario in 1959. The oak and maple trees which lined the streets of London were garbed in the pale green hues of newly budding leaves. The forsythia in front of many of the houses was in full golden-yellow bloom. There was a warm breeze in the air, and the sky was blue and clear.

Captain Michael Baldwin left home early and drove to work in his 1957 Pontiac. He was particularly proud of his car, the first he had been able to afford. He had worked hard, and continuously scrimped on his meager finances, to put himself through years of university education to become a doctor. In medical school, he had enrolled in the Canadian Army's Regular Officer Training Programme, whereby his tuition and board were paid for him. He was required to complete three summers of military training between school years, and to attend the Canadian Officer's Training Corps parades, which were held once a week in the evening, throughout the university terms. On completion of his rotating internship year, he reported for active duty with the Canadian Army, for a duration of three years. He was now in his second year of service as the Regimental Medical Officer of an infantry battalion, stationed at Wolseley Barracks in the heart of London.

This battalion was an integral part of the small Canadian peacetime Regular Army, and had a reputation for total "spit and polish". It was fiercely proud of the traditions of the regiment to which it belonged. Duty, discipline and meticulous turn-out when in uniform, both in and outside the Barracks, were stringently demanded of every private soldier. The morale of the unit was high. Its officers and other ranks pursued their programme of continuous training with vigorous determination, to maintain razor-sharp efficiency as a combat unit.

Michael Baldwin soon learned, after he had been taken on strength, that he was required to be an effective military officer first, and a doctor second. Whatever private thoughts he had about this, which involved medical ethics and at times led to conflicts in his dual role for the battalion, he kept to himself. He learned the ways of the infantry battalion, identified strongly with his adopted unit, and learned that he could function well both as a caring doctor and as a competent officer to the thousand men in this command. In time, the officers and other ranks of the unit learned to respect and trust him, and they accepted him as one of their own. Whatever was required of the men in their training courses and "schemes" - simulated battle maneuvers - he insisted on doing with them. This willingness to participate actively in all of the battalion's duties and functions made him singularly different than most of the Army's medical officers, who detested any service with "line units", preferring the comfort and familiarity of hospital postings. Michael Baldwin thoroughly enjoyed playing soldier in the peace-time Army.

Although he was not an infantry officer of the regiment to whose battalion he was posted, he was required to wear the uniform and rank designations in a manner peculiar to the regiment. He wore its three brass "pips" on his shoulder, which needed daily polishing, unlike the cloth pips worn by the other officers in the Medical Corps. He wore its regimental buckle on his web belt. His carefully creased battle-dress trouser legs were by regulation stuffed into his brown jump boots, with about two inches overlapping the top of the boots, held down over the boots with lead weights. However, as if to emphasize his hybrid role with the battalion, he wore the maroon, blue and yellow shoulder flashes of the Royal Canadian Army Medical Corps, and its badge, consisting of the Caduceus staff, serpent and maple leaves on his khaki forage cap. Also he wore the red patch of the First Canadian Infantry Division on both sleeves, required of all ranks of the Army which belonged to this formation.

Michael Baldwin drove up to the main gate of Wolseley Barracks, a sprawling military complex which was home not only to the battalion, but to various ancillary units of the London garrison, including the regimental recruit depot. The gate guard, which was mounted by the battalion, recognized their medical officer, saluted with their C-1 rifles, and lifted the wooden barrier. Michael drove through the gate and up the wide road on an incline, to the unit's lines. These consisted of a large asphalt parade square, surrounded on all four sides by white-washed cement buildings, the barrack blocks, quartermaster stores, mess halls and the administration building. This latter building housed the battalion headquarters offices, the company offices and the Medical Inspection Room. The M.I.R. was Michael's domain, and actually consisted of several rooms; his office, which doubled as an examination room, the documentation and treatment area, the dispensary and a waiting room. He parked behind the building, and walked in.

He passed through the waiting room, where several soldiers were seated, waiting their turn to see the medical officer. To report sick, each soldier had to be in his company office by seven in the morning, with his small pack, in which he carried his tooth-brush and sundry items, "in case you have to go to the hospital". This was a blatant example of ancient military bureaucracy, which was supposed to serve the purpose of dissuading soldiers who wanted to avoid distasteful duties by reporting sick. The men had learned that with this M.O., they would receive prompt care and concern for legitimate medical problems, but the lead swingers were rapidly identified and despatched back to their companies.

Captain Baldwin commanded the battalion's medical section, which included a sergeant and five corporals. All were from the Army Medical Corps, posted "for all purposes" to the battalion. All were qualified technically in the medical corps. The sergeant and four of the corporals held technical grouping as Medical Assistants. One of the corporals was a Hygiene Assistant. When the unit was in barracks, these men formed the staff of the Medical Inspection Room. When the unit was in the field on schemes, each Corporal M.A. was assigned to each of the unit's four rifle companies, and in effect became each particular company's private doctor. This left the medical officer with the sergeant and the hygiene corporal to run the Regimental Aid Post. In time of war, casualties would be evacuated from the companies to the R.A.P., where the battalion doctor provided triage and initial treatment, before they were evacuated further to the supporting casualty collecting posts and the surgical units in the rear areas. When the battalion was in the field, Michael Baldwin was handed the twenty-odd men from the battalion's Corps of Drums, the drummers and buglers of the battalion, commonly and derogatorily dubbed the "rain makers", or the "corps of bums". Michael had trained these soldiers to function as stretcher-bearers, and once the unit was away from barracks, these men were distributed to the companies where they came under control of the medical corporals. Usually, two or three remained with the R.A.P.

"Good morning, sir!"

The medical sergeant and the corporals greeted their M.O. as he walked through the M.I.R. to his office.

"Good morning, gentlemen! I see we've got seven on sick parade today."

Michael often used the term "gentlemen" when he addressed his men together. This was a form of greeting normally used between officers, who customarily never used the term when addressing other ranks. With some humour, along the lines that only officers were gentlemen by act of parliament, they nevertheless relished the term when used by their M.O. In the Canadian Army, there had always been a very firm and definite line drawn between officers and other ranks. They could not socialize together, except on formal occasions when, for example, the officers once a year were invited for drinks to the sergeants' mess. The top priority of this exercise was to get the officers very drunk. Michael had devised a fool-proof system to prevent this fate befalling him, by arranging for one of the corporals to call the sergeants' mess at a pre-designated time, to ask for the M.O. because there was a serious medical emergency. The sergeants never caught on.......

However, with this small medical section, all of whose personnel had been attached out of the parent medical corps to this infantry battalion, there had always been a close tie between the men, and a more relaxed level of communication, rather different from the rest of the battalion. Yet the line between Michael and his medics was scrupulously maintained, and from it he learned what was meant by "the loneliness of command". But in the Canadian Army, rank alone did not merit respect; the officer had to earn it. Thus Corporal Allen, his Hygiene Assistant, with whom he worked most closely of all of them, once said to him: "Sir, I would follow you to hell itself, as long as you didn't act stupid!"

"I think you had better see Private Oliver from Bravo Company first," said Sergeant Scott. "He's running a temperature of 103. Seems pretty congested."

"O.K., send him in right away, Sergeant Scott."

Sergeant Scott was forty-two, some thirteen years older than Captain Baldwin. When Michael was posted to battalion, soon after his internship, Fred Scott resented coming under the command of this "whippersnapper", and the tough sergeant proved to be difficult to manage. But as time passed, and he discovered that the young M.O. was not the sissy he had expected, could be firm when necessary, and far more "regimental" than many of the M.O.'s with whom he had served in the twenty-four years he had been in the medical corps, a more comfortable working relationship developed.

Fred Scott had enlisted in the Army in the Second World War, when he was eighteen. Because he had a grade twelve diploma, this qualified him for the medical corps. He served in Europe in an Army general hospital. In the Korean War, he was with a casualty clearing station. Had he been more circumspect, he would undoubtedly by now have had the rank of Warrant Officer. But he drank heavily, was frequently charged with drunkenness on duty, and as frequently busted in rank, only to work his way up again. By personality, he was far more suited to serve in a combat unit than in a hospital facility. He bitterly resented taking orders from the young Army nurses, all of whom were commissioned officers. As far as he was concerned, nurses were "good for one thing only" — but for him they were in this respect unattainable. Fred Scott was now approaching the age of retirement as a sergeant, with no hope of further promotion. He strove to conceal his alcohol problem, to protect his pension. He had a son who had just been accepted into the Royal Military College in Kingston, and despite his distrust and resentment of officers, he spoke proudly of the day when he would be able to salute his own son, when he was commissioned.

Michael Baldwin's office was a rather spartan affair. There was a small wooden desk and two wooden chairs; to one side was an examining table, covered with a clean white sheet. On the wall above his desk hung his Red Cross flag, which accompanied him in field exercises, when it always flew over his R.A.P. In one corner there were a number of grey-painted steel panniers, piled one on top of the other. These boxes contained medical supplies and instruments, whose contents had been originally designed and organized for the Second World War. These cumbersome cases were heavy and awkward to carry around, and were usually loaded onto the trailer which was hauled by the medical officer's jeep during schemes. In winter exercises, however, when all supplies had to be pulled by the men across the northern wastelands on toboggans, they proved to be useless. Michael preferred the airborne medical packs made of canvas stretched over aluminum wires, which were much lighter to carry. Since this was a medical matter, before his first winter exercise he requested permission from the area medical officer, a lieutenant colonel, to employ their packs instead of the panniers. The A.M.O. informed him in stern and threatening tones that "what was good enough for me on the Normandy beachhead is good enough for you." Risking court-martial, Michael left the panniers behind, and took the packs instead. The A.M.O. never found out.

Corporal Ken Allen, the H.A., brought Private Oliver into the office. Sick as the lad was, he did not fail to stand to attention and salute the medical officer.

"Sit down here, Private Oliver. Let's get your battle-dress blouse off so I can see what is going on. You have had this cough for some days......"

There were ominous rales on auscultation in Private Oliver's chest. The boy looked flushed, and felt light-headed. He could not stop coughing. A provisional diagnosis of pneumonia was made. Michael Baldwin completed the necessary forms. "Corporal Allen, get this lad to the London Station Hospital by box ambulance right away. Better go with him. Make sure to keep him warm."

"Right away, sir. Let's go, Oliver. Wait till you see them pretty nurses at L.S.H. They'll fix you up in no time flat!" But nothing could have been further from the young soldier's mind. He felt very sick, and could not wait to be admitted to hospital, so he could crawl into bed.

Corporal Allen had total trust in his M.O. Like the other medics, he fitted comfortably into the structure of the battalion. These corporals had all been well trained in their trades, and in the battlefield conditions would have served their M.O. and the battalion. Ken Allen was twenty-nine, the same age as Michael Baldwin. He had served in Korea, and preferred duties with this battalion, to those in a hospital or base unit. And like Michael's other medics, he was determined to show the "foot sloggers" that he could do whatever they did, and better.

By ten in the morning, the day's sick parade was completed. Michael was preparing to accompany Ken Allen on a hygiene inspection of the mess halls when the M.I.R. received an unannounced visit from the commanding officer of the battalion, Lieutenant Colonel Bob Banfield.

"Commanding Officer!" announced Fred Scott, as the colonel entered, and all ranks stood to attention. A soldier was still on the treatment table, under a heat lamp, because of a strained back. The medics were in shirt sleeves, without battle-dress tunics or web belts. None wore the blue forage caps, required of the non-commissioned ranks. They were after all still working with the remaining patient, and this lapse in correct dress was expected in the medical establishment. Being without headdress, none saluted the colonel, according to Canadian Army regulations.

"Good morning, Sergeant Scott. Carry on, please. Is the doctor in?"

"Yes, sir, he's in his office. I'll get him for you."

Without waiting for a reply to his knock, Sergeant Scott opened the door, poked his ruddy face through, and said: "C.O. wants to see you."

Michael was just completing the last of the sick parade paper work. He got up and met the colonel at the door.

"Hello, sir."

"Ah, there you are, Mike! Can I come in for a chat — unless you're still busy with the sick and the lame ......"

"No, sir, we've just finished with sick parade. Please come in, and sit down."

....

Colonel Banfield rarely visited the M.I.R., unless there was something he wished to discuss away from his office. Medical matters were something of a mystery to him, and it was his policy to leave them entirely to his medical officer, allowing him considerable freedom to run his section the way he saw fit. On field exercises, Michael had experimented with different forms of organization and procedure in field treatment and evacuation of casualties, often in direct contravention of the prescribed routines, but the C.O. patiently accepted the M.O.'s novel methods, and enthusiastically supported him in the firm conviction that it was all for the good of the battalion. In turn, Michael had a deep affection and respect for his colonel. There was nothing pretentious or stuffy about Bob Banfield. He was singularly even-tempered, quick to see humour in adverse circumstances, with always a good word for his men. He was consistently fair in his dealings with all the ranks, whether he had paraded before him some hapless private on charges of A.W.O.L., or some subaltern trapped in an affair of the heart.

Bob Banfield took his profession of arms seriously, and thoroughly enjoyed his calling. Almost fifteen years ago, as a platoon sergeant, he had brought back the few survivors of his platoon, in the first disastrous attempt of the Canadian Army to capture the Verrières Ridge. With his rank of sergeant, he was given command of his platoon, which he led in the subsequent battles leading to the destruction of the German armies in Normandy.

Verrières Village ..... Rocquancourt ..... Caillouet ..... Clair Tizon ..... Falaise. With dedicated, consummate skill, he had led his platoon, consisting mostly of raw replacements, from one successful action to another. At Caillouet, on the morning of the second day of Operation TOTALIZE, his battalion was ordered to charge into this forward bastion of the German defences before the Laize River. For his personal heroism under heavy enemy fire, which led to the capture of this village, he was awarded the Military Medal. The higher authorities were by then fully convinced of his leadership qualities, and once Falaise fell, signalling the end of the Normandy campaign, Bob Banfield was abruptly removed from his battalion, and sent back to England on a crash officer cadet course, at the Royal Military College at Sandhurst. He was the only Canadian on his draft, the others being sergeants from the British Army. The war with its invidious drain on junior officers, particularly in the infantry, had made this opportunity for the young sergeants, who had risen from the ranks to become commissioned officers; they would never otherwise have had the chance to attend Sandhurst.

Bob returned, a newly-commissioned lieutenant, to his battalion which was committed to holding a segment of the winter line on the Maas River in Holland. This was fortunately a relatively quiescent time for the Canadians at the front, and provided a respite for their three battle-exhausted divisions. By this time, there were very few of the original officers left in the battalion from the Normandy days. The officers welcomed Bob back, now as one of their brother officers. He found it painful to relinquish his close relationship with the senior N.C.O.'s, and the men of his old Three Platoon, now that he had "crossed the line."

By February of 1945, Bob Banfield's battalion, as part of the Second Division, fought in the final offensive battles of the war. The Rhineland .... Groningen .... Oldenburg ..... Then came "Victory in Europe Day". The Second Division was moved to the Amersfoort area in Holland, and by October, it was disbanded. The battalion was transported to England, and then back to Canada and its home city, Toronto, where they were de-mobilized. Bob came home to Canada with them. With the rank of Captain, he transferred to the Canadian Army (Regular), determined to make the Army his career. He had various postings, including service in the Korean War, as a major commanding a rifle company. His last promotion came three years before, when he was posted to command this present battalion in the rank of Lieutenant Colonel.

Michael Baldwin knew something of the colonel's background. He knew that he had been a hero in the Northwest Europe Campaign, where he had won the Military Medal, whose ribbon was clipped with the other campaign ribbons on his battle-dress blouse over the left breast pocket. This meant that he must have been commissioned from the ranks. Bob Banfield was thirty-eight, but there were relatively few of these "old soldiers" left in active service, and most held field officer rank or were senior N.C.O.'s or warrant officers. The majority of the young officers of the battalion had never experienced combat, although some had served in Korea. The "old soldiers" were always a group apart, who seemed singularly reluctant to talk about their war experiences, except amongst themselves.

....

Michael Baldwin looked intently at his commanding officer, wondering what the purpose of his visit was. Bob Banfield was, as always, immaculately turned out in his battle-dress uniform. He was a robust man, in excellent physical health. The sideburns below his forage cap were already greying. As did so many of the officers of the Army, he wore a meticulously trimmed moustache.

"Well, Mike, I'll come directly to the point. The Ipperwash route marches are starting in a week. Charlie Company goes first, then Delta Company. Headquarters Company comes next, which means that Major Niles and all his odds and sods will be on the march in three weeks. At the last "O group", you said that you wanted to be on this march with Headquarters Company yourself."

"Yes, sir....."

What was the C.O. leading up to? The Ipperwash route marches were a rite of spring for the battalion. Each of the six companies — Headquarters Company, Support Company, and the four rifle companies took turns on this exercise. Each was trucked out to Camp Ipperwash on Lake Huron, some fifty miles from London, where the soldiers engaged in the annual rifle qualifications on the ranges. Following this, each was required to march back to London with weapons and full gear, the march to be done in forty-eight hours; there would be two nights when the soldiers would bivouac in the field. The route was along township roads, away from heavy civilian traffic. It was a gruelling march, a test of physical endurance for the men.

Route marching was very much part of the stock-in-trade of the rifle companies — and even Support Company, normally vehicle-transported on field exercises, made certain to prepare its men with fitness programmes at the Barracks. But it was another matter for Headquarters Company. This consisted of the Signals Platoon, the Transport Platoon, and a motley collection of administrative personnel, including the provost section, the quartermaster staff, the battalion's cooks and the main orderly room staff. Many of these soldiers were very much desk-bound, and caused continuous concern for the colonel, who wanted his entire battalion to be, in his words, "lean and mean". Furthermore, it was always difficult to spring these people out of their specialized services, for any preliminary toughening-up training.

Michael Baldwin always assigned one of his corporal M.A.'s with a few stretcher-bearers from the Corps of Drums to accompany each of the sub-units, to treat the inevitable blistered feet and other problems incurred on the march. However, he always made it a point to drive out to meet each of the companies when they arrived at their second night's bivouac, which was when they needed his services the most. But Headquarters Company usually ran into the most difficulties, and he decided this year to accompany it himself, to do the march with it. He was physically in top condition, and he looked forward to getting away from the Barracks for a couple of days, and living like an infantryman. To do this, he had to arrange with the Area Medical Officer to provide temporary coverage for the battalion's sick parades, until he returned. The A.M.O. readily concurred, but privately concluded that there was something unbalanced about this young medical officer, to want to participate in this ridiculous business, of which Bob Banfield seemed so fond, undoubtedly because he too, the poor infantry sod, was likewise unbalanced......

"I am concerned about Jim Niles," the colonel continued, referring to the officer commanding Headquarters Company. "I'm no doctor, but the man seems to be depressed or something. Since he was posted to the battalion less than a year ago, he has never shown any enthusiasm for his job. He lives in the Officer's Quarters, and keeps to himself. In the evenings, he goes to the Mess, gets himself quietly plastered — and then goes to bed. I'm damned glad we did not need him for one of the rifle companies, or there would have been real trouble. The sigs and transport people pretty well run their own show. The H.Q. Company C.S.M. has expressed concern to me. Jim shuts himself up in his office much of the time when he is on duty. No interest in training. Leaves the administrative work to the C.S.M.

"Jim approached me the other day, requesting that Leo Toland lead the company on the march, instead of him. Wanted his transport officer to lead the march! Needless to say, I refused him permission. Damn it, it's his company! Mike, keep this to yourself. I hate to have to discuss one of our field officers like this, but I have no choice. Not yet, anyway. When you are on the march, will you keep on eye on things, please? You're the doctor; I need your professional help with this one. If there is a problem, get back to me soonest. I'll want a briefing, when you return."

"Yes, sir, I understand. I've wondered about Major Niles. He seems to be so lonely ... really unhappy. Is there something in his private life?....."

"I'd rather not go into it right now. I'm afraid that whatever I'd say might not be particularly objective, or impartial. Since you have been with us, you have been a top-rate M.O., and a damned good officer for the battalion. If there is trouble on the march, you are going to have to deal with it, as our M.O. If I were to discuss Jim further with you, it might influence, shall we say, your professional judgment.

"I realize that I am imposing a difficult task on you, Mike. You see — I'm not asking you to spy on Jim Niles for me. Regardless of my personal feelings, I am deeply concerned for the man. For a long time, he has been carrying something pretty heavy. I believe you may be the only one of us who can help him.

"Well, now, I'd best be off. Sergeant Morgan has a hell of a pile of paperwork waiting for me. Cheers, Mike!" He got up and moved towards the door, which Michael opened for him.

"Good-bye, sir."

The C.O. bounded through the M.I.R., and with a wave to the medical section, was gone.

....

Michael Baldwin left with the Hygiene Assistant, Corporal Allen, for the round of inspection of the mess halls and kitchens. Ken Allen was his usual keen-eyed self, and pointed out to the kitchen staff where improvements could be made regarding cleanliness and the correct storage of provisions. As they walked from mess hall to mess hall, the two chatted about "shop" matters. But it was difficult for Michael to concentrate on this routine task.

What did the colonel know about Jim Niles that he did not wish to divulge? The peacetime Canadian Army was small, and it would be inevitable that officers would run into each other on their postings. Both the colonel and the major wore Northwest Europe campaign ribbons on their uniforms. Was it possible that they had served together in the same unit in the Second World War? If so, had something happened between them to account for the noticeably strained relations between them? But then, Jim Niles was distant with everyone.

The colonel was obviously concerned about how Jim Niles would conduct himself on the Ipperwash march. What was he, the M.O., supposed to look out for? And how was he to help this man? He knew nothing about him. There was something mysterious about the whole situation; there was intrigue, and personal enmity. Yet the colonel seemed genuinely concerned about Jim.

Michael Baldwin had an uncomfortable feeling that he was being inexorably drawn into a constellation of tragic circumstances involving Jim and Colonel Banfield. There was also an uneasy sense of obligation closing about him, from which he feared he would be unable to withdraw.

CHAPTER SEVEN

At Wolseley Barracks, the two officers' messes were located some distance behind the battalion's lines. These buildings, adjacent and identical, were of cement block and stucco construction. One belonged to the officers who served with the area headquarters, service units and recruit training depot of the Western Ontario Area. These officers were disposed to keeping their distance from the incumbent infantry battalion, whom they regarded as the "Poor Bloody Infantry". The "P.B.I." was frightfully "gung-ho", and insufferably "spit-and-polish", and its unique traditions were awkward and incomprehensible.

The mess closer to the battalion's lines belonged to the officers of the battalion. For these thirty or so officers, the mess was their regimental home. There was a large dining hall with an immense mahogany table and chairs to match. On its walls were large paintings depicting battle scenes from the glorious history of the regiment. There was also a large photograph of the Queen and her consort, hung above the head of the table. There were three lounges with leather-upholstered easy chairs, more paintings of battles on the walls, and also row upon row of group photographs of the generations of officers who had served in the battalions of the regiment at different times. One lounge also contained the bar, and a smaller one the regimental library. The entire mess had the atmosphere of a graciously comfortable private men's club. On very special occasions, the officers' ladies were invited to visit. Otherwise it was very much an all-male domain.

Behind the battalion's Officers' Mess, and connected to it by an enclosed passage, was a similarly-constructed building, containing the Officers' Quarters. Here, in rooms reminiscent of a college dormitory, lived the young bachelor officers, and others who were separated from their wives, or who were with the battalion on temporary assignment or on courses. Exchange officers from Britain and other Commonwealth countries lived here as well. There was a common bathroom and toilet area. Also a room was set aside for use by the officers' batmen, private soldiers assigned to the duties of personal servant to each officer in residence, who took care of laundry, the pressing of uniforms and the polishing of boots, and other domestic requirements of each individual officer. In the field, these batmen also functioned as runners for their officers. The married officers who lived off the base had no permanent batmen; they were required to assign one of their men to perform these functions when the unit was in the field, on exercises.

Once a month, every officer in the battalion was required to "dine in", whether he lived in quarters or not. This was regarded as a parade, meaning that all the officers were ordered to attend. Dress for the occasion was the dress blues or patrol uniform, consisting of a tunic with a collar buttoned up to the neck, and trousers with a stripe down each outer seam, identifying the particular corps of the wearer — for example, bright red for the infantry and maroon for the medical corps. A sash about the waist was also worn, with the same corps color. The purpose of "dining in" was to promote brotherhood and camaraderie among the battalion's officers, and to detach the married officers from the connubial bliss of their own homes for this purpose. The meals were consistently well planned and prepared by the mess cooks, correctly and tastefully served, as became a dining place for gentlemen.

Michael Baldwin, as R.M.O., was required to attend. Although he thought of it all as rather a chore, as it took him away from his home after duty hours, nevertheless he found the occasions pleasant, and enjoyed socializing with his brother officers. However, he kept his eye on the colonel, for when the Old Man had had enough and left for home, this was when it was permissible for him and the others to leave as well.

....

It was for one of these occasions that the officers of the battalion had gathered in the mess lounges. A number were at the bar, happily imbibing their pre-dinner drinks. Lieutenant Colonel Banfield was there with his guest for the evening, Lieutenant Colonel Newhouse, commanding officer of their sister battalion, stationed with NATO forces in Germany. He had returned to London for a conference and was invited to the dining-in. Eventually, the senior mess steward approached Colonel Banfield, and said, "Dinner is served, sir."

"Thank you, Corporal O'Reilly. Well, gentlemen, shall we?"

The noisy chatter subsided, the officers trooped into the dining hall after their colonel, and stood at their designated places at the table. The C.O. and his guest were the first to sit down, the C.O. at the head of the table and Colonel Newhouse on his right. The others sat down after him. The majors were seated closest to the head of the table. Then came the captains, and finally the subalterns, the most junior Second Lieutenant at the very end. The courses of the meal were served by the mess stewards, dressed in white jackets and dress blues trousers, with yellow chevrons on their sleeves if they held the rank of corporal or lance-corporal. With each course was a carefully selected wine. This was a merry gathering; the officers joked and chattered, with occasional raucous guffaws. They obviously enjoyed each other's company. As Michael Baldwin listened, he marveled at how they never ran out of conversation, despite the fact that they worked with each other every duty day, and never got away from each other when the battalion was on scheme.

The battle adjutant, a captain, sat next to Michael, and eagerly related in detail his various amatory escapades on leave in Germany some years previously. But Michael's mind was on Major Jim Niles, whom he watched sitting quietly, talking to no one, methodically drinking a great deal of wine as the stewards repeatedly filled his glass. Michael sensed impending danger from this excessive drinking. The C.O.'s words came back to him: "carrying something pretty heavy".

As the mess dinner approached its conclusion, and the dessert and coffee had been consumed, there came the moment of solemn ritual, shared by all units of the Canadian Army at these formal mess dinners — the toast to the Queen. The president of the mess committee, a captain who was elected by the members that year for the purpose of conducting mess functions, struck his wine glass several times, bringing the chatter to a halt. The port decanter was then passed from officer to officer around the table without being allowed to touch down, and each officer charged his glass. The PMC then rose from his chair, which was the signal for all to rise with their glasses in hand. He announced: "Mr. Vice, the Queen!"

This was the cue for the most junior officer in the mess, traditionally dubbed the vice-president of the mess committee, to give the toast. Holding his glass up, the young officer said: "Gentlemen, the Queen!"

"The Queen", responded the officers, and sipped their port.

"Gentlemen", said Colonel Banfield, turning to his guest, "A toast to Colonel Newhouse and his Royal Canadians!"

"Colonel Newhouse!" intoned the others.

"Gentlemen," replied Colonel Newhouse, "And here's to Colonel Banfield and his Royal Canadians!"

"Colonel Banfield!" responded the officers.

By this time Major Jim Niles was quite drunk on the wine he had imbibed with each course during the dinner. To a hushed audience, he blurted: "And here's to Guy Lombardo and _his_ Royal Canadians....." With that, he collapsed face first onto the table, sending plates and crystal crashing in all directions. The major had passed out.

This gross breech of mess etiquette and flagrant violation of correct gentlemanly behaviour at dinner completely stunned the officers, who stared in horror at the prostrate form on their table. No one dared to acknowledge the humour of this fourth toast.

Michael Baldwin knew he had to act fast. Addressing Colonel Banfield, he said: "Sir, may I have your permission to remove Major Niles to his quarters?"

"Yes, Mike," replied the colonel, quickly collecting himself. "I want an officer to give Captain Baldwin a hand."

The officers, however, continued to stand frozen in place, and for an agonizing moment, no one volunteered. Then, Lieutenant Peter Forsythe, who commanded Three Platoon of Alpha Company, spoke up, "Sir, may I have your permission to help the M.O.?"

"Yes, Peter, get on with it".

Peter and Michael succeeded with some difficulty in lifting Jim Niles off the table, and the two dragged and carried him out of the dining hall, through the mess building, and over to the Officers' Quarters building and to his own room. There they removed his dress blues uniform and put him to bed in his underwear.

"Peter," asked Mike, "could you get a jug of hot, black coffee from the kitchen — and a cup?"

"Roger, Starlight, wilco, out!" Peter replied, as he hastened off. Michael Baldwin was faintly amused at this ridiculously incongruous use of correct radio telephone technique by the young officer in the awkwardly embarrassing situation. "Starlight".... the radio code for the medical officer.... the very same, now in attendance on a drunken field officer....

Peter Forsythe returned with a mess steward in tow, carrying a large pitcher of coffee. The lance-jack's eyes were straining with curiosity about what was going on, with the M.O. here in Major Niles' room, and Mr. Forsythe in such a dither.

"Thank you, Corporal Simms — put the pitcher down here. You may leave now".

"Yes, sir! Sure you don't need me for somethin' else?"

"No, Corporal Simms, I can manage." When Simms left, Peter closed the door behind him. It would not do for other ranks to see their officers involved in this shabby business. There was a highly efficient grape vine in the Barracks, and it was mandatory not to disclose to the mess stewards anything more beyond the scandalous events they had already seen and heard at dinner.

Jim Niles began to stir. "Doctor, is that you?"

"Yes, Jim. We've got some coffee for you...come on, Jim,...sit up...that's it...Peter, pour it into the cup...here you are, Jim, now drink...O.K., here's another cupful..." To Michael's relief, the major seemed willing to comply with his ministrations. He drank cup after cup of hot coffee.

Eventually, Michael said, "Peter, I can handle it now myself. Best you get back to the mess. You've been a great help. Will you present my compliments to the colonel, and tell him I'm going to stay with Jim for the next while?"

"Sure, Mike, guess I'll stand down now. Glad to have been of help." Peter glanced at the major, and left.

Gradually Jim Niles sobered up, and as he did, the full enormity of his shameful behaviour at the mess dinner permeated his consciousness, and with it came mortification and fear. "Conduct unbecoming an officer..." read the Queen's Regulations (Army), and the phrase reverberated within his clouded sensorium. Was this to be the disgraceful end of a miserable career in the service of the Queen? Poor morale and lack of motivation... cowardice in the face of the enemy...drunken and disorderly behaviour on parade...

More coffee.

Banfield...What did Banfield intend to do? Full inquiry and request for the resignation of his commission? Colonel Banfield. Colonel Bob Banfield...Sergeant Bob Banfield...Verrières Ridge...Three Platoon, Able Company...Damn Three Platoon — Banfield was welcome to those people...He was never the type for combat command...war sickened and revolted him...war and soldiers...God how he hated the Army...R.M.C., England, Normandy...Verrières Ridge...and the fifteen years of indentured servitude which followed...The brigadier, his Old Man...there was a real professional soldier, not a scrap of humanity in him...Duty. Honour. Country...

More coffee.

Three Platoon... Jesus, Peter Forsythe commanded Three Platoon in Alpha Company in this battalion. How ironic, that he was the only regimental officer who was prepared to help him. His "brother officer". Likely the same age he was, fifteen years ago, in Normandy. Was Peter a better platoon commander...of course he was...but Peter had never had to lead men in battle, had never "seen the elephant", to borrow an American Civil War term.

Jim Niles looked at the young medical officer in his room, who had given generously of himself in this whole sordid situation. The man was a doctor, but he was in uniform. How could he function as an officer in the Army, whose role was to defend the country from whomever the current politicians had decreed was the enemy, to kill and if necessary to be killed?...Officer...and doctor...If he was a doctor, he was supposed to have committed himself to the service of humanity...to cure its ills of soul and body sometimes, but to render comfort and show compassion always...this was what he was trained for, and he must have had the intelligence, motivation and drive to persist through the long years of medical education...But what was he doing in the Army? What a colossal damned waste...

More coffee.

What sort of officer was the M.O.? This was an R.O.T.P. product....Regular Officer Training Programme....he recalled attesting these young medical students at the university where he had served as resident staff officer. The Army provided them the financial means to attend medical school, and the Army saw to it that they were trained all too effectively in the summer officer cadet courses, to mould them into Army officers. Captain Baldwin, doctor and officer. On the battalion's weekly parades, he was always present on the parade square, and knew the drill and commands like any infantry officer....What about that time when he, Major Niles, was not available to go on parade, and Michael Baldwin found himself the senior ranking officer for Headquarters Company? Baldwin had actually taken command of the company on the parade, which seemed to amaze and amuse all ranks for weeks later!

But this young M.O. had never been in battle...unlike that poor bastard on the Verrières Ridge, right up with the Tac HQ, desperately trying to cope with the flood of wounded and dying soldiers lying in the mud all about his R.A.P.....the blood....the screaming....the horror of it all....the sickening, pointless horror of war....

He saw Michael Baldwin looking at him, with perplexed concern. "Jim, its none of my business, but....hell, it *is* my business. I'm your M.O., the only one you've got! I am your doctor, but I am also your brother officer. I would like to help you, but I don't know where to start...."

Jim smiled for the first time. "Take it easy, Doc! You're doing fine! You have done a great deal for this broken-down, besotted old soldier tonight — and I'm grateful."

"I'm no head-shrinker, Jim, but I know something is bothering you, in fact tearing the living guts out of you. You're drinking an awful lot. What happened at the mess dinner tonight was an outward expression of all the anger and resentment churning inside you. I think you're trying to blot out a lot of unbearably painful feelings. There are a lot of people in the battalion who are concerned. Your mind is not on your job. You want to be alone all the time. You isolate yourself from these people, and they don't understand, and they get anxious and then hostile. Colonel Banfield...."

"Colonel Banfield, ...yes, Colonel Banfield.... I must be a real thorn in his side.... The ineffectual field officer, never gung-ho like himself....let the battalion down, eh? Has he ever said anything to you about me?"

This worried Michael. The only way to help this man at all was somehow to get to know him, to allow him to unburden himself of whatever it was which was inexorably destroying him. This was his responsibility as a physician, but he must also be a friend. He could lose this opportunity, if Jim Niles convinced himself that Michael was there exclusively as a medical officer under command of the colonel to determine how to dispose of him. Furthermore, the major outranked him, and he was some eight years older. How was he to cope with all of this, so that Jim Niles would confide in him?

"Really no more than any of the other senior officers; they are all concerned about what is happening to you. They don't know what to do for you. There is a great deal at stake. You're an intelligent, cultured man. You're a field officer. Your career...."

"My career. My God-damned career. The profession of arms....We're legalized killers, Mike. The defence of the nation. How do you justify defending Canada many thousand miles away in a foreign land? We were expected to kill the Hun.... Kill or be killed.... A soldier is supposed to die for his country....But die in France? The war cemeteries there are full of Canadians who will never return. We destroyed the Nazi regime at terrible cost in Canadian lives, and people maimed for life. And now the Germans have an army again, and are supposed to be our allies. Now the Russians are our prospective enemies....it makes so damned little sense to me....Wars make no sense. Armies make no sense....Soldiers.....soldiering....My God, I'm trapped in this career, Mike. I detest the Army, but I cannot get out."

"I don't understand, Jim? Why trapped? You're an intelligent man. There must be other careers — you're still young."

"My father was a regular army officer. He was an R.M.C. graduate. He was a hero at Vimy Ridge in the First World War. I was an only child. I was raised in army camps across Canada. My father retired as a brigadier. His greatest disappointment.... barring myself....was that he was not given field command in the Second World War. He was too important to be released from his directorate post at D.N.D. Headquarters in Ottawa. I was expected....programmed if you wish....from the start to go to R.M.C. after high school. There was no problem getting in. I'm sure there were others far more qualified by temperament for military college, but I was Brigadier Niles' son. Brilliant military career before me, like the old man had had.

There was simply no other option but to be a professional soldier, and the proscribed way was through R.M.C.

"My mother was a colonel's daughter when the old man married her. Perfect match. She knew all the social graces, dignity incarnate in the infernal reception lines. She was indispensible for my father's career, but they hated each other. In fact, there was no love at home. Duty, honor, country....isn't that the motto of West Point?....well, the Yanks got it from good old dad and mum....rather father and mother, which they demanded I call them.

"When I left Ottawa for Kingston, at the train station I got a firm handshake from father, and not so much as a peck on the cheek from mother. He said: "Now I want and expect you to be the best cadet R.M.C. ever had!" When I came home on Christmas leave in uniform, I was expected to salute my father on every possible occasion. At the end of my pre-embarkation leave before going over to England on my draft in 1944, both of us were in uniform at the station. No hand shake then, but the very necessary exchange of salutes and, 'Do your duty to King and Country!' That was it.

"Shortly after I arrived in England, in the Spring of 1944, I was posted to a battalion which was part of the Second Canadian Infantry Division. The battalion had been badly clobbered at Dieppe. It had taken the best part of two years to build the division up again with raw recruits. We had a commanding officer who was not regular army, and he knew nothing of military command and control in battle. He loved parades, and revelled in playing soldier, and playing colonel. There was no....tradition....in this man. I could not respect or trust him. However, I was assigned to command a platoon in a company where the company commander was also from the militia, a school teacher, I recall. But he was deadly serious about the war. He had been at Dieppe, and had no illusions about the German Army, and what it was capable of in battle. He was determined to master his temporary trade as an infantry officer. He was a leader and a brave man who could be trusted. Then there was the brigadier who was from the regular army. He had been in the Italian campaign. He was a professional soldier....and damned dedicated....like my father....but he was *human*....a warm and concerned officer.

"I took over my new platoon without enthusiasm, not looking forward to the task ahead. Second Div was to land a month after the assault on D-Day, as a build-up formation, expected to be a part of the breakout operation from Normandy and France itself. We were to have a whole Canadian corps in the field, and eventually a full army. To win the war we had to destroy the German Army. I was to command a rifle platoon which would inevitably end up in the front lines. Platoon commanders had a very high casualty rate and a short survival time on the battlefield. I was frightened....I guess we all were....I didn't want the job....I would have far preferred to have waited out the war in a training post back in Canada. But my father....my father wanted a hero son. And R.M.C. saw to it that any Niles must surely serve in the combat arms. My marks were too mediocre for any other corps but the infantry. At twenty-two, everything in my life was inexorably propelling me in the direction of battle....to Normandy.

"I was never....am not even now....interested in command. I found the common soldier detestable....uncouth.... I never liked my men. I had grave doubts from the very beginning about leading my platoon successfully. I had a platoon sergeant who was a year older than me. He had been at Dieppe....He was a good Senior N.C.O.; the men looked up to him....not to me. His name was Banfield, Bob Banfield...."

"Our colonel!"

"The very same. We crossed over to Normandy. Then there was Operation ATLANTIC....Verrières Ridge...."

"What ridge?"

"Verrières — an extension of the Bourgebus Ridge. Second Div was to assault and capture the ridge, to break through the German lines."

"What happened, Jim?"

"The attack was a total shambles. Our battalion was temporarily detached to the brigade which was selected for the assault. The brigade sent one of its battalions ahead of us. They reached their objective in part, but were cut to shreds by the Germans. We were supposed to establish a firm base for them in their rear. But their survivors came streaming back and through our position. Then we were hit. The artillery....the God-damned mortar shells fell everywhere. Then their machine guns....high-pitched rapid firing tore into us....I was paralysed with fear....God, I didn't want to die....not there, on the slopes of that God-forsaken ridge....blood, broken bodies, guts and arms and legs....the yelling and screaming....the profession of arms....God damn the Army — all armies....God damn all wars...."

Tears were streaming down the major's cheeks. It frightened him to see the agony this man was in, as he spoke deliberately, quietly, and bitterly, about these distant experiences.

"Jim, what happened to you on the Verrières Ridge?"

"My dear doctor, I have talked enough. I have never had the chance to unburden myself of all this rot, and I thank you for listening. Odd, but I feel better for it....like some weight has at least partly been lifted off me....Now I think I'll turn in. Undoubtedly a momentous day awaits me on the morrow....Goodnight, old chap!"

"Goodnight, Jim."

....

When Michael left the Officers' Quarters, the dining in evening was over. The lights in the mess were turned off. Wearily, he climbed into his Pontiac, and drove home, his head reeling with the events of the evening. It seemed a hideous travesty on the part of the Army's directorate of personnel to have posted Jim Niles to a unit where his commanding officer had served as his platoon sergeant at that fateful time.

A stream of doubt assailed him. To an extent, he felt that he had helped the major to bring out into the open many of his bitterly painful experiences — fear, shame, inadequacy as a battle leader, hatred of war and the military, rejection by his parents, then by the Army itself, total isolation and abject failure. The hell of Verrières Ridge seemed to have lingered on in this man's life, as though there were no possible end to his soul-destroying suffering. His spirit had been crucified on the Verrières Ridge, but the crucifixion continued.

But Jim had not talked about his personal experiences during the climax of the Verrières assault. Regardless of all the wine and the coffee, he was not prepared to get into this critically important part of his life. If he did so, would his emotional defences break down entirely? And if so, what would be the consequences? Did Jim need expert professional help beyond what Michael could provide? If so, he knew that the major would almost inevitably be categorized as mentally unfit for military service and be released from the Army. If this happened, would it destroy him totally? Was he serving some sort of penance by staying in the Army? Or was he trying hopelessly to prove something to his parents?

Michael found himself drawn even more deeply into the tragic and dangerous situation. He would have to learn more about the events which occurred fifteen years ago, in a foreign land, where so many had died, where so many others had survived maimed and scarred - and, in the case of Jim Niles, wounded in spirit and never healed.

CHAPTER EIGHT

When Michael Baldwin arrived at the M.I.R. the following morning to begin the day's work, it became rapidly apparent to him that the battalion's grape vine was as usual working at peak efficiency; it seemed that all ranks had heard about what had happened at the Officers' Mess the previous evening. Evidently the mess stewards, never having been sworn to silence regarding the escapades and indiscretions of the officers they served, had started deliciously intriguing rumors, that Major Niles had fatally disgraced himself and that he would be dishonorably discharged from the Army, and so it all went.

"I heard something happened at your Mess last night, sir!" snickered Sergeant Scott, his ruddy face contorted in a leering grin. The medical corporals busied themselves in preparation for the morning sick parade, but they were straining their ears to catch any comment which the M.O. might make.

Michael, however, merely smiled, and walked by into his office, calling for the first patient to be brought in. He was in no way prepared to discuss anything of this nature with his "other ranks". Sergeant Scott had served long enough in the Canadian Army, and was sufficiently familiar with his M.O., to know that he would get nothing out of him, yet he could barely conceal his disappointment. What a hit he could have made in the Sergeants' Mess, relaying in intimate detail the part his own M.O. had played the night before. Bloody tight-lipped officers....

In the mid-morning, after sick parade, Michael walked over to the Officers' Mess. A few of the members had gathered for coffee, but no one was using the small lounge, where the regimental library was kept. This was an unclassified collection of books on military history, sports and other subjects. The officers were encouraged to browse and to take out books, with no provision for signing them out, and no time limit on how long they could be kept. Michael began to look through the volumes, until he came across "The Canadian Army, 1939 - 1945", written by Colonel C.P. Stacey, the official military historian for the Army. This was the first volume of a series to be published on the Canadian Army in the Second World War. He removed the book from the shelf, looked up the "General Index", and found: "Verrières Ridge: 189-93, 198." He sat down in one of the leather-upholstered chairs, and began to read:

> "Four miles or so south of Caen, between the Orne and the National Road, stands a kidney-shaped eminence, an outlying foothill of the higher hill-mass closer to Falaise. It is covered with cultivated fields and is usually called, after a hamlet situated upon its northern and eastern end above the road, the Verrières Ridge. It is of no great height — its loftiest point, at the west end above Fontenay-le-Marmion, is 88 metres — but it completely commands the ground to the north. For this natural outpost of the new German line there was to be desperate fighting for a fortnight to come, and on and about it much Canadian blood was to be poured out. It was on 20 July that we first set foot on those perilous slopes....."

Michael read on. There was a map attached to Page 194, but it had very little detail, and no mention of the individual units involved — simply "2nd Canadian Div" before the small light-brown blob with "Verrières Ridge" in blue print over it. He became absorbed and indeed obsessed with what he read. War, he knew, was replete with horror, but this battle had a particularly gripping horror of its own. He became more intensely aware that the soldiers who were slaughtered in waves in their attempts to wrest the Ridge from the enemy served in the same Canadian Army, fifteen years ago, as he himself did now. The loss of life more than matched that at Dieppe, and by the same infantry division; why was it that so few Canadians knew about the Verrières Ridge? He recalled the perfunctory effort made to teach some Canadian military history to the C.O.T.C. cadets at McGill during the winter evening parades when he was in medical school. The emphasis, curiously, was on the First World War. He learned about Vimy Ridge, but not about the Verrières Ridge. So typical of Canadians, he thought. We are supposed to know all about Iwo Jima, Stalingrad, El Alamein, the Battle of the Bulge — God knows there were enough movies based on these battles! But there was never any concerted attempt to teach Canadians about their own Army in the schools — not even by the Canadian Army itself! We are a peace-loving nation. We are expected to shun war and all its insane, wasteful destruction. And to be alert and to prepare for it, should it be unavoidable....but in the nuclear age, did this make sense anymore?

But the men of the Verrières Ridge battle....surely they deserved to be remembered, for what they had lived through, for what they tried to achieve. He thought back to what Jim Niles had tried to tell him; to die in France, to be buried in those manicured cemeteries, never to return home. But if you were dead, what did it matter anyway? Damn it, it did matter! It mattered for those who survived, and for the nation never to forget ....Remembrance Day ....the poppies.... For the first time in Michael Baldwin's life, the memories of the old vets, standing in the rain, their chests emblazoned with medals, the mournful "Last Post" sounded by the bugles, seemed to have more meaning.

As he tried to comprehend the terse descriptions in the military history text, struggling back in time to sense what the young Canadians of that time had experienced in the frightful battle, he noticed a uniformed figure at the entrance of the lounge. It was Colonel Banfield. Michael stood up with a start.

"Good morning, sir."

"Good morning, Mike. I've been watching you for the past ten minutes. You seem so damned preoccupied! I see you've got Stacey's book out. Trying to find something?"

"My God," thought Michael, "you were there on that Ridge. You survived the holocaust. You and those others with you are now truly part of our history. Not long afterwards, you won the Military Medal. You must have been still a sergeant — the Military Medal is conferred exclusively on "other ranks" for bravery in battle. What the hell is it like to be a hero? You're a great C.O., yet you don't come through as some sort of bigger-than-life demi-god...."

"Mike, why are you staring at me?"

"Oh, sorry, sir, I was lost in my thoughts! I was reading about the Verrières Ridge battle...."

"Jim Niles talk to you about the Verrières Ridge last night?"

"Yes. It took quite an effort to sober him up, after Peter Forsythe and I got him back to his room. I stayed with him for some time. We talked about his background and his past. He got on the subject of the Verrières Ridge battle, then abruptly refused to discuss his experiences there any further. I had never heard of it. I thought I'd look it up. Stacey's book mentions something about the units of Second Div which were involved. But there are so many questions. Jim said that you were there."

"Mike, have you heard of the American poet Alan Seeger? He died when he was still in his twenties, in the middle of the First World War. I was reading his stuff some time ago, and came across these words:

"I have a rendez-vous with Death

At some disputed barricade....

"Well, this is how I recall the Verrières Ridge. There was a lot of bravery, and also a lot of cowardice. I guess a lot of us were more frightened of being cowards than of being killed. The brass pulled some real snafus during that offensive. We should never have lost so many good men. Jesus, it still burns me, when I think of it....Poor administration, poor intelligence, poor co-ordination of all arms. But we were soldiers. We took orders. So were the Germans, and they took orders. Only they were a hell of a lot more experienced and better led than we were. Second Div had been badly clobbered at Dieppe. The Verrières Ridge business was our first offensive operation after Dieppe. Most of the men were very green. We were committed to a major offensive less than three weeks after we landed in Normandy, and we weren't ready. The Germans had seasoned veterans against us. And they sure as hell were ready. But, in time, we learned the hard way, and we finally beat them.

"More important than battle doctrine was leadership. Canadians are not born soldiers, Mike. The Canadian soldier has always been something of a rugged individualist, and with the right leadership, he is unbeatable. So many of our officers in Normandy were from well-heeled families. They had attended universities, and R.M.C. But when the crunch came, many of them didn't have the balls to lead men in battle. No stomach for the killing stuff. 'Lack of intestinal fortitude', I believe was the old Brit expression! They could never acquire what Montgomery called the 'light of battle in their eyes'. After the Verrières Ridge battle, a lot of heads fell. We lost a lot of officers that way, particularly senior officers, as well as to enemy action. But Second Div toughened up as a result. We became professional soldiers, and we won the war.

"I was platoon sergeant then. I was twenty-three. Jim Niles was posted to us a few months before we crossed over to Normandy. Jim was just out of R.M.C. He had no combat experience. But more than that, he never got the feel of commanding men. The details of running the platoon were always left to me. The men never got to know their platoon commander, and he never allowed himself to get to know them. And then we were right into it. We had a C.O. who ran the battalion by the book. He was fine on parade, and at the military social functions — even got to shake hands with the King, on a round of inspections just before D-Day. But he proved to be worse than useless commanding a battalion in battle.

"Our battalion was detached from our brigade, and in short order handed over to Six Brigade for the second part of Operation ATLANTIC, which was the assault on the Verrières Ridge position. We were to follow up on the South Saskatchewan Regiment, and to provide a firm base for them, half-way up the slope. But the Germans smashed the Sasks, and drove them off the Ridge. Then it was our turn; that evening, the Germans counterattacked with tanks and infantry, and drove in our forward companies. My platoon was with one of them —Able Company. Well, that dates me, Mike! The old terminology was "Able", before it was changed to "Alpha". There wasn't much left of Able or Charlie that night. The next morning, they succeeded in over-running our position, and that was the end of the battalion as a fighting unit. The survivors made it back as best they could. But we took on replacements immediately, and in five days were back into it.

"Another battalion, the Black Watch from Five Brigade, was the next to be loaned to Six Brigade. This time, there was better co-operation with the tank regiments, who had been convinced by brigade that discretion was no longer the better part of valor. We lost a lot of Shermans, but the Black Watch gained all the territory we had lost. Then there was Operation TOTALIZE. We were in on that one, about two weeks later. And the Verrières Ridge was taken. But we lost a hell of a lot of men."

"You're still avoiding the important issue," thought Michael. Out loud, he said, "What happened to you and Jim Niles?"

"Well, when we were advancing up the slope, in the old extended line, two companies up and two behind, the enemy mortars and artillery caught us in the open. The noise and smoke and flying hardware was pretty awful. Before we had time to dig in, their machine-guns opened up on us. We had no artillery or air support because of the weather. Our men were falling everywhere. Jim got lost in all the shindig. I had to take over command of the platoon. When the battalion was overrun, I was cut off from the rest. I made it to a shell-hole with the two men who were left of the platoon. There we spent an uncomfortable day, with the Germans charging around all around us. The Black Watch saved the day for us, and we high-tailed it home, the two privates and myself.

"Well, in the meantime, Jim Niles had joined us, and we brought him back with us. He was — treated in a battle exhaustion unit in the field, and then repatriated to Canada."

"What happened to him in the battle, sir?"

The colonel glanced at his watch. "Mike," he said, "I really have to get going. I've got orders parade coming up — some bloody private from Delta Company bashed his corporal! Imagine that! We're getting to be like the French Foreign Legion! By the way, for your information, I'm not taking any action about what happened last night at the Mess. Major Niles has agreed to write a letter of apology to Colonel Newhouse. Can't let him think that we run a rowdy, drunken bunch of officers in our battalion! As far as I am concerned, that settles it. But he had better learn to curtail his drinking habits, at least in the Mess, or there will be serious trouble.

"Mike.... keep an eye on him. It's the Ipperwash march I'm concerned about. He'll be leading a dog's breakfast of odds and sods. We're talking leadership, now. Leadership and morale. Something to do with the ten principles of war, eh, doctor!"

"Thank you for talking with me, sir." The colonel waved, grabbed his cap and web belt from the rack in the foyer, and left the Mess.

....

Michael Baldwin sat down, and stared at the red-covered book, with the coat-of-arms of the Canadian Army embossed in gold on its front — the crown, crossed swords with a sprig of three maple leaves. As he flipped through its pages, he concluded that he would need to read the entire book to put into historical perspective the events which occurred on the Verrières Ridge that July of 1944, fifteen years ago. The book was about his Army, and he was determined to learn more about it. In time, for this young physician, the study of military history became a consuming interest and absorbing hobby. For the moment, however, it was the Verrières Ridge which obsessed him. He wanted to know what happened to the Canadian soldiers in that momentous battle, and in particular how it had affected the major and the colonel, and their relationship as it stood now.

Colonel Banfield, always the professional soldier, had given him a detailed account of the military situation as it had applied to his battalion, and the tactics employed by the Canadians and the Germans. He could have been describing a war game or simulated battle scheme. He spoke about what he knew best, with an almost irritating aplomb and objectivity. One was a soldier, had to fight a war, and this was how it went.

Major Niles, on the contrary, had spoken to him the night before with agonized revulsion about the same battle, with bitter recrimination of war and armies, and in particular the Canadian Army in which he was somehow compelled to serve. It was as though he were in a penal colony, where he had to serve his time.

Neither officer, however, seemed prepared to discuss the events at the end of the battle. What did the colonel mean, when he said that "we brought him back with us"? What happened at the battle exhaustion unit? Why was Jim sent back to Canada? And why was he still in the Army? And why, in turn, did Major Niles suddenly balk at Michael's question about what had happened to him, during the battle, before he was "brought back" by his sergeant and the two privates?

Michael had volunteered to go with Headquarters Company on the Ipperwash march, because it would in many respects be enjoyable to get away from barracks duties, and would be a test of his own physical fitness. Furthermore, this was the company which was always in most need of medical services on endurance marches. But the events of the past few days had turned the coming march into something of a dreaded ordeal. He did not know that many of the questions which perplexed him about the relationship between Jim and the colonel would be answered, and that for Jim, the march would become a critical turning-point in his life.

CHAPTER NINE

Sharp at eight in the morning, the jeep from Transport Platoon arrived outside Michael Baldwin's duplex apartment. Its body was painted dark green, then the standard color for all vehicles of the Canadian Army. Attached to its front bumper and to its back, beside the spare wheel, were the "tac signs" of the battalion, red with the figures "51" in white superimposed. Its canvas top had been fastened in place, but the doors were not attached. The driver, a private, was neatly turned out in battle-dress uniform, with shining web belt and boots. He had been exempt from the forthcoming march with his company, because he had a special duty to perform; to convey his medical officer the fifty miles to Camp Ipperwash, to join up with the marching troops before they moved off. He was lounging against the hood of his vehicle, happy in his good fortune; he would not have to slog the fifty miles back to London, carrying a full pack and a C-1 rifle. After he had dropped Captain Baldwin off, he would be returning to the infinitely preferable comforts of the Barracks.

Michael emerged from the front door of the duplex, waved good-bye to his wife and little sons and walk towards the jeep, with his arctic rucksack and medical satchel slung over his shoulder. The M.O. was dressed in the dark-green bush uniform, with the soft cloth cap, the prescribed attire for field exercises in the warmer months. The driver stood to attention and saluted. He could barely conceal his amusement at seeing his M.O. kitted out for the march. "Boy, this is friggin' nuts," he thought. "Why the hell does the M.O. have to go on this bloody march? Could've given himself excused duties"!

"Good morning! Are we all set for Ipperwash?"

"Yes, sir! Climb aboard!"

Michael threw his rucksack and satchel into the back seat. In the rucksack he had packed his sleeping bag, toilet articles, extra socks, a khaki sweater — and a chunk of salami sausage that his wife had insisted he take with him, in case he got hungry. His canvas satchel, with the red cross painted on it, contained medical instruments and supplies, to supplement the ample stock of medical equipment which Corporal Ken Allen had taken with him in the jeep ambulance, which accompanied Headquarters Company on its journey.

The trip along the highway to Camp Ipperwash on that bright sunny morning was pleasant and uneventful. The M.O. tried to make small talk with the driver, but the lad was taciturn. Sitting next to someone with three brass pips on either shoulder hardly seemed conducive to chit-chat. The jeep left the highway after an hour's drive, and pulled up on a field just outside the military camp. The men of headquarters Company had been at the camp for two days, for the annual rifle qualification shoots, and were now assembling for the march. Although none had any illusions about what was ahead of them, the young soldiers were in a jocular mood as they formed into platoons and adjusted the straps of their rucksacks and rifles. Their ribald laughter echoed across the field.

"Well, sir, this is where you get off! Enjoy your hike!"

"Yeah, thanks, Johnson. See you back at the Barracks!"

Michael picked up his rucksack and satchel, and walked over to the parked jeep ambulance. Corporal Allen, standing by the vehicle, grinned and saluted.

"Good morning, sir! Hope you're in good shape today!"

"Good morning, Corporal Allen. All raring to go! How have things been with you these last couple days?"

"Not bad. A few bruised chins from the firing range. Them cooks are no fuckin' shakes when it comes to firing the C-1 rifle! Can't seem to hang onto them mothers tight enough! A couple of minor cuts. Didn't have to evacuate any of them. We're 'fat' for supplies in the back of the jeep amb. Lots of elastoplast strip dressings and syringes!"

Michael had taught his medical corporals to aspirate foot blisters with a syringe where necessary, before applying a dressing. He calculated that on the average it took one yard of elastoplast per company per mile on these marches — but for Headquarters Company, one never knew. Corporal Allen would be following the marching column with the jeep ambulance, and would be available to attend to the men on rest stops, and when they pulled in for the night bivouacs, when a routine foot inspection of all ranks would be carried out.

There was a group of officers at the head of the assembling column and Michael headed in their direction. Major Niles, the company commander was there, with the company sergeant-major, Jan Kovacs, Captain Leo Toland, the Transport Officer and Captain Eric Fisher, the Signals Officer. Michael saluted the company commander. "Good morning, Jim."

"Good morning, Mike. Glad to have you with us."

"Well, hello, there, Mogey! So we now have the medical corps with us in force, eh? Think you'll last the fifty miles, old chum?" This was from Eric Fisher, who delighted in bantering with the Medical Officer, for whom he felt a mixture of respect for Michael as a doctor, and utter contempt that he was not a "real soldier" like himself. Both were keen chess players, and had engaged in many games on schemes and exercises, when they had time off together. Eric at twenty-eight was a year younger then Michael, and shared with him the distinction of not being from the regiment, having been attached to the battalion from their respective corps. Eric, from the Royal Canadian Corps of Signals, was an R.M.C. graduate. He was an aggressive young officer, committed to his military career, loved his job with the battalion, and ran his Signals Platoon with a tight grip.

"I'll match you mile for mile, Eric. And I'll be there to patch your blisters long before I need to take care of mine!"

"Hi, Mike!" Leo Toland, in contrast to Eric, was a quiet man, who had been commissioned from the ranks. He was a lance corporal when he had been selected by his commanding officer to attend the Officer Candidate School which was periodically conducted at the Royal Canadian School of Infantry at Camp Borden. He had served as a platoon commander in Korea. Now he had the responsibility of running the battalion's Transport Platoon and the vehicle pool.

"Hi, Leo!" Mike sensed uneasiness in this officer. Leo had had very little by way of close working contact with his company commander, and had been horrified when Major Niles collapsed dead drunk at the mess dinner. He had always been in awe of R.M.C. graduates, and envious that he had been commissioned from the ranks, without the advantage of higher education. The Army traditionally looked to the R.M.C. graduates for its future senior commanders. Next in hierarchy came the university graduates who were commissioned through the university officers' training programmes; it was rare indeed for an officer commissioned from the ranks to advance beyond the rank of Major, their own colonel being an exception. But Major Niles never behaved as Leo expected from an R.M.C. graduate, and this perturbed him. He never knew how he stood with him, and was painfully aware that the major had no interest in the Transport Platoon, and left the running of it entirely in Leo's hands. Nevertheless, Leo ran his platoon with quiet efficiency. He had made every effort to master the complexities of auto mechanics, and had a good grasp of what his men were required to do.

Major Niles gave his orders to move. "Captain Fisher, I want you to lead off with your Signals Platoon, right behind me. Captain Toland, you and your transport people next. Sergeant-Major Kovacs, you and the M.O. will bring up the rear with the cooks, provost personnel, Q.M. staff, battalion orderly staff and the rest. Fall in your men, in single file. We move in five minutes."

The officers raced off to take their positions. All ranks hoisted their rucksacks onto their backs. Rifles were slung over shoulders. With a brusque, "O.K., let's go!" Major Niles strode out of the field and onto the road, with Headquarters Company, a hundred and twenty strong, in a long line behind him.

....

The prescribed route had been carefully planned by Colonel Banfield, before the first of the rifle companies ventured on the march that spring. The route left Lake Huron at Camp Ipperwash, and moved inland, across the northeast tip of Lambton County, into the gently rolling terrain of Middlesex County. The route was along dirt country roads where possible, and where it was necessary to use county roads, the soldiers were to keep to the left of the pavement, on the gravel shoulders. Each marching company was required to do twenty miles the first day, twenty again the second day, and the final ten miles on the third, which took them to Wolseley Barracks in London. In the built-up part of London, the soldiers would march on the right side of the selected streets. Bivouac areas had been requisitioned from farmers where the men were fed with meals cooked on the battalion's field stoves, which were always set up and operating on the bivouac site before they pulled in. There they would camp for the night — and there the medical personnel would conduct their foot inspections, and attend to medical needs.

Route marching was then very much part of the stock-in-trade of any infantry unit. All ranks, and especially the officers, knew that the conventional infantry pace was three miles an hour. This meant that the first day's twenty miles should comfortably be accomplished in eight hours, with occasional rest breaks. But Jim Niles seemed determined to ignore this rule, and doggedly forged ahead, his hands gripping the shoulder straps of his rucksack, rarely bothering to look behind. In keeping with his characteristic manner of running his company, having as little to do with it as he could, he set a gruelling pace. He was not in fact leading them. In many respects he seemed to be stretching every muscle and sinew in his body to get away from his own men.

The men of the Signal Platoon, accustomed to accompanying the rifle companies on frequent schemes and exercises, were generally in top physical condition. Sweating and panting behind their platoon commander, Eric Fisher, they kept up with Major Niles, mile after mile, along the dusty road. However, this was no simple test of endurance for them. They had a long march ahead, and the pace the major was setting was foolhardy in the extreme. And each cursed his company commander in muttered tones which Eric Fisher chose to ignore.

The pace soon began to tell on the rest of the company. The men from Transport Platoon, vehicle-borne in much of their soldiering duties, were unable to keep up, and a gap lengthened between them and the signals people in front of them. In the weeks before the march, their platoon officer Leo Toland had tried to organize "toughening-up" marches along the streets of London, but because of battalion demand for vehicles and drivers, he simply could not spare enough of his men for sufficient time to get them into hardened physical shape. Captain Toland, having come from the ranks, knew and respected his men. Although he was concerned that this would likely cause trouble for him with the company commander, he set his own pace for his men, and kept to it. He was determined not to exhaust them in the first day out.

The third group on the march, the composite platoon formed from the odds and sods of the battalion, the cooks and bottle washers, those least practiced in the art of foot-slogging, ran into difficulties quickly. No provision had been made by the company commander beforehand to provide them with any physical training. Many became badly winded, their leg muscles ached and spasmed, and their feet were quickly painfully blistered. CSM Jan Kovacs, who led them, viewed all this with alarm, for not only were his men unable to maintain the pace the major had set, but many were straggling behind so that his group was stretched out badly. Some were doubled up with cramps, and lay panting by the wayside, attempting again and again to catch up once they had rested for a brief time. "God damn that black-souled son-of-a-bitch!" Jan Kovacs spat through his teeth. Life was so much simpler when he had served as a Company Quartermaster Sergeant with Alpha Company. Those rifle company lads were fit, not much between their ears, they took orders, the drill and organization was so simple .... and now he was expected to handle this lot of trades people, like a bunch of God-damned civilians! This man's Army was becoming too bloody complicated! And the damned major never gave a shit for anything or anyone — least of all his CSM.......

Since he was not required to command, Michael Baldwin had positioned himself directly behind the Battalion Orderly Room Sergeant, Theo Morgan. Theo had a demanding job as the right hand man to the adjutant. The two attended to the administrative and personnel needs of the battalion. Theo was also, in fact, executive secretary to Colonel Banfield. All the papers pertaining to the business end of running the unit passed through his hands first. He never tired of working his long hours, but because of the sedentary nature of his duties, he was a little overweight. Michael could see that he was starting to flag, the sweat pouring off his face.

He tapped the orderly sergeant on the shoulder. "Sergeant Morgan, will you let me carry your rifle for a stretch?"

Sergeant Morgan was nonplussed. Now here was something wierd and totally unexpected, he thought. No officer was ever expected to carry a rifle — let alone one belonging to an "other rank"! Besides, this was no ordinary officer. He was the bloody M.O., for Chrissakes! For him to carry a weapon was in thundering violation of the bloody Geneva Convention! But the prospect of eleven pounds of steel weapon off his aching shoulders for a spell could not be dismissed lightly.

"Thank you, sir! I would be most obliged!"

The weapon changed hands. Michael slung it by its strap over his shoulder. The two of them trudged on. It had been a while since Michael had carried a rifle. In his first summer of the officer candidate course at Camp Borden, his rifle accompanied him everywhere, for the hours of drill every morning on the parade square, to the classrooms and to the mess for lunch, on all the route marches and to the rifle ranges. At night, after supper, he would have to clean and oil it, to pass inspection the following morning. For that whole summer, it was literally like having a third arm. But at that time, the Army was still issued with the old Lee Enfield. He had never carried the new C-1 rifle before. He had, however, been very carefully indoctrinated on the officer candidate course that the welfare of his men was always of paramount importance. And Sergeant Morgan merited his concern now.

After the first ten miles, Major Niles ordered a fifteen minute rest break. The signals personnel whipped off their rucksacks and weapons, and collapsed at the side of the road. It was then that the company commander realized that most of his men were far behind, and out of sight. It took ten minutes before the transport people caught up.

"Captain Toland!" Jim Niles shouted, before Leo had the chance to fall his men out for the rest stop. "You will oblige by getting the God-damned lead out of your men! They are infantry like the rest! I will not tolerate any lagging behind on this march!"

"Sir, they're tired. They'll do the march, but they are not a rifle platoon...."

"God damn it, captain!" Jim persisted, in front of all present. "They'll do what I want them to do! And we are moving off again in five minutes." Looking down the road, he saw the first of CSM Kovac's men appear around a clump of trees, a half mile behind. "Where....in hell....are the rest of them?....Captain Fisher!"

"Yes, Major Niles!"

"I want you to get down there to see what is going on. Tell the CSM, because he has permitted his men to lag so far behind, that there will be no rest stop for them. They are to continue on the march to catch up with the main party, or they can damn well drop in their tracks!"

"Roger, Jim, I'll handle it!" Having just completed ten miles of marching, he dropped his pack off at the side of the road, and ran off at a steady lope to find the CSM. For Eric, soldiering was a serious business, and he relished this opportunity, as a Signal Corps officer, to blast the lagging infantrymen in the rear for their tardiness. Eric Fisher was fully aware of what the men thought of the major, but this, after all, was duty, he was obeying an order — albeit with sadistic delight — and the major could take the consequences.

He quickly reached Jan Kovacs, at the head of his straggling column. Without taking time to catch his breath, and walking alongside the CSM, he delivered his message: "Sergeant Major, Major Niles' compliments. He wishes to know, what in hell seems to be holding your group up. This is totally unacceptable. You have to do better!"

"The men are having a rough time keeping up, sir. The pace was too fast...."

"Too fast? The pace has been brisk, Sergeant Major, not too fast! Get along with it, will you? Company commander's orders are that there is to be no rest stop for these men. Best way for them to catch up, would you not agree?"

"Yes, sir! We'll make it!" Jan Kovacs, seething with indignation, tightly clenched his fists around his rucksack straps. He knew the young signals captain enough to conclude that had he, Kovacs, been a sergeant or corporal, Eric Fisher would have used his most polished military sarcasm. But this damned officer was addressing a warrant officer, and his language was accordingly patronizing. Damn him and damn the major! Neither showed any consideration for these men, who should not have been on the march in the first place, but for the Army's chickenshit obsession with top physical fitness for all ranks and trades. Some tolerance surely was in order here. Jan Kovacs regarded himself as much of a career soldier as Captain Fisher. He had fought with the infantry in Northwest Europe and in Korea, and had been on many exhausting marches. But those marches were tactical and operational necessities. And here was this young R.M.C. type telling him to move his butt! Some of these young officers today seemed to know more about commanding and less about leading. He knew, however, no matter how he detested his company commander, his orders must be obeyed. But he consoled himself with wry satisfaction that whereas the officer corps of the Army was the brains of the Army, God damn it! the non-commissioned officers were its backbone!

Michael Baldwin missed this interchange between the CSM and Eric Fisher. He saw the latter run off, to rejoin the head of the company column. Jan Kovacs turned to Mike. "Captain Baldwin, we're in a bit of a snafu hereabouts. Will you take the head of this platoon group. Keep it at three miles per hour — please, no faster! Me and the sergeants here will have to crack about to get the lads to haul ass so we can catch up with the major."

"Sure, Sergeant Major, gladly! If there are any bad problems, let me know. Corporal Allen is bringing up the rear with his jeep amb, and will be picking up those who have fallen out of the march." And so the battalion's doctor, still hefting Sergeant Morgan's rifle, led the remnants of the motley platoon, while all senior N.C.O.'s rounded up the stragglers. He knew clearly now that he would have his hands full once they reached the bivouac area, when he reverted to his functions as a physician. It was a struggle for him not to share the resentment all ranks felt towards their major. With each mile of this march, his apprehension and concern about Jim Niles mounted. Would he make it through the next two days, without serious trouble with the rank-and-file? He was more acutely aware than ever of the importance of his special mission, conferred upon him by Colonel Banfield.

....

By late afternoon, the company reached its first bivouac site, a flat grazing field, with a small brook flowing across it, a tributary of the Ausable River. The battalion's cooks — those who were not sacrificed for the march — had set up their field cookers, and were busily preparing a meal of soup, steak and vegetables, with cake and coffee. As the first two platoons stumbled past to their allotted areas, there was a cry of delight as they detected the delectable smells of their forthcoming dinner in this rural setting. They dropped their rifles and rucksacks, and began snapping together their ponchos, to construct the makeshift hoochies, under which they would sleep that night. Some took off their boots and socks, and waded in the little stream. Others simply collapsed on the ground, too exhausted for anything else, and awaited their turn to be called to the chow line.

Two arctic tents, without liners, had been pitched in a corner of the field, one for Major Niles, and the other for the three captains and CSM Kovacs.

Shortly after the lead troops arrived, Jim Niles repaired to his tent, and stretched out on his sleeping-bag, not waiting for the rest of his company to pull in. He ordered his batman to bring in a basin of hot water so he could wash, which he used with no word of thanks to the young private, who had done the twenty miles with the rest of them, and who was just as tired.

The major knew that it was an inviolate tradition in the Canadian Army that the men in field exercises were always fed first, and that no officer was permitted to eat until all the men had been served. With resentful resignation, he was prepared to wait until he was called.

The sergeant cook yelled: "Come and get it!" The young soldiers rushed to line up, with their rectangular aluminum mess tins, and enamelware cups. Never did Army food taste so good as after such a long route march! The food was always well prepared and plentiful. Once they were served these young men ambled back to their respective areas, sat on the grass, and chowed down.

The last group under CSM Kovacs stumbled onto the bivouac area as the cooks had finished serving the signals and transport troops. Sweating, dust-covered and aching, some were simply too tired to fall in line for food. The jeep ambulance pulled in, with three men on two stretchers, two on the hood, and one sitting next to the driver. Corporal Allen had given up his seat, and marched the remaining four miles with the others.

Michael Baldwin was alarmed at what he saw. He asked a passing soldier to carry his rucksack over to the officers' tent, and proceeded, with Ken Allen's help, to examine the jeepload of casualties who needed his immediate medical attention. He would get around to conducting the foot inspection later, after the men had had their supper and cleaned up. Swiftly, he examined the casualties, made his diagnoses, and instructed Corporal Allen regarding their disposition. Then he walked over to Major Niles' tent, to report on the medical situation.

"Can I come in, Jim?"

"Oh, hello there, doctor! I was expecting you. A SITREP, no doubt, on the sick, lame and lazy."

"I haven't had a chance to take a close look at the sigs and transport people yet. I am going through with a foot inspection for all ranks right after supper, before the lads settle down for the night. But, Jim, the march has been devastating on the odds and sods group. I am going to have to evacuate six of them by our jeep amb. They are unfit for further marching...."

"What the hell is this all about! God-damned malingering bastards! What happened to them?"

Michael was dismayed at the callousness of these remarks, but chose to ignore them. "Your orders were for these people to keep up, Jim. I must tell you, without qualification, that they tried damned hard. But without any fitness training, physically they broke down. Many were doubled up with cramps. On my orders, Corporal Allen picked some of these men up in the jeep ambulance, and carried them for a couple of miles, to rest them, or they would never have made it here.

"Corporal Sykes of the Q.M. Stores came down with prolapsed haemorrhoids. Private Benvenuto from the men's mess-hall has some kind of strangulated hernia, which he tried to conceal when he went on the march. Both of these men are to be admitted to London Station Hospital, and I have sent them off in the jeep ambulance. The four others, two from the officers' mess, a provost corporal and one from the battalion orderly room, all have badly blistered and bleeding feet — beyond anything now except excused duties until their feet heal. The jeep amb will have to make a second run back to London with the three remaining foot casualties. I'll wait up for it, to make sure they get away O.K."

"My great God, Mike, what sort of bloody Army is this? Haemorrhoids, hernias, bleeding blisters, all of this in an infantry unit?"

"These are all healthy young men, Jim. Haemorrhoids and hernias can happen with anyone. But as far as blisters and sore muscles go, I must point out again that the cause of these problems lies in the fact that many of the men in your company are not in physical condition to do this type of march. The sigs and transport people have officers who ensured that their men underwent hardening-up training as much as possible. The others provide essential administrative services, and nothing was laid on for them. They should have been left off the march."

Jim Niles stared past the M.O. His fists and jaws clenched. It seemed to Michael that he was struggling with his feelings, attempting to come to grips yet again with his persistent, agonized conflicts about the Army and his role as a field officer.

God damn the Army, and these filthy soldiers whom he was forced to command. To hell with this march, and to hell with all their aches and pains. He had problems enough of his own without concerning himself with these men.....

But this young M.O. did the march with us, when he did not have to.... and, for God's sake, he enjoyed it. Even carried a rifle during much of it. Then he had to examine and treat the casualties at the end of the day. And he's planning to do the routine foot inspection with his medic, after supper. And he is intending to stay up to make sure the second jeep ambulance load gets off tonight, before turning in. The men all admire and respect him. This damned doctor has proved to be a real officer, concerned for their welfare. He, Niles, was directly responsible for all the additional work which has been imposed on him. But Baldwin takes it on without a word of complaint.....

My God, where does that leave me. I am the professional soldier, the infantry officer..... Damn me to perdition for what I have done! So infernally wrapped up in my miseries, with nothing left for these men in my own company. What in hell is the answer to all of this?

Jim looked sadly at Michael. "I am getting the drift of what you are saying, and it horrifies me. As company commander, I should have seen to all of this. It was my responsibility....."

"Major Niles, sir!" It was Private Brandt, his batman.

"Yes, what is it?"

"The men have all been served, sir. Officers' turn for chow next."

"Thank you. Well, doctor, here is where we eat — at last."

The four officers and the CSM gathered at the food line. Jim Niles received his rations, and returned to his tent, to eat alone. The four others ambled over to a comfortable spot, and ate their meal out of their mess tins, sitting on the grass together. They were not, it appeared, to have the honor of their major's company.

....

Michael had work to do. As soon as he had eaten, he washed his mess tins and utensils in the buckets provided, and stuffed them back into his rucksack in his tent. The men of the company were lined up in rows, sitting on the grass in their bare feet. Corporal Allen had already started on the all-too-familiar job of treating blisters. Carefully, the medical officer checked every soldier, and worked deftly with his medical hygiene corporal wherever there were blisters to be treated, which presented in profusion after that first day's march, particularly among the men of the composite platoon. Fortunately, there were no more so seriously affected as to require evacuation, although Michael wondered how many of his plaster jobs would hold up for the next day's march.

The sun was setting by the time the last soldier was checked out on the foot inspection. Many of the young soldiers had already crawled into their sleeping-bags. Bone-weary, the medical officer found a basin which he filled with water from the water trailer, stripped to his waist, and washed himself down with one of Corporal Allen's medical towels. "Well, that was quite a job, eh, sir!" said Ken Allen, as he put away his equipment in the canvas bags.

"Sure was! Some of those feet looked God-awful! I'm damned glad I had you with me! You have really got pretty slick at aspirating blisters!"

"Yeah, you should talk to the man who taught me! Boy, I sure was glad to have you here today after that piss cutter. I hope the good major is not going to push them this way tomorrow."

"Are you going to be comfortable tonight, Corporal Allen?"

"Oh, sure, Captain Baldwin, you know me, the old arctic fox! Got me a hoochie I rigged up with the tarps off the jeep amb, and a couple of sticks I pulled off that old fence yonder!"

"O.K. You better turn in. I'll wait up until the jeep amb returns to pick up the last three lads, before I do. Have a good night!"

Michael returned to his tent. Jan Kovacs was out, chatting with his sergeants. Leo Toland, in true old soldier fashion, had already crawled into his sleeping-bag, and fallen asleep. By the light of the naphtha lamp hanging from the tent pole, Michael and Eric Fisher were settled down over a quick chess game on the miniature set the sigs officer always carried.

"Captain Baldwin, sir!" It was Major Niles' batman outside.

"Yes?"

"Major Niles' compliments, sir. He wishes to see you in his tent."

"O.K., Brandt, I'll be right over."

"God-dammit, Mogey; just when I'm about to beat you in this game!" Fisher was irked by his departure. "Well, if the master calls, his word is our command...."

Michael pulled back the entrance flap of Niles' tent, and stepped in. "Ah, thank you for coming over, Mike. How was the foot inspection? Any further bad news?"

"No, Jim. I think we were able to patch up those who needed patching. Most of them just need a good night's sleep. I am waiting for the jeep amb to return, to pick up the last three I'm sending back. Was there something you wished to see me about?"

"Well ... I've had time to do some thinking since supper. I ... well, I wanted to thank you for what you did for me today. I'm not sure I could have managed without you. This whole thing could have ended in a real bloody mess. Well ... there's something else I have to thank you for. You see, it really hit me how remiss I have been in my responsibilities as O.C. of Headquarters Company. What happened to those men today really struck home. Damn it, Mike, I should have made certain that those who were to go on this march were fit for it. I don't mind admitting that I found it damned odd that I should learn about the responsibilities of command from you. You're a doctor. No harm meant, old man — but you're not a soldier — well, not a real one ... but pretty close, though...."

"From an infantry officer, I take that as a compliment, Jim! I wasn't required to come on this march. But, I wanted to do some real soldiering with you people. I thought it would be fun to get away from the M.I.R. for a couple of days. Anyway, as it turned out, I was needed as a doctor as well."

"Mike, you must be mad, to want to get into this type of thing. You may not have been ordered on this march, but I'm damned certain that Bob Banfield had something to do with it ... wanted you to keep an eye on the problem major!"

This made Michael uneasy. "The Old Man was very concerned. What happened at the mess dinner upset him. I think he was glad that I was to come with you. The welfare of the battalion is very much part of my job. This includes the welfare of our majors. I enjoy my job. I like the Army...."

"For God's sake, what's likeable about the Army! I detest the Army, and I detest the common soldier. I think it was Wellington who called them the scum of the earth!"

"You come through loud and clear, Jim. And that is your prerogative. You have seen war. I haven't. Something terrible must have happened to you over there. If you feel so negative about the Army, why did you stay in, after the war?"

"There is nothing mysterious about that. There have been professional soldiers in my family for several generations. Great things were expected from me in the service. Well, I was no hero in the war. On the contrary..." For a moment, Jim Niles stared in front of him, obviously struggling with painful feelings, which he was not prepared to share.

"When I returned to Canada, my father was enraged and disgusted. Far from returning as a hero, I was a total failure. No V.C. or M.C. — just a physically intact son. I know he would have preferred to have received news of my glorious demise on the field of honour instead! For him, it was better to be a dead hero than a live coward........

"Without any leave, I was posted to an advanced training unit near Brockville. My father was determined to watch me closely. Within a year, the war was over, and the Army overseas returned. The brigadier insisted that I was to serve as an officer in the peacetime Regular Army. He said that this was necessary to give me a chance to _redeem_ myself, and clear the good name of the Niles family. And because of my heritage and my upbringing, I believed him. There was really no other option. At the age of twenty-two, the label of 'coward' was branded onto me, and 'redemption' was all I had to look forward to. I was to 'redeem' myself in the Canadian Army, an institution I have hated and despised all my life.

"There were a number of dingy postings, as decreed by the 'Palace Guard' at D.N.D. Headquarters in Ottawa. I served in staff positions in recruiting depots, processing these miserable, stupid little men, good for nothing but cannon-fodder in another war. Then I was Resident Staff Officer for the C.O.T.C. at a university, my main function being to convince the cultured and the educated, or rather partially educated — like you were, doctor! — to train to become officers, so they could lead these miserable, stupid little men to great heights of glory.....oh, Jesus... it's nauseating, all of it. There were also various postings at Army H.Q., aide to this or that directorate chief, accompanying these generals on their eternal social rounds, announcing guests at the gala occasions, all under the nose of my father....

"Somewhere along the line, I was promoted to Captain. Then came the inevitable captain-to-major course. I was sent to Staff College in Kingston, and rather amazingly, passed. With my majority came the clarion call to the colors — I was deemed ready again for service in an infantry battalion! And this, my dear doctor, eventually led to where I am today, in a bloody tent, on some farmer's field, and expected to march my brave and stalwart company of Canadian soldiery all the way back to London town..."

Under the sardonic humor, there was so much bitterness and pain; Michael Baldwin strove to understand. He felt pity and compassion for this tortured man. The pieces of the tragic story were coming together, but an important piece was missing. What had happened to him on the Verrières Ridge? Although Jim was not aware of it, Michael's sincere efforts to help him, his willingness to listen, were gradually drawing him out of himself. For the first time he was encouraged to re-examine the circumstances and emotional forces which had led to his relentless guilt and pain.

"Well, Mike, we had better turn in. Another twenty miles of this nonsense tomorrow, and I'll need a functioning doctor again at the end of the day! See you in the morning!"

"Goodnight, Jim."

Michael returned to his tent. The others were sound asleep. The naphtha lamp was still burning. He stretched out on his sleeping-bag, using his ruck-sack as a pillow. Very soon afterwards, he heard the distinctive chortling of the jeep ambulance, as it drove into the bivouac area. Wearily, he got up, went out to check with the driver who assured him that the two soldiers had been admitted to hospital, and assisted the last three casualties onto the vehicle, which took off once more for London. Walking back to his tent, he noticed that a deathly quiet had descended on the bivouac area. There were no sentries posted on picket duty. No orders had been given to stand to at dusk and at dawn. For the few veterans in this motley group, including their major, it must have been very different, fifteen years ago in Normandy. He wondered how it was, the night before Bob Banfield and Jim Niles marched up the slope of that ridge, which irrevocably shaped their lives to come.

Once again back in his tent, he removed his bush uniform and boots, and crawled into his sleeping-bag. As he drifted off to sleep, he wondered how a man could be so programmed by his upbringing, to be driven to serve in an Army he detested. How could he function in military life with such anti-military convictions? How could he have survived as a young officer on the battlefield, having totally isolated himself from his brother officers and his men, when unit cohesion and unity of purpose were vital to survival? With his sensitivity, how could he have kept his nerve in the violent fury of a pitched battle without disintegrating under the strain? And what happened to him on the Verrières Ridge, which had emotionally lacerated him, and had compelled him to stay in the Army, to redeem himself.....

....

Dawn came early. The air was crisp with a heavy dew, a reddened sky to the east. The battalion's cooks were first up, and the smell of frying eggs and bacon, and coffee brewing, permeated the bivouac area. The men rose in small groups, and lined up for breakfast. Following this, there was a little time available for ablutions. The men were required to shave and clean up before packing their gear. The officers and CSM Kovacs were called to attend a brief "O-group" with Major Niles. The men started forming up in their platoons. Again, there was the usual ribald banter, as they concealed their fear that the major would again drive them on the march the way he had done the previous day.

But the major seemed changed. He ate his breakfast with his officers, and even engaged in conversation with them. At his "O-group", he announced that the same order of platoons would be maintained on the march, but this time he would keep the pace to three miles per hour. All were relieved at this decision. The company formed single file in platoons, and off they went.

The men marched throughout the day, under a warm sun. Water-bottles, which had been filled from the water trailer before they left the bivouac area, came in handy at the rest stops. There was none of the straggling which had occurred the day before, but the march took its toll nevertheless. When the company reached its second bivouac area, Michael Baldwin had seven more blister casualties to send back to London. This time, the jeep ambulance was not required. A three-quarter ton truck had arrived with provisions for the cooks; it returned to the Barracks with the seven footsore men aboard.

Michael noted with relief that this time there was no rancorous recrimination from Major Niles. On the contrary, on the foot inspection after this second day, he accompanied Michael and Corporal Allen on their round of ministrations. He expressed concern when he saw Ken Allen attending to Michael's own blisters, developed, to the M.O.'s disgust and embarrassment, after the second twenty miles. He even allowed himself to chat with some of the other ranks, and contrary to his expectations, discovered that they did not hold him in vile hatred, but that they were pleasantly surprised that the second day had not been as gruelling for them. In that short while, many of these young soldiers had actually toughened up. Without letting their sentiments be known to the party concerned, many of the lads had concluded that their fearless leader had himself begun to run out of steam! Jim Niles was learning something about leadership and command, despite himself.

....

On the third and final day of the march, the men rose in superb spirits. The ten final miles were a mere cake walk. Even those who had the most sedentary jobs in the battalion convinced themselves that they were now lean and mean, just like the colonel wanted, and they could march to hell and back if necessary. The company of odds and sods had found itself.

As Major Niles led off, the young soldiers strode off behind him, one platoon tightly following the other, chatting happily amongst themselves. All looked forward to the forty-eight hour pass they were entitled to when they got back to the Barracks. As he marched along, behind Sergeant Theo Morgan, Michael Baldwin listened with amusement, then with consternation, to the boastful talk from these lads, about the second thing they would do after the first, once they took off on pass, and were let loose on the flesh-pots of London! Fervently, he hoped that they would remember something of the stern lectures he had delivered to them, regarding the dangers of venereal disease! He hoped that Sergeant Scott, back at the M.I.R., had stocked up on the mechanical prophylactics — if only these lustful young yokels would come in for them......

A half mile outside the Barracks, well into the city, Headquarters Company was met by the regiment band, which Colonel Banfield had laid on, for the final lap. The company formed up in platoons of three ranks, and marched home to the stirring martial music of the drums and brass — even though the only tune, played over and over, was the regimental march! Michael had not marched behind a band since his passing out parade at Camp Borden. He noted the effect it had on these young soldiers, who swung down the street with their heads held high, weighed down though they were with their weapons and gear. And so it has been throughout history. So many glorious armies and their marching bands, which had led young men into the hell and horror of war. Follow the drum ....into eternity....

Jim Niles led his men through the north gate of the Barracks, and onto the parade square. There, he brought the men into column of platoons, facing front at attention, as the last bars of music were played out by the band behind them.

Standing to attention, the major faced his company. He addressed them: "You men of Headquarters Company did well on this march. I am proud of you, as I am sure your commanding officer will be, when I tell him how well you did." Standing in front of the composite platoon, Michael could scarcely believe what he heard.

"Company, fall out!"

With this final command, the young soldiers made a smart right-turn, and broke ranks. Having just completed fifty miles of route marching, they raced across the parade square to their barrack buildings, yelling and whooping like a bunch of rowdy children, finally free of their officers, and eager to begin their forty-eight hour passes.

The officers and N.C.O.'s marched off the square with martial dignity more appropriate to their status, towards the administrative building.

"How's that for morale, eh, Mogey!" exclaimed Eric Fisher. Michael smiled. He was more concerned with the morale of the major. He felt greatly relieved that nothing more disastrous had befallen Major Niles and his company. He had carried out Colonel Banfield's wishes. He knew that he had contributed significantly, in helping his patient when it was most needed.

Michael checked in at his M.I.R., and dumped his rucksack on his desk. Corporal Allen had already arrived, having been dropped off at the M.I.R.

by the jeep ambulance driver on his way to the vehicle pool. Sergeant Scott and the other medical corporals stared at their M.O., coated with dust and soaked with sweat, with a mixture of amusement and admiration.

"Sir," said Fred Scott, "you'll make a soldier yet!"

After taking care of matters which required his immediate attention, which had accumulated over the days he was away, he left the M.I.R., to report to Colonel Banfield, before returning to his home for a long-awaited bath.

CHAPTER TEN

Captain Michael Baldwin, Regimental Medical Officer and, of late, foot-slogging infanteer, walked into the battalion's orderly room and saluted. This was the custom in the Canadian Army, that a soldier of any rank saluted on entering a military office, regardless of the rank of those present. The battalion clerks on duty grinned, seeing their doctor in his crumpled bush uniform, coated with grime and sweat from the march. The orderly sergeant, Theo Morgan, had not yet gone home either, and hobbled around the orderly room on his painfully blistered feet and aching legs, similarly attired and soaked in sweat, attempting to bring some order to the pile of paper which had accumulated during his absence. He looked up, and returned the medical officer's salute.

"There you are, sir! C.O. is expecting you. You're to go in right away. Major Niles is with him now."

Michael felt decidedly uneasy about the prospect of having to report to the commanding officer with Jim Niles present. The relationship between the two senior officers had been strained at best, and he had no wish to be spectator, or worse yet, arbitrator for them. He had tried to learn what had affected this relationship so severely during the last fifteen years; neither seemed willing to provide much detail as to how their distant battlefield experience had scarred Jim Niles so deeply.

The march had taken a toll on Headquarters Company, but it could have been worse. He was concerned that the C.O. might want an account of Jim's performance on the march. He did not wish to jeopardize his rather tenuous relationship with the major, which he had worked hard to foster over the past while. He was acutely aware that Jim Niles still needed all the help he could provide.

Michael left the orderly room, and walked down the corridor to the first office. On its door the sign, in the yellow and blue regimental colors, read "Commanding Officer". The Colonel answered his knock immediately;

he opened the door and saluted. Banfield was sitting behind his desk; in an easy chair acrosss from him sat Major Niles.

"Good morning, sir."

"Ah, good morning, Mike. My God, you look a sight! Major Niles marched the living hell out of you, I hear! Bet you can't wait to get home for a damned good hot bath! Sit down over there; you must be tired."

"Thank you, sir."

"Major Niles has told to me about the march. I am concerned about the men who fell out. I understand that there were two you sent off to hospital."

"Yes, sir. I had to evacuate six after the first day, then seven after the second day. The two who were admitted to the station hospital have been booked for surgery. The Area Medical Officer will board them with me. Temporary categories until they will be fit for full duty again. The other nine have badly blistered feet. A few days' excused duties should be sufficient. We'll look after them at the M.I.R."

"Mike, what are your conclusions here? We did not run into this kind of thing with Bravo and Charlie Companies. From your medical point of view, what happened?"

This was very awkward, very fast, and required the utmost diplomacy. "We had no particular difficulty with the sigs and transport people. Eric Fisher and Leo Toland saw to that, by marching their platoons on practice runs, before the big one. Sergeant-Major Kovacs organized a crash fitness programme for a group of odds and sods a month before the march, which I tried to attend as often as I could get away; I personally felt it was very helpful and necessary. But inevitably there were Q.M. and clerical personnel who couldn't get away for this training, and they got into trouble."

"Can you comment here, Jim?" the colonel asked.

"I agree with Mike. If the entire battalion is to be in top physical shape, then all troops must be have regular fitness training. This would apply to Headquarters Company as well. In this, I must admit that I've been remiss..."

"Yes, well, we'll discuss that later. Mike, we still have Alpha and Delta Companies to go. Are you medical people ready for them?"

"Yes, sir. Corporal Lanthier will be with Alpha, and Corporal Latimer with Delta. Both are top-rate M.A.s. They have been assigned to each of these companies in previous exercises and schemes. Both company commanders seem to believe that they are their doctors, and want no one else! And as I have done before, I will make it a point to get out to them at their second bivouac site to lend a hand."

"Good show, doctor! Anything you want to bring up before Mike leaves, Jim?"

"No, except to say that the M.O. was truly invaluable to me on the march. Without wanting to embarrass him, I have to say that I have never served with an M.O. who was both an exemplary doctor and top-rate officer as well. I think we're fortunate to have him on strength."

Colonel Banfield smiled. It seemed, for the moment, that this was all he needed to know from his medical officer. The lad had done his job well. Headquarters Company and its major were back in the Barracks, and all was well.

"Mike, you have my thanks as well. Now go home and get soaked!"

"Yes, sir!"

....

The colonel turned to face Jim Niles. "What did you mean that you were 'remiss' - in what?"

"When you interrupted me, I was about to say that I was remiss as the company commander in not making sure that all ranks had some form of fitness training before this march. It was my responsibility."

"I interrupted you because I did not want this sort of thing sorted out with the M.O. here. It would have been uncomfortable for him. This is between us only."

"Yes, of course. I wanted to acknowledge my responsibility. I was not attending to my duty. It may seem strange to you, but I came to this conclusion with Mike Baldwin's help. He never shirked his duty. He is a doctor, not a professional soldier; I was impressed with how he went about his medical work after marching all day. He must have been dead-tired like the rest of us. I could see how the men looked up to him. He also took time to talk with me at the bivouacs. I know damned well you had ordered him to keep an eye on me."

"Yes, I did that, but out of concern. Whether you will accept this or not, I have been concerned about you since you were posted to us. Frankly, you've worried me."

"I'm sorry I have been a burden to you, but I'm perplexed that you should be concerned. You and I are totally different. For a start, your whole philosophy about soldiering and the role of the Army seems so tied up in the military realities of fifteen years ago, when we were committed to a conventional war on the European continent. We are now in the nuclear age, and it seems to me we are facing a totally different situation. Your insistence on total fitness for all ranks in your battalion for example: if we got into a nuclear war with the Russians, no amount of physical fitness would protect this Army from being vaporized on the battlefield. It seems even more ludicrous to have the admin personnel brought to this level of 'Superman' fitness...."

"Damn it, man!" retorted Colonel Banfield, "I think *you* are missing the real point! I hope to God we don't get into a nuclear confrontation with the Russians; I'm sure they think the same way. But the Canadian Army could still be committed to a limited conventional war. Look at what happened in Korea. Something like that could happen in the Middle East. We have been designated as a United Nations standby unit for some months; any or all of us could be posted overseas at a moment's notice. If we have an army at all, it has got to be properly trained and equipped. And fit, if we have any chance of success, or survival for that matter. Furthermore, morale is of paramount importance. Morale and good discipline. A professional army must possess these elements in spades. Physical fitness is very much tied in with morale; if a soldier is in top physical condition, he will have confidence in himself whatever mission he is given. And this applies to everyone, particularly in a line battalion, whether he is a rifleman or a cook or clerk."

The two senior officers glared at each other, each harboring his own animosity for the other. Bob sat upright in his chair, livid with the effort of controlling of his anger and contempt for the man in front of him. He repeatedly reminded himself that he was now Jim's C.O., that he outranked him, but although his record of service reflected bravery in battle, devotion to duty and unsurpassed skill in leadership, he possessed none of the formal education, military traditions and social background he envied in Jim. Nevertheless, he saw himself as very much more a professional soldier than Niles could ever be. But what the blazing hell was he to do with this man?

Jim continued to sit back in his chair, his outward calm belying his own turbulent feelings. Banfield, his former sergeant, was now senior to him. With what had transpired in Normandy when they were young men, being a company commander under this man now was well nigh unbearable. Bob was everything Jim detested about the Army, yet he was expected to emulate him.

"We seem to be so diametrically opposite in everything. I am sure I have been a disappointment to you since I was posted to your battalion. The whole thing has been a travesty of fate. Since the Verrières Ridge, it was my constant fear that we would sooner or later be serving together again. It has been very difficult for me — and no doubt for you, too. But something happened to me on that march. I am going to try to be a better company commander for you, even though I detest the posting, and resent having to serve under you. I.... I simply want to reassure you...."

There was a painful silence. Bob feared that Jim Niles was about to break down. He could dismiss the major with the trite remark that Jim must "do his duty" more adequately. But here was an opportunity to resolve at least some of the bitter enmity they had shared between them for so long.

"I'm relieved to hear it; I accept your reassurance." What was all this leading to.....

" God damn it, this is so bloody difficult to talk about, especially with you," Jim continued. "It has never bothered me that I have been at best a mediocre officer. I have always rationalized to myself that I despise the Army and all it means to me, but I am trapped, like a prisoner, detesting my captivity, but unable to break out.

"No, it is Verrières Ridge. When we were advancing up the slope, under intense enemy fire, I had convinced myself that I was not going to survive. It was then that the bloody obscenity of it all overwhelmed me: I was going to die before I had ever had a chance to live. My whole life up to then had been one long close-order drill. I did what I was told, went where I was ordered to go, acted the role that was expected of me. I had never had the chance to do what I wanted, to experience meaning in my life, some warmth or joy, some positive purpose, some happiness — in other words, to *live*. I felt caught in a gigantic machine, which was propelling me inexorably towards a terrible and bloody end, and then there would be nothing.

"During the advance up the slope, I began to shake so much I was afraid that the men would see. I started falling behind more and more from the platoon line. You'll remember what it was like, when the German barrage hit us. The Saskatchewans were withdrawing through us. In all the noise and horror and confusion, I lost the few leadership abilities I possessed. I became one man, incapable of commanding the platoon, expecting to die. A mortar bomb exploded close by, lifting me off the ground, and dropping me into a shell-hole. I thought I had been killed. I felt a terrible coldness. I was shaking violently; there was no sign of blood or broken bones, yet I felt paralysed. The company behind us — Dog, I believe — passed me. As far as they were concerned, I must have been just another junior officer, dead in the ditch.

"During the evening, when the German counter-attacks hit the battalion, I could hear the firefight, but the noise seemed very distant. A strange feeling of complete detachment possessed me. I experienced myself floating up out of my own body; I recall looking down on myself, and all the death and destruction going on about me. I could actually see the bloody hand-to-hand combat, and the soldiers of both sides falling and dying. It was hideous — like a movie with something wrong with the sound-track. Christ, I must have gone insane!

"A while later, I came back into myself. It was night. I was out there alone. I was physically unable to crawl out of the shell-hole, to rejoin the unit. I lay there all night. When the Germans attacked again in the morning, I assumed that this was the end. The survivors of the battalion ran past me. I was weeping uncontrollably, but not so much out of fear; I was grieving for myself — like a mourner at my own grave.

"That was when I was found by a group of Germans who hauled me out of the shell-hole, and dragged me behind a wrecked Mark IV tank. The corporal in charge aimed his Schmeisser at me but a colonel in panzer uniform came up and ordered him not to shoot. I have no idea why; in that battle, no quarter was given, by either side. It was nothing but maddened killing on both sides. He looked at me with utter contempt. 'Lieutenant', he yelled over the deafening noise, 'You have deserted your men! If you were a German officer, I would have ordered the corporal to shoot you, as he was going to!' Then he ordered the corporal to guard me, and he walked off. The corporal glared at me with a furious hatred, as if hoping I would provide him with an excuse to kill me — I think he would have killed any officer gladly at that moment. Later, a German sergeant took over, and I was dragged over and thrown in with you. I really didn't care; I was totally numb. When the Black Watch rescued us, I realized that I had survived, but a part of me had died in that battle. I had lost all respect for myself. I am a complete failure as an officer. I cannot forgive my own cowardice in my first and last battle. And many times in the years since, I wished to God that I had died there.

"It was a long road back to Canada. First the encounter with the company commander and the brigadier outside Ifs. Then the battle exhaustion unit at Thaon, where I was examined by the division psychiatrist. Then the trip back to England with the wounded in the LST. More inquiry at the reinforcement unit in England, and at CMHQ. The shame was damned near unbearable. Then I was put on a troop ship, also full of wounded, and returned to Canada. My father met me in Ottawa. I shall always remember the utter scorn with which he greeted me. 'You have disgraced the Niles name', the old man said. 'But I expect you to continue to serve in the Army, and if you are fortunate, there will come a time when you will be able to redeem yourself'. God, how do I do it?"

As Bob Banfield listened to this agonizing recounting, vivid memories of the battle flashed before him. In quick succession, he recalled his subsequent battles in the European theatre. The smashing of the German defences before Falaise and the capture of the town, where he won his Military Medal. The drive to the Seine, the Reichwald Forest and Operation VERITABLE. The crossing of the Rhine and yet another final offensive, into the heart of Germany, the capture of Oldenberg and the German surrender. Then the Pusan perimeter in Korea. But none of these battles had had the same impact on him, nor were the memories so painfully acute, as the Verrières Ridge. Now, Banfield, the colonel, was able to understand Niles, in a way which Banfield, the sergeant, who had lost his platoon officer in disgraceful circumstances, could not.

"Jim", he said quietly, "In the name of God, forgive yourself for what happened so long ago. We were both very young and very frightened. I had many advantages over you then. I had been in battle at Dieppe. You had never faced that type of situation before. You were forced by your background to take on a job which by your very nature was impossible for you to succeed in. I came from no such background, had no military traditions to uphold. My father served as a sapper in the First World War, and when he returned he spent the rest of his life as an engineer with the C.N.R. I was not compelled into the profession of arms. But because of my own nature, I took to military life quickly and easily. In fact, I thrive on being a soldier. Leadership came easily to me. Men looked up to me and depended on me. I learned the skills of survival in battle. You are a cultured and sensitive man; you could never become a killer, and you could never lead killers in the job. You never acquired the detachment so important to survival in battle.

"I am trying very hard to get across to you that it was not your fault. You are no less of a man because of it. And I feel the awkwardness which was imposed upon us both, when you were posted under my command here. I want to tell you that I think.... I understand."

"I wish to hell there was something I could do to convince you to give up all that guilt, and shake off this damned business of redeeming yourself once and for all! You have lived with some kind of God-damned curse which your father put on you. To hell with your bloody brigadier father! We are both in this man's Army, but I enjoy it, it gives me a sense of purpose and belonging, despite all of the bureaucratic bullshit that comes with it. But I know you don't enjoy it. No army on earth is worth the suffering you go through. You still have a lot of living in front of you. Jesus, if I were you, I would say, 'screw the Army' and get into some other life."

Niles watched Banfield as he spoke. The bitter anger and resentment on his face slowly changed, first to puzzlement and then to relief, mixed with despair. This was no longer a confrontation between a superior officer and his subordinate. This was a deeper communication between two men who had shared desperate times. He looked away, agony in his eyes as he stared out through the window, struggling for control.

"Thank you for saying that, Bob." The colonel recognized that this was the first time Jim Niles had addressed him by his given name. Normally, no major in the regiment would permit himself the familiarity of using the colonel's first name, particularly in uniform and on duty. "As to forgiving myself," he continued, "I don't think I shall ever be able to do that."

The Colonel shook his head. "What happened between us on the Verrières Ridge is over for me. I wish it was over for you, too. I don't think we're cut out to be close friends, but I would like us at least to serve together with friendliness if not in friendship. I need you — we need you — to command your company as a competent field officer, as long as you're here. Will you do that?

"I have one more important request — a favor, not a command. You remember the two privates who shared that God-damned shell-hole with us? Well, Ronnie Matthews finished the war as a sergeant; Tom Brennan never went beyond the rank of private. Both got out after the war. The three of us get together about once a year. Sort of a private reunion for three old vets. They're going to be in London to spend the day with me next Saturday. Will you join us after dinner, at my quarters? I feel it could be important for all of us."

Jim Niles was surprised and disturbed by this request. Recently, events were coming at him in rapid succession, and all of them connected with his Verrières experience: the posting to Banfield's battalion, the disaster at the mess dinner, the persistent efforts of the young medical officer to get him to talk, the march, this meeting with Banfield, and now he was expected to meet with two other participants in that fearful occasion. Wryly, he thought that the only missing party was the German tank officer! It was all coming together like some form of bizarre 'shock therapy', yet he knew that he could no longer avoid facing up to his past, and perhaps this agonizing re-living could exorcise at least some of the demons which had ripped at his soul for so long.

"Thank you, Bob, I'll make it a point to come over."

The two officers stood up. The colonel held out his hand. The major shook hands without hesitation, stepped back, saluted his commanding officer, and left the office. Bob Banfield returned to his chair and sat down. He felt drained; but out of this, would he get a better officer to command Headquarters Company? More important, would it prove helpful for his tormented brother officer?

Colonel Banfield was not left long in his reverie. There was a knock at the door. It was Theo Morgan.

"For Chrissakes, Sergeant Morgan, don't you know enough to go home!"

"I'll be on my way pretty damn' soon, sir! I wanted to wait until you were through with Major Niles, to sort out some pressing business, before I leave. We got a call from the battalion provost sergeant. They have Corporal LaChance from Transport Platoon in the cooler. Remember, he went A.W.O.L. two days before HQ Company left for Ipperwash. The Central Command provost finally picked him up clear back at Lafontaine, just outside Penetanguishene, his home town. He was with his parents. The report indicates that he took on the provost. It got quite ugly before they subdued him. I called Transport Platoon, but Captain Toland had already left, but CSM Kovacs is there. How do you wish to handle it, sir?"

Corporal LaChance had been a troublemaker from the start. A mechanic, trained in the Army, he had been posted from his parent corps of the Royal Canadian Electrical and Mechanical Engineers to the battalion as a vehicle mech two years ago. Arrogant, surly and explosive, he was frequently on charge for insubordination and neglect of his duties. To avoid the Ipperwash march, he had gone "over the hill".

"O.K., Sergeant Morgan. Let's keep the good corporal in the guard house for the night. Tomorrow morning, have him paraded before Major Niles, who will prepare charges. Make sure Major Niles is fully briefed by Captain Toland and the CSM beforehand. Then put him on the next orders parade for me for sentencing. I think this time it will be thirty days in the digger, and my recommendation for release afterwards."

Sergeant Morgan shuddered. The regional detention barracks was at Camp Borden. Commonly called the "glass house" by soldiers, it had the reputation of meting out the harshest discipline to all who had the misfortune to be sent there. Its punitive approach to prisoners stripped all dignity and identity from them. It usually succeeded in breaking even the toughest of its inmates. Very seldom did a soldier return to serve another sentence.

"Very good, sir."

"Thank you for staying around to take care of this damned nonsense. Now, man, go home and enjoy your forty-eight!"

Colonel Banfield knew that this nasty business was going to be a stiff test for Major Niles. He had to be fair, but this corporal needed firm handling. This time there was no question of leniency. Ironically both the major and the corporal were misfits in the Army. Although he fervently hoped that the major would now be able to sort out his own personal difficulties and to come to terms with his military career, he had no illusions that the corporal could do likewise.

CHAPTER ELEVEN

When Major Niles returned to his room in the Officers' Quarters, a batman, on loan from another officer, was waiting for him. His own batman, Brandt, had been on the march with him, and was off on his well-earned forty-eight hour pass. Jim emptied his rucksack, shed his crumpled bush uniform and dusty boots, and handed the clothing to the private soldier to be laundered, and the boots to be polished. He noted with satisfaction that the battledress uniform which he had sent to the cleaners before he left for Ipperwash had been returned, and that the batman had already polished the crowns and clipped them to the shoulder tabs. The lad had polished his web belt and its brass buckle as well. He took a long, hot shower, got into formal civilian clothes, and went to the Mess for some lunch. He was off duty for the rest of the day. He spent the afternoon lying on his bed, reading, had dinner, and retired early.

He fell into a deep sleep. As the new day was dawning, he woke from a terrifying nightmare. In the dream, he was back on the march again, in the spring sunshine, leading his company. Then, the sky turned dark, the fields and countryside disappeared, and he found himself struggling through the ruins of a city in the midst of a raging battle. He no longer led the column; another major was in front of him. They were wearing the battledress of 1944. Jim had two pips on his shoulders, and not the crowns. He was filled with dread. The major ahead of him kept yelling: "Look out over there! Can you see it! The Ridge! It's called the Verrières Ridge! Verrières Ridge!"

He was drenched in sweat. He could not return to sleep. He had to be in his office by 0800 hours. When a rifle company returned from the Ipperwash march, all ranks other than a skeleton staff in its company office went on the two-day leave. But this pleasant custom could never apply wholly to Headquarters Company. The cooks, after all, had to get back to cooking, the clerks to clerking and the drivers to driving on battalion business. Other than the signals personnel, few of Niles' company could get away on pass. As the officer commanding Headquarters Company, Jim

Niles was no exception. There was a pile of work waiting for him on his desk. For the first time in his military career, he was determined to apply himself to his responsibilities. He intended henceforth to run his company effectively.

He shaved, put on his battledress uniform, and went to the mess for breakfast. Walking to the Administrative Building, he passed platoon after platoon of soldiers on the march to their various duties and functions. At the start of the new day, Wolseley Barracks was alive with the rhythm of marching feet, and the staccato commands of the N.C.O.'s.

He walked up the stairs and into his company headquarters area. Outside his door stood his Transport Officer, Captain Leo Toland and the Company Sergeant-Major, Jan Kovacs.

"Good morning!" Jim said, after the customary exchange of salutes. "Please, come in and sit down. Well, now, to what do I owe the honor of this early visit? And on this day, of all days, the day after the march!"

"Jim," said Leo Toland. "We have some nasty business to deal with." He related the details of R.C.E.M.E. corporal LaChance, who had gone AWOL, and was now detained in the guardhouse, waiting for charges to be proffered by the company commander within the hour. The corporal's personnel file was on Jim's desk. CSM Kovacs went through the file with him. It was filled with documentation pertaining to previous charges. Repeatedly, the phrases "insubordination", "conduct prejudicial to", "absent without leave", "confined to barracks", "extra work and drill" appeared on the forms. It was clear that this soldier was habitually in trouble, was consistently defiant of authority, and fitted poorly to service in the Army.

Although Major Niles had previously dealt with soldiers charged with having been AWOL, nothing of this magnitude had ever come up before him. Here was a soldier who refused to soldier. LaChance seemed to hate the Army as much as Niles had. But he was from a farm background, with limited formal education, trained and qualified as a "vehicle mech, group 2"; Patrick LaChance had had none of the support from the Officer Corps traditions which had been so rigorously programmed into Jim Niles; this young corporal behaved badly without guilt. He had continuously vented his hatred through his insolence and insubordinate conduct, never learning from his mistakes; he was repeatedly punished, yet continued his private war with the Army with apparent relish. This was his sixth year of service; he must have signed on for a second three-year term. He could obtain his release in three months; why was he making it so difficult for himself?

Then again, why was Jim Niles making it so difficult for himself, staying on when he had the privilege as an officer to resign his Queen's Commission at any time? Duty.... Tradition.... Redemption; the God-damned brigadier. He almost wished he could exchange his crown for the two stripes of LaChance....

"Does the corporal have a family?"

"Just his wife, sir," replied Jan Kovacs. "Laura LaChance. A nurse at Victoria Hospital. His records show that he was married in Lafontaine when he was a buck private, two years into the service. I believe she is from Lafontaine also; childhood sweethearts. I don't think it's been a happy marriage. The fellow is something of a 'horse's ass'. But so far she has stayed with him. No children."

"O.K., Sergeant-Major, parade him in when he arrives. Leo, I'll have to handle this pretty firmly. I'll get in touch with you later."

"Thanks, Jim." Leo was relieved to "pass the buck" on to his company commander. He had had his fill of attempting to bring the recalcitrant junior N.C.O. into line. Before Leo was commissioned from the ranks, when he was "on the other side", he had had some painful experiences living and working with habitual troublemakers like LaChance. They were worse than useless, and a dangerous menace in battle. They were far better off released from the Army — and everyone else better off with them out. It always seemed pointless to him, that the Army required every soldier to serve out his enlistment term to the very end. But Leo, the "old soldier", clung to his faith in the wisdom of R.M.C. graduates, "the real educated professional officers". They knew best how to handle this sort of nonsense.

....

The telephone rang in the company headquarters. "....Yes, Sergeant, hold on...." The clerk turned to CSM Kovacs. "Provost Sergeant on the line, sir! Wants to know if you're ready to have Corporal LaChance brought over for charges."

"Here....let me have the phone....Hello, Sergeant Gallant, you old Spud Islander! Kovacs here! Got some business you want us to attend to, I hear....Yeah, well, I think the clown has finally done it!....O.K., Willie, have your lads escort him over....Yes, I'll be waiting here for him....Yes, charges to be laid now, and he'll be on C.O.'s orders parade tomorrow.... Ciao, Willie!" He stepped over to the open door of Major Niles' office. "Sir, prisoner being escorted over now!"

"Thank you, Mr. Kovacs. March him in when you are ready."

Shortly, Jim heard the clattering of boots outside his office, and then the voice of his sergeant-major, as he went through the familiar drill.

"Prisoner and escort, fall in! Prisoner and escort, mark time! Prisoner and escort, right turn. Quick march! Left wheel! Right wheel! Halt! Left turn!"

This brought the prisoner and the two provost corporals on each side of him, in line, at attention, in front of Major Niles' desk, with the CSM on their left. The provost corporals were resplendent in battle dress with spotless white web-belts, and bright red bands around their blue forage caps. In stark contrast, the prisoner was attired in crumpled black coveralls, with no belt or cap. The laces of his boots had been removed.

"Sir! Sierra Bravo Two Niner Three One Zero Niner, Corporal LaChance, Patrick, on orders." Reading from the charge sheet in his hands, CSM Kovacs continued. "Absent without leave from approximately thirteen hundred hours 15 May 59. Apprehended approximately eleven hundred hours 22 May 59. Resisted arrest when apprehended. Sir!"

Major Niles looked directly at the young corporal before him. Tall and powerfully built with curly black hair and brown eyes, the corporal glared down at him defiantly. Having been brought back from Lafontaine to London like a dangerous criminal, caged overnight, stripped of rank markings and personal dignity, he faced a very certain fate as a prisoner of the universally dreaded detention barracks at Camp Borden, without any sign of fear or remorse.

"Thank you, Mr. Kovacs. Will you now remove the escort. I would like to speak to Corporal LaChance alone."

Jan Kovacs was shocked. This could be releasing a maddened young bull in the proverbial china shop! He doubted that the major could manage the miserable punk, without getting himself into a shindig he wouldn't be able to handle alone. Was it damned stupidity, or a genuinely courageous gesture? He quelled his doubts.

"Yes, sir!" CSM Kovacs replied. "Escort, fall out!" The two provost corporals turned a smart right, and marched out of the office, with the CSM behind them. Jan Kovacs closed the door.

"Stand easy, Corporal LaChance", said Jim Niles calmly. "This charge sheet indicates that you were A.W.O.L. for some seven days, and that you resisted arrest when you were apprehended. I have been ordered by the commanding officer to lay charges against you. But I want to hear what you have to say for yourself."

Patrick LaChance held his fists clenched, his feet apart, still glaring his rage and defiance.

"What the hell difference does it make what I have to say for myself? I'm going to be sent up anyway. So what I will say, is, fuck you and fuck your God-damned Army!"

"I must warn you, Corporal, you are adding insolence and insubordination to these already serious charges. When you address an officer, you will address him as 'sir'."

"Then fuck you, _sir_!"

"The hell is the matter with you? I know you are in a bad jam. But why are you so damned angry with me? I have never seen you on orders before. In fact, I have never met you before."

"You said it! What sort of shit-head company commander are you anyway? I was here when you took over Headquarters Company. You never came around to Transport Platoon, to see what we were doing. Not that I gave a God-damn anyway. Toland was the one who ran the platoon...."

"Captain Toland to you, Corporal!"

"O.K., Captain Toland. But he's another shit-head officer, in this shit-head outfit!"

"So this is a shit-head outfit! So you hate all officers! Is there anything about the Army that you like at all? You keep getting into trouble. Look at your file; it's full of charge sheets. You don't do your work satisfactorily. You can't take orders without going off at the mouth. Seems to me you can't do anything properly. Why the hell did you join up in the first place? And why did you re-enlist?"

"Well, now, that's the most sensible question I heard so far!

"Sir!"

"And I say again, the hell with you, sir!"

"You haven't answered my question."

"Why I enlisted ain't any of your damn' business. Now I want to get out! Can't you get that into your God-damned head? I ain't takin' orders no more from none of you bastards. I want to get out of this chicken-shit Army. I want out now! I'm not waitin' no three more months. A month in the D.B. ain't goin' to be that friggin' bad! Jesus, I'll show them! They'll be glad to see the last of me there. And I'll be laughin'."

You poor young fool, thought Jim Niles, struggling to maintain his composure. They'll break you in there! What's more, they'll keep you there until you are broken. And no matter where you go after that, you will hate the Army for the rest of your life. Army discipline was designed to make you a man, to provide you some purpose in life, and an opportunity to serve your country. It could have made a better citizen out of you. It should have been an experience you could look back on with some satisfaction — even gratitude. But you have rejected everything it offered you. And no matter where you go in life afterwards, you're going to run into trouble. On civvie street, there will be damned little concern for your welfare from your employers, and if you continue with your adolescent attitude, they will only fire you.....But what in hell am I doing? Here I am, defending the Army. God, what is happening to me?

And then it struck him. This young corporal, white with anger, effectively reflected his own anger. He hated the Army, because it represented parental authority to him. His parents had utterly failed to prepare him for life, and he was incapable of accepting any form of army discipline. Trapped in his own immaturity, ignorance and intolerance of any demands placed on him, ever seeking immediate gratification, with no consideration of the needs of others, he had failed miserably in his short military career, which was soon to end ignominiously.

But he, Niles, had not so much hated the Army; he had hated himself. For all these years, he had bitterly blamed the Army for all his personal woes and disappointments. In effect, he too had rebelled against parental authority, against his father, the brigadier. It was by his choice, and not his father's demand for him to redeem himself, that he had stayed in the Army. His stubbornness reflected his determination to show the brigadier that he could survive in military service, and he had come very close to destroying himself in the attempt. Unlike the corporal, he could now let his anger go.

Jim Niles then came to the most important realisation of his life. He had a choice. He could leave the Army if he wanted to. And having realized this, for the first time he felt a sense of belonging to the Army with all its imperfections, and aggravating customs and rules. Like the miserable corporal in front of him, he had fought it, despised it and all those who served in it. Yet, despite himself, it had tolerated and sustained him. For God's sake, he thought, it forgave me for my blasted cowardice on the Verrières Ridge when I could not forgive myself. He was the commissioned officer, the professional soldier, and out of choice, for however long he wished to serve in it, he belonged to the Army.

Jim Niles began to smile. This was as disconcerting to himself as it was to the corporal in his guardhouse coveralls across from him. "Corporal LaChance, I feel sorry for you...."

"Shove it!"

"I feel sorry for you. You made a big mistake when you decided to be a soldier. You want badly to get out of the Army, but you're taking the wrong way out. And, sadly, you will continue to run into trouble after you are out — until you do some growing up. Also, I feel sorry for your wife...."

"You keep my wife the hell out of this!"

"No, I can not! Until you leave the battalion, I am still your company commander. Your welfare is my concern, and that includes your private life as well. I believe you have made life hell on earth for your wife. Why she has put up with you so long is beyond me. If you carry on the way you are, you will very likely lose her.

"However, you do have a point. I have never taken time, so far, to get to know the people in Transport Platoon, or for that matter the other sections of Headquarters Company. I intend to rectify that. But it will be too late for you."

"The hell are you talkin' about?"

"Something you could never understand. Nor did I until now. Now I am going to ask you once again, is there anything you want to bring up, before I prepare charges?"

"And I still say — fuck you, you God-damn' officer! And without the sir."

"Sergeant-Major Kovacs! I'm ready."

"Sir!" Jan Kovacs opened the office door, looked in, and was relieved to see that both the major and the office furniture were still intact.... "Escort, march in and take position! Prisoner and escort, Attention!"

"Sergeant-Major, complete the charge sheets against Corporal LaChance forthwith, for being absent without leave, for resisting arrest and also add gross insubordination, prejudicial to the conduct of good discipline. The prisoner is to be removed to the guardhouse and is to appear on orders parade before the commanding officer tomorrow."

"Sir! Prisoner and escort, right turn! Quick march! Right wheel, right wheel...."

Jim Niles picked up his cap. He had decided to walk over to the battalion vehicle pool, where he would brief Leo Toland regarding the disposition of his vehicle mech, and learn something about Transport Platoon.

CHAPTER TWELVE

For Lieutenant Colonel Bob Banfield, the day started unpleasantly. In the morning, he held orders parade, a periodically scheduled function in which he presided over the summary trials of defaulters, soldiers who had been charged under the "Code of Service Discipline", a part of "Queen's Regulations (Army)". This legal authority was conferred on the commanding officer of a unit, to try, convict and sentence defaulters, within proscribed bounds. If the charge was sufficiently serious, the accused could be given the choice of summary trial, accepting the C.O.'s judgement and punishment, or a full Court Martial. The C.O. could deem the charge too serious, and remand the accused for Court Martial. He would be assigned a defending officer, the Judge Advocate General branch of the Army would designate one of its legal officers as prosecutor, and there would be a tribunal of judges, of general officer rank. However, no such arrangements were available for a simple summary trial, whose historical antecedent was the drum-head trial of yesteryear; its process and subsequent disposition were just as swift. The commanding officer's punitive powers were limited, the maximum sentence being thirty days in the "digger", the regional detention barracks.

Colonel Banfield dealt with two private soldiers from Charlie Company first. They had been in a brawl in a tavern in London, and had been picked up and returned to the Barracks by the Area provost. Their sentence was to be confined to barracks for two weeks, with extra work and drill. By late morning, the hapless lads were doubling around the parade square with full packs, rifles at the port under the command of a corporal in their company.

Then the case of Corporal LaChance came up. The colonel had all the information he needed on the charge sheets; within five minutes, it was all over. He gave the accused no choice regarding Court Martial. Had he done so, the sentence would have been much heavier, considering his previous record and the leniency with which his prior charges had been disposed. The colonel was convinced that the battalion — and the Army in general — would fare considerably better without this man. LaChance was to be returned to the guardhouse, there to await transfer to the detention barracks at Camp Borden, where he was to serve his thirty days. He was to be demoted forthwith to private rank with the recommendation that he be dishonorably discharged from the Army after he had completed his time.

....

Before Patrick LaChance left for Camp Borden under close guard, his wife, Laura, upon her request, was permitted to speak with him. She had arranged for time off duty at the hospital for this purpose. She did not have her car, since her husband had taken it when he went "over the hill", and it had been left in Lafontaine. She took the city bus, got off at Oxford Street, and walked down a side street to the main gate of Wolseley Barracks, where she was admitted and escorted to the guardhouse.

Corporal LaChance was not allowed out of his cell; they had to talk through the bars. There was not much time. She had never seen him in this grim situation before, and it upset her. LaChance was his usual rude, arrogant self.

"Shit," he said with a bitter laugh. "What the hell are you doing here, you slut? Regular whore of the battalion, ain't you? Can't wait to see me gone, so you can screw all the studs here! Goddam nurse! That don't mean nothin' to me. You're all whores!"

This was too much for one of the provost corporals standing by. "Shut your mouth, LaChance! There's a lady present!"

"Lady? You fuckin' meathead, she ain't no lady, she's my wife! You think the likes of me would marry a lady!"

"LaChance, if you don't button your lip, I'm going to come in there and deck you proper!"

"That will be enough, Corporal Dinsdale!" Gallant, the provost section sergeant, interjected. "Mrs. LaChance, ma'am, you don't have to put up with this. Do you want to say something to your husband before you go?"

"Yes, Sergeant, thank you. Patrick, I've had enough of you. I was concerned about what was happening to you. I wanted to see you before they took you away. I felt there might be something I could do to help you. But you are no different now from how you have always been with me. I'm not going to put up with your rudeness anymore. I'm through with you. I don't want you back when you get out. Our marriage is over."

"The hell it is, bitch! We're Catholics, remember? You married me for life. What are you going to tell your God-damn' priest back home?"

Laura was in tears, shaking. Sergeant Gallant took her into his office. He had made tea and offered some to her. Tough and unbending when it came to handling soldiers, he fairly melted in her presence. He was sickened by her husband's behaviour, and filled with compassion for her. Gradually, she composed herself.

"Sergeant," Laura asked. "Is it possible for me to talk with Colonel Banfield? I want to know what to expect. Patrick has never been in a detention barracks before; I want to know what dishonorable discharge is going to mean."

"Sure. Let me see what I can arrange." The provost sergeant telephoned the battalion orderly room and spoke with Sergeant Morgan. Laura could see him frowning and nodding, and then he hung up.

"Colonel Banfield, the second-in-command and the adjutant have all left for a conference at Command Headquarters in Oakville. The orderly room sergeant is arranging for you to see Major Niles, your husband's company commander. Major Niles will be waiting for you in his office. I'll take you over myself."

When they arrived at the Headquarters Company offices, the company clerks stared in wide-eyed delight at the young woman, and both immediately stood up at their desks.

"Mrs. LaChance to see Major Niles, Corporal," said Sergeant Gallant.

"Yes, Sergeant. This way, ma'am."

Laura turned to Sergeant Gallant. "Thank you, Sergeant, for your help. I'm very grateful."

"It was my privilege, Mrs. LaChance. This must be a very difficult time for you. I'm sure Major Niles will be able to answer all your questions. Good day, ma'am!" The sergeant saluted her and left.

The lance-corporal led Laura to Jim Niles' office.

"Mrs. LaChance, sir."

"Thank you, Corporal Suzuki." Jim stood up. "Good morning, Mrs. LaChance. I'm Major Niles. Please sit down." He closed the door.

Outside, the two young company clerks looked at each other, and grinned.

"Man, did you get a load of that? I sure would like Santa to put her in my rucksack for Christmas! Wouldn't need no wrappin', neither! Man, I go for older women! Did you see them legs...."

"Shit, Porky! It's my sack, not my rucksack, I'd like to have her in! Jeez, what a fuckin' waste on that LaChance! Wonder what's goin' on in Niles' office now. Fuckin' officers have all the luck!"

"She sure beats Molly at the Silver Dollar, eh?"

Both chuckled and went back to their work, each with his fantasies of the dark-haired beauty who had briefly invaded the humdrum, masculine world of the Barracks.

....

Jim Niles, at thirty-seven, officer and gentleman, was by age, rank and social status light years away from his nineteen year old company clerks, but her impact on him was no less startling. He had imagined a poor, drab, long-suffering woman who endured the misfortune of being married to the fool he had charged the day before. Instead, before him was a poised young woman of exceptional beauty, and her presence intrigued and disturbed him. Throughout his adult life he had had limited experience with women. He lived a socially restricted existence, preferring to wallow alone in his guilt and personal agony. He had convinced himself that he had neither the time nor the inclination to involve himself with women. There had been the odd dalliance on annual leaves. Then there were the infernal military social functions, when he was commanded to escort and entertain members of the fair sex, deemed eligible for marriage to a career officer, but he had always been polite and distant in these brief encounters, and had not pursued any relationship seriously.

Laura, at twenty-six, was truly beautiful. Slim, erect in bearing, meticulously yet casually dressed, he thought she was positively regal. The soldier in him admired how she stood and how she sat, and he wondered whether nurses were taught to maintain their poise during their training! She had on a dark maroon knit dress, over which she wore, unbuttoned, a light, pastel pink spring coat. Without her heels, he guessed that she was about five foot six. She had dark-brown hair, thick and in waves, which fell across her shoulders. She had wide-set hazel eyes, a pert, straight nose, wide cheekbones, and full lips, neatly made up with brick-red lipstick.

Jim Niles cleared his throat. "I am told that there is something you want to talk to me about."

"Yes, Major Niles. It is about my husband, Corporal LaChance of your Transport Platoon. He was arrested for being A.W.O.L. Colonel Banfield has sentenced him to thirty days in the detention barracks. He is supposed to be discharged from the Army when he gets out. I need to find out what is going to become of him. I wanted to talk to Colonel Banfield, but he was away. I was told you could see me instead."

"Yes, that is true. Your husband has a bad record going back to his first days in the Army. I guess you know he has been charged and punished before. This time, Colonel Banfield had to impose the maximum sentence. It includes automatic release after thirty days in the D.B."

Laura pondered, then said: "I understand it is pretty awful in the D.B."

"Yes, it will be hard on him. He has been repeatedly warned about his unacceptable behaviour. I don't think he should ever have enlisted in the Army. We have a code of discipline as every army must have. Soldiers have to take orders. They have to obey. He couldn't or wouldn't. I'm sorry to say this, but he deserves his sentence. He brought it all on himself."

"I understand that, Major Niles. I don't think Patrick ever grew up. He was badly spoiled by his parents. He was an only child. His mother doted on him; there was never any discipline when he was growing up. I have known him since we were kids. Somehow I thought by marrying him, I could help him. I also thought the Army might teach him responsibility. I guess it never happened.

"I knew what he was like when I married him. We both come from Lafontaine. We were both farm raised. We went to school together. There is a small Catholic, French-Canadian enclave up there. We started dating early. I went into nursing training here at Victoria Hospital, where I work. Everybody back home expected us to get married. The summer I graduated, we did. I had a lot of doubts, but I come from a large family. I think my parents wanted to see me safely off their hands! It seems so pointless now

..... even silly ..... Do you understand, when I say I was pretty well forced into this marriage by family pressure?"

God, what is she saying? thought Jim, spellbound by the rich tones of her voice. Forced into marriage; same damned parental programming. Different circumstances, different time. He felt a strong bond between them, as if he had always known her. This was ridiculous, he had better get hold of himself.....

"Yes, I think I do." He was becoming increasingly uncomfortable. He had better get back to her husband, and why she came. "Patrick is a trained mechanic," he continued, "and the Army saw to it that he got his 'Class A' licence. He will have no civilian criminal record. He should be able to get a job."

"I know that. But he can't take orders from anyone. He is arrogant and insensitive, completely wrapped up in himself. I am afraid for him."

"What about you? When he gets out, are you going to move away with him, to wherever he gets employment?"

There was a silence. Laura said: "No. I don't plan to leave London. I have a good job. I can continue to keep my apartment. But I don't think we are going to get back together. I've had five years of marriage to him; he is not the man I want to spend the rest of my life with. But we are Catholics, and that is a problem. I'm going to have to do a lot of thinking in the next while. I saw him for a few minutes at the guardhouse .... he's brutal ...."

Jim Niles stared at her, transfixed. He had never met a woman like her before. He was experiencing a wild confusion of feelings; anger at what had happened to her in her marriage, profound compassion and concern such as he had never known before, and intense physical attraction and desire. Confused, he found himself groping for surer ground.

"Um...you have learned a lot about the Army in these last years."

"Oh, yes. Would it surprise you to know that I come from a military family? Oh, not like you, Major Niles! My father served in the Army in the First World War, and was wounded at Vimy. There were nine of us children. I am the youngest. My oldest brother joined the RCAF in the Second World War and was shot down and killed over Hamburg. Three of my brothers served in the Army during that war. One brother was killed in Normandy."

"What!"

"René. He was twelve years older than me. He was with the Second Canadian Infantry Division at Dieppe. Then he became a corporal, a section commander in a rifle platoon. He was killed in July 1944 at a place called Verrières Ridge. Were you overseas at that time, Major Niles?"

Jim felt the blood drain out of his face. "Mrs. LaChance, what was your last name before you married?"

"Charlebois. Why?"

He groped in his memory. There was a Corporal Charlebois in his platoon, but he could not recall his first name. There were after all only three corporals, one in charge of each of the rifle sections. Could his first name have been René? Banfield would remember. But all nine infantry battalions of Second Division were committed to the Verrières battle, at one time or another. All had been involved in heavy fighting and several were virtually destroyed. Charlebois was not that uncommon a name. My God, are you yet another part of this whole reliving I have been through? Having charged your husband, could it be possible that I was your brother's platoon commander, and that I had abandoned him at the time of his death........

"Yes, I was at the Verrières Ridge battle. There was a Corporal Charlebois in my platoon, who was killed. I was not with him when he died. I'm not sure if he was your brother. You realize that there were a lot of Canadian soldiers in that battle ...."

"René was buried in the Canadian War Cemetery at Bretteville-sur-Laize, a few miles south of the Verrières Ridge. Some day I would like to visit his grave. Two of my brothers visited after the war. They said it is pretty and peaceful out there. They keep the graves in good care .... His death really broke my mother's heart. He was her favourite boy. Full of life .... He used to pull my pigtails when I was a little girl. In his letters, he said he would bring home a doll for me. It was not to be ...." With that she smiled wistfully. Jim trembled. "War does terrible things to people, would you not agree?"

So frequently, he had heard that it was the professional soldier who detested war more than anyone, but who, nevertheless, by choosing the profession of arms, was prepared to endure war and if necessary to lay down his life in defence of his country. To preserve peace, one must prepare for war. What he had seen of war was too horrible to justify. Until now, he had been convinced that neither his country, nor his family, nor above all the Army itself, was worth dying for. The absurd thought entered his head — would he die to protect Laura, this young woman whom he had never known before today? The perturbing feeling again overcame him, that he had known her for a long time, that this meeting, by chance of circumstances, was not by chance at all.....

"Yes, war does terrible things. Do you resent soldiers? Do you resent me?"

Laura laughed. "Why, Major Niles, I don't resent you! I hate war but I believe Canada must have an Army. My husband has been a failure as a soldier. But he is not like you. You are intelligent and you're educated. I believe that you have an important job. You are a professional career officer. You are so different from me, but you are kind and sensitive. I'm glad that I have met you."

Never had anyone spoken to Jim like this. It was always assumed that he would perform as a competent professional soldier and commissioned officer. He never expected any appreciation of himself or what he did. But she had no idea of how much of a failure he had been in his military career. What would she think if her brother had indeed been in his platoon, and that when he was killed, facing the enemy, his platoon commander had been cowering in a rain-filled shell-hole, paralysed with fear, hallucinating?

"Can I ask you something, Major Niles?"

"Yes."

"Are you married?"

He flushed at the unexpected question, yet strangely did not feel that it was out of place or presumptuous on her part. It seemed natural, even necessary to answer.

"No."

"I think some woman has missed out on a good man. You have been very kind to me. I must confess something. I said that I came to inquire about my husband's situation. But what I really wanted was to speak to a professional soldier who could assure me, that as a soldier's daughter and the sister of soldiers, regardless of what happened to my husband, somehow I would still be — I guess the word is accepted — by the Army. I can't explain it any other way. And now I had better be going. I'm sure you have a lot of work to do. Thank you, Major Niles, for talking with me."

"Mrs. LaChance, if ....."

"One more favor. Will you call me Laura?"

"Laura ... yes ... If you need to talk with me again .... I mean if something happens ...."

"I will get in touch! Goodbye, Major!"

"I hope to see you again, Laura."

The young woman left the major reeling within himself, shaken by feelings which kept him awake all the following night. He had never felt towards a woman the way he felt towards her. It was perturbing, perplexing, yet with it there was a strange feeling of exhilaration, of urgent anticipation. He had to see her again; it was as if his very life depended on it.

CHAPTER THIRTEEN

On a pleasant Saturday morning, Ronnie Matthews drove off from his home in Kitchener in his old black Volkswagen, and headed west on Highway 7, bound for London. His route took him through St. Mary's and Stratford to Elginfield, where he turned south on Highway 4 to London. Just outside Elginfield, there was a ramshackle corner store, and it was here that he was to pick up his friend from army days, Tom Brennan. The two of them would drive on to Wolseley Barracks in London, where the third member of their unique veteran's group, Lieutenant Colonel Bob Banfield, would be waiting for them at his quarters. Since these three men had returned to Canada from the Army in Europe some fourteen years ago, they had followed up on their pact to stay in touch, and to get together if possible once a year. Bob Banfield proved to be the main obstacle to their annual reunion plans, because he was periodically posted out of Ontario and thus could not attend. One such posting was when Bob was serving in Korea as a company commander. But Ronnie and Tom met regardless, anticipating when Bob could again be with them.

As Ronnie drove along, across the gently rolling hills of Waterloo and Perth Counties in the warm spring sunshine, he thought about their friendship, and how it began. It was to Three Platoon that he and Tom had been posted, when they and that big Pole, Jack Sipulski, had arrived on their draft from Canada. Those were fun days in England; pubs, the English girls, even the grueling battle training and those incessant route marches in full battle gear were not really that bad. But then in July of 1944 the inevitable finally came. They were transported across the channel to Normandy.

Normandy and war and killing and destruction. Lord, how frightened he was. Stomach all in knots. Body shaking like a bloody leaf. The awful dryness in his mouth and throat. Stark, gripping terror. The horror of it all becoming more unbearably horrible with each successive day. The march through the burning ruins of Caen. Dead bodies and pieces of bodies and blood everywhere. Second Div goes into the offensive. Operation

ATLANTIC. The advance in an extended line up the slope of the Verrières Ridge. The German counterattacks. The utter insane carnage. Cold, wet and terrified. Three Platoon butchered, trying to hold the line. Jack Sipulski killed; Corporal Charlebois killed; the platoon officer lost. Bob Banfield, the platoon sergeant taking over the platoon. Being cut off from the battalion. That muddy shell-hole. Bob and Tom and me. The rest were gone.

That shell-hole. The young German lieutenant, badly wounded, falling in on top of us. Then the German tank colonel appearing above us. And in a weird macabre exchange, they remove their lieutenant and we get our lieutenant - - Niles was his name — pushed in with us. Niles in severe shock. The barrage. The rescue by the Black Watch. The walk back to Vaucelles across flaming hell of the Verrières battlefield. We never saw Niles again. Bob and Tom and me, sole survivors of the old Three Platoon. We could have all been killed. We must never forget. If we survived the rest of the war, we must stay in touch. We had gone through too much together.

Ten months more of war, before the German Army is finally defeated. During this time, Bob commands the platoon, and gets his Military Medal in the fight for Falaise. Bob goes off to England for officer training. Returns in the winter to command another platoon. Despite my fears and my stomach aches, the Army thinks that I have become a good soldier, and rewards me with stripes. One after the other. More stripes, more responsibilities. I turn twenty, but I am an old veteran already when I become a platoon sergeant. Not with Three Platoon. More casualties, more replacements. No battle experience for these new lads, or even adequate training. They get younger all the time. Kids to be fed into battle. Many don't last a day.

Nigmegen, Operation VERITABLE, the drive into Germany. Finally, V.E. Day. But Tom Brennan stayed with Three Platoon to the end. "Shit!" he would say. "I got enough on my hands to look after me in this fuckin' war, without lookin' after some other poor fuckers!" Tom refused all promotion. Maybe in the long run he had the right idea.

....

By the early months of 1946, they were all back in Canada. Ronnie recalled the feeling of estrangement each felt on returning home. It became quickly apparent that few who had not shared the experience of serving overseas in battle were interested or concerned with what they had lived through. Although both he and Tom were very glad to be out of the Army, they missed the camaraderie and feeling of purpose and belonging, and the pride they felt for their battalion, which had sustained them throughout. Now, they had just themselves. Bob, a commissioned officer, stayed in the Army. But he always remained their old platoon sergeant. The reunions became increasingly important as time passed.

When Ronnie got back to Canada, his stomach bothered him badly. He recalled his experiences at the D.V.A.'s Sunnybrook Hospital in Toronto, the "upper G.I. series" (horrible tasting stuff), the medicine he was required to take for ulcers and the threats on the part of the D.V.A. doctors that they might have to remove his stomach. ("No way, doc, I'd rather die first!"). Yet regardless, he took full advantage of what the country had to offer for returning vets. The clothing allowance, the rehabilitation grant, the war service gratuity, and most important of all, the education grant. Ronnie enrolled at the University of Toronto, was assigned to the campus for veterans, located in a former munitions plant in Ajax, and started his years as a university student, to obtain his B.A. degree. He worked hard and put in long hours to maintain his marks and academic standing, to continue to qualify for government assistance. Eventually, he earned his degree and he became a teacher. He got his first job teaching elementary school with the Kitchener School Board, and in time became a principal. He met Beth, another teacher, and married her. They now had three kids. He adored his family. Children for him were the true memorial to his comrades and all the other Canadians who had died on the fields of battle. He dedicated the raising of his own children and his teaching of the hundreds of others that passed through his classroom to them.

Yet nothing of this sort had happened for Tom Brennan. Tom had a difficult time adjusting to civilian life. He rejected any form of assistance the country offered to the vets after the war. He resented anything which had to do with the society he lived in. He never held a job for very long. He fitted in poorly in any working environment. He felt keenly that he was betrayed and rejected by those with whom he was required to associate, for whose freedom he and the other vets had fought and many had died. He seemed to hate everyone and everything. He drank a lot and got into trouble with the law. ("Another God-damn' drunk vet!") During all of this time, with Bob Banfield away so often, his only constant friend was Ronnie

Matthews, a friend who never gave up on him, no matter what trouble he got himself into.

Then, some years ago, Beth discovered from another teacher that there was an old man who owned a country store outside Elginfield, who needed an assistant. The store was getting to be too much for old Amos Warwick. Amos had served in the Canadian Army in the First World War. He insisted that the only man he would hire had to be a vet like himself. He accepted Tom, at a time when Tom had pretty well hit the ultimate skids in his life. Finally, Tom found what he was looking for, and so did old Amos. Amos was a talkative old fellow, and he and Tom argued incessantly about who had the worst war experiences. "Tom," he would yell, in his high-pitched voice, "you blokes were on a picnic in your war! Nothing like the trenches at Passchendaele, Vimy and the Somme, where we were!"

Ronnie felt a deep gratitude to Amos, for what he had done for his friend Tom Brennan. He anticipated that when he picked Tom up, he would not be able to get away without having a cup of tea with Amos, and once again submit to the inevitable loud boasting about what Amos had gone through in the trenches, about his escapades on raiding parties in "no man's land", and how he hated "those damn' officers", almost as much as he hated the Huns!

....

The black Volkswagen pulled up at the main gate of Wolseley Barracks. The corporal of the gate guard approached Ronnie. "Good day, Corporal. Ronnie Matthews and Tom Brennan here to visit with Colonel Banfield."

"Yes, sir, Mr. Matthews. Colonel Banfield is expecting you. Will you park your vehicle over there, please? No place for visitor parking where the C.O. lives. My orders are to take you and Mr. Brennan over to his residence in my jeep."

"O.K., Corporal. Neither of us has been in a military jeep for some years!"

"You were in the Army too, sir?" This was directed to Tom Brennan.

"Would you be hearin' that, Ronnie, me boy? The corporal here callin' me 'sir'! Better lock up the car, or these lads in uniform here will steal all you've got inside, and then the VW too!"

"Never mind him, Corporal," Ronnie reassured the puzzled young N.C.O., "Tom here was the biggest thief in our battalion!"

The two climbed in the jeep, and were driven up the driveway to the battalion's line, then left, past the officer's messes, to the old grey stone, three-sided building complex, surrounding a small parade square.

Ronnie and Tom got out of the jeep; Ronnie thanked the corporal, Tom nodded, and they walked up to the front door and rang the bell. Bob opened the door immediately.

"Hello, Bob!" said Ronnie.

"Hi, there, Ronnie, welcome! So glad you guys made it down! Hi, Tom!"

"And a good day to your worship, Colonel, sir!"

"And to you, you Irish son of a whore! Come in! Mary, they're here!"

Mary Banfield joined her husband at the doorway. "Bob", she scolded, "what a terrible way to greet Tom! Tom, do forgive his crudeness! And how are you, Ronnie? And Beth?"

"Just fine, Mary! Beth sends you her love. Good to see you again. How has this soldier been treating you? Remember at your wedding, when I told you that I would kill him dead if he was ever mean to you!"

"Yes, indeed, Ronnie! But you know Bob. He has always been as good a husband as he has been a soldier! And me, well, I'm just a dutiful 'soldier's lass', I just 'follow the drum' and all that!"

Mary Banfield at thirty-six had lost none of the beauty and charm she possessed the day Ronnie had met her, when she and Bob were married in Kingston eight years before. The following year, Bob, by then a major, left for Korea, and was gone for two years. Mary had been a physiotherapist at the Hotel-Dieu Hospital. She was pregnant when Bob was sent to fight in Korea. There were complications. The baby died shortly after birth. Bob could not obtain compassionate leave to return home, so Ronnie and Beth arranged to be with her during the difficult time. Bob never forgot what the Matthews' had done for Mary. There were no more children. Mary followed her husband wherever he was posted, after he returned to Canada, and worked in her profession where she could obtain employment. Now, she was working part-time at Westminster Hospital in London.

Ronnie looked with affection and admiration at the petite blond with her striking, well-proportioned figure. Tom simply gawked. When he addressed Mary, it was usually as "ma'am". He always envied Bob. How the hell do you get a dame like that? Well, the officers get all the breaks anyway....

The four of them chatted through the afternoon, catching up with what had happened in their respective lives since the last reunion. Mary was delighted to hear that Tom seemed at last to be permanently and happily settled. Ronnie was always anxious to be brought up to date with the Army, a subject which held very little interest for Tom. And Bob and Mary wanted to hear about Ronnie's career. They had dinner, a delectable roast prepared by Mary, replete with Yorkshire pudding and Burgundy wine. Then Mary knew she should leave them to their "men talk", knowing full well how important it was for them to renew their old war-time bonds. She excused herself, and left to visit with friends in the City.

....

The three of them were sitting in the living room, enjoying their after-dinner beer — the 'champagne of privates' — when Ronnie stood up. Their own particular reunion ritual began.

"Sergeant!" called out Ronnie, assuming, for the moment, the role of the imaginary officer.

"Sir!" yelled Bob as he and Tom stood up.

"Call the roll for Three Platoon!"

"Sir!" replied Bob Banfield. "Private Matthews, R.!"

"Sir!" cried Ronnie.

"Private Brennan, T.!"

"Sir!" answered Tom.

"Sir!" continued Bob, once again the platoon sergeant to the imaginary officer, "All present and accounted for! Sir!" Then to Ronnie and Tom, "Platoon, prepare to advance in review!" All three then grabbed their beer mugs. "Platoon, right turn! By the right, quick march!"

The three then marched in step out of the living room, to the dining room. There they continued marching around the dining room table, guzzling their beer, merrily singing the old war-time barrackroom ballad, the unofficial anthem of their old battalion.

"Fuck 'em all! Fuck 'em all! Fuck 'em all!

The long and the short and the tall!

Fuck all the Sergeants and W.O. Ones

Fuck all the Corporals and their bastard sons!

For we're saying goodbye to them all..."

On came the ribald verses, until they had exhausted every profane verse, and themselves as well.

Before they sat down again, Bob said: "Ronnie, Tom. Here's a toast to those who died in Three Platoon, and in all the platoons in that damned war! To their everlasting memory!"

"Too all our comrades who died!" said Ronnie solemnly.

"Yeah — and even the officers as well!" added Tom.

"And here's to our friendship, Tom, and Ronnie. To eternity!"

"To our friendship," the other two repeated. They sat down. A poignant sadness gripped them. In silence, they allowed themselves to remember.....

....

Bob glanced at his watch. "Gentlemen, this time I have arranged for something of a surprise for you".

Ronnie looked at Bob with puzzlement.

"What the hell is this, Bob?" asked Tom.

"Tom, you were always the one back in Three Platoon who would ask me the God-damnedest questions at the God-damnedest times! Well, this time it has to do with Three Platoon. And the Verrières Ridge."

"What is this about, Bob?" asked Ronnie.

"Lieutenant Jim Niles. He's a major now, O.C., H.Q. Company in my battalion. He'll be over to join us soon."

"Jesus Christ", remarked Tom, "Thought I'd never see that bastard again! How did he come out of the woodwork?"

Bob Banfield explained the recent events which had taken place regarding Jim Niles, and put it to them that he now needed their help for the man who had abandoned them fifteen years ago, and who had shared that shell-hole with them before they were finally rescued.

Ronnie and Tom wrestled with their feelings about their former platoon commander, which had lingered with them since that battle so long ago. Bob was their very close friend and comrade. They would do anything for him. But he was also a colonel, and Jim Niles, by the perverse logic so commonplace in the military, now served under Bob. And after all that had happened years ago, Bob wanted them to help him!

The doorbell rang, and Bob walked to the front door and opened it. The three at the reunion were attired in casual shirts and slacks. He was relieved to see that Jim Niles was similarly dressed. He had never seen the major out of uniform. The civilian clothes made him look younger.

"Come in, Jim!" Bob said. "I am delighted that you were able to make it over. This is a momentous occasion for all of us! I would like you to renew your acquaintance with Ronnie Matthews and Tom Brennan!"

Jim Niles looked searchingly at the two civilians. He was uneasy and uncertain as to what reception he would get from these former privates in his old platoon. Both had aged over the fifteen years. Ronnie Matthews was still his slim, tall self, but his hair was thinning and beginning to turn grey. Tom Brennan had put on a fair bit of weight around his middle, but the stoop he had as a nineteen-year-old, the despair of drill instructors and his RSM, was still plainly there.

"How are you?" Jim said, hesitatingly.

Ronnie walked over to him, and held out his hand. "I'm very glad to see you again, Jim. It has been a long time. Say, you look far more dignified now than the shave-tail just out of R.M.C. we knew way back then!"

Jim smiled, and shook his hand warmly. "Thank you, Ronnie! But so do you! I understand you are the principal of a school in Kitchener."

"That's correct. I'm into another sort of battlefield now!"

Jim saw Tom Brennan staring awkwardly at him. He went over to Tom, and offered his hand. "Hello, Tom."

"Good evening, Major Niles."

"Cut that, Tom!" interjected Bob Banfield. "Tonight, he is Jim to you, and all of us. No rank. Just four old vets, who shared that living hell on the Verrières Ridge. We survived .... that's what matters. Hell, lads, we've got something to celebrate! Jim, the fourth survivor of the old Three Platoon, is now with us. Let's have a round of beers on that!"

The four sat down. There was a great deal to talk about. Ronnie expressed interest in the various postings in which Jim had served since the war. Initially, Tom remained awkwardly silent. But, as the evening progressed, he overcame some of his reticence, felt more assured that this "damned officer" had accepted him without reservation, and the four of them chatted comfortably together.

As veterans do, when reunited, they talked about their experiences in the "old Army", sharing humorous anecdotes and memories of the hardships, and the homesickness which had affected them all when they were so young and so far away from home. Gradually, they got onto the subject of their battle on the slope of the Verrières Ridge. Ronnie took it upon himself to bring Jim Niles out of the shell which he had built so tightly around himself. As Jim became aware that they held no grudge against him, he was able finally to share his own terrifying experiences with them. As Bob Banfield had hoped, this meeting provided the opportunity for a long-delayed catharsis of feelings for Jim. The three recognized the courage Jim was showing, as he talked with them, and they made certain that he knew this. With all of this, Jim began to learn that he could also forgive himself.

They talked about the old Three Platoon. With a great deal of regret, Jim admitted that he had never taken time and effort to get to know the men in the platoon. The names of some of the men were brought up. Did Jim remember the big Pole Sipulski, who was always getting into fights in the English pubs? They reminisced about RSM Stuart Reid (sending shivers down Tom's spine), and about Major Dick Mitchell, Able Company commander, who had dubbed Ronnie, Tom and Jack Sipulski the "Soldiers Three". They then got onto the subject of the platoon's section commanders, the three corporals. They came to Number Two Section. Did Jim Niles remember Corporal René Charlebois?

So his name was René? "I don't recall much about Corporal Charlebois. I want to hear more about him."

Ronnie Matthews gladly told him about his old corporal. He commanded the section in which he and Tom Brennan had served, both in England and in Normandy up to and including the assault on the Verrières Ridge. Bob said that he and Charlebois had attended the junior N.C.O. school together after they returned from Dieppe. Both had been section commanders, and then Bob was sent on the senior N.C.O. course, and returned to the platoon as platoon sergeant. They talked about their memories of the little man from Lafontaine. Ronnie described how he had seen René Charlebois killed, trying to hold back the German counter attack, as Three Platoon abandoned its forward position.

This was the confirmation Jim Niles had been waiting for, since he met Laura LaChance. "Bob," he said, "you know the R.C.E.M.E. corporal I recently charged, who was up on orders before you; you sent him to the D.B.? LaChance?"

"Yes."

"His wife, Laura, came to my office the day her husband was sent off. She wanted to speak with you. You were off at a conference at Command, so I saw her instead. Her maiden name was Charlebois. René Charlebois was her brother."

Banfield let out a low whistle. He had no idea that there was any connection between that fool LaChance, and his old comrade, Charlebois. However, even if he had known, he would have decided on the same punishment for LaChance. René, *mon ami*, Bob thought, Jim Niles was no use to you when you were killed, but maybe he has been able to help your little sister at this difficult time for her. Rest in peace, old friend.....

....

Jim left before the others, knowing that they needed more time together. He thanked them for their warmth and comradeship, and their help in his task of resolving the bitter conflicts which had plagued him. He thanked Bob for arranging the meeting. Ronnie and Tom told Jim that they hoped that the four would meet again. As events were to unfold, this was not to be.

PART THREE

LONDON, FALL 1959

CHAPTER FOURTEEN

It was Saturday afternoon in early October. The trees in the city of London were rapidly turning. The splendor of their autumnal foliage glowing with yellows and reds was little diminished by the windy, drizzly weather.

Major Jim Niles sat in his easy chair in his room in the Officers' Quarters, his feet propped on the bed. He was off duty for the week-end, and was dressed in casual clothes, reading the Saturday edition of the London Free Press. The newspaper seemed devoid of anything of interest, and he soon let the paper drop. He stared out of his window at the old stone regimental depot building. The rain-drops pelted against the window panes, tapping hypnotically. His thoughts wandered over recent events in his life, and then back to the previous May, recalling the series of significant events which had begun at that time.

Wolseley Barracks appeared deserted. There were no marching troops, no sergeant or corporal yelling out commands, no military vehicles chortling and clattering past. For this was fall, and for the infantry battalion stationed here, a relatively quiet season in the annual cycle of training activities. When it returned from the summer brigade concentration at Camp Petawawa, most of its personnel were sent on a month's annual leave. As the troops trickled back in September, the battalion settled once again into its routine garrison duties. Every Wednesday morning, there was the formal battalion parade on the vast asphalt parade square. At specified times, the guard was changed at the main gate with the customary ceremonial. Orderly duties were attended to, and the perennial inspections carried out, ranging from weapons and equipment to hygiene in the mess halls. This was also the season for individual training courses. The junior and senior non-commissioned officer's courses were being conducted, necessary for promotion in the ranks. Many of the officers had left London for various career courses at military establishments across the country.

Major Niles' Headquarters Company continued to attend to its many and varied administrative functions, on which the battalion depended each day.

Even when most of the troops were away on annual leave, there still had to be a skeleton staff on duty. The men who remained for guard duty and other functions had to be fed. Vehicles had to be maintained. The battalion's orderly room never shut down. But the battalion was now back to full strength, less those men who were away on course. Jim Niles noted contentedly that the demands and pressures inherent in his job had eased considerably, compared to how they were in June, when the battalion was preparing for its four-hundred-mile move to Camp Petawawa, on the Ottawa River, and its summer brigade training exercises there.

An army, according to Napoleon, marches on its stomach. A contemporary axiom must surely be that a Canadian infantry battalion in 1959 marches into the field on what its Headquarters Company and all its subunits provided. Last June, he had waded into his work with a determination and vigor which surprised his subordinate officers and N.C.O.'s, and himself as well. He recalled with amusement the expression on Colonel Banfield's face, when he dropped over to see how H.Q. Company was getting on, as if he could not believe the change in the O.C. of the company. The company was working hard and working together, with a growing respect for itself and its commander.

Jim thought of his Quartermaster, Captain Joshua Kirst, Royal Canadian Ordnance Corps, who with the "R.Q." and his other stalwarts had wrestled the necessary supplies and equipment into their two-and-a-half ton trucks for the brigade concentration. And Sergeant Gallant, the provost sergeant ....had his section revving those Harley-Davidsons every day before the move, to make sure they were in operational condition .... meat-heads on motorbikes! Then the cooks, resentful about having to leave the familiar comforts of their ultra-modern mess kitchens, for the rigors of cooking in the field .... almost had to drag them, kicking and screaming, into their "deuce and a half" kitchen marquee vehicles ..... And then there was the medical platoon .... good old Mike Baldwin, physician and gung-ho soldier .... he always took care of his own bailiwick with minimal direction from above ......

Captain Leo Toland and his Transport Platoon ..... the vehicles ..... the God-damned jeeps! Ridiculous orders from Central Command. Their battalion was on "U.N. Standby", was it not? And if they went overseas, what vehicles would they be issued? Why, jeeps, of course. You'd need them for the desert, dear boys! So why not use this God-sent opportunity to transport the battalion in jeeps to Petawawa? Good way to shake your lads down .... never been tried before, what? Good show, Colonel Banfield, we knew you would see it our way. And we need a full report, in quintuplicate, regarding your observations and experiences with a jeep-borne battalion ..... Banfield: "Jim, I have news for you. We're going to Petawawa loaded on jeeps. Now before you get hot under the collar ....."

Then came the frantic effort to scrape up enough jeeps from Western Ontario Area. The London garrison's Central Ordinance Depot on Highbury Street was primarily responsible for pulling the jeeps out of their military hat ... and they did a rotten job. They drove dozen upon dozen of these vehicles onto the battalion's parade square, where they were taken on strength by Leo Toland's people ..... mad efforts on the part of pioneer platoon to paint on the battalion's red tac signs, front and back .....

Leo Toland: "Jim, you had better come down and take a look at this last batch! Jesus, I can't believe what they sent us. Pure shit-buckets! I don't think they're roadworthy! Where in hell did C.O.D. find them — in a Boer War museum?"

Colonel Banfield: "Dammit, Jim, you and Leo are going to have to patch them up as best you can. Our orders are that we must take them with us —-four men to a jeep."

Toland: "Sir, them rust-buckets are going to break down all along the road from here clear to Petawawa!" And he was right .....

Banfield: "No way around it, Leo. But Command has promised an L.A.D. which will be on our tail all the way." ... Light Aid Detachment .... glorified military wrecking service, courtesy of the Royal Canadian Electrical and Mechanical Engineers ....

0800 hours, 28 JUN 59. Entire battalion, having been previously assembled on the parade square, appropriately organized in "packets" of six vehicles each, rolls off. First bivouac, Blackdown training area in Camp Borden: hot and sandy. Troops lay, stripped, in the sun ... some got badly burned. Next day .... Barrie, Orillia, Gravenhurst, Highway 60 into Algonquin Park. Bivouac area cordoned off in a large field .... Were they trying to keep out the tourists and campers, or the black bears? No effect on the swarms of mosquitoes .... it was on the second day that the jeeps began to break down .... they littered the entire route. Terribly embarrassing .... this was the Army which had to defend the country, come what may?

On the battalion command net: "Hello Flamingo, Hello Flamingo, from Flamingo Three. Fetch Sunray. Over." Charlie Company O.C. looking for Banfield.

"Flamingo Three from Flamingo. Sunray on set. Send message. Over."

"Flamingo Three to Flamingo. My forward packet reports figures four one over four ton trucks non-serviceable. Awaiting your orders. Over."

"Flamingo to Flamingo Three. Dismount your lead platoon. March them in single file, repeat, single file, on the shoulder of highway. Implement Contingency Plan Zulu. Use remaining vehicles to shuttle your call-sign to Area Tango. Provide regular SITREPs. Out .... Hello Flamingo One, this is Flamingo. Sunray on set. SITREP. Over." Banfield wants to know how Alpha Company is faring ......

"Flamingo, this is Flamingo One. Figures one zero vehicles hors de combat, Sunray. Have implemented Contingency Plan Zulu. My entire call-sign on their feet and headed in general direction of Area Tango. Will muster available vehicles to pick up troops in rear platoon, will then leap-frog advance platoons. Will provide SITREP's, over."

"Flamingo to Flamingo One. Good show, Art. Gives your lads a chance to exercise their feet. No sweat after Ipperwash! Cheery-bye, out." Banfield at his best .... the man never seems to get discouraged ... he loves playing soldier ... with the whole of southern and central Ontario to play in!

On the command net: "Flamingo Four to Romeo Three. Over." O.C. Delta Company to the Medical Section.

"Romeo Three to Flamingo Four. Send message. Over."

"Flamingo Four to Romeo Three. Fetch Starlight. Over."

"Romeo Three to Flamingo Four. Starlight speaking. Over."

"Flamingo Four to Romeo Three. Mike, my lead vehicles just passed a provost corporal three miles east of Barry's Bay. Lying in the grass beside the road, next to his motor-cycle. Bad belly-ache. I think he needs your attention. Over."

"Romeo Three to Flamingo Four. Roger, Sam. Wilco. Am now about ten miles west of your location. One jeep amb right behind me. Out." So now there is real live human break-down, to go with the jeeps ..... Thank God Mike's jeep amb remained serviceable ... took the corporal directly to Pembroke hospital ... hot appendix, Mike later told me.

Final assembly area, fifteen miles into the bush from the built up area of Camp Petawawa. Christ, they must fear for their wives and daughters in the P.M.Q.'s, to put us this far out! But we're on the Petawawa River ....a natural bath-tub for us all, a Godsend after the three-day trip.........

....

Third day at Petawawa. C.O.'s jeep pulls up at my tent. Bob Banfield, covered with dust. Just got back to battalion lines from brigade H.Q. located near the base. (Where else? Brigadiers love their comforts, and close access to a well-stocked mess....) "Jim, we have an important change in our command structure. Art Robertson has been transferred to brigade H.Q. for staff duties during the concentration. His 2/IC as you know is not with us, off on his course at the Staff College in Kingston. As of now, you are to take over Alpha Company for the month we are here. I want Leo Toland temporarily to run Headquarters Company, as well as keep an eye on Transport Platoon. CSM Kovacs is a good head. Your company is in good hands — you deserve a lot of credit for that."

Again, Banfield at his best. Credit where credit is due. .... Takes getting used to, this type of thing .... But, hell, why me? I've never commanded a rifle company before .... he could have one of the 2/IC captains from the other rifle companies ..... The man seems determined to make a professional soldier out of me ... restoration to its accustomed status, the military glory of the Niles name ... God, will I let him down? .... Will I let me down? Alpha Company ... Able Company ... Verrières..... And Three Platoon .... Lieutenant Peter Forsythe, the only one of them all who had the courage to help this drunken sot of a major at the fateful mess dinner. — he and the M.O.

Better pack my rucksack. Decided to take my batman with me, because I don't know any of the "little green men" in Able Company ..... I must remember that the word is Alpha, damn it, not Able....

....

A hot, humid day. Dense bush on the western edge of the battalion's training area. Fieldcraft training for the company's sections. Sweat pours off the faces of the men as they practice stealth, creeping through the underbrush. And the sweat streaks their blackened faces.....

Sections patrolling the northern defensive perimeter report sighting of a "significantly large enemy force" moving up the gravel road, in front of their concealed positions. Enemy tracked by each section as he passes across their front, his position at each moment radioed in to Company H.Q......

Enemy then moves off the road, and bears directly towards my H.Q......

"Alpha Niner to Alpha. Do we intercept? Over."

"Alpha to Alpha Niner. Put your enemy in the bag and bring him to my Hotel Quebec soonest. Out."

Two of the young soldiers jump out of the bush, two yards away from the enemy. Expertly camouflaged, he did not see them until he was right on top of them.

"Good day, Captain Baldwin, sir. You're our prisoner. Major Niles wants you for interrogation!"

"For Christ's sake, Private Walters and Private Cormier! Put down your rifles! You scared the hell out of me! I've come peacefully on a visit to your lines, and this is the reception I get!"

A pleasant short visit with Mike Baldwin. Guess he got bored at Tac H.Q. and left his R.A.P. in the tender hands of his medics to hike the two miles out to us. Or did he want to check up on me, to see how I was faring, with the weight of command of a bloody rifle company on my shoulders?.....

....

One more unit exercise, before the brigadier has his chance to play general with all three of the infantry battalions now gracing this sodding camp, plus the artillery regiment and the armored squadron. Tanks had two rounds of twenty pounder shells for each Centurion to fire during the whole concentration — and these were blanks. Artillery had no shells for their 105's, except for that one demonstration of a battalion in the attack, when there was an ad hoc miniscule "barrage" to "shoot them in". The Canadian

Army in peacetime. The smartest dressed, the best fed and paid — and the most poorly equipped of the NATO forces.....

The Mattawa Plain, a stretch of sand and scrub used by generations of Canadian soldiers for field training, running alongside the Ottawa River for some miles, the land gradually rising to a ridge of sorts, rather cliffy directly above the river. Our battalion was designated to provide the demonstration. A whole bunch of brass from Ottawa to observe on the side-lines. The approach march to the assembly area. Moving out to the forming up point. Deployment in line prior to crossing of the start-line. Alpha Company on the left, Three Platoon on the extreme flank. Banfield with me at Company H.Q. before we cross the start-line. Someone is required to fire a burst from a Sten gun over to the west side of the assaulting troops, to signal the crossing of said start-line. All officers committed to the exercise. The M.O. was sitting in his jeep amb close by. Banfield gets his brain wave....Mike Baldwin is to start the war for us. The artillery fire phase begins and is soon ended. Dust and smoke on the ridge facing us, our objective. This is Mike's moment of glory. Banfield waves the O.K. to him. There is a clump of bush thirty yards from him. He is to shoot in this general direction. He fires off the whole mag in the Sten. Thud-thud-thud-thud-thud. We found out afterwards that the entire general staff from Army H.Q. in Ottawa was on the other side of the bush. Mike could have got them all! Pity.....

The mortars and machine guns of Support Company join in the assault. The three platoons of Alpha Company advance in extended order, up a gradual slope to the ridge. (Will the Army ever learn?) The men fire their C-1's as they move ahead. I see Peter Forsythe right up front with his men. I begin to move my H.Q. behind the three platoons. We pass old armored vehicles, used as targets undoubtedly for countless schemes.....but these "tanks" seem to be changing shape.....they look like burned-out German Mark IV's.....the whole ground around me erupts violently.....everything turns grey.....the noise of explosions becomes deafening.....mortar fire onto us.....artillery shells in air bursts, the shrapnel screaming at us.....the terrifying swoosh of the 88's.....we continue to advance up the slope of the ridge.....Christ, what is happening to me?.....I must be going insane.....Peter Forsythe, platoon commander, Three Platoon — where is he? Dear God, let him be with his men, not abandon them, hide in a sodden shell-hole.....

"Major Niles, are you O.K., sir?" It was Private Brandt, my batman. "Jeeze, sir, you suddenly turned white and began to shake, then kinda hunched down on your knees....."

"Yes, I'm O.K., Brandt. Bit too much sun, I guess! Thanks for your concern. Now, lad, let's get up there on the objective where the three platoons must be by now."

"Very good, sir!"

My God, my God.....Will I ever be free of the Verrières Ridge.....

....

At the conclusion of the Petawawa concentration, Art Robertson returns to the fold, and I hand over the command of Alpha Company to him. Damn it, despite myself, I enjoyed serving with them. Got to know the officers well, and many of the other ranks. Leo Toland was glad to hand back H.Q. Company to me. He spent the month feverishly trying to get the jeeps overhauled and roadworthy for the trip back to London. Many were too far gone. Somehow, Command found twenty deuce-and-a-halfs, which ensured a much smoother return journey.

Then came annual leave.....Prince Edward Island.....Savage Harbour on the north coast.....Heather Cottage.....Ancestral summer home of the Niles clan.....Father and Mother.....the esteemed Brigadier James Lowell Niles, D.S.O., M.C., C.D., Q.R.S.T. and even U., and his ever-loving wife.....they had long lost interest in the little wooden cottage on the top of the red sand-stone cliff, overlooking the ocean, and only occasionally availed themselves of the rustic, sea-side haven from life's travails and disappointments.....God, how I love the place.....Old Angus McLean from Mount Stewart nearby, who was caretaker for my parents.....always saw to it, before I arrived each late summer on leave, to stock the place with food — even the inevitable bottle of home-made elderberry wine, and a case of beer — never took money for all of this. "It's good to see you again, Major, me darlin', sorr!" Angus, who was "mentioned in dispatches" was at Passchendaele in 1917.....

The red earth, the bright green of the fields, the blue sea all around. Alone, and at peace. Walks along the quiet beaches. Grasses covering the dunes. Brisk swims in the cool sea. Time to reflect, to replenish, to think.....

Laura. I can't get her out of my mind. There has not been a day since I met her, that I have not thought about her. Her beautiful face, her hazel eyes.....that thick, dark hair.....the faint scent of her perfume.....the grace in her movements.....how she walked.....the enchanting rich tone of her voice.....that bewildering sense of intimacy.....as if I had known her all her life.....as if I had known her for a thousand years.....Laura. What has happened to her since last May? That fool LaChance would surely be out of the D.B., and out of the Army, by now. Could she have gone back with him? A thought too repugnant for words.....

....

Jim Niles sat up abruptly, dumped the newspaper on his bed, and glanced at his watch. Sixteen hundred hours. Damn it, it's not sixteen hundred hours, I'm off duty, so it's plain old four o'clock on a rainy afternoon in London Town. Still time to pick up a book to read over the week-end. He pulled on his raincoat, and walked out of the Officers' Quarters to his green MG roadster. He got in, started the motor and drove off, past the battalion's lines, down the road to the main gate. The guard recognised the O.C., H.Q. Company, lifted the barrier, and saluted as Jim drove through. He waved at the young soldiers, the rain dripping off their ponchos. Out of uniform, no soldier in the Canadian Army was permitted to salute.

He drove out onto Oxford Street, to Richmond Street, and turned left. He was headed for the Wellington Square Mall, and his favourite bookstore.

CHAPTER FIFTEEN

The bookstore was crowded. Jim Niles set about examining what was available, with no particular subject in mind. He glanced at the section on War. There was Chester Wilmot's "The Struggle for Europe"; Liddell Hart's edited "Rommel Papers"; "El Alamein to the Sangro" and "Normandy to the Baltic" by Field Marshall Montgomery; "Panzer Leader", an English translation of the book written by the German general and architect of blitzkrieg, Heinz Guderian; and also the first two official Second World War histories of the Canadian Army, "The Canadian Army 1939-1945" by Stacey and "The Canadians in Italy" by Nicholson. Jim knew that Stacey's first volume was in the library of the Officer's Mess at the Barracks. Nicholson's book was part of the required reading for the forthcoming "Captain to Major" course. But Jim passed this section without stopping. Although he was a professional soldier, he had no interest in the study of war — especially not the Second World War — unless he was required to read military history in a career course.

He moved on to the History section. There was Winston Churchill's four-volume "A History of the English Speaking Peoples". Not really what he wanted either. Beyond this section were novels by Agatha Christie, John Steinbeck and Leon Uris. Uris' "Exodus" caught his eye. He removed it from the shelf for a closer look.

He immediately felt a strange, uneasy sensation, a disturbing foreboding, followed by a peaceful feeling, a quiet warmth which suffused his body. The hubbub outside in the concourse of the mall seemed to subside. For a moment, he was afraid that he was entering another of the bizarre, hallucinatory experiences which had come over him before.

"Hello, Major Jim Niles!"

The young woman's voice was unmistakable. Before he turned around, even before she spoke, he was acutely aware of who was behind him.

"Laura!"

It was almost five months since he had met her in his office. The impact of seeing her, of being in her presence, was almost overpowering. She wore a pale beige raincoat over her white nurse's uniform, white nylon stockings, and white oxfords. The white collar of her uniform accentuated the warm, dark tones of her face, the wideset cheek-bones, straight nose and straight, dark eyebrows. He recognised again the soft, hazel eyes, and the brick-colored lipstick on her full, wide lips. Her thick dark-brown hair fell loosely over her shoulders.

"Why, yes, it's Laura! You remembered my name! I'm truly flattered!"

"Good Lord, how could I.....how could anyone forget.....I've thought a lot about you....."

Laura watched, fsacinated, as this army officer, some eleven years older than she, unnerved in her presence, struggled for words.

"I'm so glad I ran into you! I'll never forget how kind you were. It seems so long ago. And how have you been?"

"Oh, fine.....let's see.....since I saw you, I was with the battalion at Petawawa.....you.....know all about that, I'm sure. Then I was on annual leave.....usually go to Prince Edward Island.....my parents have a cottage there by the sea....."

"Oh, that must have been nice. You know, I've never been to the Maritimes — in fact, I've never been out of Ontario, except for a couple of times when my husband and I went to Detroit."

My husband and I.....God, was she living with him? Get hold of yourself.....you're behaving like an awkward school-boy. Jim fought for a semblance of control. Laura's initial amusement changed to concern and compassion for this sensitive man, who seemed so painfully clumsy before her. This is a rare specimen, she thought. All the army officers she had encountered in the past had been glib and abrupt, practiced in the manly arts of flirtation and seduction, and supremely sure of themselves when it came to women. This one was different. She sensed that the initiative must be hers, and she took it.

"Jim, I'm famished. I just got off a pretty busy shift at the hospital. There is a restaurant a few stores down from here. Would you like to come and have a coffee with me — perhaps a donut? I hope I'm not being too presumptuous....."

"Laura, I would like nothing better. I'd consider it a privilege!"

Jim knew the restaurant. It was small and unpretentious, with individual booths. As they walked over, he glanced at her frequently, hardly daring to believe she was there.

Falling into the familiar role of attentive escort, Jim recovered his poise. He ordered coffee, and Danish pastries instead of donuts.

Laura watched Jim smile at the waitress, nodding his thanks. He turned to her, and offered her the cream. You are a strange man, she thought. Such sadness in your eyes. You're attracted to me and that bothers you.

"No, thank you. I have my coffee black — a bad habit nurses get into!"

"Laura, tell me what has happened to you, since I saw you last."

"Well, when I left your office, they had already taken Patrick off to Camp Borden. I decided to keep my apartment on Grosvenor Street. I felt the best thing I could do was to continue working. My parents came down from Lafontaine to visit me. I was so angry with Patrick; I had had enough of him. I decided not to write to him. His mother called about a month later. If he had behaved at the D.B., he would have been released after thirty days. But he didn't, and they gave him another month there. His mother told me about it and blamed me! She said that I did not look after him properly! He got out in the middle of July with a dishonorable discharge from the Army. He came over to the apartment; he said he wanted to come in to pick up his things. There was.....a terrible fight. He hit me, and tried to choke me. The neighbors called the police. They wanted me to charge him with assault. All I wanted was for him to leave with his belongings, and to stay out of my life.

"It's not a very nice story, is it? *Alors, avec un canard comme lui, ca va sans dire*.....Oh, I'm sorry, Jim. When I get upset, sometimes I break into French....."

"I understand you, Laura. I am....horrified...."

"Well, since that time, I have been on my own. I've been....O.K. Sometimes he phones, usually when he is drunk, threatening me with more violence if I do not take him back. Sometimes I've seen him parked outside my apartment....."

Laura hesitated. "Why am I telling you all these very personal and painful things about my life? You must have more important things to worry about, than me, a ward nurse with a broken marriage. But somehow I feel that I know you, and that it is necessary and right for me to talk about my problems.....my marriage is over, I'm certain of that. I have seen a lawyer about a divorce. He said that the only grounds would be adultery. When I stopped trying to please him and giving in to him, and when things got bad enough that I did not want to have sex with him, he would tell me that he would find it somewhere else, and walk out. But there is no real proof. Even if I hired a — what do you call it — a professional co-respondent, I doubt whether he would agree to a divorce. He wouldn't give me the satisfaction of releasing me. Then there is the question of my Catholic religion.....

"Jim.....I feel embarrassed.....I must not dump all of this stuff on you.....Hey, don't look so worried! It will all sort itself out, one way or the other. Us Charlebois people — we're pretty tough.....*les coureurs du bois*.....and all that!"

"Please don't think that you are dumping on me. There is no need to feel embarrassed. On the contrary, I am grateful that you share these things with me. If I can tell you something....I'm not good at this sort of thing.....I.....have been concerned about you since that day in my office. Well, I have worried about you.....and I have wanted to see you again."

Laura looked intently at the man across from her. My God, she thought, I think you have fallen in love with me, and you don't really know it. You seem so naive and vulnerable. I could give you something you have never had, I think. But I am not from your social class; where could it lead?

"I have something to tell you, Jim. Last summer, when I was back home in Lafontaine, I asked my mother to let me see the letters she had received from my brothers during the war. Of the four of them, René, my favorite, sent very few. The last one was from England, just before he went to Normandy. He mentioned a Lieutenant Niles who was his platoon commander. I knew that it must be you. He was in your platoon when he was killed in the Verrières Ridge battle."

"I know, Laura. After I met you last May, I saw three of the veterans from that platoon. Two are civilians, and the third is my commanding officer, Colonel Banfield. Your brother served under me as a section corporal. I was twenty-two, just out of R.M.C. It was my first battle, and it was my last. I....am....not proud of what happened then. It has haunted me all my life. I...." He swallowed and stared at her, afraid to continue.

Laura stretched her hand across to him, and gently put her fingers against his lips. "Please, let's not talk about it now, if you don't want to. I don't want you to be sad. It is not important to me, except that it concerns you."

Jim took her hand in both of his. He did not look directly at her, but stared past her, struggling with his feelings. As he spoke, his grip tightened. Laura was momentarily baffled by his behavior. This was the first time that there had been any physical contact between them, yet this was hardly a pass. She recalled that men whom she had nursed had tried to cling to her, when they were very ill and frightened. She placed her other hand over his.

"Hey, look at me, Jim. Tell me what you're thinking."

"Well, there's really not much to tell. I don't want to bore you with all the sordid details. Our battalion advanced up the slope towards the Verrières Ridge, and we were badly clobbered. The German artillery....mortar bursting amongst us....machine gun fire....the noise and smoke....people being ripped apart everywhere....blood....guts....the rain and the mud.... Laura, the plain truth was that I was terrified that I would be killed. I abandoned my platoon, and the platoon sergeant had to take over. I lay in a shell-hole while they fought the Germans, hand to hand. The following day, I was taken prisoner. I was certain that they were going to kill me. There was a German tank colonel, who released me in a dazed state to the custody of my platoon sergeant, who had survived. He and two other men in my platoon had given aid to a badly wounded young German officer. For this, apparently, the colonel let us all go. I was sent back to Canada, declared unfit to command troops in battle.

"Do you understand, Laura? I was a failure as an officer. Your brother René was a far better soldier than I. He was killed, covering the withdrawal of his section. While I was being treated in a battle exhaustion unit behind our lines, his body was left unburied on that damned ridge, until the Canadians finally captured it, two weeks later. In the years since, I have wished many times that I had died there too. Worse, I wallowed in my guilt and self-disgust. I withdrew from people. I preferred to be left alone. I was a very poor officer. The only reason I was not forced to resign my commission was because I came from a family with political and military connections. My father is a retired brigadier, who was a hero at Vimy Ridge.

Christ, military history is full of ridges!....And mine was my undoing....God, I'm sorry! I must be boring you...."

"Of course not! My dear Major Jim Niles, you are no less for me, for what you have told me. You are not that frightened young man any more! You are still the kind man I am getting to know. It does not matter what happened years ago. That is not important. But you are important.....You are important to me.....I would like to see you again....perhaps go out with you. But you might not want that. There must be many other women for you to go out with, far more suitable than a separated nurse from Lafontaine!"

"No, Laura! There is nothing in the world I would rather do, than to continue to see you. I have never felt this way with any other woman. Laura....when can I see you again....when are you off duty....would you like to go to dinner with me?"

Laura laughed. "Why, Major Niles," she teased, "I do believe you don't know how to ask a girl out for a date! Well, kind sir, how about next Saturday? I'm not on duty, and I'll be fresh as a daisy, all bright-eyed and ready to go out with you."

"Oh, that would be marvelous. How about dinner at the Friar's Cellar?"

"That would be great! Now you have to tell me at what time!"

Jim began laughing at his own clumsiness. He worked out the logistics for the operation, as the army had trained him to do. And to his delight, the beautiful young woman across the table was more than willing to comply with his operational plans.

....

Laura had no car; Jim drove her to her apartment. He walked her into the building and up to her door, but did not go in. He thanked her for a pleasant luncheon, and left. When Laura closed her door, she went to her bedroom window, and watched him drive off in his green MG. She was intrigued: another man, in her experience, would have wanted to come in, and to try his luck with her. *Vraiment, un chevalier...*

Laura crossed to her dresser. In the top drawer was René's letter; she read it yet another time. The scrawl was barely legible, and the spelling awkward, with its "anglicised" French:

"Le 8 Juin 1944

"Mon cher père et ma chere mère

"J'écris de l'Angleterre, mais il est défendu à dire, ma location. Vous savez que les Canadiens enfin sont arrivés en France, pour combatter les Allemands. Bientôt, nôtre battalion sera là aussi. Soyez tranquil, mes parents. Nous avons un bon colonel. Nôtre sergeant était avec moi à Dieppe, un bon gar et mon ami. Je ne sais pas trôp beaucoup de nôtre platoon officer, Lieutenant Niles. Il ne parle avec nous jamais. Il n'a pas de concern pour ses soldats. Nous ésperons qu'il sera O.K., quand la battaille commence. Il faut vaincre le Boche. Puis, je peu retourner chez nous. Je vous embrasse, aussi les enfants. Dites "hello" à la petite Laura. Quand je retourne, j'apporterais une poupée pour elle.

"Priez pour mois.

"Votre fils, René."

Poor René, Laura thought. If you had not been killed, perhaps you would have liked meeting Jim Niles again. He really is a nice man....

Down the street from the entrance to her apartment, Patrick LaChance sat unobtrusively in his car, and watched as Jim escorted Laura inside. When Jim left he followed him at some distance, back to Wolseley Barracks. With mounting hatred, he watched as the guard lifted the barrier, and saluted Jim as he drove through.

CHAPTER SIXTEEN

At seven Saturday evening, Jim Niles drove up to the apartment building on the west end of Grosvenor Street, and parked in the lot provided for the tenants. He walked through the main entrance, climbed the single flight of stairs to Laura's suite, and rang the bell. Laura answered promptly.

"Good evening, Laura! I'm....glad to see you again....I....may I give you this....something I picked up on the way over."

"Well, good evening to you too, Major Jim Niles! Please come in!" Jim gave her the small package, wrapped in green paper. It was a single red rose. He observed the faint blush which came to her cheeks. She was wearing a crimson blouse tucked into a dark-brown wool skirt, the whole ensemble fitting closely, and accentuating the firm, feminine curves of her slim body. He was sure he had never seen anyone so totally and captivatingly beautiful.

"Why, thank you, kind sir! I simply adore red roses. They are my favorite flower! Let me have your coat. Do we have a few minutes before we go to dinner?"

"Yes, the reservation is for seven thirty." Jim took off his grey tweed fall coat. Laura looked at him with unconcealed admiration. A tall man, greying at the temples, navy blue blazer, the crown and maple leaves of his regimental crest on the breast pocket, blue and yellow striped regimental tie, grey flannels. His regimental cuff-links showed below the sleeves of his blazer.

"Jim, I declare! You look so distinguished!" She had not expected him to dress this elegantly. Until now, she had only seen him in battle dress uniform, and casual attire.

"Thank you. ....You have a lovely apartment."

"I like it. Since Patrick left, I've changed things around a fair bit. I bought new furniture — all on the 'never-never plan', of course! That chesterfield set is new. I did my bedroom completely over. Let me show you around.

But first, I'm going to find a vase for this beautiful rose. Would you like to come with me into the kitchen?"

Jim had never been in the apartment of a young woman before. What he saw delighted his senses. What an unbelievable contrast to the austere surroundings he was accustomed to in the military! In his different postings, his quarters had always been rather spartan, with no thought given beyond what was basically utilitarian. In some places, even the curtains were khaki! Many of the officers' messes had been lavishly upholstered and decorated, comfortable enough, but always decidedly masculine in character. Laura's apartment reflected her feminine warmth and beauty in every corner. There was nothing gaudy or affectatious, nothing giddy or frivolous. Yet the apartment expressed the joyful spirit of the young woman who lived here. With his soldier's eye, trained to observe, he perceived so much of Laura in this apartment, and he warmed to what he saw. She was a fun-loving sensual woman.

....

The Friar's Cellar. Elegant, gracious dining. Superb service. A menu which offered tantalizing variety, every dish prepared to perfection. Exquisite bouillon. Venison for the main course. Chocolate mousse. Candlelight and wine. And for both, an intimate evening which remained a cherished memory for the rest of their lives.

....

They drove back to the apartment building. Jim got out first. Laura began to open the door on the passenger side of the two-seater sportscar, and abruptly stopped. I must learn that I am in the company of a gentleman, Laura solemnly reminded herself. Jim went around the front of the MG, and opened the door for her.

"Thank you", she smiled, mustering all the grace she could, as she climbed out of the small car. "It has been such a wonderful evening, I don't want it to end. Will you come in, Jim, for a short while?"

He gladly accepted her invitation. The two of them walked up the stairs to her apartment. She took the key from her purse, opened the door, and they went in.

"Now what would a dashing army officer like for a night-cap? I've got some scotch. Or will you have a glass of sherry with me?"

"Whatever you have that is handy. Do you like sherry?"

"*Oh, mais oui, alors!* I love wine. It's the French in me, I guess. Make yourself comfortable. I'll be right back."

When Laura returned with the bottle and the glasses, Jim was sitting at one end of the chesterfield. Laura filled the glasses, put the bottle on the coffee table, and then sat down on the broadloomed floor beside him.

"I like sitting on the floor. Does that surprise you?"

You constantly surprise me. I have never known anyone so full of delectable surprises. To be with you is an endless joy. You intoxicate me. "I shall do the same." Jim got off the chesterfield, and joined Laura, sitting on the floor. He crossed his legs. It was Laura's turn to be surprised at this gesture. She curled her legs under her, and lifted her glass to Jim

"*A vôtre santé, mon cher commandant!* That is the French for 'major', is it not?"

Jim laughed aloud. "God, I don't know, Laura. But it sounds pretty impressive. *Et à vôtre santé aussi, ma chère mademoiselle!*"

"Oh, wow, I'm impressed! Such a well-educated man!" She touched his shoulder lightly with her hand. "Jim Niles, I want to know more about you. What was it like when you were growing up....."

....

The evening passed. They were insatiable in their need to know more about each other. There was always an urgency, as if there would never be enough time, as if time was running out.

Jim looked at his watch. "Laura, it is almost three. I must apologize for keeping you up so late. I had better be getting back. I'd like to see you again soon. When....that is....would you like...."

"I am on days this coming week. How about Wednesday? Would you like to come over for dinner here? How would you like a real home-cooked meal for a change?"

"I would be greatly honored....if it is not too much trouble."

"Of course not. Come over any time after you get off duty. You can watch me cook the dinner!"

"I'll be over, as soon as I change out of my uniform! Thank you for a marvelous evening. I have enjoyed being with you so much."

Et moi aussi, mon cher, Laura said silently to herself. *Tu es vraiment charmant.....*

Laura got Jim's coat, they walked to the door.

"Goodnight, Laura. I'll look forward to seeing you next Wednesday."

Dear man, thought Laura. When are you ever going to make a move! She put her arms around him, pulled herself against him, and kissed his lips. Hesitantly at first, then with a hunger and longing which seemed without limit, he responded. Eventually, they pulled apart, breathless. Jim took her hands, gently kissed them, and then her lips once again.

"Laura, I must leave. Sleep well. Can I call you tomorrow?"

"Oh yes, I'd love that!"

Jim left the apartment, and drove off. Again, Laura watched him from her bedroom window. Yes, Major Jim Niles, she thought, I will sleep well tonight. Because I have found you. And you are the best thing that has ever happened to me. But will it be so for you?

....

Wednesday evening. A warm, lingering embrace as soon as the front door of the apartment was closed behind Jim Niles. Another single red rose. Again the hunger, when they kissed.

"Hey, let me show you something about kissing....Jim, please....now, like this....that's better....now kiss me like you mean it...." Again the breathless withdrawal. "I have to....I must get back to the kitchen. I'm trying to make a great dinner for you. Now, sit down over here on that chair, and behave! Talk to me!"

....

A magnificent meal. Delicious French onion soup, which Laura had prepared the night before, complete with parmesan cheese, served piping hot. Filet mignon, bought at a small butcher's shop on the way back from the hospital. Done to perfection, with delicately cooked vegetables. Almond torte for dessert, and coffee. A robust French red wine during the meal. Creme de menthe liqueur after the dessert.

"Avez-vous bien mangé, monsieur?"

"Absolument! Tout allait comme il faut! Mes compléments!"

....

They washed the dishes together. Rarely in his life had he attended to this particular chore. In the years he was growing up, his parents had always had a cook, and often a maid, even in the dingiest PMQ's on the army bases. He thoroughly enjoyed himself. Over his slacks and flannel shirt, Laura had tied an apron. She flirted outrageously and he revelled in it. Within the growing intimacy of this relationship, for the first time in his life he could let go of the proprieties and relax the inhibitions which so controlled his relations with others. She accepted him for himself, and provided every encouragement for him to come out of his shell, to enjoy, to share — to love.

....

They returned to the living room. Jim sat on the chesterfield. "Mm....I'm all warm and cozy. Move over....there! I'm going to put my head on your lap!" Laura stretched out on her back, with her head nestled in his lap. He held her hand in his. "Mm....I could stay like this forever...."

They chatted, and grew quiet. Jim looked down at her. She wore a short sleeved pale blue sweater, tucked into her tight-fitting jeans. She had kicked off her low-heeled shoes. She was are so utterly beautiful, and he adored her. But within him was a mounting uneasiness. He desired her, and raw lust suffused his whole being. It seemed to violate the tenderness, trust and devotion he also felt. He felt paralysed.

Laura looked up at him. "Jim, I would like to go to bed with you....now." She sat up, fixed her gaze directly on him, searching his eyes for some reaction to her brazen proposition, fearing she had offended him.

"Yes."

Laura led him by the hand to her bedroom. Without hesitation, she deftly removed her jeans and sweater, and stood before him, in her black lace brassiere and panties. He was transfixed.

Placing her hands on his shoulders, Laura murmured, "Hey, haven't you seen a naked lady before?" She turned her back to him. "Now, will you undo me....please...."

A great deal of unpracticed fumbling, his heart pounding in his ears. Her back....her beautiful slim legs....exquisite form. Wild confusion....he struggled with his feelings, he stood before a blindingly beautiful goddess; he should fall to his knees and worship, but there was also torrid, insistent lust. She turned around.

"Oh, God...."

"Jim, here I am, naked as the day I was born, and you're still dressed. Come here....." She began to unbutton his shirt. To her relief, he complied. She studied him closely. "Well, now, look at you! You are gorgeous!"

Laura removed the bedspread, and turned down the top sheet and blanket. She climbed into bed, and, lying on her side, she beckoned him to join her. He took her in his arms, roughly holding her breasts, burying his face into her body, kissing her awkwardly. "Jim....please....let's take our time....I want to enjoy you and I want you to enjoy me. Here, let me...."

She taught him physical loving tenderness, total absorption in each other....touching ....deep caressing...."Wait....not yet....do this for me....I'll show you....yes, that feels good.....again!"

"Laura, I want you, now!" Laura opening to him.....the explosion within her....total exhaustion ....tender holding...."Jim, now I want you to make me come....your hand....here....yes....that feels so good. Do it some more....more...." Laura tensing every muscle, and then total relaxation.

....

Jim did not return to the Barracks that night. Neither got much sleep. They made love repeatedly, with joyful abandon. Once more in the early morning, as they gulped down coffee and orange juice. Laura scrambled into her white uniform. Jim drove her to the hospital, and then returned to his quarters. After a night of ecstasy, back into his khaki battle-dress and another day of routine soldiering.

....

They met frequently, never getting enough of each other. They enjoyed the best restaurants London had to offer. They attended plays, films and art galleries together. Drives in the country. Trips to Toronto. Above all else, Jim loved to visit her in her apartment. There they could sit and talk, and make love. There was so much to share, and there never seemed to be enough time. Jim eagerly learned the skills of an accomplished lover with an obsessed determination which startled Laura. His greatest pleasure in love-making was to pleasure her. At times their sex was pure release from blind irresistible passion. At other times, it was an exquisitely tender celebration of the rapidly deepening love between them.

．．．．．．．．．．．．．．．．．．．．

The marked change that came over Jim at work was recognized by Colonel Banfield, his brother officers and the N.C.O.'s and men in his company. With each passing week, he seemed more human, with more understanding of the needs of the others, more at ease with his responsibilities and more confident in his professional abilities. Bob Banfield observed these changes with disbelief. He was unaware that it was not merely the events of the previous spring which accounted for it.

With increasing frequency, Jim Niles spent his nights with Laura. Each time he left the barracks he was checked out by the guard on duty, and it tantalized the young soldiers when O.C., HQ Company returned in the morning, with barely enough time to get into his uniform to report for duty. The batmen at the Officer's Quarters became increasingly curious about where the good major disappeared to. The batmen, after all, supplied the unending wellspring of the battalion's rumor vine, and the rumors poured forth indeed. The batmen then decided to "recce the situation", when they were off duty, by tracking Major Niles. They borrowed a car from a civilian friend, on a Saturday evening when they were certain Jim would be off on one of his trips. They had to be back by curfew time, since they lived in barracks, and did not have the privilege of coming and going at night that their officers had. With some adroit sleuthing, the mystery was solved. The good major was dating that screw-ball LaChance's ex-wife. A major with a corporal's wife! How about that! Wait till the Old Man hears about that!

．．．．．．．．．．．．．．．．．．．．

Jim Niles then took the next inexorable step in his love affair with Laura; he invited her to attend the officers' Passchendaele Ball, held every year on the first Saturday of November.

CHAPTER SEVENTEEN

The Passchendaele Ball. Gala social event of the year for the military garrison in London, hosted by the incumbent infantry battalion in Wolseley Barracks. All serving officers, both of the Regular Army and the Militia, were invited with their spouses and guests. These guests also included the politicians and the socialites of the city and region. The battalion "ran the show", which it invariably did with the organizational precision characteristic of any of its programmes. The Army spared no expense to ensure that the ball was a memorable success each year. The "other ranks" of the battalion provided all necessary labor and attendant duties. Lavish decorations were created, which reflected a World War One theme. The ball was after all in honor of the anniversary of the regiment's role in the crucial Battle of Passchendaele. Few of the elite patrons had any knowledge of that historic battle, nor could they have cared. They were here to enjoy themselves, and being invited to the ball ensured that they had "made it" socially.

But what of the Battle of Passchendaele? Fought in four phases over a period of two weeks, from the 26th of October to the 10th of November 1917, its cost in casualties was appalling; almost 16,000 for the Canadian Corps alone. It involved the capture of the village of Passchendaele and the ridge on which its ruins lay. This was part of the Ypres salient, in the southwest corner of Belgium which the Germans never succeeded in capturing. The Canadian battle was an integral part of the "Third Battle of Ypres", during which the British armies sustained over 400,000 casualties. But the offensive broke the German will to win, although it was a whole year before the Armistice on 11th November of 1918. The battle was thus of crucial importance among all the cataclysmic battles of that war. Ever since, controversy raged in Canada as to whether it was worth the cost. Canadians continue to regard the battle for Vimy Ridge, fought earlier in April of the same year, as the military achievement which brought nationhood to Canada. The mud and slaughter of Passchendaele seemed better relegated to the history books.

Laura had doubts about attending the Ball with Jim. Although she had not been raised in an established military family, she had acquired in her life, and particularly during the month of her love affair with Jim Niles, a sensitive understanding of the social rules, both stipulated and unspoken, for how an officer in the Canadian Regular Army should conduct himself, above all a field officer in mid-career.

Laura at twenty-six was fully aware of her attractiveness and how men saw her and desired her. This very awareness enhanced her beauty. So also did her self-assurance; she had been raised by her parents to respect herself and to expect that others would do the same. She feared, however, that she lacked the subtle social skills, so necessary if she were to be escorted by this army major to the Passchendaele Ball.

"I am a ward nurse, from Lafontaine, who happens also to be a separated woman, who was married to a corporal. I am uncertain, not so much about me — you should know by now, Jim, I could go anywhere and talk with the Queen herself! — but about how taking me to the Ball would effect you. I am afraid it might cause trouble. Your career is too important...."

"Laura, I love you, you are the most important thing in my life. I have waited too long for you. There could be no other woman in my life or any life vocation more important than you. I am stating a simple fact. You are not responsible for my career. I almost said that you are not responsible for me falling in love with you, but you know damned well that that is not entirely true!

"Six months ago, the day I laid charges against your husband, I realized that I had a choice about my military career. I still have that choice. I want to share the rest of my life with you. If this will create problems in my career, then there are always other options. Good Lord, Laura, we sound like Wallis Simpson and the Duke of Windsor!"

"Yes, but Edward wanted to marry a woman who was already divorced. I'm not! I love you, I want to be free of Patrick even more now. But I am afraid that the Army will not tolerate your relationship with a woman who is still legally married to another man, who was not an officer, and who was released from the Army in disgrace. I could not stand to come between you and your career, Jim. You must be very certain....."

"I am totally and completely certain. Ironic, isn't it, that many officers are married to nurses. Some kind of perverse attraction of opposites! Soldiers belong to a profession whose purpose is to kill in defence of the country. Nurses are professionally committed to the care of people. When I was at R.M.C., there was a hell of a lot of fraternization between the cadets and the nurses at KGH. Many cadets in each graduating class married nurses. And I know senior officers whose daughters went into nursing. Laura, love, I should have met you sooner! But when you were a nursing student here, I doubt whether you would have seen anything about me then to attract you. In fact, I wonder what it is about me now....."

"Oh, Jim, you crazy idiot!! You are everything I want! And I think you are stuck with me! Your options ran out a while ago! Dear man, I'll gladly go to the Passchendaele Ball with you. I shall be very proud to do so. And both of us will take the consequences."

....

For the ladies who accompanied the battalion's officers to the Ball, there was a propriety of dress; long gown, white gloves — up to a certain length on the arms, no more or less. All the ladies were to contact the colonel's lady, who would instruct them. This was an obligation as Bob Banfield's wife that Mary Banfield detested. Each year she professed indignation at having to play the role of "headmistress to a snobbish girls' school." But each year she complied, "for Bob, my soldier boy bloody colonel!"

Major Jim Niles entered the colonel's office, and saluted.

"Hello, Jim! Always good to see you. Please have a seat. Now, what's on your mind? If it's those bloody trucks again, C.O.D. promises on a stack of bibles that there are six new ones on the way!"

Jim laughed. C.O. is acting like I am making a nuisance of myself! Gung-ho company commander, conniving to get everything he can for his company! God, what a turnaround!

"No, Bob! Nothing so banal! I am....taking a young lady to the Passchendaele Ball. I....thought I would clear it with you, for her to give Mary a call about the regulation dress...."

"Jesus, Jim, so that's all! Consider it done! Mary would be glad to provide the gen. Our number is in the directory. So glad you are coming. May I ask if I know the lady?"

"You know....about her, Bob. Laura LaChance."

Bob stared at him, struggling to mask any sign of disapproval on his face. My God, the man is serious. A fellow could get his ass trimmed for less! So this is the reason he's changed so drastically! But she's a married woman. And to that ex-R.C.E.M.E. fool....

"Jim....forgive me....it's your business, but it is mine as well, unfortunately....You know what you are doing...."

"I do. We....are seeing a great deal of each other. And when she gets her divorce, I plan to marry her."

There was defiance in his voice. This sounded like the "old Jim" Bob had had so much difficulty with in the past; better be handled with supreme tact.

"Will you allow me simply to say — please be careful. There are so many damned rules and traditions — you know about them better than I. Well, so much for that. I'm sure Mary will be glad to talk with Laura. I....look forward to meeting her."

After Jim left Bob's office, Bob sat at his desk, with his head in his hands.

Jesus, Bob thought, after all that you have gone through, after the Verrières Ridge and what it did to you, now that you are freeing yourself from all that redemption nonsense and I have acquired a top-rate company commander, you are going to throw it all on married woman! The Army has forgiven a great deal, but an affair with an ex-corporal's wife — never! Damn it, why are you so determined to destroy yourself? Damn it, to hell!

....

Laura called Mary Banfield. But Mary did more than settle for a phone call. She invited Laura to have lunch with her. They met in a little French restaurant off Richmond Street.

Although there was a difference of ten years between them, and Mary was the wife of Jim's commanding officer, she and Laura discovered that they enjoyed each other's company immensely. Mary was greatly impressed with Laura's warmth and spontaneity. Laura in turn sensed how sincere and unaffected Mary was, so delightfully different from many of the wives of senior army officers.

It did not take long for Mary to instruct Laura about how she should dress for the occasion. Most of the time, they simply enjoyed chatting with each other. Mary learned, without possible doubt, how Laura felt about Jim Niles; the beautiful young woman was very much in love.

After their pleasant luncheon, Mary drove Laura back to her apartment, and then returned to her home in Wolseley Barracks. Bob joined her after he had completed his duties for the day.

"Bob, she's positively charming! I can think of no woman better suited for Jim Niles. I really do believe that what they have between them is serious and enduring. But under the circumstances I'm afraid for them, Bob. God help them...."

....

The great occasion arrived. The large gymnasium at the Barracks was lit up with colored lights. Spotlights illuminated the wide entrance. The battalion's provost section was employed in traffic control, which included parking the cars on the nearby playing field.

Captain Michael Baldwin arrived with his wife Alison, in their blue Pontiac.

"Good evening, sir! Mrs. Baldwin! Great evening for the Ball. Park over here, sir." Michael recognised the provost sergeant, Willie Gallant, in his khaki overcoat, with gleaming white web-belt and cross straps.

"Good evening, Sergeant Gallant. Thank you."

The sergeant helped Alison out of the car, and she and Michael walked to the entrance of the gym and directly into the foyer. The cloakroom was to one side. The attendants in this area were all dressed in the uniforms of the First World War. To outfit them, the battalion had had to deplete the regimental museum. The service dress was of a coarser, darker khaki. The tunic extended below the wide web belt with its brass buckle, and was buttoned up with brass buttons to the collar. On both sides of the collar, and on the peaked khaki cap, was the regimental badge. On the sleeves was the blue patch of the Second Division, about the only part of the uniform which remained unchanged for yet another World War. Two soldiers with Lee-Enfield rifles stood at attention on either side of the inner entrance. Michael recognised both from the battalion's corps of drums, the "rainmakers", who were his stretcher-bearers when the battalion was in the field.

He handed over his khaki raincoat and peaked cap, and Alison her cape, at the counter of the cloakroom. He walked over to the young soldiers, armed and uniformed from an age gone by. "Well, you people have quite a job tonight! How long do you have to stand like that?"

Both men stared ahead, silent and motionless. They were, after all, at attention. Then, when he thought that he was safe, one of the lads whispered, barely audibly, his eyes still focused ahead: "We'll be finished as soon as you bastards are all inside!" Michael smiled. He could have charged him with insubordination. He would not have dared to speak that way to an infantry officer. But Michael knew that this part-time stretcher-bearer of his trusted and admired him enough to communicate his inmost feelings, even though he had in so doing violated the code of service discipline.

When he and Alison walked through the inside entrance, the full glory of the ballroom decor struck them. The massive walls were festooned with blue and yellow bunting and streamers, the colors of the regiment. On the walls hung huge plaques, commemorating the battle honors of the regiment from the First World War: "Mount Sorrel 1916", "Vimy Ridge 1917", "Canal du Nord 1918", and of course "Passchendaele 1917". On one end of the great hall, tables had been set up for the patrons, covered with white tablecloths, decorated with flowers and plaster-of-Paris replicas in miniature of the old army peaked cap, souvenirs to be taken home after the ball. On each table were name plates for each of the patrons. On the side, a bar. At the other end a bandstand, also gaily decorated with bunting, occupied by the regimental band, resplendent in their scarlet and blue uniforms, with white pith helmets.

The floor of the hall was filling with people. Michael looked appreciatively at all the pretty women in their colorful full-length gowns, who charmed the setting with a sea of bare shoulders. The civilian men were in black tie. The army officers were in scarlet dress uniform, their scarlet mess kits adding color to the impressive scene. Their uniforms glittered with gold and silver braid, the more senior of them with rows of medals attached to the left breast of their jackets. Michael himself was required to wear the dress blues, with his leather Sam Browne belt and cross strap, since he was officially on duty. After all, they needed a doctor around, in case some old vet collapsed.....

Just inside the inner entrance was the inevitable reception line. As the commanding officer of the resident battalion, Bob Banfield was on the line, with Mary at his side. So was the mayor of London and his wife, and the lieutenant governor of the province. And also, on the line, was Brigadier Horace Timpson, commander of the Western Ontario Area. He was tall, angular and balding, with a bushy moustache which twitched nervously when he was under pressure. He had served as a brigade commander in Italy during the Second World War. But as Canada had very few major generals in peacetime, there was to be no further promotion for him, and he was scheduled for retirement the following year. His policy was to live out the remaining time of his service career without rocking the boat if at all possible. He detested administrative problems, and was well known in his headquarters for delegating as much of the difficult work as he could to his staff officers. His wife Melinda was with him, a gaunt, shrivelled woman with a pinched face and thin, cold lips.

As the Baldwins moved to the reception line, they were sonorously announced by Regimental Sergeant Major George Walton, this being the traditional task of the RSM at formal balls.

"Captain and Mrs. Baldwin!"

"Good evening, Mike!" from Bob Banfield. "Alison, good to see you again!"

"Hello Mike! Alison, you do look pretty!" from Mary.

"Good evening," a glassy stare from the brigadier, and a mere nod from Mrs. Timpson.

"How are you, captain?" from the mayor.

The RSM carried on. "Mr. and Mrs. Montague. Captain and Mrs. McGreggor. Mr. and Mrs. Howarth-Jones. Miss Dionne and Mr. Tremblay...." On and on.

Jim Niles arrived with Laura. The RSM looked to Jim and asked: "Major Niles, sir, may I have the name of your guest."

"Laura LaChance."

"Sir, shall I announce Miss?"

"No, Mrs. LaChance."

"Mrs. LaChance and Major Niles!" came the announcement.

Jim and Laura were greeted with warmth and civility by all, except by the brigadier and his wife. The brigadier's moustache began to twitch. Who was this damned woman the major was escorting? Divorcee — or was he having a fling, and brazenly flaunting it before him! The name again — Niles was it? Good God, James Niles' son? Will have to talk with Banfield about this! No handshake for Jim, merely a stiff bow of the head. No recognition at all for Laura. The brigadier's wife simply glared at them, and said nothing.

When they had moved along past the reception line, Jim said, "Laura, I'm damned sorry the brigadier was so rude to you. What a pompous old goat...."

"It's all right! We're going to enjoy ourselves. I have never been to anything like this, and I am impressed! It's like — something from a Hollywood movie about Napoleon's time. The officers all look so handsome in their scarlet uniforms. And you, dear man, are the handsomest of them all! Let's find our table so I can leave my purse. I can't wait to have our first dance!"

....

Jim danced with Laura, one dance after the other. He could not keep his eyes off her. From the day that he met her, he had found her exquisitely beautiful, but on this night she was devastatingly so. Her thick dark hair was expertly coiffed, done up in the back, in the current bee-hive style. She wore a white satin strapless gown, closely fitting to accentuate her bust and slim waist, below which it flared outward, and down to her silver low-heeled shoes. Once again, Jim had brought her a red rose when he came to escort her to the ball, this time in a corsage, which she had decided to wear in her hair. She wore long white gloves, almost up to her elbows. Her entire ensemble complemented the dark, warm tones of her face, neck and bare shoulders. For this occasion, she wore dark red lipstick.

Laura's left hand rested on Jim's right shoulder, lightly on the gold braid and crown, designating his rank. This officer is mine, Laura kept telling herself. This is what I have always wanted. And he is mine forever.

As they danced, Laura allowed her gaze to wander, taking in all the elegance and splendor of the military ball, bathing in its delights. The regimental band had a string section as well as its brass instruments, and it played with virtuoso skill. There was considerable variety, to Laura's surprise, who expected rather staid dance music. There were waltzes, fox trots, some Latin American numbers, and to the glee of the younger set, the rock music of Elvis Presley, who was coming into vogue. When Jim hesitated, Laura said: "Hey, watch me! I'll show you!"

At the first intermission, Jim got them drinks, and they sat on the folding chairs at their table. Food was served by the mess stewards on duty. Laura was amazed that the military cooks could prepare such daintily garnished dishes. Nothing was spared to indulge the people at the ball.

They were joined by Lieutenant Peter Forsythe and another young subaltern. Both had arrived without dates. Their attendance was required, since for them the ball was a parade. But this did not daunt the young officers. They knew that after the first dances, many of the captains and majors would abandon their wives, and congregate about the bar, as if they could not do without their own company. This left the way open for the young officers to select whichever "abandoned women" they chose to dance with. Frequently, these soirées led to the most titillating extramarital affairs! Jim Niles knew exactly what these young shave-tails were up to.

"Good evening, Jim! Will you please introduce us to your charming lady?"

The music started again. Peter Forsythe asked to dance this next number with Laura. Laura hesitated, and looked to Jim for acquiescence.

"Of course, darling. I'll wait for you here."

Jim watched Laura dance with Peter Forsythe. To his amusement, consternation, and yet with surging pride, subaltern after subaltern cut in, and it was three dances later when Peter Forsythe escorted Laura back to Jim. Kissing her hand, he said: "Laura, you are unquestionably the most beautiful lady at the ball. It has been my great privilege to have danced with you. I speak for those other subalterns as well. Jim, you are indeed fortunate!"

....

"Ladies and gentlemen!" It was Captain Parsifal, the director of the regimental band on the microphone. "We have a special treat for you! Sergeant Lorne Jamieson and his vocal group will now entertain you with a medley of songs. As you know, our regimental colors are yellow and blue. And the songs are about just that! Yellow and blue! Take it away, Sergeant Jamieson!"

The young sergeant approached the microphone. He was tall, with blond hair. His rich baritone voice captivated the audience. At times singing solo, and at times in harmony with the three other bandsmen, the sergeant fill the hall with the old, familiar melodies, masterfully woven together:

"Round her neck, she wore a yellow ribbon

She wore it for a soldier who was far, far away...

"Blue, blue, my heart is blue...."

"The yellow rose of Texas...."

Sergeant Jamieson bowed to the audience, as they applauded resoundingly. "Thank you, thank you, ladies and gentlemen. And now as our final number, to get you folks dancing again, a real 'oldie' —- Blue Moon...."

"Blue Moon,

You saw me standing alone,

Without a song in my heart,

Without a love of my own.

Blue moon,

You knew just what I was there for....."

A slow, intimate dance. Jim and Laura listened to the words. To both, it seemed that the singer had especially chosen the song for them. Laura looked at Jim, locked her hands around his neck, and pressed her head against his chest. He held her around the waist.

"Jim," she murmured, "this has been the greatest day of my life. I don't want it to end. I love you, I don't want to lose you. I have waited so long. We have not had much time..." Her eyes welled with tears.

"Hey, now, it's O.K. My darling girl, there are going to be many more balls like this. You and I have a lifetime together before of us. I will never let you go, Laura, never.... You and I are married. We are as married as any couple could be. Some day, when you get your divorce, we will take care of the legalities. But we could not be more married now, if a thousand bishops had married us...."

...."Blue Moon,

Now I'm no longer alone,

There is a song in my heart,

I have a love of my own."

Laura thought. No, I will never lose you. No matter what happens. But it has all been so beautiful and wonderful for us...it cannot last...I'm so afraid...

....

The Passchendaele Ball of 1959 drew to a close. As a final salute to all the members of the fair sex who had so delightfully graced this festive occasion, the regimental band played for the last dance, "Goodnight, Ladies!" Then, the traditional drum-roll sounded, and the band broke into its forceful rendition of "O Canada". All stood to attention, officer and civilian alike. The lights in the hall brightened, and they began to depart, holding in their hands their souvenirs of the ball. Captain and major, lieutenant and civilian, brigadier and mayor, each left with his or her own fond memories.

Laura and Jim drove back to her apartment. Once again, they sat together on the floor in front of the chesterfield, she still in her gown and he in his mess kit uniform. Her head was against his shoulder, and he had his arm around her. They remained quietly that way for some time, as each thought about the ball, and the feelings they shared. For them, it had been far more than an enjoyable military ball. It had also been a public declaration that they were a couple, regardless of consequences. It had been in fact a form of marriage ceremony.

Laura turned to him. "Jim, it has been so wonderful, I don't want you to leave tonight. I want you to stay with me. I want us to go to bed — now, if we can find the energy to get up! Dear boy, I'm propositioning you. Let's sin!"

Jim laughed. "Laura, don't let me get in the way of your licentiousness! Funny, I thought only soldiers were licentious — never nurses, eh?"

"Hey, I'm going to teach you some more about nurses!"

Jim wondered how it would appear to the gate guard, for him to roll in some time late Sunday, still with his mess kit on! But he had long ago concluded that he belonged here with Laura, that the apartment had become his home as well, and that it was only a matter of time before he moved in with her, officially married or not, with or without the Army's blessing. To be with her was more important than anything else.

They went into the bedroom. Without hesitation, Laura set about to undress Jim. "You know, this is real fun, stripping an officer of the Queen in full ceremonial dress uniform! Let's do this more often!"

CHAPTER EIGHTEEN

For Jim and Laura, the weeks which followed the Passchendaele Ball were idyllic. They spent every evening and week-end together, when neither was on duty, and most of the nights. Colonel Banfield watched with increasing consternation, sorely conflicted; should he haul his love-struck major in for disciplinary measures, or stand by for the inevitable reaction from the higher authorities. Never since he had taken command of the battalion had Bob Banfield faced such a vexing situation. This was not some young subaltern involved in a messy amorous tangle. Jim Niles was a field officer. Since the major was conducting himself as if he were oblivious to the potential consequences of his affair, and since he continued to function as an exemplary company commander, Bob decided to wait. He knew that it was only a question of time before he would hear from his immediate superior, the commander of Western Ontario Area, Brigadier Horace Timpson.

....

With each passing month since his separation from Laura, Patrick LaChance brooded about the loss of his marriage. At first, he tried to convince himself that no woman, least of all Laura, would be able to resist him, and that it was only a question of time, with a little harassment, and a few physical threats, before she would see the error of her ways, that there was after all no other man with his irresistible virile charms, and she would beg him to come back. He plotted the ways he would punish her for her ridiculous transgressions against him, and on bended knee she would beg his forgiveness. He continued periodically to park outside her apartment, to wait for his chance to set matters right between them. He lived in seedy rooming houses in the south part of London. He found employment in service stations in the city, but at each job he refused to take orders from his employers, was consistently rude to the customers, and was invariably fired. When he ran out of funds, he returned to Lafontaine to live with his parents, to lick his wounds, and to be reminded by his doting mother that it was everyone else who was out of step and not he. Then he would drive back to London.

One evening, he decided that the time was ripe to pay Laura a visit. Jim was with Laura in her apartment and an ugly confrontation ensued. Jim asked Laura to call the police, while he stood at the door. Patrick lunged at Jim, but found himself abruptly thrown to the floor, with a painfully twisted arm and shoulder. Never having been trained in unarmed combat, since the R.C.E.M.E. was a service of the Army, not a combat arm, he made the mistake of taking on an infantry officer well trained in such skills. By the time the police arrived, he had run off, cursing Jim loudly with the strongest epithets in his limited vocabulary, and threatening vengeance.

To console himself, he drove to the Silver Dollar on Oxford Street, a favorite watering-hole for the soldiers at Wolseley Barracks. When he walked in, he immediately saw the two Headquarters Company clerks, sitting at a table, cheerily consuming their beer. Both were out of uniform.

Lance Corporal Kono Suzuki turned to his pal Porky. "Jeeze, man, I smell skunk. Now you're a country boy. Do you smell skunk, Porky?"

"Sure do, Kono! How the hell did it get in here?"

"Hey, you clowns, you're talkin' to a corporal! Let's have more respect!"

"Go screw yourself, LaChance! You ain't no corporal no more! You're a fuckin' civvie, and the worst type! I got no time of day for you! Get lost!"

Patrick LaChance moved towards the two young soldiers, with his fists up. "Care to come outside and say that again?"

"I told you, I got no time for a man who fucks up in the service, gets sent to the digger, and then gets turfed out on a dishonorable discharge!"

"You two morons better believe I was framed. Your fuckin' major framed me, so he could screw my wife! Did you know that?"

"Shit! We all know Major Niles has a thing for your ex-wife - get it? - your ex-wife! You were never man enough to keep a woman. A woman would have to have rocks in her head to put up with scum like you!"

"Oh, yeah? Think your Goddamn' major is any better'n me? I heard different. I heard he was a fuckin' coward during the war...."

"You shove off, LaChance! We ain't goin' to stand by and hear you insult our major! If you want a fight, you're gonna get one!"

"I'm with you, Kono! C'm on, let's get the bastard...."

"Now, hold it, both of you!" A burly sergeant in battledress uniform had entered the bar, and overheard the commotion. "I recognize you. You're LaChance. I don't want you causing trouble with any of our men! You're out of the Army, aren't you? If you were still in, I'd put you on charge. I have no jurisdiction over you, but if you don't get the hell out of this pub now, you'll answer to me. Be a good fellow, now, and leave peaceably."

Patrick got the message. One defeat was enough for one evening. Once again, screaming invectives, he departed.

"Thank you, sergeant. That guy was not worth getting into a fight with, and ending up in trouble."

"You got it! Never mind what that idiot said about Major Niles. Let's not have any idle gossip about our officers. Bad for morale! Go finish your beers!"

....

Brigadier Horace Timpson, Commander, Western Ontario Area, sat at his desk in his office, drumming his fingers on the desk and scowling at the photostatted copy of the personnel file of one SB 293109 Pte LaChance, P., who had been demoted from the rank of corporal and released from the Canadian Army last July on dishonorable discharge, having served a two month sentence in the detention barracks at Camp Borden. Next to it was a letter the brigadier had received two weeks previously, from the same P. LaChance. The letter was what prompted the brigadier to request copies of the former soldier's records, before he decided what action to take.

What he read in the file disgusted him. Really, this was too much. This man LaChance was a rogue and a shirker. He simply was incapable of soldiering. It was all absolutely no good at all. All this damned nonsense about refusing to take orders, gross insubordination, repeatedly A.W.O.L. Why, in the good old days, he would have been more than two months in the ruddy glass house. Indeed, some patriotic provost staff sergeant would have seen to it that LaChance perished accidentally while doing his punishment. In the good old days....Fighting the Hun....There was my brigade, deployed to take the next objective, two battalions up, one in brigade reserve. Div would ensure the right sort of artillery barrage. Squadron of Shermans on the crest. Great show! Damned fine lads we had then. Always took their objective .... except for that time, when Jerry gave them a bit of a bloody nose....had the supreme gall to drive them back <u>behind</u> the artillery lines. What a rocket from the div G.O.C.! "Horace, we can't have this sort of thing, old man! It simply is not laid on for the arty to have to defend itself against Jerry infantry! There's a good fellow. Do sort it out, will you? I want your infantry in front of any arty I happen to send your way!" God, that was a nasty bit of work....

But this, here. Frightful waste of a brigadier. Should be leading men in battle — not sorting out ex-corporals writing nasty letters about their wives being seduced by majors! It's all simply not done! Dreadful handwriting. Not much schooling here. No sense of propriety whatsoever. Filthy language. Why didn't the blighter challenge the major to a duel or something? And the major in question is James Niles' son! Damn the luck! Jamie and I served in Ottawa together after the war. Damned fine sort, Brigadier Niles. Rotten luck about the Army not sending him overseas for a field command during W.W. Two. Kept him at Army H.Q. all through the show instead. But Jamie knew the ropes in Ottawa. Great man to work with. Retired now....as I shall be soon....

Major James Niles. Presently serving as O.C., H.Q. Company, with the battalion at the Barracks. Bit of a dark horse, this lad. Poor show in Normandy in '44. Got the wind up at Verrières. His father wanted me to keep an eye on young Jim when he was posted to Wontarea. Disgraceful business at the Passchendaele Ball. Escorting a married woman past the reception line! And a corporal's wife at that! Simply will not do.... But she was dashed pretty....

The brigadier pressed a button at the side of his desk. Into his office walked CSM Grenier, who ran the clerical services at Area H.Q.

"Yes, sir."

"Ah, Sah'nt-major, there you are. Now here's the gen. I want you first to put a call through for me to Colonel Banfield at the battalion. Then, see if you can chase up a Brigadier James Niles who lives in Ottawa. The brigadier is retired. I want to talk to him."

"Very good, sir. I'll get Colonel Banfield first. Then I'll see what I can do to locate Brigadier Niles for you."

....

Brigadier Timpson was not altogether satisfied with his telephone conversation with Lieutenant Colonel Banfield. The colonel admitted that he knew that Major Niles was involved in an affair with Mrs. LaChance. After all, so did the entire battalion. But he felt that it was the major's business, and that Colonel Banfield had every confidence that Major Niles would in due course resolve these delicate issues to the satisfaction of all concerned, including the good name of the Army. He insisted that Major Niles attended to his duties in an exemplary manner, and that he could wish for no better field officer to command H.Q. Company.

What a bore, this man Banfield! Commissioned from the ranks, war hero and all that, but he is really not one of us! Never attended R.M.C. Good soldier, but no family tradition. But I'll say this for him — he's loyal to his subordinate officer — too much so, perhaps. Have these two known each other for long? Good God, Banfield might have been in Niles' own unit overseas!

CSM Grenier knocked on the brigadier's door. "Sir, I have Brigadier Niles on the line."

"Oh, good show, sah'nt-major! Thank you. Er....close the door after you leave....rather personal, this call."

"Right away, sir." The CSM departed.

"Hello, Jamie, that you, old chum?"

"Horace! A great pleasure to chat with you again. Let's see, when was the last time? Good grief, that was when our young Jim was posted to your Area. How are things up at the 'sharp end'? And how is Melinda?"

"Just first class, Horace, first class! And you? Enjoying your retirement, I trust? And Roselyn?"

"Oh, yes, we're fine! Well, dash it, I miss the old uniform and all that! Gets in the blood, Horace!"

"Jamie, old man, I really must get to the point of this call. It's about....well, it's about young Jim."

There was silence. "Hello, Jamie, you still there?"

"Yes, Horace. Well, what has the lad been up to? Deficient leadership skills again? Poor attitude to the Service?"

"No, no, not at all. As a matter of fact, I was just on the blower with his C.O. Claims he makes a damned fine company commander in his battalion."

"I find that rather difficult to swallow, considering how he behaved both in Normandy and since. But perhaps he has....shall we say, matured. Then what is the problem?"

"James, I don't know how to put this — really not my bag, this sort of shenanigan. Well, the truth of the matter is, Jim has been consorting with a married woman. As a matter of fact, the wife of a corporal in the battalion — that is, an ex-corporal. The good corporal was charged by your son, and convicted by the battalion commander. He was sent to the D.B. and then released. The way I see it, she put her husband out, and Jim is now actively courting her. This, of course, puts a bit of a burr under the ex-corporal's blanket. Got a rather filthy letter from him recently, claiming he was framed when he was sent to the D.B., to permit Jim to....well, have access to his wife. No legal action threatened. But it's all rather messy, what? Wanted to apprise you of these matters. What would you suggest we do?"

There was another silence. "Horace, I'm grateful to you for letting me know. I'm....disappointed in my son. It....hasn't been the only time. Can't have him sullying the name of the officer corps — or for that matter, the family name. Damned inconsiderate of him. Well, we shall have to take action. I think an immediate posting will be the answer — even on a temporary detachment basis. A few months away from London may well cool things, would you not say?"

"Yes, it sounds the way to go on this."

"Horace, I still have pretty good connections with the personnel directorate at Army H.Q. here in Ottawa. Leave it with me. You'll be hearing soon. And thank you."

"Cherrio, Jamie!"

Now here's a man! Real Army, to the bone. Problem arises, problem is analyzed, solution determined and corrective action taken. No shillyshallying around. Good old Jamie....

But his moustache would not stop twitching.

....

Bob Banfield, too, waited uneasily for what the Army would conjure up for Jim Niles and his affair with Laura. He was deeply concerned. During the past months, Niles had worked hard towards becoming a competent, respected company commander and he deserved some measure of happiness and personal comfort in his life. Laura obviously had been a true Godsend, and Bob feared a tragic ending to the affair. The Army had no business meddling in Jim Niles' private life. But he was a field officer, with the name of Niles, and the Army would not tolerate his involvement with a married woman. Bob also knew, that whereas it would often take an eternity for command approval of a certain project, or for necessary supplies or equipment procured after indent, whenever a possible scandal could in one way or other affect its officer corps, the Army would react with stunning alacrity. Yes, sir, no sooner said than done....

Bob was in his office, signing strength returns, when Sergeant Theo Morgan appeared at his open door.

"Sir, this just came from Wontarea. Posting orders. Thought you better take a look, before they appear tomorrow on standing orders."

"What have we got here, Sergeant Morgan?" The smile left Bob Banfield's face as he read the document. "Jesus Christ....and we all know why...."

"Yes, sir; it's damned unfair."

"Well, we're all in this man's Army, and we all have to take orders. Notify Major Robertson of Alpha Company, so he can alert Lieutenant Forsythe. And please ask Major Niles to come to my office right away. I will tell him myself."

Within minutes, Jim Niles was in Bob Banfield's office. Bob closed the door behind him, and beckoned Jim to sit down. Bob sat on the edge of his desk.

"Jim, I have important news for you. Posting orders have just been received from Wontarea for both you and Peter Forsythe of Alpha Company. As of 19 December, you will be temporarily struck off strength from the battalion, and taken on strength by the United Nations Emergency Force in the Sinai and Gaza. This will be a detached posting, for a period of six months. For Peter, it will be a 'swan'. For you....I know this has come at a bad time."

"Oh, Christ, Bob! After all that has happened this year, this is some reward! I knew damned well I'd have to pay a penalty, one way or the other, for my happiness with Laura. Well, I have made up my mind about her, and there is nothing the Army can do to change that. The relationship is permanent, Bob. She is the most important thing in my life. The Army takes second place to her.

"Well, I'll go to the Middle East, as ordered. But I know damned well, that whether or not Laura is successful in getting her divorce and I marry her, the relationship between us will never be sanctioned by the Army. My father and all the demigods in Ottawa will see to that. So my course is clear. When I return, I'm going to live with Laura, and shall resign my commission. The only life I've ever known has been the Army — until I met Laura. I have no bitterness or resentment of the Army anymore. It's time to look into what civilian life has to offer....seems that was what you asked me to consider, when I got back from the Ipperwash march."

They talked at length that afternoon. Time was rapidly running out, and they felt an urgency to communicate, to share feelings together. They talked about Laura, and the situation she would be facing when Jim was overseas. Bob reassured Jim that both he and Mary would maintain contact with her. They talked about U.N.E.F., the international peace-keeping force which came into being at the end of the 1956 Sinai campaign, whose purpose was to keep the Arabs and the Israelis apart along the Armistice Demarcation Line, in the forlorn hope of preventing further incidents that might lead to full-scale war. The Canadian Army furnished a reconnaissance squadron, and administrative staff. Both Jim and Peter were to be posted to the operations and intelligence branch of U.N.E.F. Headquarters.

Jim thanked Bob for taking the time to talk with him. With his characteristic optimism, Bob conveyed his fervent hope that his jaunt to the Middle East would be a pleasant one, and that he would soon be back with Laura, even if this meant that he would be leaving the Army.

Jim left Bob's office, and walked into the orderly room. He approached Sergeant Morgan.

"Well, sir, C.O. briefed you about your posting?"

"Yes, Sergeant Morgan. The next few days will be rather busy. I'll have to be equipped and kitted out for the Middle East. Thank God we've been on U.N. standby — I don't think I shall need any more needles from the M.O.! But today, there is one thing I want you to look after for me; my service will. I want to change my beneficiary. It will henceforth read 'Laura LaChance'. Will you take care of it, sergeant, so I can sign the documents before I leave?"

"Yes, Major Niles. I'll get on it, right away."

CHAPTER NINETEEN

Jim had dinner at the Officer's Mess. Laura was on afternoon shift, and would not be home until after midnight. Word about his posting had already got around. He was greeted by a number of the regulars, curious about the sudden posting, wishing him a safe trip and a speedy return, and offering their sympathy over his having to spend Christmas in "that damned desert". Peter Forsythe, however, could not contain his excitement at the prospect of soldiering in the ancient biblical land. He breathlessly shook Jim's hand, declaring to all his joy that Jim was going with him. What great fun they would have together! And did the "bints" do the strip on the Gaza Strip!

"Why do you think the two of us were chosen for this? And why now?" Peter asked.

"Each Area is required to supply officers and other ranks on rotation, for the United Nations peacekeeping commands. This type of posting will probably become more common, as Canada commits herself more and more to these operations. God knows how the individual selections are made; it's likely all left to some faceless corporal at DND." Jim kept to himself his conviction that his selection had been anything but random.

After dinner, he drove to Laura's apartment, and let himself in with his key. He poured himself a drink of scotch, and sat down on the chesterfield. While he waited for Laura to return, his thoughts turned to his relationship with her, and the love they shared. They had had so little time together, yet they had experienced so much. It had seemed like a lifetime of deep loving, intense commitment and consuming passion.

Laura got home just at midnight. When Jim heard her outside the door, he got up and opened it for her. "Hello, lover! I'm glad you're back!" He kissed her gently, then stepped back, and looked at her with loving admiration. She wore her brown woolen overcoat, buttoned over her white uniform. Her hair was still pinned up, under a pale yellow scarf.

"Hello, darling! It's so nice finding you here waiting for me!" He helped her out of her coat. She pulled the hair-pins out, and let the dark tresses fall against her neck and shoulders. She looked at him again. Instantly, she detected that something had happened; he was gazing at her with deep longing and profound sadness.

"Jim, what's wrong? What is it ..."

"Laura, I'm being posted to the Middle East. I'm leaving in a week. I'll be gone for six months. Oh God, Laura, I don't want to leave you......"

They were in each other's arms, clinging, as if to let go would be to lose each other forever.

Laura spoke softly, still holding him tightly. "Jim, lover, darling, you are a soldier. This sort of thing happens to soldiers, it always has. Only, so often they go to war, and never come back. Thank God you are not going to war. And you know when you will be back. And, darling, I will be here, as always, waiting for you! We have the rest of our lives ahead of us, to be together. Now, I think I am going to have some sherry — not that awful scotch you got for yourself!"

"Laura — will you really wait? I mean .... you're so beautiful. I know damned well that you could have any man you wanted....."

"Jim, *tais-toi, alors! Tu es mon homme, il y a aucun autre!* There is only you, Jim, only you, for ever. All my life, I have waited for you. Do you think I would be stupid enough to give you up — even for six months! I will always be with you, wherever you are, no matter how many thousands of miles away. And I know very well, you feel the same about me....."

Jim covered her mouth with his before she could finish. With reverent tenderness and unbridled passion, he kissed her. For a while, they sat on the floor in front of the chesterfield, their arms around each other.

"Jim, I told you, seems like so long ago, I don't hate the Army — not even now. I ... respect the Army. I guess that was how I was raised .... even when I heard about René ... I was so little then. Am I right, Jim, was it your father? You know, because of us. The brigadier must have .... connections..."

"I believe you are right, but I shall never know with certainty. U.N.E.F. needed an infantry major. Army H.Q. decided that Wontarea was next to provide one. And I was it. But, all this stuff about the honor of the officer corps, a bachelor field officer and a separated woman, especially ... no matter. It's done. Christ, if I had met you before you married, Laura...."

"You would have thought I was impossibly naive and hopelessly insubordinate; not suitable material for an officer's wife!"

Jim laughed. How skilled Laura was, he thought, making him laugh even under the most trying circumstances. No one had been able to do that before. He sighed. There was only a week left, before his posting. There were things to be taken care of. He wanted her to have his car, and she agreed, promising to accord it the tender care he had always given it. He was required to store his possessions, since his room at the Quarters could not be held for him. Could Laura take some of the more personal items, so they would not be pilfered by some inquisitive batman?

Laura looked at Jim. "Hey, soldier boy, wanna good time? Wanna go make love?"

"Why, you wanton wench! There is nothing I would like better!"

They undressed each other, got into bed, and made love with a slow and tender intensity. Afterwards, as they lay in each other's arms, they shared a long, quiet time of total intimacy and oneness, confirming a bond that nothing could break. Eventually, they kissed each other good night, and soon afterwards Jim fell asleep. Laura studied him as he slept. "Dear man," she whispered, "I know this is forever. But I have a terrible feeling inside me that I am going to lose you, not just for six months, but for all the time we could have had together on this earth. Is this a punishment from God? How could God punish two people who deeply love each other? Is it so evil, for a man to love a woman separated from her husband? And why is the Army so strict and unbending with its officers? Oh, Jim, my lover .... my real husband .... if only we had met before....."

....

The last week was a frantic one. There were several conferences with Colonel Banfield and the Battalion Headquarters staff, regarding the arrangements during his absence. Captain Leo Toland, the Transport Officer, was to take over Headquarters Company, and a young lieutenant, recently arrived, would run the transport platoon. Jim and Peter Forsythe were frequently at the quartermaster's stores, being kitted out for the

Middle East. They acquired the pale blue beret to go with the pale blue helmet. The United Nations blue patches were sewn on their battle-dress sleeves, to replace the red patch of the First Division. They were issued bush uniforms for the hot days, and khaki sweaters for the cold nights. To their dismay, Michael Baldwin discovered more inoculations were required before they left.

Laura managed to work exclusively on day shift, during this week, and Jim spent every spare moment with her. They went to bed together every night, and made love. Sleep itself was rare, as if both refused to waste any moment of their time together.

The day came. Major Niles and Lieutenant Forsythe were to be picked up outside the Officer's Quarters at 0700 hours. Before he went off duty for the last time, Jim spoke with Colonel Banfield. Bob confirmed that he and Mary would stay in touch with Laura, and visit with her. Jim asked Bob to convey his best regards to Ronnie Matthews and Tom Brennan, the old Three Platoon vets. Bob readily agreed, but felt a sense of foreboding in this request, as if Jim were settling his affairs before a final departure.

Jim spent the last night with Laura. The following morning, they had an early breakfast together, although neither had much appetite. He told her that he did not want to say "goodbye" in the cold, formal setting of a military camp, under the gaze of passing soldiery. "I prefer to remember you in this warm, loving place, which has been more of a home to me than I have ever had in my life." He handed her his car keys. He reminded her of the Christmas presents he had left for her on the shelf in her closet. "No opening them until Christmas Day, remember!" Laura gave him her present, a tiny box, gift-wrapped. " Darling, this is to keep you close to me, wherever you go. Carry it with you. Open it on Christmas Day. It will remind you of me, so you will never forget."

"Laura, you will be with me in my thoughts always. I will treasure your gift, whatever it is, always."

Jim called for a taxi. There was a last, lingering farewell. Laura wept uncontrollably. Jim dried her tears. "I'll write often, whenever I can. But don't worry if my letters don't arrive regularly; you know the vagaries of the army postal service."

He urged her not to leave the apartment. As he got into the taxi, he waved to her in the bedroom window, and blew her a kiss. The taxi drove off.

Laura lingered at the window, watching the taxi disappear into the distance. Her period had been late this month. Was it possible she was pregnant, or was this delay the result of all the stress and excitement and heartbreak of the last few days?

"Jim, my love, you have my love forever, no matter what happens. Please come back to me. Life would be meaningless without you. But if I am carrying our child, then I will have him to raise, regardless of what may happen. Our child, conceived in total love, would give purpose to my life, even if I were to lose you.

"Mon amour, je t'implore, retourne à moi, plus vite. Que le bon Dieu te protége......"

Sickened with heartbreak, she left the window, threw herself on her bed, and sobbed.

....

RCAF Station Marville, France

21 December 1959

My Darling,

How are you? Already, I miss you terribly. How on God's earth am I to get through the next six months, so far away from you?

We caught the flight from Dorval, which took us to London, then on to Marville in France, close to Metz. We got in here last night. Rather a rocky trip across the drink, and unbelievably noisy! North Star crews must all be deaf after flying these planes continuously. Perhaps they rev their engines to make it even noisier when they know Army people are on board. In half an hour, we will be off to Naples, which is the U.N.E.F. staging and supply base for the Gaza and Sinai operations.

Laura, please look after yourself. You are my very life — I could not live without you. Will write every chance I get. I love you, *ma cherie* — *je t'aime* — I love you.

Forever your Jim.

U.N.E.F. Supply Base

Capodichino Airfield

Naples, Italy

22 December 1959

My Darling,

Here we are in sunny Italy, except it is in the middle of the night. We arrived here this afternoon. One continuous round of briefings since then — no chance to write until now. In four hours, before dawn, we will be taking off again, this time in one of those damned flying boxcars —C-119's — which will take us across the Mediterranean to El Arish, the U.N. airfield in the Sinai, about 40 km from the Gaza Strip, which is our ultimate destination.

How are you, love? I miss you more than ever. Seems like an eternity since we said goodbye three days ago. Will you please take good care of yourself, Laura. Laura, Laura, Laura — you are on my mind constantly. And you are also with me — no matter how far apart we are.

I love you forever. Jim.

....

U.N.E.F. Supply Base

El Arish, Egypt

23 December 1959

My Darling,

What a hot, dusty, filthy place this is! U.N. airfield ringed with Egyptian soldiers. Anti-aircraft guns everywhere — they use our incoming C-119's to practice aiming at, but so far have not fired at them! These soldiers are the most unkempt and ill-trained I have ever seen. No wonder they lost the 1956 War with Israel — had to be bailed out by the U.N.

There have been more briefings, all day since we arrived. Apparently some trouble south and west of the town of Gaza. Marauding Palestinian irregulars — called fedayeen — are crossing the Armistice Demarcation Line, and raiding an Israeli kibbutz on the other side. The U.N.E.F. is there to stop all of this. The Israelis will not allow us on their side of the line.

And the Egyptians are not that happy with us on their territory. All this amounts to a rather difficult mission for the Canadians and the other U.N. troops.

Laura, I love you, and it is forever. My darling, please look after yourself for me. You are everything to me, and I yearn for the time this tour of duty will be over, so I can come home to you. On Christmas Day,I shall be thinking of you, hoping that you will like the presents I left for you in the apartment. And I look forward to opening your gift which I have carried in my pocket since I left you. You are always on my mind and in my heart.

A bientôt, ma cherie, et au revoir. I love you, Laura. I love you.

Yours forever, Jim.

....

In the afternoon of Christmas Eve, Major Jim Niles and Lieutenant Peter Forsythe, on attached duty with the headquarters staff of U.N.E.F., serving in the operations and intelligence branch, set out from El Arish in a jeep for the village of Abasan in the Gaza Strip, some five kilometers east of Khan Yunis, close to the Armistice Demarcation Line. Their mission was to contact the Indian battalion, on outpost duty in that sector, where ominous signs of fedayeen raiding activity had been reported the day before by radio to U.N.E.F. headquarters. The two Canadian officers were to report to the Indian commanding officer, who would take them to his company outposts, which had observed this activity. A patrol of Israeli paratroopers, on their side of the A.D.L., had contacted the Indians, reporting fedayeen night raids on Kibbutz Nirim, three kilometers inside their territory. The Israelis threatened to launch a reprisal raid on the Palestinian village of Abasan, if the U.N. forces could not stop these raids.

The white jeep, with the blue U.N. flags flying from its guidons, pulled up at the Indian battalion headquarters, a cluster of tents with barbed wire strung around them. Lieutenant Colonel Abid Hasnain, the Indian C.O., came out of his tent to meet them. Colonel Hasnain was a short, lithe man, with a thin black moustache. He wore the light khaki uniform of the Indian Army, with shirtsleeves rolled up, the U.N. blue beret on his head. The Canadian officers dismounted.

Major Niles saluted. "Sir, Major Niles and Lieutenant Forsythe of Operations Intelligence reporting. I understand that you have had problems in your sector?"

"Oh, I say! Jolly glad to have you with us! Bit of a sticky wicket out here! Damned rascals over there have been rather restless lately! Reminds one of those beastly sectarian riots we had to contain back home. This sort of thing has been hard on the lads, you know!"

The colonel ushered the Canadians into his command tent. His batman immediately served hot Darjeeling tea, as they examined the operational maps. Jim noticed with faint amusement that although these Indians had rid themselves of the British Raj, their army was still run very much along British lines. Their colonel spoke and acted as if he commanded a battalion of Coldstream Guards! More British than the British!

Following their briefing, they drove off to locate the headquarters of the Indian rifle company which had reported the violations of the armistice agreement. There they were greeted by Major Rai, whose headquarters was in one of the sparsely scattered outposts along the Armistice Demarcation Line. There were a few tents, surrounded by sandbags and wire. Here the Canadians were to observe, and to report back to U.N.E.F. headquarters the next day.

Through their binoculars, they could plainly see gangs of fedayeen irregulars gathering in and around the small, mud-hut village of Abasan, less than a hundred meters off the A.D.L. They were in fact within the demilitarized zone, but ignored the U.N. presence close by. They were firing wildly into the air, yelling "Alahu Akbar! Yahya Nasser!"

Dusk came, and soon after a dark, moonless night. Throughout the night, the field radio in the company headquarters tent crackled, as message after message was received from the sections manning the outposts, reporting fedayeen raiders infiltrating across the A.D.L., into Israeli territory. The Indian soldiers had been ordered to remain in their outposts. There were simply not enough troops for active patrolling of the demarcation line. Soon, explosions and small arms fire could be heard in the distance. The fedayeen were attacking Kibbutz Nirim again.

By dawn, the fedayeen had all withdrawn to their base at Abasan. Their jubilant celebration of their sortie against their hated enemy was short-lived. As the sun rose, the Israeli Defence Force reacted with its customary swiftness in reprisal. A company of green-clad Israeli paratroopers drove in their jeeps to the A.D.L., where, ignoring the U.N. outposts, they dismounted, and moved in assault formation across the line and towards the fedayeen-held village. Machine gun, rifle and mortar fire was brought to bear on the Arab defenders. With their superior training and fire discipline, the Israelis quickly took a fearful toll of the fedayeen, whose dead and dying soon littered the parched ground surrounding the village. The village then caught fire. The few ragged villagers who still remained fled from their burning huts, directly into the crossfire between the combatants. None survived.

Lieutenant Peter Forsythe observed all of this with mounting alarm and horror. "Oh, Christ, Jim, how the hell can they be doing this to each other?"

Jim replied quietly. "In the land of the bible, we are now witnessing 'the sword of the Lord and of Gideon'. Peter, lad, take a good, careful look. You are seeing for the first time what war is all about. People dying, soldier and civilian alike. Utter and total mad, wanton destruction. This is what being a soldier means; death and destruction are our stock-in-trade. And so it will ever be, unless the time comes when sanity prevails, when armies and soldiers like us will no longer be needed."

Through his binoculars, Jim observed an Arab man and woman running towards the U.N. outpost, in a desperate bid for safety. They had two children, a little girl of about six, and a baby carried by the woman. The fedayeen opened up on them with AK-47 machine carbine fire, killing both the man and the woman. With her last breath, the woman crawled over the baby, to provide it some protection. The little girl sat by her dead parents, screaming in terror.

Without a further word, Jim Niles put down his binoculars, climbed over the sandbag wall and the wire fence, and ran towards the stricken family.

"Major Niles! Major Niles!" yelled the Indian major. "For God's sake, not to be doing this, sir! You will be killed!"

Jim ran headlong across the fifty yards to the children, swept them up in his arms, and began running back with them. He had almost reached the wire fence when he was struck in the back by fedayeen fire. He staggered to the outpost, where two Indian soldiers grabbed the children before he collapsed. He was carried into the tent, bleeding badly from his wounds. His face was ashen-white, his breathing labored and gasping, and he was coughing up streams of blood.

Peter Forsythe stared at him, aghast. An Indian stretcher-bearer frantically applied shell-dressings to the gaping wounds.

"Jim, Jim, please....hold on, Jim. We've put a call in for the medics. Oh, God, Jim, please hold on...."

"Peter....no....no....it's over....listen....tell Laura....there is a locket around my neck....her Christmas present....please take it back to her....my father.... redemption.... now that I don't need it any more ... Laura....Laura...."

Major Jim Niles died at 8:03 A.M. on Christmas Day.

Peter Forsythe wept, cradling Jim's lifeless body in his arms. Gently, he lowered the body. He removed the identification tags, and also the locket. It was a small, silver heart-shaped keepsake, which Laura must have found in an antique store, or perhaps it had come down to her through her family. Peter opened the locket. In it was a photograph of Laura, cut out of a colored snapshot. Opposite the picture was an inscription:

"To Jim, *te amo ad infinitum*, from Laura."

....

Laura retired at about midnight on Christmas Eve. She had placed the presents that Jim had left under the small Christmas tree in her apartment, intending to open them on Christmas morning, before she left to spend her three days off with her parents in Lafontaine. She had barely fallen asleep when she woke from a disturbing dream. In the dream, she saw Jim standing in front of her. His face was pale, and he looked sad and perplexed. He was reaching out to her with both hands. There was blood on his bush uniform. She moved toward him, calling his name. But gradually he receded into the distance and disappeared.

Laura shivered with cold. She sat up, hugging her knees under the bedclothes. She began to sob, repeating to herself, "Oh, Jim, no, please, don't leave me, please." It was 1:03 A.M. in London, seven hours behind Middle East time. Laura could not get back to sleep. She had to maintain a vigil; waiting for the news she knew would inevitably come.

....

Shortly after 7:00 A.M. the telephone rang in Brigadier Timpson's quarters. He was still in bed. He was annoyed at being awakened this early on Christmas morning.

"Yes?"

"Good morning, sir. Sorry to have to wake you. Lieutenant Longstreet here, Orderly Officer on duty. We have just received an urgent message from Central Command which I felt you should have. Can I quote, sir?"

"Yes, for heavens' sake, Longstreet, what does it read?"

"Major James Niles serving with U.N.E.F. killed in skirmish on Armistice Demarkation Zone Gaza died 0603 hours Zulu Time. Inform battalion commander Wolseley Barracks, also N.O.K. Posthumous citation for bravery in service of Canada now being considered at Army H.Q. Detailed info to follow."

There was silence. "Sir, do you copy?"

"Yes, yes! Telephone Colonel Banfield immediately. The telephone number for Brigadier Niles is available at the Area orderly room. Call him....er....as you were....put the call through and have it transferred to my quarters. I shall speak to the brigadier myself."

"Very good, sir."

....

Melinda Timpson, lying in bed beside her husband, stirred. "What is it, Horace?"

"That damned young Niles. Got himself killed out on the Gaza Strip. What a frightful mess!"

The brigadier got up, his moustache twitching, and made himself a cup of tea. How many young men, he recalled, had he sent to their deaths in battle, when he commanded his brigade in Italy in the Second World War? Damn it, it was necessary then. After all, we simply had to win the war. It was not the dead which bothered him. It was those infernal field hospitals, full of ghastly wound cases, which he was required periodically to visit. But this business about young Niles was a different matter. Damn it, it was not his responsibility. After all, it was the lad's father who had arranged for the posting. Had to get him away from that beastly scandal.

As he sipped his tea, the story of David and Bathsheba came to mind. The brigadier had always prided himself as a student of the Old Testament. What was that passage? And then it came, as if trumpeted by Gabriel himself. From II Samuel:

"And he wrote in the letter, saying, Set ye Uriah in the forefront of the hottest battle, and retire ye from him, that he may be smitten and die."

But something did not fit the biblical story here. Ah, yes! In II Samuel, it was the husband who was killed, not the lover. But in the case of poor Niles....well, that was not his concern now.

....

The news of Jim Niles' death shocked and sickened Bob Banfield. It seemed so pointless. Jim had died when he was finally beginning to live. But what, after all, is a good time for a soldier to die? What had Jim said in Bob's office, which seemed so long ago now? Duty....honor....country....and the thing about redemption. Well, Jim, brother officer, comrade of the old Three Platoon, you have finally redeemed yourself. You died a hero's death saving those kids, when you no longer sought redemption.

Laura. Bob lost no time. Laura had to be informed. Without hesitation, Mary agreed to take care of it. She called Laura. Then she drove over to Laura's apartment.

....

The two women held tightly to each other. Laura cried quietly in Mary's arms. Mary wanted Laura to come home with her. Laura declined. She intended to drive to Lafontaine to be with her parents. The two women agreed to stay in close touch. In the hour of her extreme need, an important and enduring friendship was forged.

PART FOUR

NORMANDY, APRIL 1986

CHAPTER TWENTY

From his room on the third floor of the Hôtel Moderne, Michael Baldwin heard the persistent bleating of a siren, swelling louder until it ceased abruptly outside the French window. He walked over to the window, and opened it. It led to a narrow balcony with an iron railing. Below, across the street, parked at the curb, was an ambulance and a police car. The white-clad ambulance attendants were carrying a man on a stretcher out of the adjacent bistro, then deftly loading their charge into their vehicle, marked "Service de Secours". The ambulance drove off, its siren once again blaring into the night. A dishevelled, drunken man staggered over to the police car, and began to argue volubly with the policemen. The bedraggled inebriate repeatedly attempted to get into the police car and the gens-d'armes, with matching vigor, fended him off.

"Allez! Allez!" ordered the police. Finally, in disgust, they drove off, leaving the drunk by himself on the street.

"Les maudits flics! Maudits bâtards!" he shouted, and eventually stumbled out of sight.

This was Caen, major city in the département of Calvados, in Normandy, its myriad of streetlights stretching into the distance. Almost forty-two years ago, when Michael was fourteen, the mighty Allied armies had crossed the English Channel to liberate Europe, and had landed on the coast close by, the nearest beaches no further than ten miles from the heart of the city. The German defenders had fought with grim determination to hold onto this key city, and it took over a month of bitter struggle before Canadian troops finally captured Caen. There could not have been much left of William the Conqueror's ancient city after this battle, but in the intervening years, the French had rebuilt Caen, retaining many of its narrow, convoluted streets, designed for an age long past, before the advent of the automobile. Present-day Caen was a motorist's nightmare.

Michael had arrived two days previously at Charles De Gaulle Airport outside Paris, having taken the night flight from Toronto. He picked up his rented Renault-5, drove around Paris on the "Peripherique", and exited on the A-13, the "Autoroute Normandie", which took him all the way to Caen. The hotel had been advertised as the "second best in Caen". Located at the corner of Avenue Maréchal Leclerc and Rue des Jacobins, it was an unpretentious cement block building of immediate post-war construction. Compared to Holiday Inns in Canada, it was austere and diminutive — small lobby, small front desk, small dining room and small rooms. The room Michael rented contained a bed, a miniscule wooden desk and side chair, a night table and little else. There was a small bathroom with a shower stall. Although there was barely enough space to swing the proverbial cat, the room was comfortable, and would do for the purpose of his two-week holiday.

Caen itself had few attractions, although it possessed magnificent medieval churches and abbeys which had miraculously survived the war; and also a large castle in the centre of the town, built by William the Conqueror a thousand years ago to withstand the ravages of battle, even those of 1944. The Norman hinterland was pretty enough in the early spring, with its multitude of little stone villages and small farms enclosed by hedgerows. For the ordinary tourist, France had a great deal to offer beyond Normandy. There were after all Paris, the Loire Valley and its many chateaux, and the Riviera. But for Michael, this was no ordinary touring holiday. It was in fact a pilgrimage.

His thoughts turned back to the spring of 1959, twenty-seven years before, when he had first heard about the battle for the Verrières Ridge. Bob Banfield had been there, and so had Jim Niles. This particular battle had profoundly affected the lives of these two army officers, and dominated relations between them. He recalled the difficulties he had encountered in extracting a clear account from either of them of what had actually happened to them, beyond general information about the battle, which had been so costly in casualties. Later, after Jim Niles' death, Bob Banfield had filled in the missing details regarding the experiences of the survivors of the old Three Platoon, and what they had endured during those fearful days in July of 1944.

Michael's involvement with those two officers, and what had subsequently transpired in their lives, had led him to an absorbing interest in the Verrières Ridge battle, which had quickly become an obsession. He obtained whatever books he could find on the subject. This in turn led him to the Normandy campaign in general, and thence to the role which the Canadian Army had played in the Second World War. Eventually he realized that, sooner or later, he would have to come to Normandy, to visit the old battlefields. He wanted more understanding of what that generation of his countrymen had lived through, which now no longer seemed to be of importance to most Canadians, other than the veterans themselves.

He had seen veterans in his practice. Most were reluctant to talk about their own battle experiences. But once they knew he genuinely wanted to listen, frequently an enlightening oral history would tumble out, as long-bottled-up memories and feelings poured forth. Like their fathers before them in the First World War, these young Canadians had enlisted and had gone overseas to fight for what they fervently believed in. Thousands upon thousands never returned, and many who did were permanently maimed in body and spirit. The men of the Second World War were aging. For Michael, they were more than the bemedalled ranks who paraded before the nation's cenotaphs each Remembrance Day. The poppies worn each year took on a deeper meaning. All he had heard and learned led him here. He was on his way to the Verrières Ridge.

Michael spread out his Michelin road maps of Normandy on his bed, and an array of sketches and notes he had compiled. On the night table were copies of Colonel C.P. Stacey's "The Victory Campaign" and Reginald Roy's "1944 The Canadians in Normandy", two books he found invaluable in the study of this campaign. That evening, he was preparing for the next day's touring, which would take him across the Orne River to the Verrières Ridge.

In order to maintain some form of historical sequence, Michael spent the first two days of his trip visiting the landing beaches and the build-up and lodgement areas of the invasion campaign. On the first afternoon, after checking in at the hotel, he drove off through the city and found Highway D-7, which took him directly to the coastal village of Langrune. He turned left there, and was immediately onto the "Canadian" beaches and the villages adjacent to them, which were captured on D-Day, June 6th 1944, by the Third Canadian Infantry Division and its supporting units. The JUNO landing sector was no more than five miles wide, and its villages seemed to blend one with another, with very little space in between. For the most part they were deserted at this time of year. Summer and the crowds from Paris had yet to come.

St. Aubin-sur-Mer. The North Shore Regiment from New Brunswick landed here. The old ten-foot high stone seawall still standing. A rough-looking beach, strewn with pebbles and shale.

Bernieres-sur-Mer. The old three-storied gabled house, recognizable from the D-Day photographs, boarded up until the summer holiday-makers arrived. Row upon row of wooden change huts, strung along a dirt road, which was named "Rue the Queen's Own Rifles of Canada", after the Toronto unit which had captured this village.

Courseulles-sur-Mer, by the little River Seulles. East of the river, a wide expanse of flat beach and a long wooden pier. The largest of the "Canadian" villages, since expanded as a resort and fishing port. Strange multi-tiered apartment building by the harbor, looking like a truncated pyramid. Lots of boats. Here was where the Regina Rifle Regiment landed.

Then, across the Seulles, a parking place beside a cement slab, which supported a wooden effigy of a bayonet, twenty feet tall. Its inscription: "Royal Winnipeg Regiment, 6 June 1944". And close by a white metal mast, flying the Canadian flag.

The following day, Michael toured the lodgement area, crossing and recrossing the countryside along its tortuous and narrow country roads. Ancient stone villages were everywhere, many of which were critically significant for the Canadians in the 1944 battles. Creully, Pierrepont, La Fresne Camilly, Rots, Cairon, Buron, Authie and the ruins of the Abbaye d'Ardenne. And south across the Caen-Bayeux highway, Norrey-en-Bessin, Putot-en-Bessin and Carpiquet. The stone monument to the Ninth Brigade near Les Buissons, its plaque reading: "Hell's Corners, *Le Coin de l'Enfer*". The monument in Buron to the Sherbrooke Fusiliers.

Michael had thoroughly enjoyed himself. Amidst the quiet, pastoral scenes of the Normandy countryside, for him, Canadian military history came alive. Little had changed, once one got away from the expanding city of Caen, which had swallowed up some important landmarks. As he roamed the battlefield areas, with map and compass and binoculars, he found that he was able to trace the paths of individual units, as they had crossed this same terrain in 1944, fighting for every yard.

And after each touring day, there was a magnificent French dinner to sit down to, in one of the many restaurants in Caen. In this land by the sea,

Michael took full advantage of the delectable fruits-de-mer. This was Normandy — sea-food, apples (les tortes Normandes — formidables!) and cheese. *"Que voulez-vous, Monsieur — Camembert, Livarot ou Pont l'Évêcque?"* Could the waiters possibly know that each of these towns, for which these delectable cheeses were named, had been of military importance in the Normandy campaign?

....

The last months of Michael's active service in the Army — the first months of 1960 — came back to him in poignant memories. Major Jim Niles had been killed on Christmas Day in far off Gaza. His body, in a sealed casket, had been flown back to Canada. The Army, more in respect to his brigadier father than to poor Jim, had arranged for a military funeral beyond what one would expect for a major. Jim's body was buried in Ottawa. Many of the ranking general officers of the Army attended. The brigadier was in his serge uniform, with the traditional black band over the left sleeve of his greatcoat. Mrs. Niles was dressed entirely in black. The battalion had dispatched an honor guard. This consisted of soldiers from each of the companies, commanded by Captain Leo Toland, Jim's former Transport Officer. The three rifle volleys over the grave. The mournful bars of the "Last Post", from the bugler from the Corps of Drums. And in the back of the gathering at the cemetery, the figure of a young woman, in her brown overcoat with a pale yellow scarf over her head, standing in the bitter cold with her head stooped.

After the ceremony, Michael walked over to Laura. She had just thrown a single red rose into the grave. Michael heard her say softly: *"Répose bien, mon amour. Attende-moi. Je serrais avec toi plus tard. Te amo, ad infinitum....."*

They were joined by Bob and Mary Banfield. The mourners were returning to the cortege of limousines, parked along the road which wound past the open grave. They saw Brigadier Niles helping his wife into one of the cars. But before he climbed in, he turned and looked at Laura. He had never met her, had not spoken to her during the burial ceremony. He stood there for a moment, gazing at her, without rancour, sadly. Then he was gone.

The following summer, Michael Baldwin left the battalion, concluding his active service with the Canadian Army. The Area Medical Officer, who had attempted rather perfunctorily to convince Michael to make a career for himself in the Army Medical Corps, told him that he would be leaving a sorrowing battalion. But the young medical officer had other plans. He had enjoyed his years in the Army, but he was a trained physician, and he wanted to specialize in psychiatry; the direct care of patients who needed his skills was more important to him than continued military service, which, with promotion, would inevitably have led him into administrative duties.

....

In the winter of 1985-1986, Michael Baldwin made up his mind to go over to Normandy. Alison could not take time from her work. Besides, the thought of crawling over old battlefields had no appeal for her. He would fly over alone in April. This provided some time, when his busy practice permitted, to study in depth the Normandy campaign, in any books and maps that he could obtain on the subject.

Then, one Saturday afternoon, two weeks before he left, his doorbell rang. At the door stood a young officer, dressed in the modern green uniform of the Canadian Armed Forces. On the cuffs of both sleeves were the two broad gold bands of a captain. He was tall, dark, and strikingly good looking.

"Yes?"

"Dr. Michael Baldwin?"

"Yes, I'm Dr. Baldwin."

The young officer saluted. "Sir, I am Jim Niles."

Michael was stunned.

"Oh, it's O.K., doctor! I'm not here to draft you back into the Army, if that's what is bothering you! Dr. Baldwin, do you remember a Major Niles when you were with his battalion at Wolseley Barracks, in London? Well, I'm his son. I'm Laura's son."

"My God....Come in, Jim....please come in. You're Jim Niles' son....I....can't believe it...."

They walked into the living room, and sat down.

"I am serving with the Canadian mechanized brigade group in Germany. I'm the 2/IC of a rifle company, stationed at Lahr. I've been back in Canada for a short leave. Most of the time I was with my mother in London. She's a nursing supervisor at Victoria Hospital. I'm flying back to Germany tonight. She has spoken so often about you. I wanted to meet you. She looked you up in the Canadian Medical Association Directory. So here I am. I don't have long. I hope this is not an inconvenient time...."

"Good Lord, no, Jim! I am honored. It seems so long ago that I saw your mother last. I want to know all about what has happened to her. And I want to know about you. Your father....I've never forgotten him....and you never knew him...."

As if he had found a long-lost family friend, the young officer chatted happily with Michael. "I had a great time growing up. Laura was a fantastic mother. We had a hell of a lot of fun together. For as far back as I can remember, I called her Laura — only 'mother' when I was in trouble, when she addressed me as 'James'. Then I knew I was going to get it with both barrels! By the time I was born, my father's service will had been processed. With the money he willed to her, my mother bought a small house on Magnolia Crescent in the northeast part of London. That's where I grew up. When Laura was working, there was a nice old lady who lived next door, who babysat me. Each summer, we always spent Laura's holidays in Prince Edward Island, at my grandparents' cottage. What a great place for a kid in summer. The beach was one great big sand box! Usually, the old brigadier and granny would get out there for a few days to stay with us. I loved the old man. I remember playing soldiers with him when he and gran would come to London to visit. By the time I started kindergarten, I knew all about soldiers and army organization. I miss those old people. Grandad died in my second year at R.M.C., and gran the following year."

This news that the elder Niles had reconciled themselves to Laura and to young Jim's existence, and even welcomed them into the family, moved Michael tremendously. "So a little good came out of that tragic mess after all. And our old C.O., Colonel Banfield...."

"Oh, Uncle Bob! Well, we saw a lot of him and Mary while I was growing up. Now there was a soldier! He had as much to do with my choosing the profession of arms as Grandad! He retired as a brigadier-general; he and Mary live in Ottawa now. He looked me up when I was at R.M.C.. Boy, what a splash that made with the other cadets! His last tour of duty was with NATO HQ in Brussels."

"And you, Jim. Where has your career taken you?"

"When I graduated from R.M.C. I could have chosen any other branch of the service, but I decided on the infantry. Like father and grandfather, like son! I was at Wolseley Barracks for two years, so I saw Laura often. Then, I was posted to Germany. We write to each other frequently. And a real chunk of my pay goes into long-distance telephone calls! Laura is worth it! She's my mum, and she's my oldest friend! She's fifty-three now. She never remarried. Dr. Baldwin, if you're ever in London again, you really should visit her! She's some lady!"

"I know, I should!. I'm sorry we lost touch with her. I've thought about her and your father a lot. Has she told you much about him?"

"About my father....Well, I have visited his grave in Ottawa. Laura and I sometimes go through the pictures they took before he went to the Middle East. They had so little time together....just enough to get me started, I guess! She told me about what happened on the Verrières Ridge in 1944. I'm going to visit there after I get back to Europe. Laura has a silver locket which she gave to my father before he left. It was brought back to her by a junior officer who was with him when he died. It's her most cherished possession. When I was little, sometimes I would find her crying, with the locket in her hands."

There was a short silence. Michael felt a pang of regret for the life Jim had missed, for the pride he would have felt in his family.

"Well, Doctor Baldwin, it has been a great pleasure, sir! I had better shove off, or I'll miss my flip! And there's Anita waiting for me in Lahr! Now that's a real German *schatzi* for you! A devastating blond, five three, perfect build! She's something else....I might even marry her some day. She works in a travel agency in Lahr — that's how I met her — wanted a weekend in Vienna. In the summer, we're planning a trip to Israel. May even get a chance to see where my father was killed....But there's something else, about Anita. Her father is an accountant. He was a lieutenant in the German panzer grenadiers during the big war. He was badly wounded on the Verrières Ridge. He's a nice fellow. Told me his life was saved by a bunch of Canadians during the battle; they took care of him until his own people came on the scene. I've often wondered about that. A bit too much for just a coincidence, from what I've been told by Bob Banfield."

When Captain Jim Niles left, each wished the other a safe trip to Europe, and hoped to see each other again.

....

Michael came back to the present. It was getting late. He had a lot of interesting touring planned for the next day. Morning would soon come. And the Verrières Ridge was beckoning.

CHAPTER TWENTY-ONE

Michael Baldwin had breakfast in the hotel, the traditional croissants and coffee. He packed his maps, camera and binoculars into his shoulder bag and walked down the three flights of stairs to his car in the basement parking place. Once again he drove out onto the convoluted streets of Caen. He was stopped at a red light, when a truck driver ambled over to him, asking for directions to Cherbourg. This was something else, he thought. Even the French have difficulty getting through this town! He drove on to the River Orne, and crossed the bridge into the drab suburb of Vaucelles. There was the highway sign: "N-158, Falaise 30 km." N-158 — this was the "Glory Road", the "Voie Sacrée" of the Canadian Army in 1944, the main axis of advance to the closing of the Falaise Pocket, and the end of the Normandy campaign. As he drove through Vaucelles, he noticed graffiti sprayed in white paint on a wall: *"Les flics hors de Caen"*. The French here seemed to have something against their police! Perhaps forty-two years ago their fathers may have sprayed: *"Les boches hors de Caen"*!

In no time, he found himself at Ifs. Vaucelles had obviously expanded southward. Ifs had expanded in all directions, and now included three villages incorporated into one commune. He drove off the highway, and headed for the centre ville of Ifs Bourg. He passed by a little stone church with a small spire. He recalled discussing the battle with Bob Banfield after Jim Niles' death. This must be where Bob's platoon had assembled, behind the stone wall surrounding the little cemetery, before they were committed to the battle. A short distance south, and Michael was at the village limits. There was an old stone farm-house, behind a crumbling stone wall. This was surely where the Sixth Brigade headquarters had been located. And in front, across the fields, must have been that battalion's start-line.

He drove onto D-235, a paved country road which led south. The French had since built this road, where, at the time of the battle, there had been an unfinished railway bed. Michael was now driving through "Second Canadian Infantry Division country". Before him, bare fields undulated gently, with hardly a tree anywhere. Now, in late April, the grain was up no further than ankle-height. To his right, about a mile away, was a slight rise in the terrain. This must have been Point 67, which had been captured by the Calgary Highlanders, and held as a start-line for the Cameron Highlanders, who were in turn to advance south to capture the twin villages of St. Martin-de-Fontenay and St. Andre-sur-Orne. On either side of the road, Bob Banfield's battalion had advanced, in extended order, towards the Verrières Ridge, his own company on the left.

As Michael drove over a low rise in the terrain, there before him in the distance lay the Verrières Ridge. He could see a road cutting across the northern slope of the Ridge, past a cluster of farm buildings to the left. It had to be the old Beauvoir Farm, scene of the vicious fighting which the Fusiliers Mont-Royal had encountered. He stopped the car, and got out.

The Verrières Ridge....how peaceful and how quiet it seemed today. He struggled to relate the cataclysmic events which had occurred here forty-two years ago, to what he now saw before him. Colonel C.P. Stacey's words, in his first book, "The Canadian Army 1939-1945" were:

> "Four miles or so south of Caen....stands a kidney-shaped eminence....It is of no great height — its loftiest point is 88 meters — but it completely commands the ground to the north. For this natural outpost....there was to be desperate fighting for a fortnight to come, and on and about it much Canadian blood was to be poured out. It was on 20 July that we first set foot on those perilous slopes."

He recalled the night of the mess dinner, and his efforts to sober up a very drunk Jim Niles. Jim's words had been: "The attack was a total shambles....the artillery....the God-damned mortar shells fell everywhere....then their machine-guns.... high-pitched rapid firing which tore into us....I was paralysed with fear. God, I did not want to die....not there....on the slopes of that Godforsaken ridge....blood, broken bodies, guts and arms and legs, the yelling and the screaming...."

Then the time when Bob Banfield had spoken to him in the mess library: "There was a lot of bravery, and also a lot of cowardice. I guess a lot of us were more frightened of being cowards than being killed....We should never have lost so many good men....Jesus, it still burns me, when I think of it. But we were soldiers. We took orders...."

Michael returned to his car, and drove the short distance to the crossroads, where the lateral road D-89 intersected D-235. This paved road had since replaced the dirt road of 1944. He parked again, and got out. He was now at the furthest point that Bob Banfield's battalion had advanced on that day. To the left of the crossroads and just over D-89 was where his Three Platoon must have held their position. Again, his words returned:

"It was our turn to be clobbered. That evening, the Germans counterattacked with tanks and infantry, and they drove in our forward companies....The next morning, Jerry came at us again... They succeeded in overrunning our position...."

Here, on this spring morning, no sign remained of the flaming hell and destruction of that battle. There was no vestige of the old slit-trenches, no rusting remains of tanks, no rain-soaked shell-holes and no graves of the fallen. Here, a whole Canadian infantry division had been committed piecemeal to wrest this ridge from the German defenders, and here thousands of young Canadians had been killed and wounded. Yet there was no monument anywhere to the Second Division. It seemed that Canada and the Canadian Army had chosen to forget what had happened here. This was to be no Vimy Ridge, memorialized in perpetuity. Only in the history books was there any record of the battle for the Verrières Ridge. But the Canadians who had fought here had prevailed against heavy odds and the humiliation of initial defeat. Their story was one of valor, endurance and determination. They deserved to be remembered.

Somewhere on the field below D-89, in a rain-filled shell-hole, Bob Banfield and the two young privates, Ronnie Matthews and Tom Brennan, must have cowered, on that terrifying second day, expecting at any moment to be discovered and killed. Here was where the German panzer colonel had found them, desperately attempting to save the life of the young German lieutenant, who had fallen over them. Here was where a battle-shocked Jim Niles was dumped on them by the withdrawing enemy, and the last agonized fifteen years of his life began, until, so tragically soon before he was killed in Gaza, he had met Laura.

Alan Seeger's poem came to mind:

"I have a rendez-vous with death

At some disputed barricade....."

This was Michael Baldwin's rendez-vous with the Ridge of Death, something he had anticipated for many years. Gazing at the pastoral scene before him, he strained his senses, attempting to perceive something from across the forty-two years. He began to hear the sounds of battle, growing louder. Explosion after explosion, the earth about him erupting. The irregular sizzling of the Spandaus, and the rhythmic dull thudding of the brens. The horrifying cries of the wounded, and frantic commands yelled through the maddened din. And everywhere, pale, ghostly figures in khaki with the blue patch on their sleeves, clambering up the slope of the Verrières Ridge. But, quickly, the eerie reverie subsided, and he was once again alone at the cross-roads.

Michael got back into the car, and drove off south over the crest of the Verrières Ridge, then left on a narrow farm road through the village of Verrières. This village, now totally rebuilt, had been captured by the Royal Hamilton Light Infantry. He drove towards the main highway, the N-158. He knew that he must find that other place, so intimately and irrevocably associated with the Verrières Ridge battle.

At the village of Lorguichon, Michael Baldwin turned right onto the broad national highway which led south, straight as an arrow, pointing to Falaise. He was again in heavier traffic, in contrast to the county roads running across the Verrières Ridge, on which only the occasional farm vehicle moved. He passed the hamlet of La Jalousie. Then, about three miles on, he picked up the sign he was looking for, on the right side of the road. It was green, with white lettering, and read:

"Tombes de Guerre du Commonwealth

Commonwealth War Graves

Bretteville-sur-Laize

(Commune de Cintheaux)

CANADIAN WAR CEMETERY

CIMETIERE DE GUERRE CANADIEN."

He turned right off the highway, and followed a short roadway to a parking place, in front of a marble arch. The arch was supported by four columns. Attached to a flagstone wall on either side was a brass plaque, with lettering in English on the left and French on the right. "Bretteville-sur-Laize, Canadian War Cemetery, Cintheaux, 1939-1945".

Michael walked through the arch to a short gravel path, to the entrance of the cemetery. The entire cemetery was surrounded on its four sides by a tall hedge. The entrance consisted of low pillars on a white stone base. Between each pair of pillars were iron gates, bearing Canadian flags wrought in copper. Directly inside was a narrow courtyard, extending the full width of the cemetery, another hedge separating it from the main cemetery. There were stone benches on either end, set on a meticulously kept lawn. Dividing this hedge, in the middle, was another marble arch of eight columns. This was a free-standing portico, and on either side of it, sheltered from the elements, set into the wall, were brass containers, each with a lid which could be opened, like a safe. In one of these containers were the books which cross-referenced the graves by name and location; in the other was a book for visitors to leave their names.

Michael walked through. Immediately before him was another marble edifice, like an altar, with three steps leading up to its centre, on which had been engraved the words: "Their Name Liveth For Evermore". Beyond it was a tall marble cross, bearing an iron sword. On either side of the main aisle were the three thousand marble headstones of the Canadian war dead, gleaming in the sunshine. Row upon row of these graves extended to the far end of the cemetery. The headstones had been lined up in perfect symmetry, in blocks of sixteen by eight — eight by eight on the extreme flanks — each block with its own floral border, in which the tulips were blooming in profusion. The aisles between the blocks of graves were carpeted with beautifully kept lawn. The whole cemetery was like a park, a park in which had been held the last parade of these dead soldiers and airmen. Their headstones stood at attention. But on this parade there was no concern with rank. A brigadier was buried here next to a private. Majors and corporals, lieutenants and sergeants, row upon row together. Every regiment and corps was represented. One could tell by the regiment's name and the date the soldier had been killed, inscribed on each headstone, when and where in the Normandy campaign he had fallen. And the Verrières Ridge dead were here, those who could be located, and subsequently transferred to this final resting place, from their shallow, temporary graves, where they had fallen in battle.

Michael had never seen a Canadian war cemetery before. He stood there, in the peaceful silence, staring at the rows of headstones before him. There they were, the thousands of his countrymen who had died forty-two years ago when they were all so young, for a cause they had believed to be right. Under the sparkling headstones, their mangled remains would repose in this foreign land, for the rest of time, so terribly far from Canada, and home. Was it all worth it? But with their lives, they had liberated Europe from tyranny. And had they not done this, would we today be under the domination of an enemy power, totally without freedom to live our lives, as had happened to the people of this land in which they lay buried?

The full impact of the utter obscenity of war hit Michael. This was after all the ultimate meaning of war, beyond anything that the study of the history of war and visits to the old battlefields could convey. His stomach churned. His eyes filled, and tears streamed down his cheeks. "Oh, God, my God, how can this be?" he asked himself over and over. The dead at the Bretteville-sur-Laize cemetery reached out to him and he mourned for them. Never having known any of them in life, he felt that they belonged to him, and he to them. It occurred to him that had he been born a few years earlier, he could have been killed in this campaign, and his remains buried here with the rest. He wept for these men, with an agony of soul which would not let go.

Slowly, he moved among the graves. For each grave of the Army dead, there was a maple leaf at the top of the headstone. Below this was the regimental number, the rank and name of the soldier, his regiment or corps, and the day he was killed, and his age at that time. Below this was a cross — or the Star of David — and further down the headstone, close to the ground, for some there were additional inscriptions, requested by relatives.

"We gave a jewel to the fabric of victory, our son."

"Lovingly remembered by his wife Jane and son Timothy."

"So long, Scotty. We will never forget you."

"Some corner of a foreign field that is forever Canada."

Michael walked on. Silently, he continued to weep, as he stopped for a moment at each headstone. He had never been of a morbid nature, but for the first time in his life, he fully recognized the debt he owed to the people buried here. Eventually, he gained sufficient composure to attend to the other task he had set himself, before coming here. He returned to the portico, and looked up the location of the grave of Laura's brother, René Charlebois. He would take a photograph of the grave, and send it to Laura when he got back home.

He found the grave with no difficultly. On its headstone was inscribed:

"B 108165 Caporal

R. Charlebois

Le 20 Juillet 1944 Age 23

Il est tombé loins des seins

et de son pays

Vous qui passez

Priez pour lui.

And next to his grave was buried another soldier from his regiment.

"B 150769 Pte

J. Sipulski

20 July 1944 Age 19."

No additional memorial inscription for this poor lad who died when he was only nineteen. Likely no family who cared. Had he survived, René Charlebois, the farm boy from Lafontaine, Bob Banfield's old friend and fellow veteran from the Dieppe raid, would like Bob have been sixty-eight. A sergeant and a corporal. The sergeant went on to retire from the Army a brigadier-general. The corporal died, and his remains lay here. Laura's favorite brother.

Michael recalled the verse, traditionally recited at the cenotaph services across Canada on Memorial Day:

"They shall grow not old, as we that are left grow old;

Age shall not weary them, nor the years condemn.

At the going down of the sun and in the morning

We shall remember them."

He prepared to leave the hallowed place. He hoped that some day he would return. There was another Canadian war cemetery in Normandy, at Bény-sur-Mer, close to the invasion beaches, where over two thousand had been buried. He felt obliged as a Canadian to visit there also, before he left for home. Yet these were but two of the great many cemeteries where the Canadians who died in both World Wars had been interred. Well over a hundred thousand had died. The bodies of thousands had not been located. Many who had been buried had no identification. On these headstones, below the maple leaf, the inscription read: "A soldier of the Second World War", or, "A sergeant of the Essex Scottish Regiment".

His visit to the Verrières Ridge and the cemetery at Cintheaux had had a profoundly moving — and exhausting — effect on him. This was enough for one day. He would continue with his tour of the battlefields the next day. It was time to return to his hotel. At the steps of the portico, he turned one final time to look across at the ordered ranks of headstones. He stood silently for a moment. Despite the self-concerned machinations of the Canadian politicians of that time, and the execrable bungling of the higher command, these young Canadians had not been found wanting when called upon to face the terrifying ordeal of battle, sacrificing their lives in the cause for which they had fought.

It occurred to him, despite the years which had passed since he was in active service in the Canadian Army, that he was still very much a soldier. If he were in uniform, he would unhesitatingly salute the dead of the Cintheaux cemetery. In the Canadian Army, only in uniform was one be permitted to salute. But here, alone with the three thousand dead, they would not object..... Quietly, he lifted his right hand, palm outwards in the manner of the salute of his time — and theirs — and touched his forehead. For a brief moment he stood silently, then lowered his arm, turned around and walked away. He located the visitor's book in its brass container in the wall of the portico. He wrote the date, his name and address. He searched for something meaningful to add in the column for comments. He wrote: "In grateful memory". There could be nothing more, or less.

Glancing at the page in the book, he noticed that a German from Lahr had visited this cemetery two days before. Michael thought of the panzer grenadier lieutenant who had been "traded" for Jim Niles in the Verrières Ridge battle: he remembered young Jim's story of meeting someone who could have been that man. Could this visitor be he, or just someone who wished to pay his respects to the dead of yesterday's enemy? He had written: *"Nimmer Weider Krieg".*

The German words conveyed with stark simplicity what must have been a yearning of peoples throughout history, and of the multitudes of soldiers of countless armies who fought its battles and campaigns. These words were indeed fitting in remembrance of the dead who lay buried here.

"Never Again War."

The tumult and the shouting dies;
The captains and the kings depart:
Still stands Thine ancient sacrifice,
An humble and a contrite heart.
Lord God of hosts, be with us yet,
Lest we forget — lest we forget!
Rudyard Kipling, 1865-1936

LEST WE FORGET.

For more copies of

the RIDGE

send $14.95 plus $3.00 for GST, shipping and handling to:

GENERAL STORE PUBLISHING HOUSE
1 Main Street, Burnstown, Ontario
Canada, K0J 1G0
(613) 432-7697 or 1-800-465-6073

OTHER MILITARY TITLES

The Ridge	$14.95
Black Crosses Off My Wingtip	$14.95
The Memory of All That	$14.95
To the Green Fields Beyond	$14.95
The Canadian Peacekeeper	$12.95
Ordinary Heroes	$14.95
Fifty Years After	$14.95
One of the Many	$14.95
The Surly Bonds of Earth	$12.95
No Time Off for Good Behaviour	$14.95

For each copy include $3.00 to cover GST, shipping and handling.
Make cheque or money order payable to:

GENERAL STORE PUBLISHING HOUSE
1 Main Street, Burnstown, Ontario
Canada K0J 1G0